Brain Frieze

'Barnaby Goes Home'
and 20 more stories
of humor, mystery, sci-fi,
and the mind

Brain Frieze

'Barnaby Goes Home'
and 20 more stories
of humor, mystery, sci-fi,
and the mind

Allen Cobb

at play in the sapient cranium

Mulberry Knoll
Fairfield, IA USA

First Mulberry Knoll edition, 2014.

Cover design by Stuart Friedman, Design Works, Inc.

ISBN-10: 0-9792104-6-1
ISBN-13: 978-0-9792104-6-4

Publisher's Cataloging-in-Publication Data:
    Cobb, Allen T., 1946-
    Brain frieze: 'Barnaby Goes Home' and 20 more stories of humor, mystery, sci-fi, and the mind. — 1st Mulberry Knoll ed.
    336 p.   2 cm
    ISBN-13: 978-0-9792104-6-4
    ISBN-10: 0-9792104-6-1
    1. Literature
    PS370-380 (American prose fiction)

Mulberry Knoll
www.MulberryKnoll.com

To Someone

You know who you are.
Ha! Like that could ever happen.
Let me know when you've got a
plausible answer to that question.
Until then, act like you do,
and the reader will be generous.
Readers always are.
It's the writers you have to watch.

... perhaps they have carried me to the threshold of my story, before the door that opens on my story, that would surprise me, if it opens, it will be I, it will be the silence ....

Samuel Beckett, *The Unnameable* (c. 1953)

The memory came faint and cold of the story I might have told, a story in the likeness of my life, I mean without the courage to end or the strength to go on.

Samuel Beckett, *The End* (c. 1946)

Contents

Preface 1

Barnaby Goes Home 5

The Knock 27

The Journalist 37

Interview with the Zombie 55

Our Lady of the Ellington 61

The Meaning of Life 73

The Mirror 89

Hoobner on the Post 103

Signs 113

16 Degrees of Correlation 119

Little Torments 153

Rocky Mtn High [*performance 1*] 167

The CD 175

Am Not / Am [*performance 2*] 201

Another Threnody of Hope 215

Writing in Restaurants 245

Underground 251

Deaths in the Family 261

No Brainer 273

The Beginning 291

Glass Onion 303

Afterword 315

Also by Allen Cobb 325

Preface

To my great delight, the short story form has been enjoying something of a renaissance in the last few years. This change may be a side-effect of the gradual acceptance of eBooks and the new marketplace that feeds all the various e-reader devices. It may also reflect our increasingly short attention span. Whatever the cause, it's good news for me, because every time I start to write a novel, it turns into a short story. This is good news for you too, dear reader, as it means there's much less reading that needs to be done. The 21 stories in this volume are much better off in the short form—some are so short it took eleven of them to make one.

Amid these widely varying voices, I believe I may have afforded the reader with an analog to the astronomer's "oblique viewing" technique. Star gazers know that to see a very faint star, one should look off to the side rather than straight at it. This moves the image from the fovea onto the more light- and motion-sensitive receptors nearby, making the faint star easier to see, although at a somewhat reduced resolution. In other words, we can see a bit more by looking slightly away, but what we do see is less sharply defined.

There is an opposing technique, more commonly employed, of examining something, say a gnat, ever more closely. We might call this approach "ferocious viewing," if for no other reason than that it precipitates scowls and frowns. The benefit of examination, concentration on details, is of course knowledge of the minutiae, one or another of which may turn out to be crucially important. What is lost is the vision of the original object and, more to the point, its context.

What, then, is this common thread that appears dimly peripheral to the stories? If I could define it in prose, believe me, I would, because this fuzzy internal meme is what moves me to write in the first place. But it seems the only way it can be glimpsed is through a number of fictional forays that never aim directly at it. My apologies for leaving its identity unresolved, but that seems to be the nature of things when you look very closely, and when you look to one side, you cannot discern its outline.

Some stories do have specific aims, while others may just be recreational excursions. Where I felt I could shed any further light on one or another story, I have provided some notes in the Afterword. These notes are not intended to assist in reading the stories, however, and may even hamper their enjoyment. Therefore, I urge the reader to enjoy the stories in a spirit of discovery, and save the notes for last—or skip them altogether.

I'm delighted to extend special thanks for their generous review and encouragement of my work to Jack Forem, Jim Weidle, and Ellen Metropole, and I am especially grateful to Stuart Friedman of Design Works, Inc. for his extraordinary and wonderful cover design.

Finally, I must thank the reader for your time and attention, and pray that you will find something engaging, meaningful, or amusing in the following miniature flights of fancy.

—*Allen Cobb, Fairfield Iowa, 2014*

Ω

1

Barnaby Goes Home

Barnaby was vibrating like a hardware-store paint mixer. The unused triceps on his upper arms flobbled about as he leaned into the handle-bars, and the wind billowed his slack lips. The ancient BMW motorcycle rattled and throbbed in a deadening drone that had persisted for hours now, sounding hollow going up-hill, poppy and buzzy going down.

Vermont springtime had moved from patchy snow to unmitigated mud, the leading edge of summer, but Barnaby managed to stay on pavement all the way from Brattleboro. Cars whizzed by whenever the curves and center line allowed, often with a taunting horn blast. Not much respect for 40-year-old 250 cc motorcycles, especially when they were driven by 65-year-old hippies.

The old saying about happy motorcyclists was true: Barnaby's perpetual gawk was decorated with more than a few smashed bugs among tiny glints of gold. Some had gone up his nose, too, blasted by the relentless 50 mph wind in his face.

Barnaby was oblivious to life's little annoyances, because he was on his way home. His heart was filled with the dull joy that comes when something that should have taken a few hours is finally finished after weeks and weeks of nearly fruitless labor. His mind reverberated with layers of falsified and enhanced images of a past no-one ever experienced. His eyes squinted into the roadway dust while tears coursed back across his temples in the wind.

Home wasn't his birthplace, or even where he had grown up. Home was a myth that had emerged in the darkened corners of Barnaby's dim brain-pan, growing like mold across the cranial interior. Home may have once been more or less real, perhaps during his college years, but now it was much too late to confirm anything.

The blatting thump of the little BMW lowered in pitch, and he turned into a small run-down gas station just outside an anonymous 45-mph town. Barnaby rated Vermont towns by their maximum speed limit. Anything over 45 didn't qualify as a town at all.

The bike used to get about 75 miles per gallon, but now it burned oil and the mileage was way down. There was a crack in the tank near the filler cap, so Barnaby never filled it much above half.

He stopped the motorcycle alongside the gas pumps, stepped off, and heaved the ungainly contraption onto its center-stand. He blinked at the pumps, trying to find the credit-card slot. His stance was a little unsteady after so many hours rattling and thumping along winding country roads.

An old geezer sat in a cane chair by the open garage door, staring at him.

It appeared there wasn't a slot in the pump for credit cards.

Barnaby looked over at the geezer. "You take credit cards?" he asked.

"Dunno," said the geezer, not moving.

"You don't know?" Barnaby wrinkled his nose in surprise.

"Not my store," said the geezer.

"Oh. Is the owner around?"

"Dunno."

Barnaby pulled the ignition key from the bike and walked over to the office door. Its big spring played a sproingy tune as he walked in.

The office was dark, with a big desk littered with papers and junk. Ancient vending machines stood like suits of armor in the shadows.

"Hello?" Barnaby said.

There was no answer, but he heard the distinctive clank of a wrench against concrete, and spied the grimy door into the shop.

He pushed the door open and saw a rounded lump of overalls hunched near the floor at the back end of a rusted Cadillac. He walked over.

"You the owner?" Barnaby said.

The overalls unfolded and stood up. "Yup." The owner was impossibly old and fat, and his bib-front work clothes were almost black with grease and oil.

"You take credit cards?"

"Nope."

"Cash?"

"Nope."

"Nope?" Barnaby was taken aback. "How the hell do you sell any gas?"

"Don't. Pumps been dry since '95. Just fix-ups here." The owner stuffed his hands deep into the overalls and planted his feet, as if preparing to remain standing for a very long time.

"No gas?"

"No gas."

"Look," Barnaby said, "I'm almost out. Where's the nearest working gas pump?"

"Oh, these pumps work OK," said the owner. "That ain't the problem."

"I don't understand," said Barnaby.

"Already told you. No gas. Dry since '95."

"Right. OK." Barnaby looked around, but there was nobody to appreciate the conversation. "So where can I get some gas around here?"

"Sinclair. 'Bout two mile," said the owner.

"Which way?" Barnaby gazed out into the bright sun, where the BMW perched like an elaborate steel toilet at the pumps.

"Well," said the owner, "just the way you're pointin'."

"Pointing?" Barnaby hadn't been pointing.

"Your moped out there's pointin' ain't it?"

"It's a motorcycle, not a moped."

"Pointin' down the road, eh?"

"Well, yes." Barnaby peered back into the gloom behind the owner. The interior of the garage was far too dark to get anything done. Even more so after looking out into the afternoon light.

"Two miles back you'da druv past it."

Barnaby frowned, realizing that indeed he would have seen it driving by. Life weirdly made sense sometimes.

"Right," Barnaby admitted, under his breath.

"Then you be gettin' on down the road, eh?"

Barnaby shrugged. "Yup. Thanks. See ya."

He picked his way over tires and car parts into the daylight. The BMW was down to a splash, but easily good for another 20 miles or more.

•

There was a slight breeze in the town of East Glover, carrying the cheeps and twitters of hundreds of birds scattered through the woods and across the open fields. On the hillside a sizable flock of blackbirds picked in the grass. Closer to the road, blue-jays scavenged at the back of a plywood ice-cream shop, hopping over empty boxes and a pair of garbage drums. A massive old refrigeration unit hummed and buzzed. There was an occasional swoosh as a car sped past on the nearby pavement. East Glover was a 45-mph town.

A squirrel was foraging at the edge of the woods a few yards up-hill. It grabbed an acorn in its paws, froze, jerked erect, started to the right, froze, dashed half-way toward a picnic table, froze, jerked erect, spun around, leapt a few feet closer, darted to the left, took one quick step to the right, noticed something across the road, and then remained frozen for a long time, hoping to disappear gradually into the predator's optic fatigue. Then it dropped the acorn and ran all the way back into the woods with its huge tail flowing behind like smoke.

A faint thumping emerged in the distance. A metallic clanking mingled with the low staccato and the beat slowed, growing louder, and with a crunch of gravel Barnaby swung into the ice cream store's parking lot. He parked under the tree, picked some debris from his hair, and went to the serving window.

After a minute, an old woman appeared and thrust an alarmingly wrinkled scowl over the counter. "Watcha want?" said the ice cream vendor.

Barnaby looked up at the sign: "Ginger's Hut." *More like Baba-Yaga's,* he thought.

"Make up yer mind, sir," Ginger snapped, "We ain't waitin' all day."

Barnaby looked around. There was a family of four at one of the picnic tables, but the rest of the enterprise was deserted.

"OK, well, I guess," he said, "I'll have, uh, one of those orange freeze things."

"You mean an orange freeze?" said Ginger.

"Yeah, that's it."

"Size?" she said.

"Oh, uh, medium, I guess."

"Well, is that it, or are you still guessing?"

Barnaby flinched and bounced a little on the balls of his feet. "Uh, yup, medium."

"We don't got medium," said Ginger. After a suitable pause she added, brusquely, "You mean Regular."

"I do?" said Barnaby, his mind having wandered.

"It's the size between Kids and Tall," she said.

"Oh," said Barnaby. "OK."

"One sixty-nine," said Ginger.

"What?" said Barnaby. *That's a really weird sequence of sizes: kids, regular, and tall; sounds like shirt sizes.*

"You gonna pay?" Ginger demanded. "You gotta pay in advance."

Barnaby fished out a pair of ones, and Ginger handed him his change, slammed the window shut, and set about concocting his orange freeze.

Barnaby selected an unoccupied picnic table beneath a tree, and sauntered over to it, his bell-bottoms flapping around his ankles. This place reminded him faintly of Home, although the witch wasn't supposed to be part of it. *I must be getting into the vicinity,* he thought, and sat down.

Almost immediately the ice cream shop's loudspeaker crackled, and the witch's voice rasped out across the parking lot. "REGULAR ORANGE FREEZE!"

Barnaby leaned back, sorry to be standing up again so soon, and stretched.

"MAKE IT SNAPPY!" said the amplified witch.

Barnaby jumped up and hurried back to the order window. Ginger handed Barnaby his drink, and slammed the window before Barnaby could ask for a napkin. He watched for a moment as she stormed away into the maze of frozen food equipment.

Returning to his table, Barnaby sucked a mouthful of thick orange slush, savoring the way it infused hyper-orange into every nook and cranny of his awareness.

Time stopped, and Barnaby sat on the bench in a sugar-induced orange daze while birds twittered. Squirrels scampered; a few cars swished past. The family of four was struggling to coordinate a return to their station wagon.

Eventually, his straw sucked air and the blazing stasis faded away. Barnaby suddenly wanted to be back on the road. He stood up, slurping the final splatters of slush. "Gotta go," he said. He strode quickly to his motorcycle and heaved it off the center-stand.

The old bike coughed and wheezed, and then burped into life. Barnaby straddled the rattling and thumping machinery, kicked it into gear, and roared sluggishly out onto the road.

Up ahead, a sign on the right read, "Barre 12 Miles." He glanced over his shoulder as he pulled away. At the ice-cream store, a grey squirrel was engaged in staccato maneuvers across the parking lot.

•

The Sinclair station turned out to be farther than he thought, and the BMW was running on fumes when he pulled up at the pumps. He shut off the engine and it emitted one loud pop of protest and stopped dead, ticking and clinking as it cooled.

Barnaby looked around. There was nobody in sight, but the station appeared to be open. A large green dinosaur sign presided over the empty yard and its lights were on.

"Yo!" Barnaby shouted. "Customer!" The office was closed, but he thought he could see movement inside. He hauled the bike onto its center stand and went to the door.

It was locked. Pressing his nose to the glass, Barnaby could see most of the little store, and there was no sign of life. He banged a few times, but there was no response.

He went to the big roll-up garage doors, stood on tiptoe, and peered into the gloom. Again he thought he might have seen some movement, behind the grease rack, but there was no response to his banging and yelling, so he gave up and returned to his bike.

He removed the cap from the gas tank, peered inside, and gave the bike a shake. The tank contained little more than a splash, but even a few more ounces would get him the rest of the way into Barre. He looked around one last time, and then pulled the gas pump hose over and propped the nozzle in the filler hole. He slowly lifted the hose over his head, and an ounce or two dribbled into the tank.

After draining the hoses on the other two pumps, Barnaby figured he probably had enough, and he put the gas cap back on. He was adjusting his goggles when the State Police car pulled up.

A lanky officer got out and put his police hat on before turning to Barnaby. The hat was immaculate and brimmed with a perfect-ly flat disc of felt. Barnaby took off his goggles.

"Nice evening, eh?" the officer said, striding over.

"Sure is," said Barnaby.

"Up for the foliage?" said the officer.

"Uh, no," Barnaby replied. "Foliage in the spring?"

"Yep, we got foliage in the spring," the cop replied. "Comes back every year." He gestured at the dense green trees and grass stretching for miles all around the gas station. "I'd call that foliage," he added.

"I thought you meant fall foliage," Barnaby said.

"In the spring?"

"Well, I—" the cop was looking at him. "Um, never mind."

"You got a lens for that thing?" the cop said.

"A lens?"

"Your taillight. It's not red, you know. Supposed to be red."

Barnaby looked at the light fixture over his license plate mount. Sure enough, the red plastic part had shattered again from the vibration, leaving a bare bulb. "Oh," he said. "Sorry. I keep replacing it, but the vibration—"

The officer nodded. "Happens all the time," he said. "You got some lipstick or nail polish on you?"

Barnaby frowned; he couldn't think of an answer that didn't sound like a wisecrack.

"You should paint that red," said the cop. "In the dark I couldn't tell if you're coming or going."

"OK, I'll pick up some nail polish next time I see a store."

"Good man. Where you headed?"

"Home," said Barnaby.

"Near here? I don't believe we've met."

Barnaby began to fidget. "Well, it's not exactly my actual home."

"That's interesting," said the cop. "What is it, if it's not your home?"

"I guess it's where I feel like I'm at home."

"Ah. And this place is nearby?"

"Yes, exactly."

The cop glanced at Barnaby's Massachusetts plate. "You don't live in Mass?"

"No, I do live in Mass, Cochituate."

"Then you're heading in the wrong direction!" The officer looked unreasonably delighted with this observation.

"No, no," said Barnaby. "I'm heading to where it *feels* like home, is what I meant. I'm not at home in Cochituate."

"Cochichuate? Where is that, exactly," said the cop.

"Cochituate. Outside Boston."

"Co-TICH-uate?"

"Co-CHIH-chew-it. I-90, a little North of Framingham."

"What's wrong with Cochituate?"

"Well, it's not Vermont, for one thing," Barnaby said.

The officer nodded sagely.

Barnaby continued, "And like I said, it just doesn't feel like home."

"You feel more at home in Vermont?"

"Yeah. That's what I meant."

"Where, in Vermont?"

"Well, here. Hereabouts. Central Vermont. Barre, Montpelier, Winooski River, Green Mountains. You know."

The officer removed his immaculate hat, dusted it off, and looked up and down the road.

"Gonna pay for that gas?" he said, putting his hat back on and settling the brim just so.

"Huh?" Barnaby glanced at the closed station. "I wanted a fill-up," he said, "but they're closed."

"The gas in the hoses is still worth something, don't you think?"

"Well, yeah, but it's only a few ounces. Just a dribble. I mean—"

"Got some money on you?" the cop looked serious.

Barnaby fished around in his pants. "I've got a couple of fives, and some quarters, and—"

"Gimme four of those quarters," the cop said, holding out his hand. He wore fine, skintight leather driving gloves.

Barnaby picked out a short stack of quarters and handed them gingerly to the cop, who immediately placed them on top of the nearest gas pump.

"That should cover it," said the cop, turning back to his car. Before getting in, he called over the roof, "Enjoy your trip home. Come on back any time." The cruiser's rear tires spun out as he drove off to the South.

Barnaby wondered if the trooper meant home in Cochituate, or "home" in central Vermont. He eyed the quarters on the gas pump and resisted the urge to put them back in his pocket. For all he knew, the cop had already parked out of sight and was watching him through binoculars.

Then he kicked the start lever a few times and the old BMW thumped and rattled back to life. He licked the bug bits on his front teeth and his kidneys braced themselves for the next leg of the journey. Soon his tangled hair was blowing in the wind.

•

On the outskirts of town, Barre was still recognizable as the former granite capitol of the world. Barnaby rattled past old stone-cutting shops, all shuttered and decaying, and battered granite-hauling flatbeds, their frames sagging from decades overloaded with stone. Despite the proliferation of defunct businesses, Barnaby was relieved to see the small city finally taking shape along the road.

Endless vibration and clatter all the way from Massachusetts had taken its toll. His ears rang, his vision was blurred, his body was sore, and his lower back felt like he'd been carrying his preposterous motorcycle for the last hundred miles. Up ahead, relief waited at the Barre Hotel. He would eat a light meal, get a full night's sleep, and then head on up Route 14 to the North. Somewhere along Route 2 into Plainfield he would find his home.

A few minutes later, Barnaby jounced through a deep pothole filled with muddy water and pulled into the parking lot behind the Barre Hotel. He had stayed at this same hotel 40 years ago when he visited the nearby college for an interview. It was an old, classic downtown establishment, with a dingy wood-paneled lobby, a dark slow-motion dining room, and small dark bedrooms.

The pothole water splashed onto the BMW's rattling exhaust pipe and muffler. A cloud of steam rose into the air, lending a dimly apocalyptic aspect to Barnaby's arrival. The bike was still hissing and ticking as he stomped up onto the hotel porch.

The main entrance was locked. Barnaby pressed his face against the window and peered into the wood-paneled gloom. His nose left a large greasy clear-spot on the glass. This hotel was definitely out of business.

He looked across the porch at the rest of downtown Barre. The city still had a deteriorating look about it, just as he remembered. It seemed incredible that a city could be deteriorating for four decades and still exist at all. But in the distance, down certain streets, he could glimpse a few signs of urban renewal, and he imagined that new hotels were being planned, and new buildings would arise, and artists would move in, and soon Barre would turn into the Portland Maine of Vermont.

This vision didn't assuage the road fatigue, hunger, and sore muscles, so he trudged back to the side lot and restarted the motorcycle. His lower back and glutei maximi were not pleased to reassume Barnaby's hunched riding position, but finding someplace to rest and recover was paramount.

As he waited at the pothole for a pedestrian to pass, he asked for directions to the nearest hotel.

The pedestrian, an elderly lady dragging a heavily laden shopping cart, paused and looked him up and down. She squinted at the antique plumbing of his motorcycle and said, "Beemer?"

"Hotel Beemer?" Barnaby replied, puzzled.

"BMW," she said, pointing at the black and white emblem on Barnaby's gas tank. "I used to ride one of those."

"You did?"

"Why, you think I can't ride?" She was visibly perturbed.

"Sorry," Barnaby said. "I didn't realize you were referring to the bike."

"Well, it's obviously not a 750i," she retorted.

"Do you know of another hotel around here?" Barnaby repeated.

"Ain't no ho-tels around *here* anymore," she said. "Ain't no ho-tels pretty much *anywhere*, far as I know. Plenty damn *strip mo-tels* outside of town, though. Far as the eye can see."

She started to walk away, and Barnaby said, "I know what you mean. I was hoping to avoid staying in a motel, actually. Are you sure there's nothing else?"

She stopped. "There's always Chez Marie," she said, over her shoulder. "Not a hotel exactly, but no damn strip *mo-tel*."

Barnaby remembered the old road-house up on Route 2 near campus. "You mean the old bar?"

"Only one Chez Marie," she said, walking away. "If you knew where it was, why'd you ask me?"

She had moved on too far to warrant a response, so Barnaby kicked into first gear and wobbled through the pothole onto the street.

Up Maple Ave. until it turns back into 14, Barnaby thought, watching the downtown area bounce past, jogging his memory. *Then right on Route 2 in East Montpelier.* The BMW popped and wheezed at each stop sign. *Still not many traffic lights,* Barnaby thought, *but I'm almost home.*

Maple Avenue quickly blended back into a two-lane state road winding through nondescript Vermont countryside. The clattering BMW reasserted its uncanny ability to locate every imperfection in the pavement. Barnaby's kidneys and vertebrae suffered the endless jouncing with less and less grace as the blown shocks on the R27's front swing-arm amplified every bump.

Back on the open road, the BMW crept back to maximum cruising speed, mercifully achieving the state speed limit. Bike and rider bobbled down the road as one, vibrating and flapping into a dull blur of pain and somnambulism.

Eventually, East Montpelier hove into view, a 45-mph town.

Route 2 branched off to the right, heading East along the filmy Winooski River. The countryside slipped farther to the rural end of the civilization spectrum. A few tiny farms swept by, first on one side of the road, then on the other. A new hardware store, unconnected to any population center, went past on the left.

Then the road crossed the meandering Winooski and the old road-house-from-farm-house came into view, and Barnaby sighed with relief. The motorcycle sighed, too, and began to buck and snort as he pulled into Chez Marie's gravel parking area. When he reached for the key to shut off the engine, it ran out of gas and died.

Shit, thought Barnaby, but his attention turned to the prospect of sitting on something that didn't vibrate and pound his flabby body into mush. He pried himself off the unforgiving saddle, which must have been designed by the Reich, and half waddled, half staggered up the wooden steps into the bar.

Chez Marie was red on the outside and red on the inside, but it was a lot dimmer inside. Squinting, Barnaby went straight to the nearest table and collapsed into a chair. The bar looked the same as it had 40 years ago, and it still smelled of stale beer and cigarettes, with a subtle fruity finish of vomit.

Two men sat at the bar, hunched over their drinks, not talking. The bartender was a young woman, probably from the college, with a chunky look and a distant demeanor. She steadfastly ignored Barnaby's presence until he waved repeatedly and started to get up.

"Ya want?" she called from the bar.

"Beer," Barnaby called back. The two drinkers at the bar turned slowly, gave him a brief country stink-eye, and returned to their drinks.

"Brand?" the bartender called.

"Tap," said Barnaby. "Whatever."

A minute later the bartender plunked a thick glass mug of beer on the table and held out her hand. "No tabs," she said.

Barnaby fished out a few dollars and she took them without offering change.

What the hell, he thought, addressing the beer. It was cold and watery and did a good job clearing the dust and bugs from his mouth and throat. Half-way through the mug, he rested his head on the table, just for a second, and began snoring.

•

"Hey, buddy," Ernie said. He towered over the squashed middle-aged hippie sleeping on table 6. Ernie's perfectly bald head gleamed with sweat and kitchen grease, and big stringy muscles rippled beneath his sleeveless undershirt. His skin was covered with tattoos and leathery wrinkles, devoid of even a single cell of fat.

The hippie mumbled and settled deeper into the vinyl tablecloth.

"Buddy," Ernie said, louder. "Time for you to be moving on. We're closing soon. Get up, son."

Barnaby roused and looked around at the dim, bleary interior of Chez Marie. A seven-foot giant stood over him, gently shaking Barnaby's shoulder. His cheek felt sticky where it had lain on the table in a puddle of beer-drool. Ernie continued shaking him.

"OK, man," said Barnaby. "What's going on?"

"You passed out," said Ernie. "Time to pack it in. Let's go outside."

"What time is it?"

"Ten. We're closing. You got a ride?"

Barnaby scratched his head. "Yeah, I'm on a bike."

"You got a headlight?"

"It's a motorcycle."

"Can you stand up?"

That seemed like a good question, so Barnaby stood up. Though still half asleep, he felt a whole lot better. "Yeah, I'm OK."

Ernie took his arm and eased him firmly toward the door. Barnaby sensed that Ernie's grip could have been much firmer if it needed to be.

Ernie! This really was Ernie the cook. Barnaby twisted around to look at the cook's face. *My god, Ernie must be 100 years old!* He'd been the cook when Chez Marie first opened in 1966, already wizened and wiry, surely at least in his forties back then.

"Ernie?" he said, as they squeezed awkwardly through the front door. "Zat really you?"

Ernie stabilized Barnaby on the porch and peered at him with new interest. "I know you?"

"Sort of. I was at the college. Came here a lot in the sixties. I can't believe you're still here."

"Why the hell not? It's a good job."

"But you must be—" he paused. Maybe Ernie didn't like being thought of as elderly. Couldn't blame him for that.

Ernie looked down at Barnaby's big cloud of frizzy hair and smiled. "I'm 82 years old, if that's what you're worrying about."

"Well, no, I wasn't worried. Just surprised to see you after all these years. Seems like old times."

Ernie guided Barnaby down the wooden steps. "Not to me," he said. "Where's your bike?"

Barnaby pointed at the BMW, the only motorcycle anywhere in sight. It was slumped over precariously on the side stand.

"I'm not drunk," said Barnaby, trying to pull away from Ernie's grip. "I'm just tired. Been riding all day."

"That's nice," said Ernie, releasing Barnaby's arm.

There was a crash behind them, around the corner of the bar. Ernie looked over his shoulder. Another crash, and a stocky blond-haired man staggered out of the gloom into the parking lot floodlights. He wore a torn plaid shirt and jeans, and there was a big bruise under one eye.

"You son of a bitch!" he slurred, and continued staggering toward Ernie, who straightened up and turned to face the new arrival.

"Dave, I've told you before, we don't tolerate no drunks. You need to get on home and see how Eleanor's doing." He turned back to Barnaby. "Have a nice night," he said, and headed back to the bar.

Dave, undaunted, or perhaps inspired, by Ernie's extraordinary stature, had picked up a large scrap of wood and was poking at Ernie erratically, like a dim-witted sword-fighter. Ernie ignored him and mounted the steps.

Uttering a guttural wheeze, Dave wound up and swung the two-by-four with all his might against Ernie's broad back. The wood splintered, and Ernie staggered to his knees with a grunt.

"You ain't, ain't, fucking bastard, all the time, god dammit," cried Dave. His curses faded as he lost track of the specifics.

Ernie stood up and walked slowly back down the porch steps, apparently unfazed by the two-by-four. "You shouldn't do that kind of thing," he said, in a low calm voice. Dave danced around with some difficulty, waving his fists like a cartoon pugilist, and spluttered incoherent threat fragments.

Ernie walked swiftly up to Dave and put his huge hand on Dave's head. His fingers wrapped around the skull like the thing from *Alien*. Dave's eyes went wide; he started to yell another string of besotted cursing, but went silent when Ernie picked him up off the ground, palming his head like a basketball, and effortlessly flung him through the air onto a nearby car.

Dave flopped to the ground and lay still for a minute. Then his remaining faculties rebooted and he got up and lurched away into the shadows, muttering and coughing.

Barnaby stared at Ernie in awe. Ernie turned when he reached the front door and gave a kind of helpless shrug. "Kids," he said.

Barnaby kicked frantically at the starter lever for a while, and then remembered the motorcycle was out of gas. He considered going back inside to bum a cupful from someone, but Ernie might not want to see him again just yet. Perhaps after another 40 years.

So Barnaby set off on foot to the college. It was not far, and the summer night was clear and less humid than usual. The Winooski was alive with chirping, chugging, and harrumphing frogs, and the fields buzzed with crickets and katydids.

Away from the glare of Chez Marie, fireflies floated a few feet above the grass. The sky was moonless and the Milky Way arched overhead. It was good to be walking, and good to be almost home.

•

The official entrance to campus was off Route 2 on 214, but Barnaby remembered a shortcut through the trees that led up onto a manicured hillside below the Manor House. As he clambered through the underbrush, he could hear faint voices ahead. When he eventually broke out of the bushes onto the wide front lawn, he could just make out a dark huddle of people, faintly illuminated by starlight.

Four or five students were sitting in the grass, laughing and giggling. There were a few wine bottles and beer cans, and one of them was passing a joint. When they saw Barnaby, a voice said, "Shit! Cool it! It's a nark."

"No it's not," said a girl. "There aren't any narks around here."

"Especially in the middle of the night," said another.

"You wanna toke?"

Barnaby was wide awake again, and welcomed the invitation. He drew the hot smoke deep into his lungs, and felt it burn his throat. The pungent smell of pot triggered his rhinoencephalon, and his brain flooded with rich 40-year-old memories of losing consciousness elaborately, from a variety of causes, mostly chemical.

"This is some seriously good shit," he said, by way of thanks.

"Bet your ass," someone replied.

The pot was much stronger than Barnaby remembered. Perhaps the botanical prowess of local growers had improved. "This," he said.

The Milky Way had turned blue, and he lay back on the grass to admire it. The kids continued chattering in a language Barnaby knew instinctively was English, but the phonemes no longer worked. "If," he said.

Someone farted and someone else laughed. The grass prickled on his neck. His brain floated in dark soft swells.

"You got a place?" said a voice.

Barnaby squinted into the darkness.

"You can crash up here," someone said.

"Wow," said Barnaby.

A couple of the kids led him through the darkness into a building. The lights were all off, but they found him a couch, and he stretched out on it gratefully, luxuriating in extraordinarily soft supple upholstery. The building was silent, so the exterior symphony of bugs and amphibians filled his ears with endless variations.

•

"Sir?" A woman's voice, sounding very concerned.

"Eh?" said Barnaby, scrunching deeper into the couch.

"Sir?" she repeated. "Sir, you can't sleep here."

"Huh?"

"The meeting's about to start. Are you in the conference?"

Barnaby sat up. He was surrounded by folding chairs. His couch was at the front of a large living room, across from a big stone fireplace with fancy woodwork. A painting of an English country scene hung above the wide mantel. A lectern had been placed on the hearth, facing him.

A nicely dressed woman stood over him, her face wrinkled with worry. She tugged at his sleeve. "We have to get the room ready," she said. "You're not a speaker, are you? We have to move the couch."

Gradually Barnaby comprehended what was going on, and let the woman guide him out of the big room into a kind of library or office. It seemed familiar. This might have been the room where he had his first admissions interview.

Although the pot had mostly worn off, the thought of spending the night conked out in the middle of the Manor House was unsettling. He looked down at his wrinkly, grass-stained clothes. He could smell a little pot, some gasoline, and a lively streak of old sweat. If he could smell it himself, others would probably be overwhelmed.

The woman had rushed out of the room, but he could hear several other people rushing around as well. He poked his head out of the library, and another woman hurrying down the hall almost crashed into him with a cartload of teacups.

"Oh my god!" she exclaimed. "I'm so, so sorry. We're late for the last session. They'll all start arriving any minute now."

"No problem," said Barnaby, shrinking back and holding his arms tightly to his sides.

The woman wheeled on down the hall. "Oh my goodness," she said, to no-one in particular.

True enough, within only a minute or two people began appearing in the hallway, chatting and laughing on their way to the last session, whatever that was. Barnaby kept well back from the door and watched a parade of well-dressed women go by, mostly in their forties and fifties, and a few men, a few people who seemed quite old, but all dressed like they were going to church. Except that in Plainfield, church, if any, usually meant little more than clean overalls.

The commotion lasted ten or fifteen minutes, during which

Barnaby worried about being discovered, being asked to leave, and being smelled.

Another unfamiliar woman darted into the library. "Are you coming? We're about to start."

Barnaby looked down at his disheveled clothing and shrugged. "I'm not really—"

"Do you need to freshen up? There's a lavatory just through there," she said.

"Oh. Yes. I could use that. My car broke down—"

"I could probably find you a shirt."

"Could you? That would be terrific. I'll make it quick." The woman ran out before he finished speaking. A constant chatter came from the living room. The last session was about to start.

Barnaby cleaned up as best he could, executing a classic sponge bath in record time. He was brushing the grass from his hair and pants when the woman knocked on the door and handed him a bright red Vermont shirt. It was too big, but most shirts were too small, so Barnaby was relieved. He deposited his own shirt in the wastebasket.

He was about half-way down the hall away from the living room when yet another busy, friendly woman encountered him. "Oh, no, it's this way," she said, trying to turn him around.

"No, you see—" he began, but she shushed him and leaned very close as if to tell him a secret.

"We can't talk. It's starting."

"But—"

Barnaby gave up and allowed himself to be propelled back down the hall to the living room, which was now filled to capacity with conference goers. A woman wearing a flower hat was at the podium.

"Ah, yes!" she said. "And here he is now."

The crowd turned and stared as Barnaby lurched into the room with his attendant. They didn't seem to react to his wrinkly grass-stained bluejeans and ill-fitting plaid shirt, but Barnaby felt painfully out of place. *Who the hell do they think I am?*

He stood dumbly staring at the crowd until the woman at the lectern began waving at him. "Come on," she called. "Don't be shy!" She emitted a gay little twitter and the crowd chuckled.

He started to explain that he wasn't the person they thought, but the crowd was applauding now, and his mumbled protest went unheard. His handler was pushing him again, down the narrow aisle between row after row of folding chairs filled with nicely dressed audience members.

Suddenly he was standing behind the lectern, looking out at a sea of smiling faces. Some people were holding smart phones to take snapshots or videos. Cameras and camcorders stood on tripods at the back of the room. The women in the front row were gazing at him in what looked a lot like fawning bedazzlement.

What in god's name am I supposed to say?

The woman in the flower hat said, "So now, without further ado, allow me to present Mr. Mortimer. Mr. Barnaby Mortimer!"

Barnaby drew back, a look of shock splayed across his puffy face; beads of sweat broke out on his forehead. Shakily, he pulled the goose-neck microphone closer and stepped up against the lectern.

"Hello," he said, uncertainly.

The crowd muttered "hello" in response.

"Well," he said.

The crowd hushed.

"Um—"

They waited.

He leaned closer to the mic. "A funny thing happened on the way here today."

The crowd erupted in gales of appreciative laughter that went on and on.

In the parking lot at Chez Marie, the side-stand of an old BMW sank deeper into the loose gravel, and the ancient motorcycle slowly toppled over onto the ground.

Ω

2

The Knock

The house sits on a side street, fairly tidy among various levels of disrepair. In the night, many shadows move inside, behind drawn curtains, though I live alone.

•

There was a loud knock on the front door.

I woke instantly and looked around the bedroom. It was pitch dark, and there wasn't a sound from anywhere, even the refrigerator.

I replayed the knock in my head. Whenever some noise wakes me up, I can usually still hear the last second of the sound. The knock had been quite loud and authoritative.

The police? A fire? The house was silent. Fedex? A passing car?

I put on my bathrobe and went to the front door and peeked out through the venetian blinds. The street was dark, and there was nothing in sight that moved. A prank? Some kid on his way home from an all-nighter, ringing doorbells and knocking on doors?

It was chilly standing there in my bare feet, so I went back to bed and drifted off to sleep again.

A loud knock woke me. This time, I sprinted to the door and had it unlocked and open within seconds. My little sister stood there, which was pretty much impossible, since she lived a couple thousand miles to the left.

I looked again and noticed that Marcy had an AK-47 with a big curved ammo clip. That was just wrong.

"What are you doing with an assault rifle?" I asked.

She stepped back and looked to either side. There were six or eight other women just behind her, in the shadows. They all carried automatic weapons, big clips, ammo belts.

"Why are you so violent?" I asked.

"Maybe because they gave us all assault rifles, and sent us out here to kill people," she said scornfully. "You think maybe *that's* why we're violent?"

She was right; war is like that. I nodded, feeling a wave of empathy for her and her sisters in arms. Then I woke up again, only this time there was no replay of anybody knocking. The house was silent, and it was still dark.

I remembered one night, decades ago, when I was just falling asleep and suddenly heard, very distinctly, the voice of my father, furiously shouting my name, just once. If he ever *had* shouted at me like that, it could only have been because I was about to hurt myself and hadn't heard his first warning. But this mental echo of his voice bounced around in my brain for some time as I sat bolt upright, wondering what the hell was going on.

Back then, I couldn't think of a plausible explanation, other than losing my mind. I rarely recall people's voices, even my parents. That kind of sensory memory just isn't in my brain's repertoire. But this one shout was so distinctive, so unmistakably my father, that it didn't seem like a memory at all. The *replay* was a memory, very short-term, just half a second, but what woke me up was a real shout, from nearby, very loud and clear. My name. Abrupt. Angry. Warning.

As a kid, until about nine, I dreamt a lot, and after a few especially colorful nightmares (one involved a pair of ghosts playing ping pong with meatballs on my model railroad table), I decided to do something about it. I soon found myself inside the dreams, aware that I was dreaming. Knowing it was a dream meant that it didn't matter, and before long I figured out how to control them.

For the next few years, I did whatever I wanted in dreams. I dreamt that the fearsome headmaster of my school was glaring at me, alone in his office for some unknown infraction, so I yelled at him that he was a stinker and a meany and walked out. Through the wall.

Apparently, however, the biological necessity of dreaming must have reclaimed my dream machinery, and I stopped having dreams altogether. According to the experts, of course, I did still have dreams, but they were forgotten so fast and fully that I was no longer aware of them. Over the course of my life, dreams have come and gone a little, but by and large, I don't dream.

In any case, I don't think my father's angry voice ever happened again. But I still don't believe my father's shout in 1970 was just a dream, and here I am forty years later still remembering it. I also don't think it was really my father, shouting.

Anyway, a few years ago, I started dreaming again, but these dreams were all amazingly boring and irrelevant. In fact, just thinking about them in the morning made me feel tired and bored. I began to dread going to sleep, because I knew I'd spend thirty or forty dream-hours standing around in large groups of people talking earnestly about nonsense, or walking through some vast over-decorated house filled with furniture and equipment and artifacts and memorabilia from someone else's life. There wasn't much variety, but it was repeated in endless permutations until sometimes I woke up from the sheer intensity of the irrelevance.

So now, instead of dad shouting my name, I'm still waking up the same way. This last time it was a knock, not a shout, but it felt the same.

A few weeks later, sound asleep, I heard the doorbell. Snapping awake, I replayed the sound, and that's when I realized it was the doorbell from another house, one I had owned decades ago, before I began living alone. I lay back down, very quietly, listening for any faint clue that the doorbell was real. I knew it wasn't, but one hopes.

I must have drifted back to sleep, because I suddenly found myself bolt upright again, replaying the sound of an old telephone ringing, the kind with real metal bells. I hadn't heard one of these since I was a teenager and phones had dials.

I listened intently. Silence. Then, the sound of my front storm door opening; the latch has a distinctive scrape. So I crept out of bed, put on my bathrobe, and tiptoed to the front door. I only had to bend a few slats of the venetian blind to see there was nobody there, and the storm door was still latched. I opened the inner door a crack and locked the storm door. Then I returned to bed.

Another few weeks passed without disturbances, and then I awoke suddenly to the sound of a big dog barking *inside the house*. It was one quick bark, just the size of my replay memory, and it really got my attention. I jumped up, grabbed a large flashlight, and ran out into the living room. As I expected, and sincerely hoped, there was no dog, but I could still faintly hear that deep, peremptory bark. A warning bark.

•

The next day I searched the internet and discovered an article on "Exploding Head Syndrome" which described exactly what I was experiencing. Or almost—people with exploding head syndrome don't usually have dreams directly related to the loud noise. The clinical name seemed unnecessarily ludicrous, but the initials EHS have been assigned, so it's official. Now that I have a name for what's been happening, I should feel better about it, right? It's a Known Thing, and that's a start.

Curiously, the word "start" is also a clinical term for that violent full-body twitch one sometimes experiences while falling asleep. The twitch is also called a hypnagogic jerk. But I digress.

•

I decided I had to do something, at least to check my sanity, so I looked for a shrink who was reputed to know about dreams.

I found Dr. Hälftegehirn in the yellow pages among specialists in more psychological disorders than I had ever heard of. His receptionist said he had an opening on Thursday, so I spent the next three days worrying about what he might say. Was I losing my mind? Did I have a brain tumor?

On Thursday, I arrived early at his office in an outlying medical building and sat fidgeting in the waiting room for an hour. The nurse called me in at precisely 3:00 PM.

His office was sparse and bright; Dr. Hälftegehirn was, too.

I took a seat in the proffered easy chair, facing him. "I think I'm suffering from Exploding Head Syndrome."

"Really? What makes you say that?"

"I looked up my symptoms on the internet. That's what they call it."

"Are you putting me on?"

"Of course not! Haven't you heard of it?"

"Exploding Head Syndrome? Seriously?"

"Well, that's the name. EHS. I guess it must be rare."

"Yes, it sounds rare. Perhaps you should tell me about it."

I knew he didn't believe it was a real condition. Since I had found it in the *DSM IV*, I now seriously doubted his expertise. And his attitude was more combative than supportive. Was this part of his shrink technique?

"It's a parasomnia," I began.

He scowled at me. I figured I must be invading his territory, but I had no way of knowing, so I just told him my last few experiences, the knock, the slam, the bark.

"Well," he said, "These are obviously not dreams."

I nodded. "They're too quick. But sometimes there's a dream afterward."

"Your head explodes but you remain asleep?"

"Apparently. I really don't understand it. That's why I'm here."

"You realize your head isn't actually exploding?"

"Obviously."

"Well, there's no psychological reason for these things to happen."

"It's not stress, or some buried anxiety?"

"No. Clearly, someone is messing with you." He tilted his head as he said this, and looked me up and down. His tone was ambiguous, and I couldn't decide if he was serious or not.

"Messing with me?"

"Obviously. What else could it be?"

"I don't know! I thought you would."

"Well, I'm telling you, someone is messing with you. Do you doubt my expertise?"

"Well, you said you'd never heard of EHS—"

"Listen," he said, straightening up. "Dreams have context; these 'explosions,' as you call them, are isolated, and they fit just perfectly into your replay memory. Why do you suppose that is? So they'll be the only thing you're aware of when you wake up. It's obviously deliberate."

"That's preposterous," I said, my eyes wide. "Who would do that? Who even could?"

Dr. Hälftegehirn leaned back again. "No idea," he said. "Not my field."

"What exactly is 'not your field'?"

"Messing with somebody's head."

"Well, can you recommend someone who knows about this? Someone who can help me?"

"Wouldn't have the faintest."

"Then how—"

He frowned. "Well, it's obvious, isn't it?"

"Not really," I said. "Not at all."

"Then I must leave it to you to work that out," he stated, tonelessly. He stood up and held out his hand. "Nice to have met you."

Reflexively I stood and we shook hands. "If you could please just—" I said.

"My secretary will bill you. No need to come back. Please pay promptly. Have a nice day." He turned and went back to his desk.

•

For a week I pored over listings of psychologists, psychiatrists, analysts, counselors, advisers, and life-coaches. The variety of professions surprised me, and the diversity of methods was even greater, but none of them sounded like experts in messing with someone. I was dying to ask Dr. Hälftegehirn what he meant by that, but I wasn't about to intrude where I'm unwelcome.

The next morning, a large glass shattered on my kitchen floor. I had to get up and look for the shards, but of course there was nothing there. Later, I wandered the streets, hoping to find a bookstore that might hold some clues. I stopped at a lunch counter for coffee, and sat brooding.

I hadn't noticed the old woman on the next stool until she turned to me and said, "You look-a for me."

I turned. She was disheveled, but not alarmingly so. "I beg your pardon?"

"I know-a you," she stated. "You look-a for me."

"Not really," I said.

"Oh yeah. Head boom. You look-a. I wait."

Her confidence was disarmingly intense. I told myself there was nothing mystical going on.

"I'm not into ooga booga," I said.

"No booga. Just talk."

So I swiveled my stool towards her, and the whole story spilled out, from the knocks to Dr. Hälftegehirn to this morning's broken glass. She listened intently, her eyes fixed unwaveringly on my mouth, her head bobbing in time to my speech, as if she could see the words coming out.

When I was done, she said, "He right. Messing with you, some-body."

"Really?" *What did she know?*

"Or some thing."

"Thing?"

"No booga. Messing, sure. Maybe not somebody."

"What does that mean?"

"No mean. You got-a forget."

"Forget what?"

"You forget all this business. Quick."

"You mean just drop it? Don't try to make it stop?"

"Ya, drop."

"But why? What if it keeps getting worse?"

She bent closer. "Drop. You only hope," she snapped. "Or it get real."

Get real? What was she talking about?

She wagged her finger at me. "You keep think, splode get real."

"You mean there will really be someone at the door?"

"You betch-a."

"But that time it actually was a dream," I said.

"No dream. Messing." She raised her wag finger again, and cocked her head.

"Then what do I do? I have to do something!" I couldn't believe I was seeking advice from this unknown, terse little old lady.

"No do! Forget do! Do go boom!" Her eyes were wide, and her body was shaking. I stared at her, and she gathered up her things, rotated clockwise, and slid off the stool. She stormed out of the luncheonette in a flurry of mismatched fabric.

My coffee was cold, and so was I.

•

The next day I awoke normally, and I wondered if somehow I was actually going to get past this. I didn't think much more about my problem, and the next day was also silent.

Then, for four days running, I woke to a loud pop, a screen door slamming, something heavy falling, and a splintery chopping sound. I began to obsess. Throughout the day, my replay memory would deliver up one or another of the recent sounds, and my heart would jump. By the end of the day I was close to panic.

It was impossible to sleep. I dreaded hearing the next sound, knowing that whatever it was would wake me up startled, full of adrenalin. The nights were long and restless, and I couldn't get my mind off the knocks and bangs. Was the old lady right? Was obsessing on it going to make it more and more real? That was impossible, but obsessing obviously wasn't going to help.

There was an old bottle of tranquillizers in the bathroom, left over from my air travel days, so I took a couple and fell into a deep sleep.

I woke late the next morning hung over and exhausted, in exactly the same position in the bed. I hadn't moved, and there hadn't been a sound or even a dream all night long. But it wasn't real sleep, and the day was worse than ever.

My daily routine had become erratic, and I resorted to playing loud music to drown out my replay memory. After a few days (punctuated by another dog bark, a huge metal bar, and a rat-trap snapping), I took to leaving the radio and the TV on all day, along with the music. I left the lights on. I surfed the web compulsively, hoping to stumble on something as unpredictable as the old lady. I was desperate and totally ready for ooga booga.

On Saturday, I woke to the sound of ticking, like an old alarm clock with a pair of bells on top. It reminded me of a cartoon with wires and sticks of dynamite. Then I realized it was *still ticking*— or was my replay memory just looping the echo? I pondered this for a minute, and then there was a loud click—

Ω

3

The Journalist

Eric first met Oliver Borman outside a grand country house in the Hudson highlands, where Oliver was hoeing sand and gravel from the gutter alongside the driveway. A heavy rain had just stopped when Eric arrived, after a long train ride from Manhattan.

Oliver looked up from his work and leaned on his hoe; his broad grin reminded Eric of a long-lost grandfather. He looked at Eric politely but inquisitively, and his grey gaze made Eric wonder if the real reason for this visit was no longer hidden. And then Eric wondered if he knew himself why this interview was so important.

Borman's house was large, with a weathered elegance, a relic of 19th century gentility. But Oliver himself was a visual anomaly, wet from the rain and sweat, wearing a string undershirt and baggy work pants. He pulled off his gloves: his handshake was firm and matched his obvious delight in welcoming a visitor, though Eric couldn't imagine why he would be welcome here.

"You must be Eric," Borman said, still grinning.

"I am," Eric replied. "It's an honor to meet you, sir."

"Well, it's entirely mutual." Oliver gestured at the house. "Let's go inside and have a drink."

Eric picked up his briefcase and bag and followed Oliver up the driveway toward the open garage.

"You wouldn't believe how much gravel washes away after a rain like that," Oliver said.

"I can imagine. It looks like a lot of work."

"Not really work. More like a great excuse to get outside and do something physical for a change."

Borman strode energetically up the driveway, clearly well-accustomed to exertion. He led Eric through the triple garage into the house and pointed to the hallway and the living room beyond. "Just leave your bags here and have a seat," he said. "We'll get you settled later. First I need a drink, and I suspect you do too."

In fact, Eric was still awash in headache-inducing railroad coffee and ersatz orange juice, but he nodded and headed to a couch next to the large bay window. Wet forest surrounded the house in dark saturated green.

"Beer, wine, coffee?" Borman called, presumably from the kitchen.

"Wine," Eric replied.

A moment later, Oliver strode in brandishing a glass of red and an opened bottle of beer. "Make yourself comfortable," he said, waving vaguely at the room. "I'm going to get dried off. Won't be long."

At the doorway, he turned and added, "I'm really looking forward to our chat."

Now alone, Eric realized the house was much bigger than it seemed from outside. Oliver's footsteps took a long time to fade away, and the reverberant silence evoked numerous large empty rooms. Eric wondered why someone would choose to live alone in such a large place. Perhaps it had a history.

There were three couches, a large coffee table strewn with magazines and interesting objects, a few armchairs and lamps, and a wide stone fireplace with black smoke stains reaching up over the mantel to the high beamed ceiling. Faux kerosene lamps hung between the beams, giving the room an almost theatrically rustic style.

Oliver returned in jeans and a work-shirt. "Sorry to keep you waiting," he said.

"No problem, Professor Borman," Eric replied. "It's an honor to visit your home."

"This is hardly a home," he said. "There's nobody here but me, pretty much, and I haven't given it an ounce of attention in a decade."

Eric glanced out the bay window. "Those gutters were getting some attention, I'd say."

"Necessary evil," Borman said, and then moved uncomfortably in his chair. A strange expression swept across his face, almost a grimace. After a pause, his voice was a shade deeper. "I pay property tax, too," he said evenly, looking Eric in the eye.

"Sorry, Professor. No offense intended."

"None—" Borman said, inserting an odd pause, "taken."

The man's apparently unbridled cordiality seemed to have dissipated. Perhaps it was Eric's imagination. "I didn't mean to—" he began, but Oliver cut him off.

"Please don't call me Professor Borman."

"Alright. Do you prefer Oliver?"

"I suppose."

"Or something else? Mr. Borman? Doctor?"

Oliver laughed, again showing an easy, friendly energy. "How about Doc?"

"Doc will be fine," said Eric.

"Shall we start?"

"Sure," said Eric, getting up. "We could start right now if you like."

"You'd prefer to wait?"

"No. Not at all. Let me get my recorder." Eric retrieved his briefcase from the hallway. "Time waits for no man," he mumbled, returning to the couch.

"What's that?"

"Uh, nothing," said Eric. He set his recorder on the coffee table;

the red LED glowed brightly in the subdued light of the afternoon storm.

"Nothing?" said Borman. "Nothing at all?" He sounded serious.

"No, really. I just was mumbling 'Time waits for no man,'" said Eric. *Conversing with this guy is more complicated than it should be.*

"Hardly," said Borman. He leaned forward again, smiling a little. "And you are—?"

Eric hesitated. *Did he just forget my name?*

Borman must have noted Eric's moment of confusion. "I'm terribly busy these days," he said quietly. "How would you prefer to be called?"

"Oh," said Eric, relieved. "Call me Eric. Please."

"Eric it is, then."

Eric sipped his wine; Borman ignored his beer.

"Were you born in New York?" Eric began.

"Up near Kingston. My father had a small farm."

"How long were you involved in farming?"

"Not long. Not at all, in fact. My father switched to selling farm equipment when I was a toddler, and by the time I was 12 we had moved to the city."

"Albany?"

"Schenectady. East side of the river."

"How did you feel about the move?"

"I didn't think about it much. I would have preferred staying in the country—a lot more freedom for a kid. And it was in the city that I—"

"What? Did something happen in Schenectady?"

Borman frowned, looking up into the shadows of the ceiling beams. "No, nothing happened. Not until much later."

"You seemed about to say something," Eric ventured.

"Yes. No, we'll get to that. It was only a few years ago, when I went back to Schenectady to look up an old friend."

That's something I'll be sure to bring up, thought Eric, but he needed to get the chronology clear. "How was school after you moved?"

"Pretty rewarding, I guess. I got good grades, made new friends, adapted to the new environment. And that's when I got interested in psychology."

"Really, that young?"

"I guess I knew it was in my blood from the very beginning," Borman said. "When I was a junior in high school I took my first psych course. If you can call it a course. But the die was cast—I couldn't stop thinking about character traits, relationships, personae, attitudes and fears, the way people treat each other."

Borman suddenly noticed his beer, and picked it up. He glanced at Eric with a faintly quizzical expression, and then took a long pull.

"I was fascinated by the behavior of my classmates," he said. "They were so absorbed in their own delusions. Their fantasies ruled their lives, and they didn't have a clue. I guess I figured if I could get past that, I could live in freedom." He shrugged, and pressed his lips together. "Little did I know," he said.

"About what?"

"Oh, about how far this adolescent fascination would take me. Where it would all lead." His face had collapsed into a bitter grimace, and he slumped in his chair, holding the beer bottle at a precarious angle.

Eric frowned. Was this famous psychologist, author of several paradigm-shifting books, regretting his own field of study? "Was there some other area you would prefer to have focused your energies?" Eric said.

Borman looked up, surprised. He straightened, shifted in his chair, and almost dropped the beer bottle. He set the bottle down, and smiled sheepishly. "Sorry," he said. "I sometimes get lost in thought."

"No problem, Doc," said Eric.

"Was I gone long?"

"Long? Not at all. Just a couple of seconds."

"Seemed like longer," said Borman, pensively. "But of course it's shorter and shorter, actually."

"I'm not sure I know what you mean."

"No, no, of course you wouldn't. Private joke. Not very polite of me. My apologies. There's a lot on my mind these days. Ah, where were we?"

"You were describing how you first became interested in psychology."

"I was?" He seemed genuinely surprised. "Well, it all started in my junior year, when I became fascinated with psych in a course taught by Mr. Waller. It just fired up my imagination in a thousand ways, and I never looked back."

"Was that when you realized it would become your life's work?"

"Pretty much. I've been so fortunate, really. It all came quite naturally. I didn't have to force myself to study. In fact, I couldn't stop reading all the books I could get my hands on. In psychology, that is. Those were wonderful years."

He settled back in his chair with a happy, wistful smile.

"I did miss those days on the farm, though," Borman said. "They were also very happy times. Less pressure, and I love being surrounded by nature. The city is so cold and dirty. Not real dirt, mind you, like the mud in my gutters. Just dirtiness."

"You mentioned a trip back to Schenectady," Eric said.

"Did I?"

"You said it was not very long ago, and you'd gone to see a friend."

"I said all that?" Borman looked aghast. "Are you sure? You're not trying to lead me into something?" He sounded puzzled and suspicious.

Eric pointed at the pocket recorder. "I can play it back for you, but please believe me, I don't want to push you into discussing anything you're uncomfortable with."

Borman relaxed a little. The twinkle returned to his eyes, and he said, "Eric, please don't mind my little mood swings. Perhaps I absorbed some of the neuroses I've studied for so long. I've got so much on my mind."

"Not a problem. Feel free to change the subject any time."

"You're too kind," Borman said. He drank some more beer. Eric sipped his wine. Thunder rolled softly across the sodden landscape outside.

"Would you rather not talk about Schenectady?" Eric asked.

"No, I guess it's fine. Whatever you think should be in the article."

"I was wondering about your friend. The one you were going to visit."

"Oh, Mr. Waller. My old psych teacher in high school. He was getting on in years, and I thought I might let him know what a positive influence he'd been. We so seldom acknowledge the people who change our lives that way."

"Did you see him?"

"Actually, no. I never got that far. What happened hasn't got anything to do with Mr. Waller. If I *had* seen him things might have been very different."

"Different how?"

"Well, this present situation, it might—" Borman stopped abruptly. He closed his eyes for a few seconds, and twisted around.

Eric waited, wondering if he was witnessing something personal that was none of his business.

Borman opened his eyes and looked out the bay window at the trees. Eric took another sip of wine. *Something's wrong: should I keep going?*

Borman turned back to look piercingly at Eric, a frown etched into his face. "What was I saying?" he said.

Eric decided confrontation might be unwise. "We were talking about Mr. Waller."

"What the hell did I tell you?" Borman snapped.

Eric flinched. "Just that he was a great inspiration, and that you never did get to visit him that day."

"I see," said Borman. He seemed to be growing angry, but it wasn't clear where his anger was directed.

"I gather something happened to interrupt your visit," Eric said, cautiously.

"You can bloody well say that again." Borman collected himself and tried to smile. "I must apologize. The intervals are so short now."

"Intervals?"

"Yes, I can hardly get any momentum going. Can't cover it up anymore."

Eric pondered. "Are you having some kind of episodes?" he asked.

Borman gave a short, bitter laugh. "Episodes! Yes, I guess you could say that."

"Is this something you'd rather not discuss?"

"It's something I'd bloody well rather not experience," he said.

Eric took that as a No and had another sip of wine, waiting.

Eventually Borman said, "I suppose it's too late to keep it to myself. I don't know how it will end, but perhaps your article is the place to let it all out."

Eric waited; he knew when an interviewee was loosening up.

"It started three years ago, in Schenectady. I parked near the high school, thinking I'd walk to Mr. Waller's house and take in the old sights. It was a pure nostalgia trip, of course. I don't know if I really thought I'd find Waller or if he'd even care about my life." He laughed again with a thin smile. "What a farce!"

Eric said, "What happened?"

Borman shook his head. "I really don't know. Something happened, and I've examined every minute of my life since that day, and it must have happened while I was walking, because that's the first time I lost track."

"Lost track of what was happening?" *Like you've just been doing?*

"Yes, that's about it. I was walking along Parkwood Boulevard, and suddenly I was in a hotel room in Manhattan."

"You blacked out?"

"It couldn't have been a blackout, because I'd lost a whole month. I thought it was amnesia, but there were no further symptoms for another month. And then it happened again. I was walking across the front lawn—" He gestured out the side windows of the living room. "And then suddenly it was the middle of the night, and I was sitting bolt upright in bed, upstairs in this house—" His voice trailed off.

"How long had it been this time?"

"It took me until morning to get things sorted out, but it was another month. Probably a few days less."

"But what was happening in your life while you were away?"

"That's what flummoxed me at first," Borman replied. "I started asking around, and everyone swore that I had been perfectly normal during these periods. I wasn't acting different, and nobody noticed a thing. Except that I was developing a reputation for being a bit forgetful. Absent-minded professor. Not a big deal."

"I guess not. But it must have been incredibly disorienting."

"A very big deal for me, that's for damn sure," he said, clenching his teeth. "But it wasn't just a few episodes. They kept happening."

"How often? Are they still happening? Have you seen anyone about it?"

Borman looked at Eric like an errant pupil in grade school. "Of course I bloody well saw someone about it. I know half the psychologists in the US, and all of the good ones. I've talked about it with anybody who could have an opinion, but nobody has a clue." He paused again. "Hell, I don't have a clue."

"But surely it's not that unusual. Aren't blackouts fairly well understood?" Eric asked.

"Sure, most blackouts have a cause. But we've never seen blackouts where the patient is perfectly normal during the blackout. So it's obviously *not* a blackout. It's some kind of periodic amnesia, repeating episodes of absolutely no memory."

"Wouldn't that be a completely new syndrome?"

"Well, that's what I thought, at first."

"You changed your mind?"

"That's a painfully ironic way of putting it." Borman muttered. He snatched the beer bottle and took a long drink. "I changed my mind when I started taking detailed notes. The next time I came back from a blackout, it was suddenly quite clear." He paused again, looking out the window. "As clear as it's ever going to get, I suspect."

Eric wanted to jump up and call his publisher. This interview was turning into a whole series of articles, in addition to getting a very personal exclusive on one of the most famous men in America. An unsettling, possibly tragic exclusive that could lead to headlines and bylines and possibly an entire career in the limelight.

With some difficulty, Eric took another drink of wine, fighting to disguise his excitement. "What happened with your notes?" he asked, softly.

Borman didn't respond. He was sitting quite still, staring at Eric, his face devoid of emotion. He blinked several times, and took a deep breath. "What did I just say?"

Eric suddenly got it. "Did you just have one?" he asked.

"One what?" said Borman.

"Episode?"

"What episode?" said Borman. Then he squinted and stared at Eric even harder. "You mean spell?" he said.

"Episode, spell, I don't know," said Eric. "You were describing these periods of amnesia, or something like that. Then you suddenly stopped."

Borman sat back, shocked. "You mean I've told you about it?"

"Yes. I think you just did."

"Wow." Borman sighed. Then he smiled and said, "Well, I guess

I must have thought it's the right time. I thought we were going to keep it secret a bit longer, but it's happening so fast it must be time."

"Time for what?" said Eric.

"I get these spells. I forget things, and then everything's normal again. But it's not really forgetting."

"Not amnesia?"

"Not in the slightest. It's MPD."

"Multiple Personality Disorder?" said Eric, amazed. "How could it possibly be MPD?"

"Well, it ain't your grandfather's MPD," Borman said, with a forced chuckle. "Both personalities are me. You've been talking to me, Oliver Borman, since you arrived, haven't you?"

Eric nodded.

"Well, it's been two of me. I'm cycling between two personalities, but they're both the same one. The only real effect is to give each of us periods of amnesia. But the spells alternate precisely, so in a sense I'm always here, experiencing everything, all the time. It's just that it's not the same 'I' each time."

"That's incredible," said Eric.

"We've been leaving each other notes lately," Borman said. "And as soon as we started exchanging messages, it was obvious that I was writing all of them."

Eric gaped, then shut his mouth.

Borman continued. "But that's begun to change."

"How is it changing? Another personality?"

"No, not another personality. But our worlds of experience are slightly different, so we're *becoming* slightly different. Haven't you noticed anything inconsistent about my behavior? I'm alternating every few minutes now."

Eric thought about it. Borman had been acting cheerful for a while and then inexplicably testy and annoyed. "Yes, I was wondering about that," Eric said. "I guess I'm currently talking to a happier Oliver Borman."

"Exactly," said Borman. He glanced at his watch. "In another couple of minutes you'll be talking to the other me, the one that's pissed off."

"It's strange that the two of you are so different."

"Not really. We've had three years—well, half of three years each—of different life experiences, different events, different responses. Especially at the beginning, when each cycle lasted for weeks."

"I guess so."

"The other me has every right to be angry, because of what happened when he was present. He screwed up some projects, or at least he was there when the shit hit the fan. When this all began, neither of us had any idea what was going on, and naturally we tried to cover it up. But I was the one who decided to contact my professional peers to explore the syndrome, and he was the one who got all the letters telling him he was psychotic. And he was also the one who got the termination letter from the university. And a lot more. It was just bad luck, but I precipitated all that, and he got to enjoy the results. It pissed him off, understandably, as it would have pissed me off. And I guess it changed him."

"That's incredible," said Eric.

"You said that already."

Eric laughed uneasily. "You've been repeating yourself a bit, too."

Borman laughed. This persona seemed reasonably comfortable with itself, and Eric dreaded the return of the other Borman.

Another distant roll of thunder gently shook the house.

"Rip van Winkle," said Borman.

"Yeah. Just woke up," Eric replied.

They sat for some time without speaking. Then Eric began to worry about the imminent shift of personas, and wondered if he should try to see it happening. Borman must have noted Eric's fascination, because he said, "Go ahead and study me. There's not much time left. Maybe you'll learn something we can use."

"Why do you keep saying you're running out of time?"

"I'm not sure. We're not sure. But the alternation is happening faster and faster. This morning it was almost twenty minutes, and now it's well under ten. In fact, I—"

Eric studied Borman's face, and it looked like a sheet of water momentarily rippled across, very delicately distorting the man's entire body.

Borman squinted at Eric. "How long?" he said.

"I was watching your face. I could see it happen," said Eric.

"How long?" Borman demanded.

"Six or seven minutes, give or take."

"Time this," said Borman. "We need to know."

"But *what* will we know? The whole thing is still a complete mystery."

"We have to time it, find out how fast it's accelerating."

"What can that possibly tell us?" said Eric.

"When it will end."

Eric slumped. What would happen when the alternation was every minute? Would Borman go mad? How fast could it get? Ten seconds? Half a second?

"What does it feel like?" Eric asked.

"Nothing. Can't feel it at all. Did you note the time?" Borman was visibly agitated.

"Twenty past two."

"God."

"Yeah."

They sat quietly, and Eric's head spun.

After a few minutes, Borman sat up straight. "We should be recording this," he said.

"We are," said Eric, pointing at the voice recorder.

"No, the time of each cycle," said Borman.

"We are. You started this cycle at two twenty."

"No I didn't! I just came back."

Eric looked at his watch. It was twenty-four past two. "Four minutes," he said.

"God."

"I didn't see it that time," said Eric.

"You can see it happen?"

"Yes. Your whole body sort of ripples. Just a little. Can't you feel it?"

"No, I can't feel the shift. But I can feel the discontinuity. When I'm here, I'm constantly looking back in my mind to see what's just happened, and it's kind of like a black, mental thump. Suddenly there's nothing to remember since my last period of occupancy. It's all happening in the mind, but it affects my whole sensorium. Hard to explain."

"Yeah, really hard to explain."

"Four minutes, eh? Down from seven?"

Eric nodded.

The watery shiver ran across Borman again. He closed his eyes for a second or two and then said, "How long?"

Eric looked at his watch. "Three minutes."

"Shit. That's not even time enough to talk about it."

"Sure it is," said Eric. "What do you think is going to happen?"

"How should I know?"

"Well, you're the one experiencing it. Maybe you have an insight?"

"Insight based on what?" Borman grumbled. "Maybe we'll just both go black."

"Go on."

"Or maybe it will be unbearable, and we'll go stark raving mad." He sat in stony silence. "How the hell should I know!"

Eric watched his host, who now sat stiffly, as if awaiting a jolt of electricity. His empathy for what Borman was going through had grown, and he no longer obsessed about his journalistic career. And he couldn't take his eyes off Borman.

The ripple came again.

"Two minutes," said Eric. Borman grimaced.

"You know," said Borman pleasantly, "Maybe when the oscillation gets fast enough the two of us will just merge. Probably under one millisecond the nervous system can't sustain it, so both personae will have to coexist. It could just resolve itself spontaneously."

Borman was grinning, and Eric felt a pang of compassion. This was unknown territory, of course, but some kind of merging might indeed be the most likely outcome.

There was another ripple, and Borman's body stiffened again.

"50 seconds," said Eric.

"Too fast," said Borman.

They waited in awkward silence while Eric stared at his host. Borman stared at nothing, waiting.

Another ripple.

"Wow," said Borman. "This is really strange. It's actually not so bad. I think—I hope to God, that is—that this merging idea might turn out to be a reasonable prediction." His voice was hopeful, even positive, but he was still visibly agitated.

Eric exhaled, inhaled, and again his host's figure rippled ever so slightly, and Borman's face shifted. "Bloody hell!" he said.

In a few heartbeats, there was another shift, and the other Borman reappeared, and his face snapped into the previous forced smile.

He began to speak, and then shifted again. The ripples were almost constant now, and Borman's expression began to look like a cartoon, twitching back and forth between his two personas.

"I can't—"

     "What—"

"—take—"

     "—the—"

"—this—"

     "—fuck—"

"—any—"

And then Eric saw, or felt, a kind of blur overtake first Borman's face and then his whole body, and Eric realized whatever he was witnessing wasn't just psychological. Borman was changing physically; something more extreme was happening.

Eric felt a kind of low buzz, like a muffled drum roll, and wondered if it might be more thunder from outside. He glanced out the bay window, and then back at Borman, but Borman now sat rigid, vibrating like a silent jackhammer, and Eric thought he could somehow sense it happening.

It was too much to take in. His sense of reality was crumbling, while the man he had been talking to minutes before had become a blur before his eyes. Tiny fragments of human speech were sputtering from the Borman blur, and Eric turned away again, and then realized he was going to pass out. *I've got to remain objective,* he thought, feeling a desperate sense of helplessness. He peeked back at Borman again, and the room went black.

•

Eric came to almost immediately. A far-off peal of thunder rattled the living room windows, and he opened his eyes.

Only a few minutes had passed, and he realized the room had become silent and still. Whatever was happening to Borman had stopped. The other man slouched in his chair, the beer bottle on its side, spilling onto the wood floor. Eric picked it up.

"Doc?" he said. "Oliver? Professor? Are you OK?"

Borman remained motionless. After a little while Eric summoned the courage to touch his shoulder, and then it was sufficiently obvious that the man was dead.

Eric collapsed onto the couch, exhausted and shaken. Eventually, he came to his senses and called 911. A seizure. Ambulance. He's not breathing.

The police arrived just before the paramedics, and asked the usual questions. There was no evidence of foul play. Did Eric have any notes from the interview? Yes, a few pages, but nothing substantial. Anything else? Nothing. The recorder was back in his briefcase. Eric knew the recording wouldn't do the police any good, none at all.

In the days that followed, Eric did his best to write down his recollections of Borman's dilemma and his demise, but work was nearly impossible. He spent his afternoons wandering Central Park. Once or twice he climbed the steps of the Metropolitan Museum, but suddenly realized that a deluge of diverse creativity from all cultures and epochs would only further strain his tenuous grip on reality.

After a few more weeks, Eric began to feel normal again, and his notes were starting to come together. He transcribed the recording of his interview, and pounded out a rough manuscript describing the events and revelations at Borman's house, including every detail his journalist's training could recover. His publisher had been badgering him to get a story in print while the news of Borman's death was still fresh.

Eric stuffed the printout of his latest revision into his briefcase. *I wonder if anyone will believe this,* he thought, as he headed for the elevator. A wave of doubt swept over him. He could imagine his publisher's reaction: "The public is expecting an account of a great man's last interview, not an insane fantasy. What the hell are you thinking?"

He spun around and returned to his apartment. A quick call to his publisher to postpone their meeting would suffice. He would just write up a solid, imaginary interview, describe the professor's seizure in plausible terms, and end with a respectful contemporary eulogy.

As he sat down at his desk, he blinked, and the room was gone. He was standing in a hotel bathroom with a safety razor in his hand, staring into the mirror. For a brief moment, the face peering back at him looked almost like Borman's, and then he realized he had no idea where he was, or how he got there.

Ω

4

Interview with the Zombie

The zombie sat motionless in my other leather chair. Now and then he sniffed one overstuffed chair arm or the other, as if wondering if the leather still contained food. Perhaps this confused him, if zombies can experience mental states, or any kind of states, for that matter. In any case, he was more or less still, affording me a chance to ask him a few questions.

"Do you realize what's happened to you?" I asked.

He stared at the chair arm, a dry tongue darting back and forth through his open mouth. His lips were missing.

"Do you remember your name?" I said. "Before you were—changed?"

A hoarse grunt emerged from his dessicated throat. His body shuddered and it seemed as if he might be preparing to speak. At that point, I wasn't sure if zombies could vocalize at all, but it was certainly worth investigating. After all, how many people have ever sincerely tried to converse with one?

"My name is Albert," I said.

The zombie twisted around aimlessly, opening and closing what was left of its mouth.

"I'd like to hear your point of view."

No reaction at all. Just a continuation of random motion, something like restlessness or ADHD.

"Can you hear my voice?" I asked. Then I felt stupid: obviously he could *hear* me. Zombies are attracted by noise, so yes, he could hear my voice. Perhaps it was too painfully obvious to deserve an answer.

"Do you understand English?" I wanted to shift the conversation back to a more sensible context.

A long, slow rattle emerged from his throat.

"Can you understand what I'm saying to you?"

The rattle morphed into a sporadic sandy flapping, deep in his chest, and then faded away.

I moved closer. "*Can you understand me?*" I shouted.

He turned toward me so fast that his torso twisted awkwardly. The rotting flesh dangling from his exposed ribs swung to and fro, but of course he was unaware of such things. What struck me was the look in his eye (the other one dangled from the socket, shrunken and useless, like an old grape). He seemed perplexed. His condition *was* undeniably perplexing, for both of us.

I wondered what he was feeling—some kind of undead angst?

"I'm so sorry; you don't have to reply," I said. "Don't worry."

His head bobbed around, and his eye darted from side to side.

"It's alright," I went on. "Everything's going to be OK."

Of course I was lying, but there was no need to rub his nose in it. Compassion is probably unfamiliar to zombies, but still, it might ease the tension between us. It was worth a try, anyway.

For a few minutes we sat silently, two beings in leather armchairs, sharing the mysterious gulf that loomed between us.

I asked him another question. "Do you remember who you are?"

He coughed. It sounded like "Abarth."

"I didn't catch that," I said. "Could you say that again?"

"Bendix," he said, or so I thought, making the requisite esophageal allowances.

He returned to scratching the leather upholstery.

"Please don't scratch at the furniture," I said.

He stopped scratching and turned toward me.

"Michelin?" he asked.

I pondered. Was he speaking about car parts? Was there something about cars that he needed to say? Something so deep and important that even in his extreme condition the words were fighting their way to the surface?

Then I realized all his fingernails were coming off. My heart went out to him: all along I'd been worrying about the furniture. I was such a self-centered insensitive fool. And he with no fingertips and at least two or three fingers missing completely. Oh, the vanity of the human condition!

The smell was, I hate to put it so bluntly, very intense. He smelled like—rotting flesh, what else? The room reeked of it. Another pang of guilt stabbed at my gut. Here I was, perfectly healthy, my whole future ahead of me, judging this poor creature because of his smell! We can be so petty.

I had hoped to muster some kind of journalistic professionalism. I wanted to set a suitable standard for myself. But here I was, already judging, pigeonholing, stereotyping. I fought back the urge to gag. This was not how Woodward and Bernstein would handle such things, or Edward R. Murrow.

I noticed that the leather armchair was becoming stained with colorful exudates and drippings. I wondered if saddle soap would take it out. Possibly the chair would need a full treatment with neatsfoot oil.

His hand twitched sporadically as he turned around in a series of small jerks. He was reaching toward me. I looked down—I had been gesturing with my pencil.

"Is that it?" I said. "Do you want my pencil?"

Of course! He couldn't *talk*; he couldn't articulate real words. It should have been obvious, and I had completely missed it.

But he brushed the pencil aside and lightly touched my fingertips. It was heart-breaking.

He really was reaching out. Not in a threatening way, but in a plaintive, pleading kind of gesture. I couldn't refuse him. How quickly we judge others. I let him take my hand. His eye twitched up and stared straight at me and I was filled with confusion and compassion.

He bent farther in my direction; a few loops of intestine tumbled out onto the side of the chair. Empathy overwhelmed me.

Then I realized he was gently nibbling at my hand.

He started almost as though he was savoring an hors-d'oeuvre, but the slobbering and grunts increased and I realized he was not going to stop with my fingertips. I should have pulled away, but I just didn't have the heart.

Ω

4: Interview with the Zombie

5

Our Lady of the Ellington

The grand lobby was three stories tall, bounded by high, dark-paneled walls that disappeared into shadows overhead. Out of the gloom gigantic chandeliers hung down, depending from chains fastened to unseen rafters. Over the years, simulations had replaced many of the chandeliers' elaborate brass components; now they only drew attention to a failed uniformity.

Looking up, the woman wondered what event might require the replacement of chandelier parts—had they fallen, one by one, onto the lobby floor? What a marvelous tinkling crash they must have made. Did rusting chains simply give out, over time? Perhaps the original iron eye-bolts, too high up to perceive, slowly pulled from the ancient timbers, one fiber of cellulose snapping every now and then, until the threaded bar came free and another huge tree of brass and glass plummeted the last twenty feet onto the polished marble.

She looked back across the lobby. There were no guests this late. She held her breath and listened closely, straining to hear the faint distant crackle of slowly splintering beams. The chandeliers were silent. In fact, everything overhead, even the rooms, was utterly silent for a few moments.

Once in a while, in such a silence, something far off in the hotel would make a sound—a door closing, a voice, a suitcase dropping to the floor. The sound would reverberate down the long corridors and a few of those echoes would cluster together and make their way circuitously to one of the cavernous grand entrances of the lobby. There, these softened bundles of secondary sound would float back and forth, caressing anyone who was quiet enough to listen. She savored these gentle occasional tones, feeling the hush of her blood slowly fill the long gaps between each echo, louder and louder until another impossibly faint inarticulate activity drifted past again, blotting out the sound of her own hearing.

With a rattle and clank one of the main entrance doors opened. The great hinges squeaked and groaned, and the din of traffic flowed into the lobby, enveloping a heavy-set man in a raincoat. He hauled himself through the entryway and looked around. Carrying such large bags, he would not have fit into the revolving door. He spied the front desk, and made for it with manifest deliberation, leaning forward, hauling his suitcases against an invisible hurricane.

He dropped the bags by the front desk, and looked around again. He saw no one; the woman was hidden at her far, dim-lit corner table beneath the fringed lampshade. He moved the bell on the counter closer and pressed the button three times with the flat of his hand. The bell rang and echoed through the lobby and into the back offices. The man watched the office door behind the front desk expectantly. The lobby fell silent again. The woman could hear the man's loud breathing.

After the bell faded, apparently unnoticed, the man scanned the lobby for signs of life. Finding none, he whacked the bell several times in rapid succession and then stood still, head tilted, listening.

He was just reaching out to ring the bell even more vigorously when the door behind the counter opened and the night-man hurried out, rubbing his eyes, straightening his bow-tie, trying to smile. The night-man squinted to see how many large men were standing impatiently at the counter.

"Ah hum. Good morning, good morning," he muttered, looking around with dull excitement, then fixing on the new guest and bearing down on him in an eager blur.

"About time," the man said. "I been ringing this damn bell for five minutes."

"So sorry," the night-man replied, shuffling registration forms on the marble counter top. "Caught me in the filing room. Very late, not a lot of guests this time of night. Sorry to keep you waiting. Room with a view?" He held out a form.

The man took it and said, "You got a pen?"

The night-man scooped up a ballpoint imprinted in gold and handed it to the guest with a flourish.

Wordlessly the guest filled in the form and slid it across the marble.

"Chicago, eh?" said the night-man.

"Chicago?"

"In from Chicago, I see, ah, Mr. Jensen," said the night-man. "Have a nice flight, I hope?"

"I came from San Francisco," said Mr. Jensen.

"Oh, well, that's a nice flight, too." The guest was holding out his hand for a room key, and the night-man quickly plucked one from the matrix of empty boxes behind him. He jotted down the room number. "1509," he said, putting the key into the guest's outstretched hand with a little slap, like an operatory nurse.

Mr. Jensen glanced at the key, picked up his bags, and headed for the elevator, again making good progress against the unseen gale.

The woman watched Jensen moving along the opposite side of the lobby. He heaved his bags beside the elevator doors and pressed the button. She watched the antique pointer slowly rotate around to the lobby level; the doors slid open with a metallic thump. Mr. Jensen shoved his bag into the waiting cell, walked in, and turned to survey the lobby one last time. He leaned to one side and punched his floor, straightened, and looked directly at the woman as the doors closed before his eyes. She saw a brief movement of surprise in his face just before the bronze panels met, inches from his nose.

•

Jensen was not an unusual late night arrival. She had seen many men drag themselves in from a long journey, checking in with various night-men, leaving their names on forms, slogging to the elevator, and disappearing up into the distant reaches of the hotel. They were all exhausted, curt, bundled, alone, grim, and thoroughly male—deep voices, brusque aggressive manners, determined focus, distracted by serious, professional, difficult matters weighing down their worlds.

She had seen Jensen, in another guise, another man, another Jensen, staring at her across her little marble table in the corner of the lobby. He had pushed his ruddy face close to hers, breathing heavily, exhaling hotel spices, urgently demanding, consumed by his professional distractions. She forgot the substance of their conversation, but the vibrations lingered in the spacious lobby; in her thoughts they coalesced into semi-tangible form even now, years later.

"Who do you think you are?" one prior Jensen had demanded, injured, requiring surcease. "I don't open up to just any woman I meet in a hotel bar." He shifted in his chair, crossed his legs the other way, then uncrossed them and hunched forward even more, close enough to sip her drink. "You gotta come clean with me, Doris. You can't just sit there in judgment, like some damned sphinx, for chrissake." He sat back, looked around the lobby, then turned back to her. "Aw, come on, honey. Have a heart."

She said nothing; had said nothing. His pleas weren't relevant anymore, and her mind was wandering.

He slammed his hand down on the table, but the round marble slab absorbed the impact and it made only a small high slap. He shook his head and stared at her in wonder. "You aren't gonna let me off the hook, are you?"

She remained silent; a family of five was getting out of the elevator and heading to the main dining room, chattering and giggling.

"Aw, damn—" he began again.

She couldn't let him escalate his outburst any further, so she spoke, conciliatory noises without actual meaning, knowing that her tone was sufficient to afford a little relief from whatever was annoying him. She really didn't know.

"Hush, dear," she said. "I'm not judging you. I'm not. Truly, I'm not."

"Well why are you giving me the cold shoulder all of a sudden, then? Explain me that." He sat back, already more secure, already turning the tables, instinctively.

"Oh, I'm not," she said, a little surprised. "Was I ignoring you? Did I seem distracted? I'm so sorry—those kids at the elevator, they were so happy and frantic, it was adorable."

"Honey, I don't care about some kids. Please, can't you see what this is doing to me?" He gripped the edge of the cold marble with both hands, like a steering wheel, scanning her eyes for oncoming traffic.

"Don't worry," she said. "It'll be alright. Everything will be alright." She paused, and he remained silent. To prolong the peace, she added, "When you come back through L.A. again you won't even remember this. You'll be fine." To herself she added, *And you won't be staying at the Ellington ever again, as long as you live.*

He sat back, unable to articulate the wrenching frustration that knotted his throat and churned his stomach. He stared at her like a total stranger, which she may well have been. He looked down at his hands, let go of the table, turned in his chair, and began to study the hundreds of liquor bottles behind the distant bar, hundreds of glasses hanging by their stems, the brass railings, ornate blackened mahogany cabinetry, guests perched on green leather stools, and the head-level thermocline of cigarette smoke. He heard the sound of ten dozen conversations near and far, blending in a buzz of mere phonemes.

He looked back at her again. "Doris, honey—" he began, then stopped. She was looking right at him, but he could see her eyes moving, tracking some activity far across the lobby, behind him, through him, without him. She was willing, wasn't she? She would keep talking, keep on encouraging him and saying it would be alright, but already it was obvious she could no longer even see him. He had become transparent to her, a mirage just wavering a little before disappearing completely.

She smiled at him, right at him, eye to eye, grateful that he finally understood, and then looked away.

•

The empty lobby rang out in its special predawn silence. With a discrete click, the night-man shut his door behind the counter. *Whoever was this Doris*, she wondered, fingering the marble table. It was the same table, unchanged for decades, virtually unmoved by legions of mopping and wiping custodial staff, its flowering iron base cemented to the marble floor in a thousand layers of ossified wax, ashes, and city grit, an intricate lamination of history that gripped the entire building like tree-rings, absorbing and embedding the spoor of all that passed through, rounding all the corners of the sharp-cut marble slabs.

She looked up. This latest Jensen had returned and was standing before her, peering at her curiously. "Do I know you?" he said.

"Definitely not," she replied.

He seemed not to hear, or not to believe what she said. He bent forward and peered harder, then checked himself and straightened up. "I'm sorry," he said. "I was staring, wasn't I? You seem so familiar. I can't believe we haven't met."

She smiled. "We haven't. I'm sure of it." She gestured at the table, the chair opposite. "Have a seat. I'll prove it to you."

He looked at her strangely.

"I'm joking," she said. "The bar's closed, but I'm available for conversation if you like."

"I just got in," he said, sitting. "Noticed you when I registered. Thought you looked familiar." He paused. "Damn! You really do look like someone I know. And this isn't a come-on, believe me."

"Sure," she said, and they both laughed.

"Well, it's not, honestly," he said. "But if it works, hell, that's OK, too."

She said nothing, searching his eyes.

"But I don't want to pressure you," he added, becoming uncomfortable again. "What's your name?"

She flinched at the old question. There was no suitable answer, because there was no plausible identity anymore. She was the hotel, she was Ellington, she was a lonely mirage in an urban desert, passing the time in empty chatter with strangers. She was the stranger, too. She looked at this new Jensen, and wondered if she had ever had a name.

"Call me Cathy," she said, so softly that Jensen barely heard her voice.

"Say what?" he said.

"Cathy," she whispered. "Cathy the first. Cathy the last."

"OK," he said. "I got it. Dear sad Miss Cathy."

She looked up into his face. "Who said I was sad?"

"Nobody. Sorry. I thought you sounded a little down."

"I'm fine. Happy inside, even if it doesn't show."

"OK." Jensen took a pull on his cigarette. "You want to go upstairs?"

"No. I don't go upstairs."

"Alright." Jensen was only mildly disappointed. He skidded his chair heavily, closer to the table. "So where do you go?"

"Pretty much nowhere, these days."

The chandeliers swung very slowly among the shadows overhead. The lobby was so different at night; during the day it was almost festive, if you didn't notice the dust and the grey-brown film accumulated on every surface.

"You should get out more," Jensen said.

"Get out yourself."

They both chuckled, then sat in silence.

Jensen pulled himself to his feet. "Gotta go," he said. "Meetings all day tomorrow."

She looked up and smiled, but said nothing.

"Thanks for the chat," he said, and then headed for the elevator.

"You're quite welcome," she whispered, and then, under her breath, "You always are."

Later, hours past midnight, she said to the vast empty room, "Gotta go."

She rose easily from the big chair and gathered a body back into herself. This took some effort, but soon she was all inside, ready for action. Everything worked. It was like old times.

•

For the first time in years, the woman headed for the main entrance. She paused for a moment at the revolving door, heedless of the lobby that sprawled behind her, and then pushed her way through to the street. The sea air enveloped her and she walked more and more briskly, heading into the gentle hills of Santa Monica, among the sleeping bungalows.

She crossed several residential streets, mostly devoid of lights, and came to Lincoln Boulevard, which was still blazing with cafés and gas stations, pet shops and shoe stores. She turned onto Lincoln, walking fast now, as if determined to get somewhere.

A short distance down Lincoln she found the blackened iron railing that framed the subway entrance. She felt the cold steel handrail as she descended the stairs, but her eyes were focused on something beyond the train tracks she was approaching.

At the turnstile, she fished a token from her small beaded purse and swiveled through to the platform. The station was silent. Even the sound of the nearby surf was lost in this subterranean world. She stood like a statue, feeling the still salty dampness, waiting outside of time.

A faint breath of air moved against her cheek, and then another, and then the distant rumble of an approaching train crept into the station. A subtle rhythm pulsed within the growing roar of the subway, and soon the platform was vibrating with the massive movements of rail cars and electric motors; the tunnel smelled of machinery and recent lightning. Breaks shrieked and the train shuddered to a stop; the car windows shone sallow and empty.

The doors slid open in unison with a loud pneumatic gasp. She looked down the platform and saw the conductor's head poking out at the front of the train. She stepped into the bright car and sat down by the opposite door. Another loud chorus of hissing doors, a firm jerk forward, and the train began accelerating. Masonry walls sped past on one side, the half-lit platform on the other, with small framed billboards along the tiles. Then the tunnel wall closed in and there was nothing to see but dark shadows of conduits sparsely punctuated by dim caged light bulbs.

The train steadily picked up speed, heading downtown again and again.

•

It's not all that far, by subway, from the upper Bronx down into the Village, to Astor Place. She gets off the train, and ascends the concrete stairway into a new world. The towers of lower Manhattan rise darkly all around, and there are no pedestrians in sight. Taxis cruise past without passengers; now and then a late night delivery truck.

She goes into a dingy bar with sawdust on the floor and drinks a beer and then strolls back out into the city.

She hears jazz on the empty streets and follows the sound to the Five Spot where Roland Kirk is playing, blind and eloquent. So she enters the tiny club and takes a table, watching the round little man spewing jazz filigree around the room, manzello, stritch, flute, nose-whistle, chords on his tenor sax, impossible combinations of notes in an impossible performance.

She is dismayed to feel an emptiness in the music, a missing voice among the chords and cadences of Kirk and his sidemen and his one-man brass section, but then a tall figure rises from the audience, and strides onto the little bandstand clutching a grey felt bag. He pulls a trumpet from the bag and touches Roland on the shoulder, and whispers into his blind ear, and the chords flow from the blind sax while Lee Morgan puts the trumpet to his own lips and adjusts his embouchure.

He starts to play delicate short intervals, filling in tiny voids in the brass choir from Roland's multiple horns, and then he climbs the musical staircase into the light, blowing a searing run of notes that lasts for bars, winding around the harmonies of sax and man-zello and stritch.

The woman sips her beer and taps her foot to the music; she nods at Mr. Morgan in appreciation. Far away in a distant Santa Monica, high chandeliers tremble above a marble floor.

·

The sun had not yet crowned the Santa Monica mountains, and the sea breeze was still cool and moist. Some blocks from the hotel, a local shop-keeper en route to open his doors for the new day was hurrying along the sidewalk. He was one of the few Los Angelinos who lived within walking distance of anything.

He rounded the corner of 5th Street and Strand, and stopped. Ahead on the sidewalk someone was sleeping across the pavement, most likely one of the homeless drawn to SoCal's balmy weather. As he drew closer, he could see it was a woman, an old woman. No, an extraordinarily old woman, wrinkled and almost skeletal in her frailty, her face a translucent maze of blue-veined tissue-paper. But she was obviously not homeless. She lay in a penumbra of immaculate embroidered silk and fine crinoline, looking up as if star-gazing. Her eyes were open, but they did not move. There was a broad smile on her face.

Ω

5: *Our Lady of the Ellington*

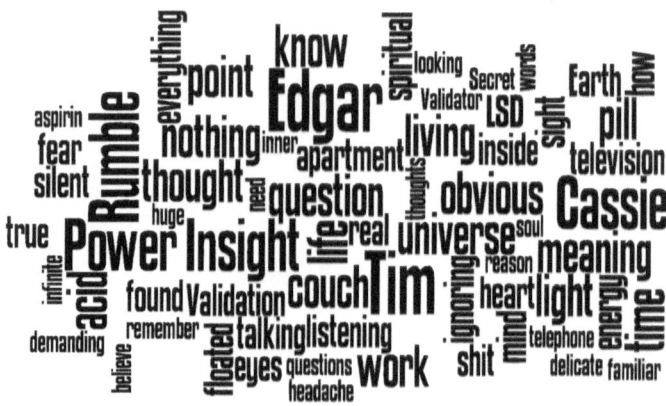

6

The Meaning of Life

The limousine floated over the cliff, tumbling as it fell, and folded like cardboard when it hit the rocks below. Seconds later, it shuddered and burst into a huge fireball as the camera pulled back and shifted into slo-mo to savor the destruction.

Tim groaned. Was this the hundredth explosion this week? Were TV stations no longer capable of telling an original story? He sighed, and went to the kitchen for alternative fulfillment. Hours later, and at least a few more explosions, he fell asleep on the couch.

Sometime after midnight, Tim half awoke and stumbled off to bed. In the morning, he felt hung over and dull.

Later that week, his girlfriend Cassie called and said she was dumping him for another guy, one of Tim's co-workers, who, she said, was a lot more interesting. Tim couldn't agree more, but his lingering depression increased. Looking back, he decided the relationship had been doomed from the start: Cassie was only interested in clothes and analyzing other people's behavior. In less than six months, playing and sharing had devolved into inconvenience and obligation.

At first, Tim coped fairly well without Cassie, primarily through increased absorption in the endless micro-variations of television. But he was gaining weight, losing energy, and becoming increasingly uninspired. *I need something to bust me out of this,* he muttered to himself, although he knew he might be really asking for it.

The following weekend he took his dog for a walk in the hills. He wandered through the trees along the edge of a small dairy farm, his attention mainly on keeping Rumble, an enthusiastic beagle, from chasing everything that moved. They paused by a muddy stream to eat a sandwich and a baggie of kibble. Tim drank half his bottled soda while Rumble slurped up watery scum from the stream.

They set off again toward the back road where Tim had parked, and soon Rumble caught sight of new prey. A rabbit was trying to freeze itself into invisibility, but Rumble's nose was too sensitive. The dog lunged forward, jerking his leash free, and the rabbit bolted zig-zag into the underbrush. Tim yelled at Rumble, but within seconds the dog's enthusiastic barks faded into the distance.

Tim spent the next two hours stumbling and crashing through the woods calling for Rumble. At some point, in a part of the forest he didn't recognize, it became obvious that Rumble had run far out of earshot. Some time later, darkness slipped in among the trees and Tim found himself standing alone, suddenly more concerned with finding landmarks than with Rumble. With some difficulty, he managed to get his bearings, and made his way back to the car just as the moon was rising over Mt. Mansfield.

He sat for a while with the windows rolled down, listening to the night sounds, thankful to be safe inside his bubble of civilization. He strained to hear faint fragments of barking while he wondered how an apartment dog might fare in the wilds with a leash fastened to its neck. His fantasies were dire and demoralizing. When the mosquitoes began molesting him, he rolled up the windows and drove home.

Monday, Tim called work to take the morning off, and drove back into the country. He wandered the area, looking for signs of Rumble, listening for a familiar bark, and eventually gave up. Back home, he watched daytime TV and didn't return to the office. When evening came, he continued watching television while consuming an entire bag of barbecue potato chips, four Cokes, and a container of ice cream. Around 3:00 AM he staggered to bed.

Not surprisingly, Tuesday didn't go well. He woke about 10:00 o'clock, called the office, and muttered a lame excuse about dental work, lingering pain, codeine, and a splitting headache. The headache was real. Lacking the resources for anything else, he defaulted to the couch and watched more daytime television. When the prime time dramas began, his interest roused slightly and he vowed to get to bed early. Every other thought was another vision of Rumble's possible fate, alone in a world without kibbles.

He woke not knowing the time of day or where he was. His windows glowed with dim light, but he couldn't tell if it was brightening or fading. Had he been asleep ten minutes or ten hours? He looked around the living room, but there were no clocks in view, and the TV had shut itself off. He walked to the bathroom and stared into the mirror. *Have I had a stroke?* A tremble of fear ran down his back.

Now fully awake, Tim rushed to check the kitchen clock. It was 6:30 in the morning. Somehow, he had slept for ten hours sitting up and not moving, and the whole night he hadn't had even a glimmer of a dream. *This is getting out of control,* he thought. *If something doesn't happen soon, I could get stuck.*

Tim ate a bowl of cereal and took a shower and called the office to let them know that today he would be in at the usual time. The receptionist told him Mr. Unger was really upset, and a pang of fear bloomed in Tim's stomach. "Just tell him I'll be in at 9:00 and I'll come see him to explain," Tim said.

At 8:30, Mr. Unger called, and told Tim not to come in at 9:00, or ever. They would send his final check and personal items by mail.

For a few days, Tim tried to assimilate his deteriorating life, but each situation was out of his control and he couldn't think of a way to deal with any of it. He began ordering pizza and staying in his apartment all day. The television's infinite nattering had become his only companion. *This is so obviously the wrong thing to do,* he thought, and then decided to check the Smithsonian channel.

A brief image of the Great Pyramid flashed on the screen, and then all the yellows disappeared and the picture turned red, blue, and purple. Tim pressed Channel Up, and Discovery was also all the wrong colors. Then the reds disappeared and he stared in disbelief at a blue man in a blue raft dodging blue rapids. White lines appeared across the screen at regular intervals, and the picture winked out.

•

Tim's first Power Insight Teachings seminar was in the basement of the community rec center. He'd been browsing in the neighborhood's last independent book store, and noticed a small flier for "Edgar" among announcements of healers, life counselors, readers, and other post-modern sooth-sayers.

There were about a dozen people when he arrived, and soon another dozen or so joined them. Apparently this Edgar had something of a following—or there had been a sudden run on Power Insight seeking.

Edgar had no last name: just Edgar. *I wonder if it's Edgar Edgar,* Tim thought, recalling a doctor he had once visited named Dr. David David. Then he remembered a comedian saying, "Never trust a man with two first names." The reason was long forgotten, but perhaps two of the *same* first name was even more suspicious than just two first names. Then again, he had no reason to believe Edgar's last name actually *was* Edgar. Of course, it could have been Edgar, and his *first* name was the missing one, but that seemed unlikely. There were probably other ways of exploring this mystery, but Tim noticed that someone was speaking from the podium, and the crowd had become silent.

"—to the Huge, Huge Secret," Edgar was saying. "There are many paths to the Secret, but with Power Insight you needn't bother with any more effort than your particular situation calls for." He paused to let his audience think about this.

Much later in the evening, Edgar said, "In other words, people, you don't need *me* to uncover the Huge Secret for you, because that's impossible. Nobody can do it *for* you. But to find it, you do need an expert like me to help you pick the one path that will work for *you*."

A person in the audience spoke up. "So you're saying I can do anything I like, and it will still lead me to the Secret?"

"Exactly!" said Edgar, striding around the podium to stand right in front of the questioner. "But it's not anything you *like*. It's whatever *works* for you. Understand the difference?"

"Not exactly. How do I know when it's working?"

"Oh, you won't know," Edgar replied. "It happens too slowly. That's why you need me—or anyone with Power Insight, of course. I'm not anything special. Anybody can gain PI with the right training. But you still need someone to keep you on track."

"I see."

"I'll keep you on track," Edgar declared to the room. "That's what I'm here for." He returned to the podium and glanced at his watch. "And we're out of time," he said. "I want to thank you all for venturing out tonight and opening the door of Power Insight with me. My books are on sale at the back of the room, and you can pick up a sheet with contact information in case you decide to get some direction into your life."

A few people in the back were already fingering the short stacks of Power Insight books, and someone was folding up a contact sheet.

"Take several!" Edgar called. "Take some for your friends and pass them around. Everybody needs something new."

A small crowd gathered around Edgar. Tim edged toward them, not really expecting to get close enough to say anything, but Edgar looked up and waved him in. "Make some room, everybody,"

Edgar said. "This fellow has some real problems to solve. Don't hold him back."

The crowd parted just enough for Tim to shuffle into the front, where several people were all talking at once, trying to get their questions to Edgar. Tim felt very uncomfortable. He really just wanted to ask if there was any hope of getting out of his rut, of getting involved in life again, but there obviously wasn't going to be any dialog in this environment. He started trying to squirm back through the crowd, but Edgar stopped him.

"Hey, brother, don't leave yet."

Tim looked at Edgar's eager, friendly face and shrugged. *I can't do anything here,* he thought.

Edgar held out his hand, a business card between his fingers. "Take it," he said. "It's my private line."

Tim took the card.

"Call me," said Edgar, and then started taking questions from the group crowding around him.

Tim pulled away and made for the door before claustrophobia swept over him. He stuffed the card into his jacket and got home as quickly as possible. The TV was still dead black, so he went to his bookshelf and selected his old college copy of *Autobiography of a Yogi.* He'd never read it, but he gave it a good try while the TV stood like a large black billboard on the credenza. Soon, not surprisingly, he was asleep.

The next day, Tim fished the card from his jacket. "Power Insight Validation," it said. He called the number, and made an appointment for a phone consultation with Edgar that afternoon. According to the secretary, he was very lucky to have gotten a slot so soon. The fee was not too steep—much less than a lawyer, at any rate—so Tim felt good about his decision. It was heartening to think there might be some help in sight.

At 3:15, the phone rang, and it was Edgar, right on time.

•

For two weeks, with Validation telephone sessions every other day to keep him on track, Tim learned how to stare at candles, hold his breath, bow to the East, soak in Epsom salts, cast *I Ching* trigrams with pennies, avoid eating refined foods, march around his apartment in time to African drums, burn the correct incense for each time of day, and press the back of a spoon onto key energy nodes all over his body.

"I just don't see how these unrelated activities can possibly all work," he said during one Validation call.

"That's just the thing," said Edgar. "They all work *because* they are unrelated."

"How's that?"

"Everything is true," Edgar stated.

Tim started to protest, but Edgar stopped him. "Just think about it," he said.

Then every time Tim began to speak, Edgar interrupted with, "You're thinking about what to say, instead of what I just said."

Eventually, Tim gave up trying to have a dialog, and Edgar complimented his growing Power Insight. "It's terrific," Edgar said. "You're really getting somewhere. What we're doing is definitely what works for you. Now keep at it, and I'll call you tomorrow."

Tim kept at it, but he was losing his optimism. Edgar's last pronouncement had taken him by surprise, and he was still unnerved by it. "Everything is true," Edgar had said. *How could that possibly make any sense?*

Edgar didn't call the next day, which was a first. Maybe his busy schedule was getting too busy. Or maybe Edgar was sensing Tim's growing discomfort with the Power Insight process.

But the day after, Edgar did call. "I've been looking at your progress," he said, "and I think it's time to move onto the next level."

"How have you been doing that?" Tim asked. "We haven't spoken for two days."

"Oh, not *physically*," Edgar replied. "In the other dimensions. I've been looking into your spiritual side. Remember, I've got to keep track of your direction."

"But how can you do that without even talking to me?"

"Tim, I've said it a million times. Your spiritual side isn't just inside your body. It's everywhere! Time and place have no meaning."

Then Edgar presented a new regime, one which Tim found especially difficult—fasting and herbs.

Another few weeks passed, during which Tim struggled to not eat anything, and then to eat bitter green blender drinks that gave him the runs, and then not to eat at all again. He went through half a dozen different diets, determined to follow Edgar's instructions until something definitive happened. Nothing did, beyond the gastronomical plane.

In desperation, during the next Validation telephone session, Tim blurted out, "Edgar! Please. It's not working."

"Of course it is," said Edgar, sounding hurt but inspired.

"It's not," said Tim. "I feel like shit."

"Oh, that's normal. The herbs—"

"No, not that I'm shitting every 30 minutes," said Tim. "The point is I *feel like* shit."

"Well, you have to—"

"All the time."

"OK. Look. I had to take you to this point so you could see the benefit of the final stage of training."

"You mean I'm supposed to feel like shit?"

"Not exactly, but it's very common. But now you're ready for the next step. Remember, that's all we've been trying to do all this time."

"Trying to *get* to the next step? I thought you're supposed to already know what's the best step for me."

"Tim, I know your innate materialism always makes it hard to believe anything, but you have to remember that *everything is true*. If you lose sight of that, nothing the New Age can provide will do you any good."

"It just doesn't make much sense, actually," said Tim.

"Don't force it to! But anyway, you're done with the hard part. Now it's easy. I'll send over a pill in the morning."

"A pill?"

"Sure. It's just a sugar pill. Well, it's an aspirin, in fact. A kid's aspirin. Just 72 milligrams. Not really anything. But there's just a little bit extra in it."

"Extra? Extra aspirin?"

"No, it's nothing, just a little kicker, sort of."

"What are you talking about?"

"You'll love it. It's so easy. Nothing to keep track of, nothing you actually have to do yourself. Just take the pill, and sit back, and you'll be swimming in Insight in no time."

"You're not answering my question."

"What question? I told you, it's just a baby aspirin. What could be safer?"

"But what's in it? What's this little kicker? I'm not going to take it if I don't know what's in it."

"Well, look, Tim, you've got to relax about this. It won't work if you're not relaxed. Well, it'll work, but not very well. It's just a tiny tiny bit of acid, and you'll hardly notice it. I'll send it over in the morning. Call me before you start."

"Acid?"

"Yes, just the teeniest amount. Almost nothing at all. A few millionths of a gram—way less than the aspirin. And it's a baby aspirin, like I said."

"You mean LSD?" Tim sat back on the couch, gawking at the black TV panel, wishing it still worked and could still lull him into somnambulance without requiring intervention.

"Sure," said Edgar. "Is that a problem? It's not like a major trip or anything. And it's very pure. The best. Costs a pretty penny, in fact. Nothing but the best for my people." His voice was confident, satisfied.

"Lysergic Acid?"

"I told you, yes, that's what it is. A little kicker, is all."

"I can't take LSD!" Tim cried. "I'm not into drugs. And I'm all alone in my apartment. What if I go crazy and jump out the window?"

"Tim, Tim, nobody jumps out windows on acid. That's an old wive's tale. But sure, if you want some company, then fine, get someone to come and stay with you for the day. It only lasts a day. Not even a whole day. Six, eight hours, maybe. Probably less."

"Why are you so up for me taking acid?"

"I'm not up for you! Heck no. I'm just looking out for your best interests. You know what you want, but you don't know how to find it. I do, because I'm a Validator, a Power Insight Validator."

"I don't know anyone to call," said Tim.

"Sure you do."

"I do?"

"Of course. Think about it. Who do you know?"

"Well, nobody at the moment. I lost my job, and Cassie dumped me, and even if Rumble was here—" Tim froze. "Cassie? You mean her? I can't call Cassie! She wouldn't give me the time of day."

"When was the last time you tried?"

"Well, never! She dumped *me*, remember?"

"You never even called her back?

"It would have been pointless. She was with Andrew. I didn't even find out until it was a done deal."

"That was months ago."

"So?"

"So from what you've told me, Cassie isn't perfect. Girls like Cassie don't usually consider *any* guy to be Mr. Right. Look, call her and then call me back if she can't come over. If you don't call back, I'll send the pill in the morning."

"OK. I'll try, but I guarantee she'll refuse."

"And Tim, one more thing."

"What?"

"Probably good to have a big breakfast first. You may not feel like eating for a while."

Edgar hung up, and Tim continued staring at the dead TV for a long time, trying to foster some spiritual growth inside.

•

Cassie arrived at 10:00 the next morning. The pill arrived a few minutes later, in a paper bag delivered by bicycle messenger. Inside the bag was a peanut butter jar stuffed with crumpled toilet paper, a small amber pill bottle nestled inside. The baby aspirin was suspended between cotton balls inside the pill bottle.

By noon, Tim was admiring the oriental rug design embossed on the dead TV panel while the apartment walls gently ballooned in and out.

Cassie was chatting about a friend of hers who had said something that implied motivations demanding prolonged scrutiny.

Now and then, Cassie would pause and stare at Tim until he noticed her and said, "Oh, yes. That's interesting. Go on."

Later, the tangibility of the apartment came into question, and Tim had to look between the molecules to see what was really there. He could feel the traffic outside as it drove up and down each of the glass bones in his body, which felt very good, actually. He had never known how sensuous city traffic could feel.

His attention was drawn to the electricity that had become the real substance of his inner organs. The bones were just filaments, of course; the real deal was the living organs, independent life-forms of pure energy.

"So that's what she *claims* is why they broke up," Cassie said, "but it's obvious that she was just showing how afraid she is about *changing* anything important. And that's why I know it was so important to *her!*"

Tim tried to look at her, but he couldn't find her face. His mind kept diving back into his internal organs, and now it was pushing into some bright warm spot that must have been inside his heart. It was. He could see the light pulsing with each heartbeat, and he realized this was where he had been living all his life.

"Are you listening?" Cassie said.

"Um, wow, yes," Tim replied.

This heart energy was really just a focal point, wasn't it? Just a reflection of the energy of the Earth, like a spiral of bright gas on the surface of Jupiter.

"Then don't you think it's obvious?" said Cassie. "I was right, wasn't I? She is so totally afraid of change, right?"

"Right," said Tim. The word floated out of his mouth in a metallic green cloud and then swelled and rushed back into him through his chest. Then it was obvious that his heart wasn't a piece of Earth energy, it was (along with the Earth) the center of all the energy in the universe. But this wasn't energy. It was Self. It was who he really is, outside of time, immortal, fearless.

"You haven't heard a word I said, have you?" said Cassie.

"Oh, wow," said Tim.

"What did I just say?"

Tim said nothing. His soul was open now, and he knew who he really was for the very first time. He was the universe. The universe was him. This was the Huge Secret, and now he would be able to do anything, take on any challenge. He was weightless.

"Are you ignoring me?" said Cassie.

Tim swam through the cosmos, soaking up the ultimate truth, expanding and expanding, feeling the stars prickle against his galactic skin.

"Tim!" Cassie sat down next to him on the couch.

Tim felt the universe swivel and right itself in response to her movements.

"Look at me," she said.

Tim opened his eyes; or were they already open? Could he even close them if he wanted to? There she was, all need and urgency.

Compassion welled up and he loved all living things. All inanimate things, too, since they were all alive inside his infinite body.

"Answer my question," Cassie demanded.

"I'm right at the center," Tim said. "I've found the answer."

"You're ignoring me, aren't you?"

Tim opened his mouth but only fiery strands of love came out; no need for voices.

"Aren't you?" Cassie demanded.

Then the phonetic machinery clicked in, and Tim watched the words materialize in his left hemisphere and flow out to his throat. "I tell you, Cassie, I'm not ignoring you," he heard himself say. "I'm just in a special place right now. It's very delicate, and I have to be silent for a minute."

"I can be delicate. Why do you have to cut me out?"

"I don't. I'm not. Please, just a minute or two of silence—"

Cassie looked at the floor and mumbled, "You're telling me to shut up."

Tim said nothing, casting about in his mind for the path back into his heart and that central spark, the tiny light that held the key to everything.

"Aren't you?" Cassie demanded, tugging his sleeve.

"No, I—" Tim could feel the spark again, but it was so small and distant he could barely discern it. The jumble of ordinary thoughts was beginning to coalesce again, casting a complex skein of language and categories over the inner light.

Cassie said something else, but all Tim was aware of now was noise, growing and intruding into his silent core until suddenly his head filled with the same old chaos he lived with every day. Confusion and fear slowly doused all the residual knowledge and clarity and one-ness. Normal life crushed back in with a vengeance, still generously spiced with LSD. Cassie continued demanding to be served.

"Never mind," he said, more to himself than to Cassie.

"But I can't!" she cried, gripping his arm tighter. "You can't just ignore me!"

"I'm not, baby," he whispered, his eyes still closed. Meaningless geometries had begun sliding across his eyelids. "Believe me, I'm not," said his voice.

"Then tell me what you're experiencing," she said. "I really want to know. I can help you."

"Yes, help me," said his voice. "Of course. You can help."

"So what is it? What's happening inside? Are you there? Are you seeing it? The Secret?"

"No," he said. "It's nothing." A steady buzz filled his head, like hiss between FM stations, with overtones of vacuum cleaner. A city bus horn floated into the apartment, or perhaps it was just the sound of one.

"But what do you see?" she insisted.

"Nothing." He opened his eyes and looked at her. Symmetrical arabesques decorated her face like Maori tattoos. "I see nothing at all," he said. "There's nothing to see."

The city went noisily about its business.

Tim's heart pumped blood and oxygen through the interstices of his body.

Cassie clutched his arm.

Familiar old thoughts and doubts and fears wallpapered his sensorium with endless text.

The apartment walls bulged inward like huge balloons in the afternoon sun, while the furniture surged hungrily upward.

Ω

7

The Mirror

Lafcadio trudged along the dark wet sidewalk, listening past the hum and swish of traffic on nearby streets, dreading the distant shuffling footsteps that surely must be tracking him. The rain had stopped shortly after nightfall, and a pervasive sodden gloom had settled over New Orleans, muffling all sounds of life, and seeping into every pore.

The sparse traffic noise faded away momentarily, and in the silence Lafcadio could hear a distant foghorn—one long, lone blast, its echo muted by the heavy wetness. The air felt as if a massive thunderhead, too heavy to remain airborne, had settled to earth, embalming everything in a dense blanket of moisture.

After the foghorn's cry, there was a moment of even more complete silence—no sound but the omnipresent dripping from saturated moss that hung like tattered clothes from the trees along Rue St. Marie.

Ever so faintly, Lafcadio heard a *whisper* emerge from the fog, bouncing randomly from the infinity of water droplets, softly reaching in from all directions. It was a whisper of another time, another world, and it filled him with dread. He couldn't make out the words, not exactly, but the intonation was unmistakable. Death was near, and had been lurking for some time, awaiting new clientele.

Shrugging deeper into his hoodie, Lafcadio hunched his shoulders and pushed on into the fog, quickening his pace. He should never have come this way, through the old streets where so many souls had already been lost. Cartloads of despair had jounced across these cobblestones in the old slave days, heading from the shipyards and bound for the paddle-wheels and unspeakable markets up-river. Desperation from centuries past still mingled with the droplets suspended in the air, swirling through alleys of indelible horror.

The whisper came again, timed perfectly in another silent gap in the muffled urban background. This time it was not entirely unintelligible: *"Return the mirror."*

That, of course, was unthinkable. Lafcadio shuddered, despite the oppressive humidity. He had gone too far to turn back now, and besides, what benefit could possibly come from returning it? *Return it to whom?* He was the only mortal soul who even knew it existed, and if he attempted to return the cursed thing it would be all too obvious what he must have done to obtain it.

No, his only choice was to press on, and find out if *any* of the old stories were true, or had at least some shred of reality to them. The fact that the mirror had been where they said it was, that was proof enough that *something* was involved. But he could never be forgiven for the desecrations he had done to remove it from the crypt.

And it was theft, pure and simple. If word got out into the Community, if even a whisper of this reached Mama Laboux, he was a dead man.

If he wasn't dead already.

•

Acrid smoke filled the basement room, glowing red from racks of colored glass offertory candles that flickered all around the altar. Tiny bones were piled high on a silver tray, bird bones, frog bones, finger bones. A high voice was humming through closed lips, tunelessly, without thought.

A glassine envelope fell with a soft slap onto the altar table, alongside the tray of bones. Spindly fingers spread it open and removed a lock of black hair, and placed the hair atop the bones. A match flared. Sulfur blended with the candles and incense. The lock of hair caught, burning and convulsing into a curl of ashes. A little cloud of grey smoke rose above the altar, adding to the cloying aromas of spice and offal.

•

Eduard awoke with a start. Confused, he sat up and looked around the room. Was this his room? Nothing seemed familiar. He sniffed, but smelled nothing, just the wet fog outside in the city. It had stopped raining, but the incessant New Orleans drip continued, audible through the open window. Not a breath of air stirred.

His head was filled with fragments of nightmare, now a familiar experience in the decades since his thirteenth birthday, but these terrors always seemed distant, uninvolving. He cast back in his mind, trying to find a thread. *Hurrying through a dark street, pursued, but alone (not pursued?). Fearful of discovery. Elated. Guilty. Danger.* Then the pile of bones, and the smoke. The red smoke.

The bedsheets were saturated and claustrophobic. He threw off the covers and got up. To his bare feet, the floor felt warm and damp at the same time, like the hide of a huge living creature. Whispers were fading all around him, echoes of whispers, those sounds that can only be remembered by the animal brain, the brain with no language.

The house creaked, as it was wont to do—a long drawn out creak that sounded like a door slowly closing. Eduard had known these sounds all his life, and each creak had a familiar feeling, like an old friend nudging him. Tonight the friendliness was gone.

He gazed out the window at the old trees along Montaigne Street: older than he was, older than his parents, maybe older than this house. In the distance, a bus slowed and turned onto Montaigne, fat tires splashing along the puddled pavement. The rain hadn't been stopped for very long.

There was a faint mixture of moon-glow and street lamps on the sidewalk, mottled by the overarching branches. Eduard craned his neck to see the stars overhead, but the sky was the color of wet ashes. The only light came from an invisible moon, and the two street lamps, one at the corner, and another half a block down the lane.

The bus came along, passing by on the other side of the garden wall. He watched the lit windows flicker through the iron fencing, dimly reflecting his house. The bus was empty, except for the driver, a large black man in city uniform, driving like a zombie through the empty streets, picking up no passengers, and dropping none off.

For a second, Eduard could see a translucent image of the whole lower floor of the house in the bus windows. He recognized the solarium, the big front porch, the tall dining room windows, the great South wing stretching out into the darkness. He shook his head in surprise. *What South wing?* It was long gone, dismantled a century ago, after hurricanes decimated the Garden District. He had seen it only in pictures, mottled silver bromide glass plates of the family's glory days.

The bus was gone, and with it the reflections of another age. Eduard frowned. This wasn't the first time he thought he had glimpsed the South wing. His dreams must be catching up with him, as his father liked to say. Late at night, thoughts lose their proportions. Things transform.

Shrugging, he yawned and considered returning to bed. It was late, but he had no idea what time it was. The house and the city were silent, and he was tired from dreaming long and difficult dreams. Then, impulsively, he dressed and went downstairs.

He opened the front door and stared out into the night. The fog softly hugged the house. Then he set out into the city, thankful for the faint movement of air against his face.

•

The beer cans were all warm, but Lafcadio was glad he had stashed them at the foundry. Since hurricane Katrina nobody ever came into these derelict blocks of half-collapsed factories and warehouses. Nobody but crazy bums or desperate fugitives.

He sipped the warm beer and his quaking limbs began to calm a little. He felt like a puppet on twitching strings. Now it was clearer that stealing the mirror was the stupidest thing he had ever done. Beyond stupid—suicidal.

A large rusting gun safe stood in the corner next to a huge broken desk. Some rich executive had sat there, lording it over everyone, making people like Lafcadio miserable and hopeless. He eyed the dilapidated condition of the desk with faint satisfaction. But then his attention returned to the safe.

The mirror was inside. The key to his dreams, and the seal on his demise.

Yesterday, after the prolonged nightmare of digging into the mausoleum and hauling the mirror back to the foundry without being seen, he had discovered the gun-safe's combination taped inside its open door. It was an invitation he couldn't resist.

He had unwrapped the mirror and glanced into it, wondering if the stories were true. It was insane to have gone through all this without even knowing if the mirror worked. Magic! How idiotic it seemed, now that he had made the commitment and his world was about to collapse.

The mirror had supposedly belonged to Jean Lafitte, or one of his wives or concubines, stolen from an unknown merchant ship in the Barbados. The legend said the mirror's owner could see through it into any place or time, like the drug stashes of the local dealers, or the secret lock boxes in closets and under beds all over the city. But last night all Lafcadio could think about was what he had just stolen, and who might feel the loss.

He had peered into the mirror, to make a quick check on its unlikely powers, but at first he saw only his own taut face, scarred and gaunt, quivering with excitement and fear. Then the mirror had fogged over and all he could make out was a pair of wrinkled hands, doing something with candles and bones. Voodoo.

He recoiled and almost dropped the mirror. What was he looking at? His mind had still been fixated on the theft, and on the person he most feared might discover what he'd done. Was this she? He had heard a faint humming song from the mirror, like an old lady doing her chores.

In a panic he had pulled the gunny sack over the mirror and shoved it into the safe. The thing apparently worked, but he couldn't control it, and he couldn't stand any more fear. Maybe later, in a few days. It was too incredible. His first real success in life, and probably his last.

He had slammed the safe door and spun the lock. Safe was a good word. The mirror was safe inside, and he was safe from the mirror. Nobody would find it here, and nobody could open the safe even if they knew about it.

Now, exhausted from another sleepless day collecting meager provisions for his lair, he collapsed onto the old mattress he had dragged in, and nursed his can of beer. Outside, the city dripped and hummed. After another warm beer, Lafcadio slept.

•

Eduard paused on the sidewalk outside his house, staring into the gloom where the old South wing once stood. The garden, if you could call it that, had reclaimed the grounds, and there was no way he could have glimpsed it reflected in the bus windows. He shook his head and decided to walk around the block.

Later, still walking aimlessly through the neighborhood, he was drawn to an avenue with a row of magnificent magnolia trees. He could just make out the ashen sky between their broad branches, and it reminded him of stories his grandmother had told about the early 20th century.

Several blocks to the East he found an intriguing wrought-iron fence that enclosed a gigantic estate with multiple houses and pathways connecting them. He continued wandering, his mind empty of thought, letting random impulses guide him this way and that, into the crooked streets of the older districts.

He walked slowly, but at a steady pace, and after an hour or more he found himself standing at the foot of a huge brick wall, a black shadow rising several stories above. He looked around, but didn't recognize this part of town.

A large opening breached the wall where a loading dock once stood. Inside, the building was pure darkness, featureless black within black.

Even as Eduard impulsively went up the steps to the doorway, he was wondering why he would venture inside. The curiosity that drove him wasn't intense, but it was accompanied by the feeling that he was doing the right thing. There might be something important in those dark rooms.

His good sense told him this was unwise, that there surely couldn't be anything of any interest in this abandoned wreck, but he thought, *What the hell? Take a chance now and then. You never know.*

He picked his way blindly through the gloom. Ahead, a large room was partially lit by the glow of nearby streetlights. Inside, a scrawny figure was sleeping on an old, filthy mattress half propped against one wall like a daybed.

Eduard stood still and stared at the unconscious vagrant.

•

Tendrils of smoke rose in a dense filigree, lit red by a circle of candles in colored glass. Bony fingers moved among the smoke trails, molding them so that they slowly solidified in the air. The fingers pushed and kneaded the congealing smoke until it floated motionlessly like a greyish red sculpture of knotted rope.

•

Eduard was content to remain standing in the dark, unmoving, while the other man slept. Then, on a whim, he spoke out loud.

"Where is the mirror?" A tiny thrill of pleasure gleamed as he said it. *Why not say it again,* he thought. "Where is the mirror?"

Every few minutes, he repeated the question, and each time he noticed a little blooming sensation of happiness deep in his body. So he kept repeating the words, monotonously, for almost an hour. Now and then a vague feeling of concern would arise, but then he would say the question again and feel better.

•

Lafcadio coughed and roused slightly from deep sleep. Something was wrong. His head was full of dark clouds and confusion. He rubbed his eyes and looked around the ramshackle foundry building, but there was nothing to see. No, wait! He wasn't alone.

A tall figure was standing on the other side of the room, silhouetted by the blown-out windows. It just stood there without moving, arms at its sides, head down. He couldn't tell if it was really looking at him or just staring in his direction.

When it spoke, Lafcadio stifled a scream. His heart pounded, and he felt his arms dampen with clammy sweat.

"Where is the mirror?" it said.

What the hell? Who is this guy?

The dark figure remained motionless, and then it said again, "Where is the mirror?"

Lafcadio couldn't decide what to do. He waited.

"Where is the mirror?" the figure said again, in the same tone as all the other times.

Every minute or so it repeated the question, like a robot.

How does he know about the mirror? Lafcadio looked desperately around the room. He could try to make a break for the door, but it wasn't far enough from the dark figure. And this unknown person was much taller than Lafcadio, and might be very strong.

"Where is the mirror?" it recited, like a man possessed.

Lafcadio leaped to his feet and lunged across the room. He

dodged to one side, and then spun around and made for the door with all the speed he could muster.

The figure jumped suddenly to the center of the doorway, in a single, impossibly swift motion. "Where is the mirror?" it said, tonelessly.

•

Eduard watched the other man wake up, recoil in surprise, and then run for the door. *I think he should stay here,* he thought, and found himself standing in the doorway while the other man stumbled back, a look of shock on his face. Moving fast like that felt surprisingly good. *I could do this all night,* he thought. "Where is the mirror?" he said, and felt a little thrill.

He remained there, blocking the doorway, for another hour, repeating the question and feeling tireless and capable. Someone must surely be very proud of him. He smiled with satisfaction, inside, but his face was blank.

The other man staggered around the room for a while, as if testing various escape routes in his mind, and then went back to the mattress and sat down. He seemed to be sobbing.

"Where is the mirror?" said Eduard.

A distant clank echoed softly through the warehouse. The other man tensed and looked around fearfully. Eduard blocked the doorway.

Footsteps crunched across the warehouse floor, followed by a rustle of heavy fabric and beads.

For no particular reason, Eduard moved to one side. A low dark mound of clothing moved through the doorway into the room, like a pile of rags.

The man on the mattress was visibly shaking, uttering tiny inarticulate noises. *He sounds like a bag of baby rats,* Eduard thought.

In the dim street light, Eduard could discern an old woman, dressed in layers of dark, ragged skirts and shawls, her long disheveled hair splayed out around her shoulders. He couldn't make out her face, but when she spoke her voice sounded like a lovely child on a summer day.

•

Lafcadio watched in horror as his worst nightmare unfolded before his eyes. He had never seen Mama Laboux, but he knew this must be she. The mound of tattered fabric shuffled to the center of the room, facing him as he cowered on his mattress, and he knew he was about to die.

"Where is the mirror?" she said, in a voice like ripping canvas.

He glanced desperately in all directions, not daring to answer.

Mama Laboux followed his gaze and noted how he avoided the gun safe in the corner. "It's in the safe, is it?" she rasped.

Lafcadio tried to deny it, but no words would come. Across the room, the tall stranger stood motionlessly by the door, watching.

The witch moved closer. "Open it," she said.

Lafcadio continued casting about in his mind for a way out, still in full denial.

"Open it now," she said. Her voice was more energetic, like a small chainsaw.

Lafcadio struggled to his feet, twitching and coughing. It was time to give up. Once she had the mirror, his life was over, and there was obviously nothing he could do about it.

He limped across the floor to the safe, trying not to faint along the way. Mama Laboux shuffled along, too, and they reached the safe at the same time. Lafcadio looked at her face, only inches away. A quarter-millennium of black magic looked back at him, and his torso jerked and twisted, and he stopped breathing.

"Open," she hissed.

Lafcadio fumbled with the dial, missing the numbers repeatedly, and then at last the mechanism clicked, and he pulled the handle and swung the heavy steel door open.

"Give it," she said.

He reached inside and pulled on the gunny sack leaning against the interior of the safe. His fingers trembled as he drew the object out into the room.

"Show me," she said.

Lafcadio was scarcely able to control his hands and arms. He loosened the drawstring on the satchel and pulled the opening wide. As he drew the bag down, his arm twitched violently and he nearly dropped the mirror. Regaining his balance, the bag swung against the safe door and he heard a faint crack. *My god,* he thought, *I've broken it!*

•

Eduard stood watching the murky drama without much thought other than dreamy contentment. The little man was standing by the open safe with the mound of rags, unwrapping something. He almost dropped whatever it was, and Eduard could see it fly partway out of the man's grasp and bang on the open steel door.

The faint *tick* of glass cracking was as loud as a thunderclap.

The dark heap of clothing reeled back, crying out like an animal beneath the wheels of a bus. As she fell slowly to the floor, Eduard suddenly slumped against the wall. *What the hell am I doing here?*

He looked around the mangled office and saw a shabby little man standing by an open gun safe, clutching a large brown bag, and shaking violently. Next to him, on the floor, a large featureless lump was writhing and vibrating, howling and yipping insanely.

He looked down at himself, and moved his limbs voluntarily for the first time in hours. *What just happened?*

He took a step toward the little man with the bag, and then he noticed that the heap on the floor was beginning to rise up.

Adrenalin shocked him into action. "Run!" he shouted, and ran out into the warehouse. As he leaped over debris toward the gaping loading dock, a strange mixture of animal sounds rang through the building.

In the street, Eduard realized he had no idea what part of the city he was in, but early dawn was brightening the eastern sky, so he began running in the opposite direction, Westward, toward civilization.

The sun was almost up when he reached the big house in the Garden District. The early morning air was fresh and the light of day made his horrific memories less and less real. He staggered into the foyer and slumped on the settee. *What the hell was that all about? Thank god it's over!*

•

Steam rose from a large vat, the size of an old iron bathtub. The vat was filled with what looked like hot mud, and its surface writhed with ten thousand wriggling worms. A scrawny shriveled arm rose from the mud and gripped the side of the rusty tub.

Mama Laboux shimmied her ancient body deeper into the steaming organic soup. A faint smile played across what passed for a face as she luxuriated in the glow of victory. The mirror was hers again, and this time nobody would ever find it. Or any of the other countless treasures she had accumulated over the generations since her beloved Jean passed away.

That wretched little gutter-rat Lafcadio was suitably punished for his transgressions. Too bad her powers didn't include possessing anyone at all, or she could have just made Lafcadio bring the mirror back himself. But dear Eduard never even knew what happened.

She sighed and allowed herself to sink deeper into the healing mud. It had been unexpectedly delightful possessing such a nice, healthy young man, her sixth-great grandson. The mud-worms wriggled against her dessicated skin. *I'll definitely have to do that again, sometime soon.*

Ω

7: *The Mirror*

8

Hoobner on the Post

Hoobner was a biker, old school. He had moved to Middle-town for no obvious reason and purchased an old wood-framed toy factory on the banks of the Manooksi River, adjacent to the sewer plant. He turned one end of the factory building into a motorcycle shop, and rented the mid-section as a residence for some local carpenters, and the other end as a workshop for a Hassidic candle-maker. The abandoned pig slaughter-house in the center of the yard was rented as a residence to a young couple, Ned & Nancy, and their 18-month old Doberman named Sufi.

Hoobner's reputation was a mystery, but there were rumors that he had killed a man. Colorful rumors were common in a tiny rural town whenever someone arrived with no connection to the community, but there was no real evidence that Hoobner was actually on the run. Apparently, he just picked a very sleepy location to hang his mechanic's shingle.

Hoobner's wife Mitsy was a bouncy, opinionated young woman known more for her bounce than her opinions. Mitsy stood up for her man. Even casual remarks seemingly unrelated to Hoobner could bring a cold glare of challenge, especially if they went over her head, as most remarks did. Although Hoobner himself was a good 300 pounds of biker, his woman was always there to protect him, and everyone took care not to rile her up.

It was also rumored that Hoobner had a pretty bad temper, but we hadn't seen anything of it in our several months living in the "mid-section" and the slaughter-house. He did stand up for his dog, though, in a rather ferocious manner—not unlike his girl's defense of himself. Altogether, Hoobner's little clan took care of its own.

Max, Hoobner's bulky black Labrador, had a well substantiated reputation for being top dog, which made his master proud. Max defended the yard from any and all shop customers, and from those of us who happened to reside in the compound. We all learned the secret password, "OK, Max. Guard the house," which if uttered in a sufficiently gruff tone would give Max the impression we belonged there, at least for the time being.

During the day, Max would lounge around in the dust, springing to life whenever something moved in the courtyard. Now and then some Other Dog would trip Max's olfactory range-finder, and he would burst into action, barking his low, mean-dog bark at the interloper, fangs bared, hackles raised, and muscles twitching, primed for battle. Generally the offending visitor would slink away, but once in a while Max would have to go and take a bite or two to prove his rank.

Ned and Nancy had gone to some trouble to put a fence around their slaughter-house, not so much to keep Max out as to keep Sufi in. Sufi was the Doberman, a youthful and almost delicate dog with the mind of a slightly dim-witted but well-meaning weight-lifter. He enjoyed flexing and preening, but more than anything he enjoyed a good run.

Unfortunately, in Vermont one doesn't let any old dog go running wherever it pleases, due to the cows. Local farm dogs, of course, and any dog who had been kicked (by cow or dairy-farmer), knew better than to chase cows, but sleek champions like Sufi, with the reflexes of an adolescent athlete on amphetamine, were a serious risk.

If Sufi—who effortlessly cruised at 40 mph for prolonged stretches—were to start playing around in a cow pasture, the consequences could be dire. Torn udders, broken legs, and lost revenue would bring righteous vengeance down on him and his owners, who were therefore extremely cautious about opening the fence around the slaughter-house. More than one errant canine had ended up on the wrong end of a shotgun while trespassing in one of the area's dairy farms.

Ned had found a cache of huge fence-posts, six or eight inches in diameter, and over many a long afternoon had built a massive fence around the slaughter-house's diminutive yard within a yard. He dug post-holes at four-foot intervals, outlining an area along one side of the slaughter-house about the size of a 1958 Buick. Around the resulting six-foot high stockade he wrapped a roll of chicken-wire, square-woven mesh whose horizontal wires were spaced closer and closer together toward the ground. Hoobner had watched the construction with disapproval—since it established an unwelcome domain for Sufi within the grander dominion of Max and himself—but he said nothing.

Sufi was extraordinarily well-behaved. He could heel and stay, and his comprehension of subtle human expectations was close to 9th Grade level. He was impetuous, to be sure, and always eager to explore new avenues of speed and agility, but that was merely his brilliant genetics, and not at all a character flaw.

Sufi's Teutonic heritage made him very literal-minded. His sense of territory was as geographically fluid as Ned's own no-madic life in those days. Sufi's world was defined by constantly changing rules about what was in or out of bounds. As a result, Sufi possessed a flexible and insightful understanding of "turf."

The slaughter-house was barely larger than a modest bedroom, so Ned and Nancy shared the carpenters' rustic kitchen in the midsection of the complex. After cooking a meal, they would of-ten invite Sufi into the kitchen area to clean up whatever bits of food fell to the floor. At other times, the invisible line across the kitchen doorway was an impenetrable Doberman barrier, and Sufi would lie just the other side, carefully keeping all parts of his body from touching the line.

It had become common practice for all parties to eat supper on a low coffee table in the living room of the mid-section. At such times, Sufi would be reminded of the "Nose Rule," which defined the airspace above the coffee table to be inviolate. Sufi would stand by, watching people eat, his nose pressed up against the edge of the table without ever intruding upon—or over—the top surface.

On one occasion, Ned had just built a sandwich of marshmallow fluff and peanut butter when some visitors arrived; Sufi was already in the kitchen cleaning the floor. Flapping his sandwich carelessly onto the kitchen counter, Ned invoked the Nose Rule and went out to greet his friends.

When Ned returned, he discovered that he had not left the sandwich (which comprised two of Sufi's most beloved ingredients) entirely on the counter top. About one-third had protruded over the side, in easy reach of a slathering, solitary Dobe. But Sufi had not reached up and pulled the heavenly treat into his mouth, as any lesser dog would have done. Instead, he had curled up his rubbery black nose, exposing the even rows of delicate white incisors at the front of his mouth. With surgical precision, he then trimmed off the sandwich perfectly flush with the edge of the counter. In no sense had he violated the proscribed air-space above the counter.

Sufi and Max had met on a few occasions, and both had lived up to their reputations. At their first encounter, cautiously orchestrated by their owners, Sufi wanted to run and jump, which drove Max into a frenzy, and Max wanted to bite Sufi to show him who was boss. In the ensuing mêlée, Ned and Hoobner were forced to grab their dogs' respective hind legs, and wheel-barrow them backwards onto home turf. Both men acknowledged the dogs would probably not become friends.

On another day, Max became fixated on Sufi's presence within the slaughter-house yard. Max decided that Sufi should not be tolerated even within Ned's interior fence, and he elected to bark his low, menacing warning until the situation was corrected. Hoobner had a limitless tolerance for Max's testicular style, however, and went on repairing motorcycles. Sufi, being a dog, quickly became deaf to the sound.

After a time, Max decided that things weren't moving quickly enough, and began to creep slowly toward the chicken-wire, barking all the while. Only a dog can fathom the strategic subtlety of creeping and barking at the same time.

Sufi lay comfortably in his yard, one eye tracking the slow movements of the elder challenger. Minute by minute, Max moved closer to Sufi's turf, until his nose was touching the chicken-wire, rubbing up and down wetly as he barked. Sufi rose and stretched languidly, his tail stump upraised like a shining black digit; but his eyes were on the aggressor.

Max by this time could not have stopped barking if his life depended on it. Every droplet of grey matter in his 3-oz. brainpan was stuck like a scratched 78-rpm record. His need to rid the area of the Doberman had probably faded into oblivion—now he merely had to bark and advance, bark and advance, until nirvana suddenly dawned.

The fence obstructed his progress, and after a time Max moved sideways a little, and discovered that his entire snout fitted nicely into one of the rectangular spaces of the fence. Sufi's eyes brightened—a visitor, by definition, even if only the first few inches.

He pranced happily over to the fence, and looked Max in the eye, hoping no doubt that Max would finish coming into the yard. Max barked metronomically.

Finally, Sufi realized that the noisome intruder was not going to play—only bark, and in an insulting tone, if you think about it. He waited for a while, perhaps hoping Max would tire, but he eventually realized that Max was stuck: the barking would go on forever if someone didn't do the right thing.

Sufi stretched his head toward Max, opened his notorious Doberman jaws very wide, and clamped down hard, taking most of Max's snout into his mouth. With a small fraction of his prize-winning 800-pound bite, Sufi calmly held Max's jaws together. A peaceful silence descended over the courtyard.

Max began tugging and struggling, but couldn't make a sound. He also couldn't get loose because Sufi's left canine had neatly penetrated the top of his snout, pinning him efficiently. Max pulled hard, his stocky shoulders bunching, dust flying as he backpedaled. Sufi stood his ground, six inches of Labrador still on his turf, where he was the legitimate ruler. A small smile crept around the corners of his mouth.

Eventually, of course, Hoobner came running, no doubt alerted by the sudden quietness. He yelled at Sufi and pulled on Max, but as long as Sufi kept his mouth shut, the dogs were joined at the fence. Roused by Hoobner's shouting, Ned emerged from the slaughter-house and told Sufi to "drop it!" This was done at once, and Hoobner and Max tumbled back in a cloud of dust and wounded machismo.

Since that time, the dogs kept their distance. Max knew in his heart he could tear Sufi to shreds, and Hoobner knew that sooner or later Sufi would get it. Sufi was apolitical: he knew that Max would make a terrific playmate, and he held no grudges.

•

Ned and Nancy had a friend who dropped in now and then, a girl who squatted secretly in the nearby village with her collection of buttons and brightly-colored ribbons. She was a tall and lanky lass, with a mind of her own, such as it was, and she delighted in the never-ending pursuit of the ultimate frill. Her name was Janella, and frills were her life.

One day, Janella came to visit the slaughter-house when Ned and Nancy were away. Finding no-one inside but the dog, she fastened a gay scrap of colored ribbon on the door and departed, leaving both the door and the gate wide open. Sufi, ever mindful of rare opportunities, emerged into the bright sun, inspected his private yard, and proceeded on out into the world beyond, eyes gleaming with youthful enthusiasm, and utterly heedless of the black Labrador snoozing in the shade beneath a decrepit Land Rover.

Glancing from side to side, Sufi began trotting around, sniffing happily for traces of excrement. His jingling collar soon caught Max's ear, and seconds later, Max was running full tilt at the hated rival. Sufi, sensing a terrific gambol, took off around the slaughter-house.

To be fair, Max truly was a daunting junkyard dog, with ample fighting experience, and plenty of speed. Few opponents had escaped his charge.

Sufi, by contrast, was an extraordinary best-of-breed from a lineage Max had never encountered. Sufi could run in sprints over 45 mph, and he always happily accepted the baton.

Within three-quarters of a revolution, Sufi rounded the entire slaughter-house and was about to lap the Lab, who had no idea he was being overtaken. Suddenly, there was Sufi, sprinting right on past, and Max redoubled his pursuit. In another few seconds, Sufi came round again, and Max's fury knew no bounds.

His confusion mounting (how many of these damned skinny sprinters were there?), Max stopped abruptly and turned for a confrontation.

Sufi stopped too, standing alongside Max like an old friend. It took a moment for Max to realize that his enemy was right next to him, and then he turned and snapped, a snap at the throat, to end it as quickly as possible.

In the twinkling of an eye, Sufi danced into the air, placing his front paws lightly on Max's back, and came to rest standing on Max's opposite side. Max's teeth clicked loudly on thin air—his prey had vanished. Quickly he turned, this time snapping to his left, but Sufi again pirouetted over his back to land again at Max's right.

Max spun around furiously, and for a moment both dogs faced

each other, panting and tense, their tongues dripping, teeth bared. Max was snarling, lips curled back, hackles straight up along his burly neck; Sufi was smiling his Doberman smile, exposing twin six-inch rows of pearly whites as he panted, but his dewlaps hung loose—he seemed not to understand this was a fight to the death.

Suddenly, both dogs froze, as Hoobner emerged from the garage, brandishing a large broom. He howled with rage, yelling to Ned (who wasn't home) that his damn Doberman was going to kill Max. Waving the broom, he ran around in circles, alternately shouting at Sufi and yelling for Ned to come out before it was too late.

The dogs stared each other down for a few heart-beats, and then Sufi took off down the street at a fair pace. Max cowered beneath his master's broom; Mitsy appeared and hauled him away to safety.

But Hoobner was not finished with his rage. His dog's junkyard crown had been tarnished, and with it the entire pride of his clan. And Mitsy was watching: something had to be done.

Hoobner hauled his massive frame over to the fence at the slaughter-house, still bellowing for Ned, who still was not home, to come outside and make things right. Nothing happened, and Hoobner's rage increased. He kicked the open chicken-wire gate, and it bounced back and bumped against him, insolently. This was the cause of the whole disaster: this damned fence.

Now howling with unbridled vitriol, Hoobner began tearing the chicken-wire from the posts with his bare hands, running back and forth while violently tugging and jerking at the wire. Within minutes, and with considerable exertion, he reduced the fence to a tangle of bent mesh encircling Sufi's tiny yard. But still his rage was not satiated.

The fence posts remained, like a spindly Stonehenge, to deny his authority over the property, so Hoobner attacked again, lunging his considerable weight against the posts. One after another, they bent a little, and worked loose in their holes, but the hard-pan kept them obstinately upright. Finally, in one roaring explosion of revenge, Hoobner jumped into the air, seeking to topple one of the damned posts by sheer mass.

For a frozen moment, Hoobner was poised atop the post, bunched into a ball, clinging with a furious grip of arms and legs, several feet above the ground. His face had gone white and puffy, and he emitted gasping, apoplectic grunts as he clung to his perch.

The fence post swayed slightly in the dense dirt that held it upright, Hoobner's obesity at its top like a gigantic round lolly-pop. Then, in slow motion, the post bent slightly, crackled in protest, snapped in two, and deposited Hoobner, still clinging to a section of splintered post, onto his back in the dust.

Silence returned to the yard once more. Hoobner's panting could be heard above the light summer breeze; birds chirped cautiously across the road. Sufi was long gone.

Mitsy came running across the yard, crying out, "You've killed him! Your damn dog has killed him!" She reached her exhausted man, and helped him to his feet.

Covered with dust and sweat, Hoobner limped back to the motorcycle shop with one arm around Mitsy. But he had defended the honor of the tribe; he had proven his rank; his dignity was restored.

Max was already inside, asleep in one corner of the garage. Ned and Nancy were still not home. And Sufi was cruising the green hills of Vermont, in search of new playmates.

Ω

9

Signs

A man sits on the sidewalk outside the McGraw-Hill building in Manhattan. His clothes are grimy and his face is so hairy and dirty that he is unrecognizable. He has been staring at his feet for a long time; his ankles are shiny and black. He wears mismatched shoes; one is wrapped in tattered duct tape. Several hundred people have stepped around him this afternoon on their way in and out of the skyscraper.

Fifty stories above, a man in a Brooks Brothers business suit stares out the window across the city. His gaze darts from building to building up the length of the island. The vast green swath of Central Park stretches into the haze.

The man in the sky glances down at the streets below his building. The people look like cockroach droppings on a narrow grey shelf. One of them is the grimy man sitting on the sidewalk. From this height he looks the same as any other dot in the steady flow of office workers moving around him.

A taxi pulls to a stop next to him and someone in a dark suit gets out and hurries past, into the building. The man on the curb looks up. The taxi pulls away, then stops abruptly and a new passenger jumps in. The car behind the taxi blows its horn. The man on the sidewalk stands. The taxi merges back into the flow of traffic.

The man looks around, puzzled, as if he doesn't recognize anything. It's true: he doesn't.

He starts walking, straight into the street. Another car blows its horn and swerves. Someone curses out of a car window, "Get the hell out of the street!"

The man stops and stares this way and that, looking for clues in the traffic. The car just in front of him moves on, leaving a gap, and he continues walking unsteadily across the street into the gap. The traffic resumes behind him.

He makes his way west, along 49th Street towards Seventh Avenue. There is a crowd at the next corner, bunched up and waiting for the light. He stands at the back of the crowd, head down, waiting for another clue.

The light changes and the crowd moves forward into the street. The man is swept along, but he isn't paying attention. Half-way across the intersection, he hears a sound, or thinks he does. Looking up, he notices a city bus passing right in front of the crowd. On the side of the bus a billboard proclaims, "West Pharmaceuticals."

The man tugs somebody's sleeve. The other person pulls away, disgusted. "Hey," says the grimy man, "Which way is West?"

The other person shrinks back. "Straight ahead," he says, and hurries off. The man moves on westward with the crowd.

Crossing Broadway, the crowd thins out and the man begins to wander. He leans against a skyscraper and looks down at his feet for a while. He does not see the caked dirt and torn shoes.

A scrap of newspaper lies on the sidewalk showing part of a headline: "Accuses Oil Lobby..." The man turns and faces the building, and then begins stepping sideways, edging along against the granite siding. He comes to a large glass door with etched lettering that reads "Lobby."

He pushes on the door, but it doesn't move. He keeps pushing, in a series of small surges of his whole body against the glass. After a few minutes, someone inside the building appears and pushes the glass door open, which shoves the man aside. He grabs the edge of the door and pulls himself in.

In the sudden shade and quiet inside the building, the man

again becomes immobile, standing a few feet from the door, looking down.

A security guard notices the man and walks toward him. At the same time, a woman hurries by from the elevator with a cluster of shopping bags and bumps into him. One of the bags has a Bloomingdale logo on it. Another has an ad for sale prices in the home furnishings department, twelfth floor.

The security guard stares at the grimy man. "What are you doing here?" he asks.

The man squints at the guard. "Twelfth floor," he says.

The guard looks at him suspiciously, and then points to the elevators.

The man shuffles to the elevators and watches while the doors open and close and people come and go. One of the elevators empties out and its doors remain open, waiting for more passengers. A poster on the back wall of the elevator reads, "New Top Floor Luxury Apartments."

A group of people hurries past and the man is swept into the elevator. Someone says, "What floor?"

"Top," the grimy man says.

The elevator doors close and it rises. On the way up, it stops and people get in and out. Eventually the man is alone. The doors close and the elevator continues up. It stops and the doors open. The man looks out at painters and ladders and stacks of wallboard.

The doors begin to close but a worker runs up. "You getting out?" he says.

The grimy man walks into the maze of remodeling. He stands still and looks down at his shabby shoes. After a few minutes a worker in overalls comes up and asks what he's doing.

He looks up at the man in overalls. A patch on the denim says, "Whitehead Roofing." The overall man looks impatient.

"Roofing," says the grimy man.

The overall man looks at the other's blackened shoes and ankles. "Over there," he says, pointing to an open door in the corner.

The grimy man goes through and slowly climbs a flight of concrete stairs. His footsteps echo forty stories down the stairwell. Eventually, he comes to another door, propped open onto the roof. Workers are swabbing a section with steaming black tar.

He walks to a low wall at one edge of the roof. The sun is behind him and the street far below is in shadow. A distant illuminated billboard is just in view around the corner of a building. The back-lit lettering reads, "MSNBC Television. Lean Forward."

Ω

10

16 Degrees of Correlation

Last night, I was surprised to receive an email from an old friend of mine, David Vivian, asking after my sister, Joan Boyce.

David's emails are quite rare; he is usually traveling the world, installing cardboard-box fabrication machines. These machines are about the size of a one-car garage, and arrive at their installation sites in multiple tractor-trailer rigs full of crates and boxes. David takes up residence nearby and painstakingly unpacks, inventories, assembles, tests, and certifies the machines, which take shape on the factory floor like elaborate mechanical sculptures. They have big red enamel panels and bright yellow catwalks, festooned with conduits and cables and conveyor belts.

For weeks, David may be found crawling over, under, around, and through this maze of steel frames and brackets, hooking things up, routing wires, bolting components in place, pushing on clevis rods, calibrating actuators, and generally losing himself in the mixed media of factory automation. An email from David always gets my attention.

My sister Joan lives in Eugene, Oregon. Her younger son attended the university decades ago, and she gravitated there, in part to enjoy his proximity. Later, her son moved to Portland, but

the mildly rural atavistic culture of Eugene, along with the rho-
dodendron and Bach festivals, held her there.

David's email didn't focus on my sister. In fact, he only mentioned her in passing: "How's Joan these days?" But my ran-
dom-access brain brought Joan's father-in-law to mind, and he
stuck there for a while. Joan is the daughter-in-law of Burke Boyce,
a popular historical novelist of the 1950's who specialized in the
young George Washington.

•

I first met Burke Boyce when I was a child and Burke was interim
headmaster of a private college preparatory school adjacent to our
home. A short time later, my sister became engaged to his son, an
astronomer, but that's another story. At the age of ten, I would
bump into Burke at various adult events, where he would inevitably ask, "How's your vocabulary?" This question never made
much sense to me, since I rarely thought about my vocabulary or
anyone else's.

Burke's remark might have stemmed from a strange joke I
memorized some years before about a nineteenth-century "big
city professor" trying to communicate with a "country bumpkin"
at a rural rooming house. The joke never struck me as remotely funny, but most adults were amused to hear the multisyllabic
language of the joke spewing precociously from a seven-year-old.

Often, when my parents had guests for dinner, I found myself
standing among them in my pajamas at bedtime, having shaken
hands with half a dozen giant adults. At such a time, my mother or
father would say, "Tell them the professor joke, dear."

I would look at whichever parent it was, hoping they weren't
serious, but they always were, so I would pull my attention away
from the enormous hands I'd just taken in my tiny grip, and ban-
ish the embarrassing weirdness of being the elf in a circle of giants.

"A big city professor," I would say, loathing the blandness of the
joke's set-up, "pulled up at a country inn in a one-horse carriage."

My little audience would fall utterly silent, enhancing my discomfort.

"The owner's little boy ran out to greet him, and the professor said:

> *Extricate the quadruped from the vehicle.*
> *Stabulate him.*
> *Devote to him an adequate supply of nutritious aliment.*
> *And when the glorious aurora doth illuminate the oriental horizon,*
> *I shall reward thee with a pecuniary compensation for thy amiable hospitality."*

The adults would then utter polite gasps and exclamations.

I would blush and look down, and then deliver the prestige: "The little boy turned and yelled, 'Hey Pa! There's a Frenchman out here!'"

After a brief period of politic laughter, one or another adult would inevitably ask, as did Burke himself on one occasion, "Yes, but do you know what all those big words mean?"

That a person might memorize a speech they couldn't understand seemed ridiculous to me, but conversing with adults was usually baffling, so I would smile and translate the convoluted antique babble into kids' English. The adults would applaud and then immediately forget the whole thing. For me, the accretion of such performances became a durable scab of blended shame and pride.

Perhaps I should also mention that the joke *per se* is apocryphal; it originated as an example of impaired communication born of pride, in a lecture by George Smith to a congregation of Mormon preachers in 1855.

•

Although I was unaware of it as a pre-teen, many years later I learned from my sister that Burke often complained about an unflattering review of his most successful historical novel, *Man from Mount Vernon*. Clive Etheridge, the reviewer, had decried certain details in Burke's book. Joan didn't remember where Mr. Ether-idge's review had appeared, but claims of factual inaccuracies always made Burke boiling mad; in his cups he would rant bitterly about these unfounded and unresolved assaults on the veracity of his best historical novel.

"If I have got one single fact wrong," Burke would mutter, "then the whole damn thing is called into question!" It was never clear whether the Damn Thing was his book, his credibility, or history itself.

Clive Etheridge's specific points about Burke's book are long lost in the temporal manifold, but they stemmed from his claim that the present curator of the Mount Vernon estate had vigorously denied certain specifics in the novel. This curator, a Mr. Frank Fellows, had apparently cited several credible historians of previous generations. Of these, the most notable was Delmar Weingarten, whose scholarly reputation is rarely, if ever, in dispute.

According to Weingarten, the original grounds keeper at Mount Vernon had been Anthony Blaine, a Virginian horticulturist originally employed at one of the early sot-weed plantations near Yorktown. Disillusioned by intractable problems with tobacco weevils, Anthony Blaine moved North and happened to meet the young George Washington at the Pope's Pub, a tavern on Pope's Creek. Washington was barely twenty at the time, but the two men became friends, and years later Blaine was recruited to manage the grounds at Washington's newly renovated estate at Mount Vernon.

Blaine, not to be confused with Anthony Wayne, the colonial military hero who drove the British from their Hudson River stronghold at Stony Point (not far from Burke Boyce's home in Cornwall-on-Hudson), was the son-in-law of a well-known pre-revolutionary doctor named Phillip Dannerston. With little success, Blaine attempted to apply early medical know-how obtained from Dannerston to the weevils in the plantations at

Mount Vernon. Soon, however, he and his wife became estranged, and his connection with Dr. Dannerston was severed.

This proved socially inconvenient for the Blaine household, because Philip Dannerston was well liked, and was considered something of a local hero. He was widely known, far beyond Mount Vernon, for having saved the lives of the entire K. P. Bellows family, including all fourteen of their children, when an outbreak of cholera from polluted groundwater swept through the region.

Colonial practitioners of animal husbandry had lost track of the "rules of run-off" from their homelands, allowing effluent from their rapidly growing herds to befoul several streams that were critical to the local water supply. More than 200 people perished in the ensuing cholera epidemic, since the disease produces severe dehydration, and the water supply itself was the origin of the epidemic. No doubt far more people would have succumbed if courageous physicians like Dannerston had not labored valiantly, day and night for months, to reverse the sanitation problem and re-establish lost hygienic practices to the population.

The Dannerston estate survives to this day, still in the hands of Dannerston's descendants. In the early 20th century, Phillip Dannerston's grandson Stanley held elaborate bohemian parties at the sprawling home, attended by young and upcoming intellectuals from his class at Harvard. Among these was T. S. Eliot, who briefly became something of a fixture at the Dannerston home until his sudden departure to Paris in 1910.

In the second decade of the 20th century, Eliot's writings were relatively unknown. But Todd Bakersfield, an obscure commentator on Eliot's work, devoted what was to become fully half of his writing career commenting on Eliot's oeuvre. The other half was, with equal persistence, dedicated to the philosophical musings of the prolific American essayist Morris Wellington. Wellington confined his writings exclusively (or so it was thought) to literary criticism of material published in the *New England Review of Lit-*

erature, a journal that was popular until well into the 1940's and of which he was editor-in-chief. Wellington's ideas and insights broke the elite boundaries of the *Review* to achieve considerable national popularity, almost entirely through the efforts of his personal "Boswell," Todd Bakersfield.

Curiously, Bakersfield himself achieved some fame or notoriety for quoting Wellington extensively, not just from the *Review*, but also from an unpublished manuscript of Wellington's essays that he claimed to have in his possession. Beyond the recognized editorials known from the *Review*, Wellington's other writings were thought to be virtually nil—apart from these additional quotations attributed to him in Bakersfield's books. Unfortunately, the provenance of the additional Bakersfield material remained uncertain. The ensuing controversy persisted for nearly a decade, most notably among literati in New York City, where it consumed several articles in the nascent *New Yorker* magazine and the literary section of the *New York Times*.

•

In 1949, Bakersfield's nephew, Bill, was patching the roof of the family home in Nyack, New York, when he came upon an old steamer trunk in the attic. After jimmying the antique padlock, he found the trunk was full of old clothes, shoes, umbrellas, a polished spittoon, four medium-sized oil paintings, and a small stack of books wrapped in foolscap and tied together with twine. Among these books was, to young Bill's amazement, what must have been the original source of his uncle's quotes, an unpublished manuscript by Morris Wellington.

The paintings were themselves also quite surprising, as they depicted strange and fantastic objects in unusual juxtaposition: perambulating inkwells, clusters of bugs, three-legged nudes on stone staircases, unfamiliar animals, levitating Conestoga wagons pulled by satyrs, and melting clocks. These paintings, as everyone now knows, were subsequently attributed to Boxer and Blaugh, the infamous colonial-Boston pre-surrealists. Years later, Charles MacKenzie of New York's Metropolitan Museum famously unmasked the Boxer and Blaugh paintings as a fraud, although their true origin has never been satisfactorily established. By the turn of the 21st century, however, MacKenzie's nemesis in art criticism had burst on the scene, a Mr. Paul M. Bowler of Pittsburgh, who surprised the art world yet again by announcing that he possessed plausible evidence the Bostonians indeed might well have legitimately preempted Salvador Dali by almost ten generations.

Paul Bowler's thesis was unknown to the art world until 2012, but just before its scheduled publication he had taken on a secretary, Miss Genevieve Delmonte, a chatty young lady from the mid-West, and had discussed his theories with her at length, hoping to arouse her interest in his work, and no doubt also in his availability as an eligible bachelor. To Bowler's disappointment, young Miss Delmonte was already engaged to a graduate student from Delaware named Arthur Yankzikov, and a few months after starting work at Bowler's office in Boston, Miss Delmonte took the train to her paramour's home town of Wilmington. She was almost giddy with excitement, since the purpose of her trip was to meet her fiancé's parents, Professor and Mrs. Frederik Yankzikov, recent immigrants from what is now Belarus.

At dinner on her first night in Wilmington, hoping to impress Paul's parents, she eagerly chattered about the Boxer and Blaugh paintings, MacKenzie's attack on their legitimacy, and—most exciting of all—her very own boss's imminent refutation of MacKenzie. Soon the paintings would be reinstated as some of the most valued art treasures in the New World, and would play a dramatic role in revising the entire history of modern American art.

The Yankzikovs listened politely, eyeing their son discreetly, and stealing an occasional raised eyebrow at each other. Their son's attention was fixed on Genevieve's animated presentation, and on the way it, in turn, animated the upper portion of her anatomy. When she paused for air and a quick sip of wine, Frederik said, "My dear, I've never heard of this Boxer Blow gentleman. Was he a painter of some renown in the Americas?"

Genevieve struggled to let go of her momentum and said, "Oh, Mr. Yankzikov, yes, he was very renown, except he was Boxer and Blaugh, not just Blow." She took another sip, hoping the interruption was but brief.

"Boxer and Blow," repeated Mr. Yankzikov. "A strange name."

"But it's two people!" Genevieve exclaimed. "They were partners. They painted together."

"I see," said Yankzikov, glancing at his wife.

"Are you pregnant?" said Mrs. Yankzikov, politely.

In the Yankzikov's home region in Eastern Europe, the Boxer and Blaugh controversy was entirely unknown, and the Yankzikovs took no further interest in their future daughter-in-law's office chatter.

However, on the train to Wilmington earlier that day, Genevieve had sat next to Dan Ringle, an up and coming publicist with dreams of starting his own publishing empire. When she casually mentioned that she worked with Paul Bowler, Ringle had recognized the name and asked a few probing questions. She had then gone into great detail about the art controversy, covering every element of her new boss's evidence validating the paintings. She prattled on almost non-stop for the entire trip, but quite early in her speech Ringle had become lost in his own thoughts, growing more and more infatuated by what he perceived as the truly vast sales potential of this pair of diametrically opposed art critics.

•

Unlike Genevieve Delmonte, Dan Ringle was on his way to meet his own father, James Haughton Ringle, who had served 30 years, until his retirement, as editorial director of the University of Delaware's closely-held printing venture, the Greenfield Press. At dinner that night, his father appeared more imperial than usual, and Dan felt himself once again emotionally regressing to the age of eleven.

Nevertheless, Dan told his father about the forthcoming publication that was sure to reignite the Boxer and Blaugh controversy. Their paintings, regardless of provenance, were worth millions. Dan emphasized the financial opportunity Bowler's writings represented, and his father immediately saw the handwriting on the wall.

"You must do it," James Haughton Ringle declared, slamming down his stein and beaming proudly at his son.

"Yes, Father," Dan replied, hopefully.

"Go to New York," the senior Ringle said. "Find out who represents this Bowler fellow, then get to Bowler in person, and sign him up."

"OK, Dad."

"Son, I'll back you on this. I've got enough cash to buy out all the publishing rights on this Bowler character."

"Sure, Dad," said Dan. "But what are you going to do with them?"

His father took another gulp of beer, and smiled broadly. "I'll get the rights. You get your World Publishing International thing set up. And then I'll just transfer everything to your company. You'll be sitting pretty."

"Wow, Dad," said Dan. "This should really get my company off the ground. Thanks!"

"It sure the hell will," said his father. "But it all depends on getting the rights to Bowler. Just see that you do it."

"Yessir! You bet!" Dan's head was swimming with thoughts of massive press conferences and a long string of best-selling books on the controversial Boston artists, no doubt further fueled by still more discrediting outbursts from the aging MacKenzie at the Met.

The next day, Dan Ringle took the North-bound express train back to New York and checked into the Algonquin on 44th Street, within walking distance of most of the major publishers. Not wishing to tip his hand to Paul Bowler just yet, he called his contacts among New York's freelance agents, and soon found that Bowler was working directly with an acquisitions editor at Alfred P. Knopf. This was highly unusual, and spoke volumes about the value Knopf evidently ascribed to Bowler's material. Publishers almost never signed an author, even the most successful, without agent representation.

As soon as he finished his call, he contacted his lawyer in Boston and directed him to finalize the paperwork for World Publishing International. It wouldn't be long before WPI was on the map, and Dan Ringle was a force to reckon with in the publishing world.

•

The acquisitions editor in question was Miss Brandy Thurston, hitherto unknown to Ringle or any of the agents he had called. She had moved to New York after a successful stint as a creative writing instructor at Bard College in Annandale-on-Hudson, about twice as far up river as Cornwall. She was not a historian, and had no post-graduate degree in literature, but her cousin knew someone at Knopf with significant pull, and she had wrangled a provisional position as research assistant in the Intellectual Property Rights department.

She took Dan Ringle's call immediately, and when she found out his reason for wanting a meeting, she had a difficult time suppressing her excitement. It was clear from Ringle's somewhat inexperienced presentation that he might be willing to spend a very large sum for the Bowler rights, and she knew from the office grapevine that Knopf was already regretting its arrangements with an unrepresented author, and was anxious to terminate the Bowler contract. This meant she could be in a very strong position to solve a problem and land a very profitable deal at the same time.

Brandy approached her boss, John J. Johnson, carefully. She hadn't been at Knopf more than a few months, and still didn't know how to read him. He was an attorney, and played his cards close to his chest. She explained Ringle's desire to buy out Knopf's rights to Bowler's work, but she didn't mention Ringle's embarrassing eagerness to close the deal. He had seemed almost desperate, and she sensed that Johnson might tend to avoid any commitments with someone he considered even mildly unprofessional.

Johnson was unenthusiastic, but he authorized a meeting, and she called the Algonquin and set up a luncheon with Ringle at the Cottage Shop, a restaurant across the Hudson in Haverstraw. It wasn't clear why Ringle insisted on meeting so far outside the city, but Brandy Thurston wasn't about to argue.

As a resident of Manhattan, Brandy had no automobile, although unlike most residents, she did have a driver's license. She hailed a cab in midtown and gave the driver the address in Haverstraw. With a sullen grunt, the driver slapped his meter into service and took off through the city towards the Lincoln Tunnel. Half an hour later, they arrived at the Cottage Shop and Brandy hurried inside, clutching her briefcase and feeling suddenly very professional. The taxi waited in the parking lot with its meter running.

In his eagerness to launch, Dan Ringle was indeed prepared to pay an extraordinary fee for the transfer of the Bowler rights to the Greenfield Press, since he had a good idea how much disposable income his father could contribute. He was almost giddy with excitement at the thought that these six-figure publishing rights would soon become the property of Dan's own World Publishing International.

After lunch, Brandy Thurston took the taxi back to Manhattan and went straight to Mr. Johnson's office, with high expectations that an unprecedented deal was about to go through. Her boss, however, felt that more market research was needed, a setback that Brandy accepted stoically, hoping thereby to project more of the burgeoning professionalism she had felt pretty much all that day.

Johnson knew that full due diligence would be critical for a deal of this magnitude, especially one destined to involve the severance of Bowler, a well-known content provider. Accordingly, he decided to send Brandy Thurston to discuss the situation with Kendall McGuire, a freelance literary scholar often employed by Knopf in fact-checking and matters of provenance.

McGuire was a fastidious, bookish fellow in his mid-sixties, who liked to stay in his upper West side apartment poring over many a quaint and curious volume of forgotten lore. He had no secretary or assistant because he conducted most of his work alone, originally through extensive correspondence and phone calls, and more recently with the aid of the new facsimile machines.

When Brandy Thurston called him about performing due diligence on both Bowler and Ringle, Kendall McGuire was startled by the jangling ring of his antique corded telephone; it had been two weeks since anyone had called him. Already familiar with Bowler's writings, and the Boxer and Blaugh controversy, this task inspired him. But he wasn't happy to be asked to check up on Ringle, who was not yet established in the publishing industry, and his enthusiasm for the Bowler portion of the project was damped by this unwanted burden. Grudgingly, although it was a foregone conclusion since he had no other paying clients, he accepted both of Knopf's projects and immediately set about contacting his myriad cronies throughout the world of books.

McGuire was a very private man, with at least a few personal secrets that would make anyone uncomfortable if they were known, and a host of other minor secrets important only to him. Among those minor secrets, and definitely unknown to anyone at Knopf, was the fact that his sister was Jane Kelly, a very famous dancer at the Copacabana, since before it became a disco, and well before the club began decades of location hopping around midtown. Jane Kelly was, in fact, the oldest continuous performer, showgirl or any other art-form, in the long history of the Copa. She still performed, well preserved and discreetly encased in flesh-colored spandex, and drew consistent applause for her famous and remarkable vegetarian hairdo.

For the last twenty years, Jane had employed a personal dresser, an unknown costume designer named Ginji Jean Jackson. There had always been very few resident headliners at the Copa, and by the present day Jane Kelly was the only one, so there was only one dresser, and Ginji Jean was it.

Every night, she would help Jane into her support hose and leotard, hook up the numerous gaudy showgirl accessories, nudge Jane's anatomy into the expected positions, attach her voluminous bustle, and then spend the next half hour painstakingly installing the huge Jane Kelly salad-like headdress. Then, once her mistress was safely positioned in the wing Stage Left, she would wait until the familiar introductory salsa music began, and watch while Jane strode out into the blazing lights, to thunderous botanically-inspired applause.

Then Ginji Jean would turn away and descend the black rear staircase to her mistress's dressing room, where she remained for the duration of the show. There she would smoke Chesterfields and work or re-work crossword puzzles from the Manchester Guardian.

Throughout the years, having abandoned a career in costume design, and apart from a dash of ostensible glamor as Jane Kelly's dresser, Ginji Jean's life had only one brief moment of color, excitement, and drama.

Ginji was raised in a working class family in the Williamsburg section of Brooklyn. She wasn't very pretty, and she never stopped snapping her chewing gum, but her body had always matched the 1980's dream-girl archetype to a T; and since her teen years she had endured pursuit by every Y chromosome in her neighborhood between the ages of 14 and 40. After decades fending off inept suitors, casual daters, malevolent intimidators, and leering masturbators, she had grown wary of all human contact and walked with her head down, bundled in shapeless coats and sweaters, in desperation not to be noticed. She was noticed, on this one colorful occasion, by someone who in fact may well have saved her life.

A few months ago, Ginji Jean Jackson was walking down Flushing Avenue with some groceries, hunched over as usual, her head covered by a dark blue scarf from which a few large yellow plastic hair curlers poked out. She wore no makeup, and had recently sprouted two or three prominent zits which were just peaking in size and vibrancy. She had been working all afternoon at one of her secondary jobs, in the stockroom of a local delicatessen, and her clothes smelled of nervous sweat, salami, and onions. Nevertheless, Ozwin Henzler, a former high school classmate, had been absentmindedly stalking her since morning. Unlucky in love, Ozwin had remained infatuated through the decades with increasingly unrealistic recollections of Ginji Jean.

It was mid-December, and the afternoon light was almost gone, so Ginji Jean was anxious to be safe at home, away from public view, as quickly as possible. She turned down a side street and quickened her pace, still unaware of the shuffling heavyweight who was following her, nursing a pint of cheap brandy.

Ozwin paused in his pursuit to take another swig. The bottle was only one fourth full by now, so he dutifully sucked down the remaining peach-flavored ounces. Then, having immediately forgotten what he just did, he became frustrated when the bottle failed to produce anything more to drink. He shook his head in disgust, which made his vision shimmy and shake for a moment, and threw the bottle at the nearest parked car.

Ginji heard the breaking glass and stole a glance behind her. There, less than 50 feet away, stood Ozwin, staring at her with his mouth open, looking even more Cro Magnon than usual. With a gasp of fright, Ginji Jean turned back and began to execute a gait between jogging and trotting, hoping to disguise her flight with something more casual, less obviously desperate. Ozwin immediately felt primal biochemistry percolate into his blood supply, and lurched into a surprisingly speedy long-legged shuffle. The two figures gyrated their separate ways down the darkening street for several minutes; the distance between them steadily dwindled.

Within only a few yards of the stoop at Ginji Jean's apartment house, Ozwin caught up with his prey. He reached out and grabbed her arm, and Ginji Jean spun round, out of balance, throwing her groceries in a wide arc onto the sidewalk and street. She screamed as Ozwin jerked her against him and wrapped his arms around her, pinning her hands at her sides. She looked up at his sweating face, his sloping wrinkled forehead, his yellow teeth, so close she could see his uvula dangling incongruously at the back of his throat. He was squeezing her so hard she couldn't breathe, and she knew this was the beginning of a whole new phase of life.

She was right, of course, but not in the way her panicked prey-mind expected. As she watched, Ozwin's slack-jawed countenance jerked suddenly to the left with a look of mild surprise. At the same moment, the right side of his head seemed to collapse a little, while a bright red eruption bloomed on the left. His crushing grip on her arms released, and he slowly tilted farther to the left, the surprised expression still painted on his face like a simian cartoon. A second later, he was lying on the sidewalk among her groceries, dark red pooling rapidly around his upper body.

Another scream, a kind of scream within a scream, struggled to burst from her throat, but she could no longer vocalize. She stood still in shock, staring straight ahead at the empty space Ozwin had just occupied, her eyes still focused only inches away.

Then, as if emerging from someone else's dream, a short man in a black coat and a black fedora strode toward her. She turned, and saw him pocket a chrome-plated gun, and hold out his hand, a look of genuine concern on his round face. He reached Ginji just as her amygdala shut down her higher brain functions, and he just managed to prevent her from falling into the mess at their feet.

Ginji awoke in the back of a limousine, driving through the dark streets of Williamsburg. The short gentleman who had saved her was sitting on the opposite seat reading a newspaper. A dark glass panel cut off the driver's compartment. The car was silent, except for the occasional rustle of folding newsprint.

After a few minutes, she decided she wasn't in immediate danger. In her mind's eye, she could still see Ozwin's strangely deformed face as he tipped over to the sidewalk. The blood seemed to be the only color in a murky twilight mental image that replayed whenever she closed her eyes.

She looked at the man behind the newspaper. He seemed to be deliberately ignoring her. Eventually, she summoned enough courage to croak, "Thanks, Mister."

Pignose Barucci folded his newspaper carefully and laid it on the seat. He looked at her intensely, from head to toe, and Ginji felt a new wave of anxiety. She shrank back into the corner of her seat.

"Hey," said Pignose. "Don't be scared. I ain't gonna hurt you."

Ginji searched his face for any evidence that he could be trusted. His skin was pockmarked with countless acne scars, and looked puffy and flushed. But his eyes were steady, and somehow she discerned that if he meant her harm, he wouldn't bother reassuring her first.

"You saved me?" she said, a half-question.

"Yeah, I guess I did."

They continued to stare at each other for a few minutes as the car bounced gently through Brooklyn and turned onto the Williamsburg Bridge.

"Where are we going?" she asked.

Pignose leaned back. "You needa get cleaned up," he said. "I'm taking you to my place."

Ginji looked around nervously.

"It'sa nice place," Pignose added. "That OK with you?"

Ginji didn't really think it was, but she nodded.

"Good," said Pignose. "We'll be there in a few minutes."

The car turned this way and that into the depths of lower Manhattan, and then dove down into a dark driveway, made another turn, and stopped. The engine shut off, and a moment later one of the doors opened and Ginji saw the chauffeur standing outside, waiting patiently. He was much bigger and beefier than the late Ozwin Henzler, and she couldn't even see his head above the door opening.

Pignose nimbly stepped from the car, and then turned to offer Ginji a hand. She took it timidly, and climbed out after him. She had only ridden in a car four or five times, all taxis, and it was awkward traversing the cavernous passenger cabin of the limo. The door was too far away, and she ended up almost crawling.

They stood in a dim concrete chamber with a roll-up garage door at one end, and polished wood double doors at the other. The man holding her hand gave a little nod, almost like a bow, and said, "I'm Pignose Barucci. You can call me Pig."

Ginji nodded back.

"Let's go upstairs and get you something nice to wear."

He started to move toward the double doors, still grasping her hand, but Ginji held back.

"It's OK," he said. "You're safe here. Nobody gonna hurt you."

Pignose Barucci was a lesser-known Don of lower Manhattan, and rumor had it that his influence in the city mob scene was not just because he was a Made Man, but he was also putative heir to both the Zamboni fortune and a substantial portion of various Brooklyn waste management enterprises. His apartment on the lower East side comprised all but the top floor of a venerable townhouse, complete with a subterranean garage with room for three cars (although they could only enter or leave one at a time). The fifth floor of his townhouse was what he called the Gilded Cage, for it was there that he boarded his current paramour, a role shared by a continuous sequence of moderately naïve young women. He was proud of his monogamy: he never had more than one girlfriend at a time. On the other hand, he never had any particular girlfriend longer than three or four months.

Pignose had always been fond of the Copa, and he was delighted to discover that Ginji Jean worked there in the evenings as a dresser. He was even more delighted that her mistress was none other than Jane Kelly, who was locally even more famous than the boss of the entire crime family, Carlo Gambino.

Ginji Jean Jackson took up residence in the Gilded Cage not long after Pignose Barucci rescued her from Ozwin Henzler. To her credit, Ginji Jean cleaned up very well, and with sufficient makeup and hair-dressing, she soon looked quite glamorous parading around the clubs on the arm of her notorious gangster.

They went steady for about three months, and then she was no longer to be seen around the hot clubs of Manhattan. That fall, her few friends and immediate family would be relieved to find her living again in her tiny apartment in Williamsburg, not far from the bridge into the city.

It happened that in nearby Brooklyn, Pignose Barucci had a cousin who ran a small-time numbers racket out of Flatbush. The cousin, Antonio Sinofoli, was a systematic operator who evaded detection by law enforcement for his entire career. He was less systematic with spouses, however, and went through them much the same way Pignose went through girlfriends, albeit on a much smaller scale.

Sinofoli married his fifth wife Bonitina (née Santorini) at a modest wedding in the Catholic church on Nostrand Ave., named after St. Jerome, patron saint of librarians (no doubt because of his fame as the first translator of the Bible into Latin). Jerome's head is rumored to be in storage near the mineral springs at Nepi, Italy, but St. Jerome's church provided a fine setting for the wedding, as Bonitina was herself a librarian and worked in the stacks at the Williamsburg branch of the Brooklyn Public Library.

Bonitina Santorini Sinofoli had a sister whose employment was more in keeping with Sinofoli's mafia cousin. Drusilla Santorini also lived in Flatbush, but she worked sporadically in the Big Apple, wherever Hollywood movie location shoots were underway. She had nothing to do with the movie business, however, but instead had developed a parasitic relationship with the film production process.

Drusilla had a cousin, Luigi Pastorelli, who worked at the Mayor's Office of Film, Theatre, and Broadcasting, which issues permits to production companies engaged in projects around the city. Luigi would notify Drusilla whenever a large shoot was being scheduled, in particular, productions involving famous names—producers, directors, stars, or other celebrities. Luigi would then scour the approved production personnel to identify someone likely to be interested in a little work on the side, and then Drusilla would meet with them to arrange clandestine access to the secured location. Her primary skill, in fact, was her ability to broach the subject of criminal activities with ordinary people without inadvertently saying anything definitive, so that both parties might plausibly deny any knowledge of what they actually discussed.

Once the production was underway, and one or another celebrity was on call for the day, Drusilla and her small band of assistants, all dressed either as extras or as additional grips and gaffers, would circulate through the prop tents, wardrobe trucks, mobile dressing rooms, and celebrity trailers, trolling for recognizable memorabilia—anything that would, once the film became famous, fetch a good price on eBay. In rare cases, her minions might come up with something that had to be fenced—a gold Patek Philippe, a Vuitton or Hermes handbag, or a mink coat—in which case Pignose's people would handle monetization of the prize.

Rumors always circulated around a Big Apple production that something suspicious was going on, but celebrities are always losing things, and many of them are *non compos mentis*, either for artistic or chemical reasons. Nevertheless, there was a persistent myth of a mob-based "showjack" enterprise operating around the city, and production companies were always on the alert. Drusilla was resourceful, however, and since she recruited her accomplices long before production even started, whenever things did turn up missing it was eventually dismissed as carelessness.

Nevertheless, as security gradually tightened at location shoots, Drusilla began looking for other venues to exploit. When she heard through the family that Pignose was dating a girl who handled costumes at the Copa, new opportunities dawned. She called Pignose's Gilded Cage and left a message for Ginji Jean. The next day Ginji Jean returned the call, and Drusilla, with consummate skill, began grooming the other woman as her next unwitting accomplice.

The first step was for Drusilla to case the backstage areas at the Copa, without giving Ginji Jean any inkling that showjacking was about to infect her domain. As luck would have it, however, Ginji Jean was idly chatting with Jane Kelly while arranging the star's salad headdress one evening, and mentioned that a friend of a friend wanted a backstage tour. Jane knew, along with everyone else at the Copa, that Ginji Jean had been out on the town with Pignose Barucci; Jane immediately suspected that the friend of a friend was probably a friend of Pignose.

Over the next few days, Jane couldn't stop thinking about the possibility of a mobster prowling around the dressing rooms and the labyrinthine corridors beneath the stage, and she was still mulling it over when she joined her brother for their usual Saturday brunch at the Russian Tea Room. Her brother, of course, was Kendall McGuire, the literary scholar hired by Knopf.

They sat in one of the big curved red leather booths, surrounded by samovars and antique-looking paintings, while Kendall told Jane about his new project for Knopf. After their coffee arrived, it dawned on Kendall that his sister wasn't listening.

"Something wrong?" he said.

Jane studied her coffee. "Well, I don't know."

Kendall rolled his eyes, mentally, and thought, *How can you not know if something's wrong? Either it is or it isn't.* Then he said, "You look worried."

Jane raised her head. "I guess I am," she said. "My dresser wants to bring in a friend of a friend for a backstage tour."

"So?"

"My dresser is dating Pignose Barucci."

"She's what?" Kendall almost dropped his cup. "A mobster? Ginji Jean is?" Jane nodded. "Ginji's dating a mobster?"

"Just the last few months. You know it won't last," said Jane.

"Yeah, it only lasts till he dumps her in the East River."

Jane looked hurt.

"Sorry," said her brother. "But Jane, you can't invite some Mafia guy in there! You know how they operate. They'll get their fingers into things, and then you'll never be rid of them."

"That's what I'm afraid of," said Jane. "But it's not Pignose himself. It's just a friend. And I don't know for sure it's a friend of Pignose. All she said was 'friend of a friend.'"

"Yeah, right," said Kendall. He looked around the tea room, scanning the other patrons for unusually dangerous ones. They were all tourists.

"Besides," added Jane, "It's a girl."

"A girl? How do you know that? They could just be saying it's a girl, and then six guys show up with shoulder holsters."

"Ginji Jean said it was a girl she knew."

Kendall thought for a minute. "Where does she know her from?"

"I don't know. I think she's from Flatbush. Ginji's from Brooklyn."

"I'm not comfortable about Brooklyn," said Kendall. "You never know what's going on over there. It's like a different world."

"Well, it's a different borough," said Jane.

"But it's so close to the City, and yet so—*different*." Apparently proximity and differentiation together implied a much greater threat to normal life.

"I don't know what to do," said Jane. "I can't just tell her no.

Staffers bring in friends all the time when there's nothing going on. She'll think I'm being mean."

"Well, it's not mean to keep criminal elements out of your work space."

"I know. But what should I say?"

"I'm thinking." Kendall's literary mind was sifting through shelves full of mystery novels he had read, looking for a comparable plot line.

Jane waited, having forgotten brunch entirely.

"I've got it," said Kendall. He lowered his voice. "Tell her some guy in a raincoat and dark glasses was poking around the Copa last week."

"Uh, yes—"

"And then let on that some of the orchestra members thought he was FBI."

Jane frowned. "OK, but what does that have to do with letting her bring a guest?"

"You've got to be subtle," Kendall whispered. "Just plant the seed about the FBI. Then, like the next day, mention that you read about some possible sting operation directed at Pignose Barucci. But don't say anything about her friend being connected with the mob."

"Well, I don't actually know that she is, anyway."

"Maybe not. But we both know that Ginji Jean is, even if it's just dating."

"True."

They both sat back, and then remembered their coffee. A waiter came, and they ordered their usual meals.

"So then what should I do?" Jane said. "What do I tell her about the visit?"

"Don't do anything. If she asks again about bringing her friend, just stall. Say you're worried about the next show. Or you have to ask your boss or something."

Jane frowned. "I guess I can do that. But what if she keeps asking?"

"Just try this much, and see what happens. Can you do it tomorrow?"

"I'm on tonight, as usual," said Jane. "I can tell her tonight."

"Good."

"And then I can mention the investigation of Pignose tomorrow, before the Sunday matinée."

"Perfect," said Kendall. He leaned back and stole another panorama glance around the tea room. "Where's our waiter?" he said. "We shouldn't breathe another word of this."

"No shit," said Jane.

•

Late that afternoon, getting her hair sculpted, Jane fed Ginji Jean the story about the man in a trench coat. She kept it short and sweet, but in the mirror she could already see a glimmer of concern in her dresser's face. Jane was tempted to reinforce the story during her headdress installation, but she resisted the temptation. At her age, she had learned to resist a lot of temptations.

After the show, she said nothing more, but she thought Ginji Jean seemed a bit more distracted than usual.

"Got a hot date tonight?" Jane asked.

Ginji Jean frowned. "Well, yes, I guess. I'm meeting someone at 11:00, and then we're going out for a while."

"You seem preoccupied," said Jane, and then decided she'd better stop probing.

"I do?"

"Not really."

On Sunday, Jane was dying to see if Ginji Jean would be acting normal when she arrived for hair and makeup. Unfortunately, her dresser seemed perfectly normal. Jane asked if her evening out had been fun, and she smiled and said yes and seemed mainly happy and a bit tired, as usual.

Finally, while Ginji Jean was pinning Jane's bustle in place, Jane said, "Did you hear about the big sting operation?"

"The what?"

"The sting. Some Mafia guy they're after."

Ginji definitely hesitated for a moment. "What Mafia guy?" she said, with a slight tremor.

"I'm not sure," said Jane. "Something about an ongoing surveillance thing, and some kind of surprise they're setting up. I don't know any details. It was just a news commentary."

"Wow," said Ginji, coming to a complete stop. She was holding some safety pins in her mouth, and remained frozen for a surprisingly long time.

Jane broke the silence. "Ginji, are you OK?"

"Huh?"

"What are you doing? Is something wrong?" Jane's heart was beating harder than it had in years, and she imagined Ginji Jean's heart was, too, though for completely opposite reasons.

"No, nothing's wrong," said Ginji Jean, and resumed pinning the bustle. She didn't say another word for the rest of the evening, and Jane didn't try to get her to speak. Jane wondered if Ginji noticed that they both were silent before and after the show, but Ginji was probably too distracted.

The next day was a Monday and the Copa stage was dark. Jane didn't see Ginji Jean until Tuesday evening. She still seemed very distracted, and didn't say much. Jane knew better than to mention anything more about the FBI or the mob.

By the end of the week, Ginji Jean was a different woman. She moved slowly, and conversed only in low, glum tones. Finally, Jane decided it would be too unusual for her not to ask what was wrong.

"My guy dumped me," said Ginji.

"Oh, I'm so sorry," said Jane.

"He just suddenly had his driver take me back to my apartment, and that was that. It's over."

"Back to your apartment?"

"Oh. Yeah. Well, I was staying at his place for the last few months."

"Really? That sounds serious," said Jane.

"I guess it wasn't," said Ginji Jean. "I thought it was, though." She paused. "I don't know what went wrong."

"Well," Jane said, "men are pretty stupid sometimes. And they're never likely to explain themselves."

"I guess not. He was pretty private."

Jane thought about it. It seemed that the ruse had worked, though perhaps a bit more dramatically than expected. Pignose must have gotten wind of the FBI rumor through the 'friend of a friend,' and then decided to play it safe.

In the days that followed, Ginji Jean made no more mention of bringing someone for a tour, and Jane called Kendall to tell him the good news.

"It really worked," she said.

"What happened?" asked Kendall.

"Well, day one, I mean two, since it was Tuesday before I saw her, she came in looking really down. I didn't dare question her, but today I came right out and asked what was wrong. It looks like Pignose dumped her right after I told her the FBI story, so I'm pretty sure her 'friend' isn't going to be asking for any more backstage passes."

"Do you know what day Pignose dumped her?"

Jane thought a moment. "It must have been the next day. I assume she told her girl friend, and then probably that day she told her about the sting. And the next day Pignose moved her out of his apartment without a word." She paused. Kendall said nothing. "I didn't even know she was staying with him."

"Everybody knew that," said Kendall.

"Well, then the whole thing's taken care of," said Jane.

"That doesn't sound good, actually," said Kendall.

"What do you mean? It solved the problem, and he would have dumped her sooner or later anyway."

"Yes, but he reacted too fast. If Ginji's contact told him and he immediately cut all ties with Ginji, that means he doesn't trust Ginji."

"Oh, I don't know about that," began Jane.

"Well, I do. These guys are very careful. And ruthless."

"I guess so."

"I know so. I've been reading about them for years. They're probably keeping an eye on you, too, Sis."

"Me?"

"Yep. And me, too, I'll bet."

"Oh come on, Kendall. That's a bit paranoid."

"I'd rather be paranoid and alive than relaxed and dead," said Kendall.

Jane said nothing. They both listened to the phone electronics for a minute.

"I've got to go," said Kendall.

"OK. I should head home soon. See you this Saturday at the Tea Room?"

There was no reply. Then Kendall said, "I don't think so. Not this weekend."

"Why not? Got something planned?" Jane knew that Kendall never had anything planned that hadn't been planned years ago.

"No," he said. "Well, I'll see you later." And he hung up.

Jane stared at the phone, and then shrugged. Her brother was always a bit of a mystery. She didn't hear from him again for months.

•

The next week, Brandy Thurston called Kendall to see if he had made progress on his investigation of Paul Bowler and Dan Ringle for Knopf. There was no answer, and as Kendall didn't have an answering machine, she couldn't leave a message.

A week later, Brandy went to McGuire's apartment and banged on the door for ten minutes, but there was no response. Finally, in a fit of investigative journalism, she peeked through the letter slot in his door. Several days' worth of mail lay in a heap inside.

The following week Mr. Johnson demanded to know why Brandy hadn't gotten back to him with results from Kendall McGuire, and she admitted that he had inexplicably dropped out of sight.

"That's odd," said Johnson. "Didn't he say anything before he left?"

"Not a word," said Brandy. "And he doesn't have a service."

"Did you try emailing him?"

"Yes, sir. No reply. The messages went out OK, but nothing ever came back."

"Very odd."

"I even peeked into his letter slot, and there's a ton of mail inside."

"You what?"

"Peeked into the letter slot in his door. Last week when I went to his apartment."

"And you didn't tell me?"

"I didn't think you'd be interested in his letter slot."

"I'm not!" John Johnson exclaimed. "But that means he's literally disappeared!"

"That's what I'm telling you," said Brandy, growing perplexed.

"When somebody goes missing for weeks without leaving a word, you call the police!"

"Well, I—"

"Listen, call them right now and report him missing. And don't mention looking through his letter slot. It'll just make them wonder why you didn't report this a week ago."

"Alright. Yes. I'll do that right now, sir."

Mr. Johnson stood up and looked around his office. "Where's that proposal?"

"Which one?"

"Ringle, for chrissake. The one you're supposed to be investigating!"

"I, oh, well, it's right here, sir." Brandy pulled a manila envelope from under a pile of papers.

John Johnson snatched it from her, opened it up, and pulled out the proposal. He flipped the pages and glanced at each numbered section. Then he abruptly held it out at arm's length. Brandy looked at him uncertainly.

"Take it!" he snapped.

Brandy took it.

"Tell him we're not interested."

"Ringle?"

"Who the hell else?"

Brandy turned and left her boss in a more agitated state than she had ever seen him. She no longer felt the slightest bit professional. She returned to her office and sat at her desk without doing anything for a very long time. Then she called Dan Ringle and told him the deal was off.

•

Dan Ringle slowly put down his phone, with deliberate gentleness. In his mind he was slamming it into the cradle with all his might, although phones with cradles hadn't been seen (outside of Kendall McGuire's office) for decades.

It took weeks for Dan Ringle to recover from his disappointment. His father listened patiently while Dan speculated about why Knopf had suddenly told him to get lost, but James Haughton Ringle was a jaded publisher himself and well understood the demands of expediency. He told his son to get over it, and suggested looking for a different line of work. Dan floundered for a few days and then called his father again, and received the same advice, framed slightly differently. This cycle repeated three or four times until on one fateful evening Dan realized that his father was simply reading aloud some text he had prepared about getting over it and looking for a new line of work.

Again, Dan Ringle gently hung up while melodramatically slamming an antique mental telephone. Then he went to the bar and asked Hoy Wong, the Algonquin's immortal bartender, for a glass of whiskey. Wong asked him what kind of whiskey he preferred; Ringle didn't have any preferences, but he swiftly consumed five of them and then staggered out into the Manhattan night.

After wandering midtown for a few hours, Ringle entered a corner diner off Lexington to use their restroom and get a cup of coffee. While sipping his coffee, still moderately inebriated, he struck up a conversation with his neighbor at the counter, a silver-haired man wearing a massive gold Rolex.

"That's one mighty fine watch you have there, Sir," Ringle said, gesturing at the man's watch.

The man reflexively pulled his arm back and studied Ringle, looking for warning signs. One doesn't walk around New York with a $17,000 gold watch and ignore people who draw attention to it. "Well, thank you," he said.

Ringle looked the man up and down. "You come in here often?" he asked.

The man smiled thinly. "All the time," he said. "I don't believe I've had the pleasure—"

"Ah! My apologies. Dan Ringle, here," he declared, holding out his hand.

The man looked at Ringle's moist palm, saw that it was probably clean enough, and gave him a quick, firm handshake. "Gerry," he said.

"Well, Gerry, I'm glad to meet you," said Ringle. "The best plan I ever had for making a name for myself in publishing has just fallen to pieces, and I'm back at square one. So it's good to meet someone who can afford a wristwatch as fine as yours."

Gerry was uncomfortable dwelling on his watch in a public place, so he quickly changed the subject. "Publishing, eh?" he said. "I think that ship has sailed, Dan."

"It sure the hell has," Dan agreed, glumly.

"Frankly, I don't see how anyone could make money in that racket these days."

"It ain't easy," said Dan, growing more depressed.

"Ask me," said Gerry, "The real money is in footwear."

"In what?"

"Well, sneakers, to be specific. One pair of Taiwan Keds costs about fourteen cents to manufacture, another twelve cents to import, about four bucks to distribute, and retails for over a hundred. Those are margins."

"That's amazing," said Dan. "But there's not much status in selling sneakers, to be perfectly frank."

"Status?" said Gerry. He held up his left arm, brandishing the Rolex. "Only about seventeen grand worth of status." Then he realized what he was doing and hastily put his arm down and pulled his coat sleeve over the watch.

An hour later, Dan was making arrangements to relocate to Portland, Oregon, to set up an import business in Asian-made sneakers.

Three days after arriving in Portland, while riding the Portland Light Rail into town from the suburbs, Ringle attempted to chat with a tall, red-haired fellow in the facing seat. This particular man was a factory automation mechanic from Providence, Rhode Island, in town to install a high-speed folding-box fabrication machine made by his employer, Emmeci Corporation, an Italian company based in Florence. Ringle had never heard of Emmeci Corporation, nor had he ever wondered how fancy cardboard jewelry boxes were made. The mechanic had little interest in imported sneakers. The two men gravitated back to their reading material and the conversation fizzled.

•

Much earlier that summer, just before the vernal equinox, Jeff Corsiglia stepped off an Alitalia 747 at Fiumicino airport in Rome. Originally from Lakewood New Jersey (not far from Lakehurst, site of the Hindenburg disaster), and whose father had been a police officer in the 23rd Precinct in Manhattan, Corsiglia was on a pilgrimage to northern Italy in search of his ancestral home. He cleared Rome passport control with the usual hand-waving and rubber stamping, and hurried on to a connecting flight to Cristoforo Colombo airport in Genoa, in the Liguria region of north-western Italy. Genoa is the front garter on the Mediterranean, opposite Venice, the garter of the gluteus maximus, of the Italian boot.

In Genoa, he rented a 1996 Fiat Punto (the Pininfarina Coupe being unavailable) and drove East on the Galleria Castelletto toward Santa Margherita Ligure and Portofino. He turned left onto the Strada Statale 333, which wound up into the northern mountains, away from the sea. A few tortuous miles later, and about thirty-thousand double-clutches, the Fiat rolled into Gattorna where Jeff refueled, had a cup of espresso, and started up the lesser Strada Provinciale 21, through the serpentine lake area in the Neirone, and pulled up in front of Pensione Braggadocio in his ancestral village of Corsiglia.

Nearly everyone in Corsiglia was related to Jeff by one or another circuitous genealogies. Corsiglia is the second most common name among the thousand or so people of the Neirone region, second only to Gardella, so it didn't take Jeff long to meet someone who was delighted to connect with a presumably long-lost relative from "I Stati." The seventh Corsiglia whom Jeff encountered, after as many cups of espresso, was Silvio Bacigalupo Corsiglia, a carpenter known throughout the area as master of on-the-fly repairs of anything involving at least one piece of wood. This included everything from umbrellas to antique dueling pistols, and soon the two Corsiglias from disparate and far-flung worlds were happily lost in a tangle of Italian and English, salted with technical terms from a dozen disciplines.

In the course of an unsuccessful attempt to bridge the language gap with a colorful example of cultural engineering styles, Jeff happened to mention an old college chum named David Vivian, who was an installation engineer employed by Emmeci, the Italian box-making machine company in Florence. This was, of course, the very same David Vivian whom Dan Ringle would eventually briefly encounter, without consequence, during a morning commute into Portland.

Coda

Naturally, I called my sister Joan, and told her the whole thing.

"It was nice of David to be thinking of me," she said.

"Yes, but what did you think of the story?"

"Well, it's a pretty incredible coincidence," she said. It sounded like she was trying not to hurt my feelings.

"But it's not a coincidence," I said. "It's a story. I made it all up."

"Still, that doesn't make it any less coincidental."

"What do you think is the main coincidence, then?" I asked.

"Don't be defensive," she said. "You called me; I didn't call you."

"What's that got to do with it?"

"Now you *are* being defensive."

"I am not." I said. "Why won't you answer my question?"

"Well," she said with a sigh, "the main coincidence is that the guy at the very beginning is the same guy as the one at the very end. Isn't that what you intended?"

"Yes," I said, "but there's no connection."

"Of course there is—you wrote it that way." She sounded like she might have added, *you idiot.*

"Yes, but there's no *actual* connection. All that stuff in between is unconnected. Arbitrary."

"You mean he didn't email you and ask how I was doing?"

"No, he did. That part was true."

"The Burke Boyce part was true, too. He was my father-in-law, you know."

"Only the first bit. He never complained about some critic finding factual errors in *Man from Mount Vernon*."

"Not to me anyway, but he might have mentioned it to you, later, when you were grown up."

"Well, he didn't."

"Then why did you put that in?" she asked, as if it was the most obvious question and I should have asked it myself.

"Because it's a story," I said.

"Well, maybe I don't understand this kind of thing," she said cautiously. "But I didn't really get it."

"There's nothing to get," I said. "The story is just one thing leading to another. I was just following this arbitrary thread to see where it would go."

"Well, I'm sorry I didn't get it."

"You don't have to be sorry—it was just a story. I don't mind if you don't get it."

"Well, I'm sorry that it didn't work the way you wanted it."

"It's really not a big deal." I paused. Joan said nothing. It was awkward. "So," I said. "What shall I tell him?"

"Who?"

"David."

"Tell him what?"

"How are you doing?"

"Oh. I'm fine."

Ω

11

Little Torments

Bentley Forester unlocked the door to his family's brownstone off Park Avenue. Home from Starkfield for the Christmas holidays, he'd spent most of the vacation with his parents at their country place, enjoying a holiday admixture of clandestine cigarettes, unrequited hormones, and purloined scotch. The charter bus back to school was scheduled this afternoon on Vanderbilt Avenue, by Grand Central Station, so Bentley had returned to New York for a rare day in the city by himself.

In the pile of unopened mail waiting inside the door, Bentley found a letter from the school, addressed to his parents. The return address was Jasper K. Morton, Headmaster, Starkfield Academy; this immediately caught Bentley's attention. His grades had arrived weeks ago from the School Office, a gaggle of mere secretaries on the third floor of the Admin Building. This letter from the headmaster was something else entirely.

He tore it open and scanned the contents. To his amazement, it contained a brief but murky message suggesting circuitously that he had been expelled. Or might have been.

After the first pang of fear subsided, Bentley realized discretion was called for, and he phoned the country house to confirm permission to read the letter, since it wasn't addressed to him. *It must have something to do with tuition, or it's a ploy for more money.*

For several months, his father had been recovering from a

stroke, so Bentley's mother answered the phone and immediately assumed the worst. Oddly enough, this time she seemed to be on target.

"Shall I read it out loud?" Bentley asked, rhetorically. She knew he had opened it; surely he had already read it, too.

"Yes, dear," she said. Her voice was tight, clipped. She'd had enough surprises this year.

Bentley began reading.

> Dear Dr. & Mrs. Forester,
>
> I realize that your family is dealing with some difficulties at this time, but I felt it was important to communicate our concerns about Bentley's continued enrollment at Starkfield.

"Continued?" said his mother.

"Yeah, I know," Bentley said. "I don't know. It goes on."

> Bentley's teachers and I have been concerned about his behavior this past year. Although his grades are acceptable, there are matters which continue to cause concern. I'm sure he can explain these issues better than I can, but we feel that it may not be appropriate for Bentley to continue here this coming semester.

"It's your senior year," his mother said.

"And my last semester, too."

"I thought you said you were on the student council."

"I am. I don't know what he's talking about."

"Is he saying you're expelled?" His mother's voice was beginning to quaver in a way Bentley hadn't heard before. He imagined his father sleeping in the upstairs bedroom with his damaged brain.

"There's a little more," he said.

> We have determined that Bentley should not come back to campus unless he is prepared to stop what he's been doing and sincerely make an effort. If he's not ready to do this, then it would be better if he does not return.

Regretfully yours,
Jasper K. Morton, Headmaster

"What in heaven's name is he referring to?" said his mother.

"I don't know. This is the first I've heard of anything. Nobody mentioned any problem last semester."

"Well, it can't be about nothing. Surely you must have done something. Some other student? Something you said? Did you hit someone?"

"No. Nothing. I didn't do anything. And JKM knew perfectly well this letter would arrive just before the charter bus."

"Oh lord," she said. "What are we going to do? This will just kill your father."

"I know." *Pretty much anything I do might kill him.*

"Well, what? You should call him. Call Mr. Morton and find out what you're supposed to do."

"Call him? Two hours before the bus leaves?"

"What else can you do? You can't just show up, not after this."

Bentley thought hard. *What the hell was JKM referring to? Why expel him in a letter, without any warning? What if the letter hadn't come until tomorrow?*

"What if the letter didn't come?" he said.

"What do you mean," said his mother.

"If it came tomorrow, it would be too late. I'd already be back at school."

"Bentley! You can't just lie about it."

"Why not? He isn't telling me not to come. It's some kind of ultimatum, is all."

"But—"

"And it's not clear what the problem is anyway. I think this is some kind of cheap shot."

"Bentley! Don't talk about your headmaster that way."

"Well, it's true. Why doesn't he say what the problem is? And why is he leaving it open for me to come back anyway?"

"I don't know," said his mother. "I just don't know."

"Well I don't either," he said. "I'm all packed. I've got to go now if I'm going to get on the charter."

"I won't claim that the letter came after you left," his mother said. "That would be lying."

"Fine. But I'll bet he never calls you. He would have called already if he really wanted to talk to my parents about this."

"It doesn't feel right."

"Look, mom, I've got to go. I'll figure out what's going on when I get to school. I'll let you know."

She didn't say anything.

"Mom, don't worry. It's my last semester. I'm graduating in three months. They're obviously not really serious about kicking me out just before I'm leaving. Besides, he didn't say I was kicked out anyway."

"Bentley," she began, on the verge of tears.

"Mom, really, it's gonna be alright. It's some kind of misunderstanding. I have to get down to Grand Central now."

"I suppose so."

"Don't tell dad, OK?"

"God no," she said. "It would kill him."

"I'll be fine. I've got to go. Bye, mom."

"Good-bye, dear. Call me as soon as you know, will you?"

"I will. Bye."

He hung up and stared at the letter. He read it over and over, trying to squeeze JKM's real complaint from between the lines. Each time he read it he became more angry. *What a cheap shot! A lame, vague threat in a letter timed to arrive just as he was leaving. What the hell did that guy want? Why couldn't he just say it?*

Fuming, Bentley jammed the last few items into his duffel bag and stormed out of the house.

•

He was relieved to find a few of his classmates were also taking the bus. Most of the guys got driven back to school by their parents, but there were always a few who had to take the charter. Nobody thought much about being on the charter, really, although most of the kids were just weenies and fourth-formers.

Bentley occupied the back of the bus with his friends, joking and telling vacation stories. They all enjoyed the obvious deference extended them by the lower grade passengers. A few cold practiced glances established two rows of empty seats between the seniors and the untouchables.

He didn't mention the letter; these friends weren't his real friends, just classmates—peers, not confidantes.

•

Spring semester of senior year in an ivy-league prep school radiates giddy excitement, transcendent social status, and soul-crushing fear of college rejections. Against this emotional counterpoint, classes continue, grades count, sporting events briefly distract, and in his way each senior begins to engage the looming Great Unknown.

Bentley told a few close friends about the letter. They were all suitably amazed, puzzled, offended, and dismissive.

"No way they're going to throw you out in your last semester!"

"They wouldn't dare."

"They'd be afraid your parents would raise hell."

"That's why they just tried to scare you into dropping out, instead of actually expelling you."

"They're all chicken-shit."

"Morton just likes to intimidate people who aren't jocks."

"He's trying to get you to admit to something."

"Did you do anything last term we don't know about?"

The whole group stopped talking and stared at Bentley expectantly. Maybe something really cool had happened.

"Not a damn thing. I swear. I haven't got a clue what's bugging him."

•

For three weeks, Bentley heard nothing from the headmaster. There was no suggestion of his having illegitimately returned for graduation. There were no oblique references when he met routinely with his faculty counselor.

"Have you heard from Harvard?" Mr. Stanton said, with a marginal smile.

"Not yet," said Bentley. "But the scout said I was a shoo-in. My dad did post-grad there, and my brother went there."

"What about your fall-backs?"

"I never really got around to them."

"Yale? You didn't apply?"

"No relatives there. And Yale's hardly a fall-back."

"Columbia?"

"I can always take a year off, if it comes to that." Bentley looked out the window at the rapidly greening fields of Connecticut. Only two months left.

"What about Wisconsin," said Mr. Stanton.

"What about it?"

"It's a great school, but you'd have a much better chance there. Just in case. You don't really want to take a year off, do you?"

"Yeah, no. I don't know." *I just want to get out of here.*

The meeting was over, so Mr. Stanton recited a few platitudes about not slacking off at the last minute, especially if the colleges were still deciding your fate. "I have a lot of faith in you, Bentley," he said.

Bentley politely acknowledged his counselor's redundant advice and left for a quick set of doubles. His tennis was nothing to write home about, but it was better than standing around in the outfield all afternoon.

•

The headmaster's unresolved threats completely slipped from Bentley's mind by mid-April. The administration offices were across from the entrance to the library, so he'd walked by a hundred times and become habituated to the little waves of adrenalin.

Wednesday afternoon he didn't get any mail, but there was a folded note in his box: *Mr. Morton will see you in his office on Thursday at 10:00 AM.*

The rest of Wednesday dragged. He confided with his friends that The Meeting had finally been announced. They all wondered what the hell Mr. Morton was going to spring on him, but nobody had any new ideas. Still, Bentley's hands were cold and damp.

The next morning, after physics class, Bentley went up to the third floor of the Administration Building. His head was full of noise and his armpits were wet.

The headmaster intercepted him in the hallway.

"My office," he said.

Now there's a surprise.

Mr. Morton strode to his desk and sat down in a large maroon swivel chair. Bentley sat in one of the school-monogrammed captain's chairs and looked up at the headmaster. *I wonder if they sawed an inch off the legs of these chairs. Or maybe JKM's chair is on a platform.*

"So," JKM said. "Of course you know why we're having this meeting?"

Bentley tried to shrug nonchalantly. "I guess it probably has something to do with your letter."

"Yes, exactly."

"OK."

The headmaster stared across his big cluttered desk with a strange expression.

"Well?" he said.

Bentley glanced around the paneled office. *Too far above the ground to jump out the window: no escape but the door.*

"You know we're not pleased with your behavior," the headmaster said.

"Well, I gathered that. But you didn't exactly say what behavior."

The headmaster pressed his lips together. "I think you know what we're referring to."

Bentley did his level best to sound sincere. "I honestly really don't. Is it something I did last semester? I wasn't aware I'd broken any rules."

"You know full well it's not about breaking a rule."

"It's not?"

"Don't be clever."

Bentley shivered. This was already going badly. "Look," he said, "I'm not trying to be difficult. I actually, truly, don't know what I did."

"Bentley, this is not a matter of something you did."

"Then what is it?"

"You're obviously not living up to the School's standards, and it's got to stop."

"But what standards? What do you mean?"

"Your attitude doesn't just affect you, Bentley. You're a senior, and the things you say and do have an influence on other people."

"Did I say something I shouldn't have?" He racked his brain, trying to recall anything that could have triggered this inexplicable reaction. Something with an underclassman? His counselor?

The headmaster was becoming visibly frustrated. Bentley was equally frustrated, but the irony was overwhelmed by growing mistrust.

"It's not something specific that you said. You know perfectly well what I mean."

"But I—"

"I'm not going to let you force me into defining something you can just argue about. What about the letter?"

"What about the letter?"

The headmaster grimaced. Bentley knew his questions must

seem uncooperative or insolent, but he couldn't defend himself if he didn't know what he'd done.

"You came back."

"Yes, sir."

"So you're ready to cooperate?"

"Sure. What do you want me to do?"

"What do I want you do to?" Mr. Morton glared at him. "What do you *think* I want you to do?" He wasn't quite shouting, but his face had lost some color, and his voice was a little shaky.

Bentley began to fear that something explosive was about to happen. "Stop doing something?" he said. *Or start doing something? Or fucking cease to exist?*

"It's quite simple, Bentley," said Morton.

Bentley waited.

"If you want to graduate, then you'd better make up your mind right now."

"Yes, sir. I definitely want to graduate."

"Your parents wouldn't be very pleased if you dropped out in your last term, would they?"

"No, sir. Not at all. I promise I won't drop out."

"It's not your choice!" Morton was definitely yelling now. He slammed his hands on the desk and stood up. His face was white.

"You'll be out of here before I open the door if I say so," he snapped.

Out the window? Bentley realized there was a white iron fire escape he hadn't noticed before. *Maybe I could climb down.*

"Answer me."

"Yes, sir."

"Yes, what?"

Bentley shook his head, then realized Mr. Morton would read some horrible meaning into it.

"Yes, um, I'll cooperate?"

"Jesus," said Morton. "Do you agree to stop this behavior for the rest of your time at Starkfield Academy?"

"Yes, sir."

"And do you agree to adhere to the School Values for the rest of your time here?"

"Yes, sir."

"And you'll live up to our standards and set a good example?"

"Yes, sir." Then Bentley added, "I'm vice president of the school council, sir, and vice president of the dramatics society. And I'm on the athletic council, too. I'll try not to do anything wrong." *I better not mention the Steam Tunnel Spelunking Society.*

"I know you've fooled a lot of people," said the headmaster, grimacing again. "But from now on, you watch your step."

"I will, sir."

"Then go ahead and stay and finish up your senior year."

"Thank you, sir."

"If I hear one report you're reverting to your old ways, you'll be out of here in a heartbeat. Do you understand?"

"Yes, sir." *Like hell I do.*

"Even if it's the day before graduation."

"I understand, sir."

"I thought you did." Mr. Morton sat down heavily, glaring at Bentley from a splotchy white face. He shook his head slowly from side to side. After a long moment, he said, "Why couldn't you just admit it at the beginning?"

"Admit what?"

"Out of here!" Morton was on his feet. "I've had enough of your evasions." He was shouting again.

"I'm sorry, sir. I—"

"Out! Get out!"

Bentley quickly exited. The office door slammed behind him and the headmaster's secretary looked up in alarm.

Bentley glanced at her, wondering what she could possibly think just happened. Did she know what his crime against the School had been? Someone must know, but it sure as hell wasn't Bentley.

He cast her a sheepish smile and hurried out of the administration building. He continued on out to the tennis courts, and
beyond into the seedy school golf course. The western edge of the
course was lined with pine trees, and he lost himself among them.

•

The next few weeks were uneventful. Bentley replayed his surreal
confrontation with the headmaster, to himself and to his closest
friends, but no insight came. He felt like Kyle MacLachlan in *The
Trial*, accused of some serious crime nobody would identify.

A month before graduation, there had been no further inci-
dents involving JKM or Bentley's obscure transgressions. Bentley
was relaxing into the concluding weeks of his secondary education. There was a lot of light now at the end of the tunnel.

One afternoon in late May, his class adviser called a meeting
in the Science building. It was time to elect a valedictorian. Some
schools just appointed the student with the best grades, but at
Starkfield the position was filled democratically. Although he was
not the most popular kid in his class, apparently a majority felt he
was the one to sum up their collective experience at the school,
and he was elected.

The next afternoon his mailbox held another invitation to meet
JKM. He went to the headmaster's office, and had to wait almost
half an hour. When the secretary finally let him in, Morton just
looked up from his desk and said, "Nice. I don't know how you do
it, Forester." His voice dripped with irony.

Before Bentley could reply, JKM dismissed him with a wave and
turned back to his desk.

That was it? He called me to a meeting just to be an ass-hole?

His friends thought it was hysterically funny, but Bentley
didn't. Mr. Morton was acting very strange, and there must have
been something much more dire than just a vague discordance
with school "values."

The semester wore on, spring bloomed and effloresced all

around, and the seniors lost more and more of their connection with secondary education, school values and all. Starkfield was morphing into a wellspring of nostalgia instead of an institute of intermediate learning, and colleges were usurping the seniors' allegiances.

When graduation day rolled around, Bentley's father was still too sick to make it, but his mother came with his brother and his maiden aunt. They sat in the parents' section under a blue June sky, fanning themselves with graduation ceremony handouts. The faculty were in their section, a grim body of academicians with varying degrees of legitimacy. Students, staff, and miscellaneous others occupied a third section. The seniors sat by themselves, like a collective ticking time-bomb.

The headmaster gave a very brief opening speech, followed by the doggedly devout chaplain, who emitted a characteristically warped spiritual metaphor (*students are like Christmas presents*).

A distinguished guest speaker whom nobody had heard of spoke much too long about setting forth on the road of life. Parents beamed, trying to catch the eye of their respective offspring. The faculty endured the proceedings as they had always done, except this time there was a new veneer of anticipation: Bentley Forester was the Valedictorian, perish the thought, and he would have the last word.

Ω

12

Rocky Mtn High [performance 1]

The rock speaks. Its voice is low, coarse, like a rock. Its declarations are all that a rock would be expected to assert: simple, solid, foundational, agglomerative, unassailable. It describes little, but when inspired, its discourse encroaches on poetry, often monosyllabic, but charged with a quiet celebration, devoid of judgment or accusation. The rock offers no dialectic; it seeks no validation. It is what it is, and its pride in innate simplicity is never far from the surface of its monologue.

The rock's dithyrambs are slow by the reckoning of other forms of life. A tree moves ten thousand times for each minute gyration of a rock. One hundred times ten thousand. The grasses clump together, rise and swell, and shrivel to be pulverized and covered with snow, while a tree watches like a scientist.

At times, they are all speaking at once, and it would be nothing but hopeless cacophony but for their widely varying time-frames. Even so, with this many plants and insects, trees and boulders, rocks and pebbles, and the exuberant variation of the tiniest grains of soil, it's hard to follow the conversations.

But the rock held my attention. It muttered and rumbled on and on in almost unbearably slow cadence and the images stole into long-atrophied corners of my brain, stirring up swirls of nameless impressions, eddies from the temporal stasis of dead ideas and forgotten lives. Eventually, I had to break the spell, and I jumped up, running toward the cliff edge where mountain birds wheeled and poised, looking down with telescopic eyes.

The rock was behind me (though its cousins and relations surrounded and I stood upon bits of its most ancestral schist), and I heard it crack. I turned and saw the dust fly and the light streaming from its exposed interior. Had I done this? Just a diaphanous human wail, the snap of mere attention severed from the rock's bare physiognomy? Do we have such power?

Deep in the fissure strange fires seethed, sending out waves of stone commentary in a heatless mirage. I pulled back, mindful of the cliff behind me, and then bent closer, entranced by the interior nakedness of the rock. It pulled me in. Or its exposure engulfed my sight, leaving nothing else.

Inside the rock was nothing but sedimentary crystallizations, agglomerations of iron, titanium, silicon, and quartz reduced from aeons of slowly cooling magma. Like pebbles among gems, granular effusions clustered all around the locus of my consciousness, bits of quartz gleaming amid the matrix, while multicolored grus and granitoids swirled around in nearly perfect motionlessness.

Then my attention was caught by rare intense beams of energy, which sparked first here, then there, then, rarely, in diaphanous coruscations all around, flared briefly and went dark again. In the inky interstices I realized there lurked tiny inclusions of uranium and radon, and as the rock spoke, or mulled its thoughts in prelude to an exclamation, the glow surrounding these radioactive microns would swell and spark faint beams of erudition which sped unimpeded into and through the surrounding stone.

These crumbled bits of dense-packed substance pulsed in the epoch-slow rhythm of the tor, one graceful beat per century, but within them stood a perfect lattice of igneous components arranged in rows and columns like a regiment of jugglers frozen in perfect equipoise, their appendages upraised, batons in mid-twirl, acrobatic cousins atop one another rank upon rank, sustaining the mineral identity.

Whole paragraphs of rocky eloquence folded upon themselves in unspoken future soliloquies, waiting for the march of magma to spawn their metamorphosis from mere notion into unforgettable expressions of eutectic intelligence.

I listened to their silent recitations while the inner structures pulled me into their arms, where super-massive spheres intertwined in a palette of inter-penetrating nuclei. A hazy aura caressed these near-fused entities, wafting afar and diving deep, knitting each one to the surrounding matrix. And the low cogitation of the rock upheld the descant sung by these amorphous revelers.

A serene, high harmony emerged, where ever finer waves of silence lapped the shores of tangibility and gave rise to chords and intervals of texture so delicate that even consciousness could scarcely find a gap. Pure resonance rang from the center of the planet through all the octaves of interaction, energizing each layer while holding them all locked in the unity of organization.

The substance of all this was nothing. Knowledge rose in waves inside the rock, to annihilate emptiness, yet nothing changed. Information unmanifest has no mass; nor does knowledge, nor intelligence. And yet I look upon this substance and it all appears, from its origin in molten chaos to the tall sandstone slabs of the Divide.

And there the rock stood, though a millennium passed, ten thousand pounds attending where I watched, it remained waiting, its most accomplished suit. The granite textures touched my skin in quartz caress. "I have so many songs to sing," it said.

•

And so I sang, too. They said it was a diatribe. A filibuster against reason, to take refuge in a wall of words against the storm of impressions. Such nonsense, to think words protect against what has never been named! Such ignorance, to think thoughts themselves could circumnavigate a soul, or a cerebellum, or the pronotum of a dung-beetle.

My thoughts were beetles in those days, but not for any reason related to the diatribe, this flail of phonemes that so pitifully characterized my attempts at penetration. [No, not *preservation*, not at all; there is no way to *preserve* any of it. It is all lost, whether the story is true or not, and even if it is not lost, we are lost to it, and the result is the same.]

This sounds like someone else, doesn't it? This is not even myself speaking—only sorry voices of the tiny id, the erect pullet of flesh that prods the massive lethargy of intellect now and then, with unbidden aftereffects, and seldom a touch of truth.

The whole assembly of concepts is falling apart, and nothing holds itself to anything else. The boundaries are a blur, and the thread which links moment to moment has been pulled taut, and suddenly released in a tangle of loose chaos. Notions with no rightful proximity are pressed up against one another in blatant contradiction. It feels like someone's visit from Mescalito on a hilltop against the fusion of June's wet seasons railing against the summer blast.

But, oh damnation and cacophony, this is not anyone else, damned be them all. They hide when they are most needed. They are the ones hiding, leafing through pages of verbal armor while I stand at the fore, bearing all the weather and erosion.

I don't even know what I am, but here it is that I take my stand, wonderingly, while the seasons compress my visions into thin strata of undifferentiable greys, like a sand-painting by a color-blind Hopi with nothing to say. Like a metaphor stretched as thin as the stratum it tries to describe. Like recursion committing its eternal incest. Praise be to sand paintings.

I have stood here on the cliff for weeks, staring out over the great valleys, watching clouds roil overhead, materializing from the blue as if by magic, winds rising and falling, hissing and roaring through the rock outcroppings.

I remember the struggle up the hills, across moraines where the scrub pine gave up, and into these cloud-cropped alpine meadows, blood pounding in my eyes and in my lungs.

Half the air is below me here, more than half, but there is no resistance to breathing and that is a relief I can't describe. At sea level the air is thick and moist and soaked with salt and a thousand spores and beings whose husks infest our trachea and fill our lungs with their residue. There the air slogs reluctantly through the nostrils as if condemned to cower in the wet spongy darkness, sentenced to one breath of hard labor, and it is almost impossible to exhale without opening the mouth. This may account for much of the excess verbalization at sea level.

The higher up you go, the easier it is to shut up. That's partly due to oxygen starvation, which makes the lungs scream out for more, but this reaffirms the simple bond between breath and death which we forget along the urban shores. We need to remember. We might remember, if the weather is kind.

But here at 14,000 feet, no Himalaya admittedly, we breathe without effort—the air slips in through the orifices at the front of my skull as if it *wanted* to be inside, away from the caustic dehydration of the sun and sky, bleached here in the mid-ground between the blue creating clouds and the crunch underfoot where lichens hug to the rock like dried stains.

The air sings into the alvioli and gives up its oxygen for a clamor of escaped carbon dioxides, who fly ecstatically back out without even a suggestion of velocity. The nasal passages slowly dehydrate and become brittle, after a lot of this breathing at altitude, but we can make that trade for the cool silver flow of tangible *prana* in and out, into and out of, effortless and insubstantial like the sky.

But here I stand, united with nothing, with the cliff and the not-cliff beyond it, with clouds and rocks like a monumental model of my pathetic catastrophe.

Betwixt and between, I should have said. I should have just said it myself. Just said it. Weeks of staring out over the immediate into the haze of distance has made no difference at all.

The dysthymia still suffuses each hillock below me, still strokes my neck with a warm hand, forcing me down until the crushed lichens are all I can see.

And I jerk my head up, trying to remember where the distant bird was sailing, which valley he was surveying, which stream-bed he could smell through the perforations in his beak, where soft and bloody prey await his fall to feed.

Ω

13

The CD

Daniel Fetter sat down in his easy chair, and opened the packaging on the new CD. Ignoring the booklet, he slipped the disc into his chair-side player and pressed the Play button. Then he put his headphones on and settled down into the cushions.

There was silence for a few moments, and then a soft chord sounded, like muffled bells struck in unison. *That's not Brahms,* Daniel thought.

A soft hum arose in the distance, farther away than the bells, and began to grow, almost imperceptibly, into a gentle throbbing, with vaguely breath-like overtones. Superimposed on the hum, varied and barely audible droning tones appeared and disappeared, like far-off sitars caught on an evening breeze. Slowly, with increasing harmony and definition, a pattern of chords and melodies began to emerge, some from far to the right and left, and others from behind. Then, dead center, a tiny point of light appeared, expanding steadily into a spot of blinding whiteness.

The white region slowly filled Daniel's eyes, and then his whole head, while the strange music grew in complexity and structure. The whiteness was all that existed, for a time, and then within it objects began to appear: figures, buildings, automobiles—indistinct but recognizably real. The music swelled, and a sound-track faded in, bringing with it the impression of a busy city, traffic and industry, people hurrying by along the sidewalk, a bus pulling up just a few feet away.

Jan stepped from the bus, waving at him. Daniel turned, startled to see her after all these years. He waved back, and pushed through the crowd toward her.

"Daniel!" she exclaimed, obviously very excited to see him. "How on earth are you?" She reached out, and they hugged through their overcoats while pedestrians flowed around them.

"Pretty well, actually," Daniel replied, scrutinizing her enthusiastic smile; he wondered just how glad to see him she really was. "What brings you to New York at this time of year? I thought you said Manhattan was the last place you'd ever be in the dead of winter."

Jan laughed. "No, not the last place—just the least likely!" The wind swirled their coats, and biting cold crept up their spines. Jan shivered and clutched herself with both arms.

"Let's get into a coffee shop," he said. "Do you have time? I'd love to chat a little."

She nodded, pulling her blowing hair away from her face, and they threaded their way through the Christmas shoppers to a nearby storefront restaurant.

The door slammed behind them, suddenly silencing the din of the city, and hot savory air swept over them. They found an empty booth and sat down, loosening their winter clothes and removing their gloves. A waiter appeared, and they ordered coffee; Daniel asked for a Danish, but Jan (as always) declined.

The restaurant was filled with people like themselves, middle aged, middle class, middle of the day shoppers and passers-by, seeking refuge or sustenance for a few moments between errands or appointments. The waiters appeared and disappeared like sparrows, darting expertly among the closely packed tables, serving or snatching plates from among the patrons. A large, elderly woman with a white mustache presided from behind an ornate NCR cash register with a crank on the side. From the kitchen came a steady hash of frying and clanking that floated on olfactory waves of baking bread, simmering gravy, frying batter, and onions.

Jan was gazing fondly at Daniel, ignoring her surroundings, and Daniel found himself watching her eyes as if they were apertures, not seeing her face. For a moment, it seemed as if her face and all the rest of the room were a realistic painted backdrop, and her eyes were small openings through the wall into another room. Fascinated, he leaned forward, and saw twin spots of light shining back at him, reflections, no doubt—the restaurant's overhead lighting, or the windows onto the street.

Then he realized that he could align his own eyes with Jan's, and somehow see through her face, into the room beyond. He leaned forward curiously, and their eyes met—and the other room came into focus. Jan seemed not to notice. In fact, she and the restaurant seemed to have gone flat and motionless, and the smells of food had vanished. But the sounds remained, changing into the soughing of wind through trees and the chirp and twitter of birds.

The room beyond came into three dimensions, and it was not a room, but a forest: steep hillsides converging on a rock-strewn brook, tangles of underbrush along the water's edge. Countless trees rose all around, blocking most of the sky except for a strip of blue directly over the nearest bend in the stream. A cicada buzzed raspingly nearby; a jay emitted a shrill whistle in the distance; robins and other small birds hopped and flew sporadically from branch to ground to branch. The ground was strewn with twigs and leaves, which crunched underfoot as he walked.

Daniel could see that the stream had almost dried up: the rocky bed was cracked and bleached for several feet on either side of the meager flow. But the water was blue and clear where it ran, and iridescent darning needles flew in tandem near clusters of water weeds. In an eddy, he could see skeets standing on the skin of the water, looking down at their own reflections in the sky.

There was a steady wind blowing, but it was high up and could not penetrate the woods with more than a light breeze. Daniel heard its soft roaring through the tree tops, and saw the slow swaying of the taller trunks. The sun was bright on the stream, but the forest floor was cool, shaded over by ten thousand intertwining branches that rose high above like a fantastic network of angular rods and cables. Ants trooped along a meandering trail up one tree trunk, picking their way over the convoluted bark.

A narrow dirt road led alongside the brook for a short distance, and then turned up the hill toward a log cabin with a Land Rover parked outside. Daniel had never seen the cabin before, but it seemed an attractive destination, so he resumed walking along the road, listening to the birds and the chatter of red squirrels. The pebbles crunched as he walked, and the stream splashed. The cicada stopped, leaving a sudden silence, and then started again.

The hillside driveway to the cabin was steeper than it looked from the stream, and Daniel made his way slowly, feeling his heart begin to pound with increasing intensity. *It really feels like I'm actually here*, he thought.

At the top of the drive, a concrete foundation supported the cabin and a front porch. Concrete steps led down from the porch, under a broad, overhanging roof. A series of clay flower pots lined the stairway with nasturtiums and azaleas. An old rug lay near the top step, matted with soil and pine needles, and an old dog lay nearby, also matted and soiled.

The dog was asleep, its tongue lolling out in the heat of the day, and now and then its legs twitched as it ran through an inner dream-field. Unseen, a pair of fleas foraged in the short hairs between the dog's eyebrows, emerging into the sun now and then as they darted back and forth, snacking on dust-mites in between blood dinners. Neither the fleas nor the dog noticed Daniel's step upon the wood planking, nor his slow paces across the porch to the front door, nor even his loud knock upon the oak paneling.

The sound of Daniel's knocking rebounded inside the cabin. There was no reply, but the door shook slightly as he pounded on it, and he realized with a start that it was ajar. Was this a vision or a lure? He didn't know where he was, and had no business entering a strange cabin in the woods, but the impulse to just walk right in was growing stronger by the moment. He paused, and then knocked again—still no response.

Finally, marveling at his own impetuousness, he tried the knob. It turned, unnecessarily, and the door swung open another inch. The dog continued to sleep; there was no sound from the cabin.

Pushing the door fully open, Daniel called out, "Hello? Anyone home?"

He heard only the forest birds and the distant rattle of a chainsaw. Perhaps the owner was out in the forest, cutting firewood. *Perhaps he wouldn't mind if I just took a step or two inside,* Daniel thought, peering into the shadows beyond the doorway.

The door creaked softly, and swung open onto a large single room that seemed dark and cavernous after the blazing sunlight. Daniel stepped inside and looked around. The open doorway flung a bright parallelogram on the floor with Daniel's own shadow centered in it, like the cover of a mystery novel.

A dark oval rag rug covered the center of the floor, with a heavy unfinished wood table upon it, and a few chairs. A big wood stove stood to the left, and a flight of wooden stairs without a railing led upward along the far wall. Sun poured in the doorway, but the windows were covered, and the whole space seemed as quiet as an empty church. In the distance, the chainsaw stopped, and Daniel could hear the sounds of floating sitars again, and a low hum.

The hum grew as he took a few more steps into the cabin. It took on the wooden quality of a low pipe-organ note, and soon was accompanied by higher organ tones, and within a few moments the whole cabin was resounding with a soft but unmistakable paean of baroque organ music. Daniel stopped, looking around for an audio system, but there was none.

Then he noticed, along the far wall beyond the stairs, a cluster of vertical shapes, almost like pipes in a church organ. He walked to the table to get a closer look, and realized that it really did appear to be a rank of burnished pipes, and the music was now distinctly coming from that direction. He stepped around the table, noticing that the chairs, which at first seemed haphazardly placed, were aligned in a single row, facing the organ. In fact, the high, curtained windows were not curtained at all, but appeared to be stained glass, with pictures of unrecognized saints bent in various tasks, illuminated in brilliant transparent colors by the bright sun outside.

The table, in fact, was gone, and the pew he stood behind was the front row before an altar of gold and marble, with brocaded purple cloth draped over it. The pipe organ was now clearly visible, with several ranks playing at once, and the music filled the church with the resonance of a very large space. Looking around, Daniel saw at least 30 rows of pews behind him, flanked by small altar-spaces on either side, with a broad aisle leading down the middle of the church to a pair of tall carved doors, one of which still stood open.

Daniel vaguely wondered if he could walk back out of the door he had just opened, and still find the sleeping dog and the exterior of a log cabin, but with that thought, the organ music suddenly ceased, and the grand interior of the cathedral slowly reverberated to silence. Intimidated by the unexpected fading echoes, Daniel stood stock still, looking from side to side for the organist, or a priest, or a member of the congregation. The silence stretched around him to the high vaulted ceiling, and the distant upper galleries, and the tall saturated windows set in thick stone walls on either side.

Then he heard a tap, from the far left corner of the cathedral, to the left of the altar, in shadows he could not see clearly. The tap echoed with a brittle bounce from various walls and stone surfaces until the silence returned—silence but for Daniel's own breathing. He cleared his throat, and the echo died away.

The tap came again, followed by the clank of an antique latch, and then the long slow creak of a large, old door opening. A sequence of patting footsteps could be heard coming nearer, out of the shadows. He stepped into the aisle and walked toward the altar to meet whoever approached.

Without warning, the figure emerged into a pool of colored light from one window, and Daniel saw a tall man dressed in a brown floor-length robe, like a monk from the middle ages. The man appeared elderly, and under his cowl Daniel could see a full white mustache and beard beneath friendly eyes that looked straight at him, smile lines playing at their corners.

"You came by a rather circuitous route," the monk said, holding out both hands in a gesture of welcome. Daniel smiled uncomfortably, and allowed the monk to take his hands and shake them warmly. He started to speak, but the monk gestured for him to be silent, and for some reason he complied, not without a small sense of relief. What on earth would he say to a monk?

"Please, don't ask questions just yet," the monk went on, still looking intently at Daniel, as if surprised that he hadn't arrived some time ago. "Let's go sit in the vestry and I'll explain everything." He started walking back into the shadows from whence he came, and then stopped, gesturing. "You will come?"

"Oh. Sure," Daniel said, and followed the dark robes into the corner of the cathedral, where a tall oak door stood open on a paneled room with a long, rough-hewn table in its center. The table reminded him of the one in the cabin.

They sat on either side, at one end. The room was filled with bookshelves, punctuated by dark oil paintings of individuals in brown robes. There was no sign of modern technology anywhere—no electric lights, no phones, no wires fastened to the stone vaulting, not even an outlet in the wainscoting. *Where the hell is this place?*

They sat in silence, while Daniel waited for the promised answers, but the monk did not speak. He seemed to be lost in thought, staring past Daniel at the floor, or at some internal vision of his own.

"Was that you I heard, playing the pipe organ?" Daniel asked, breaking the silence.

"Ah, the organ, yes, yes," the monk replied, looking as if he had just awakened from an afternoon nap. "No, that wasn't me—I'm afraid my organ playing is rather pathetic. No, I'm not a musician, not in any sense of the word. I'm more of an audience than a performer." His voice trailed off and silence returned. The enormous cavity of the stone cathedral just outside seemed to vacuum all the sound out of the vestry in a cool granite breath.

Daniel waited a polite moment or two, and then resumed, "You were going to explain everything, weren't you?" He paused, not wanting to offend the old monk, and then added, "I have quite a few questions, actually—"

The monk looked up at him again, and said, "Oh, yes, of course you do. I shouldn't let my mind wander like this, should I? It's just that each moment seems to drift across another like autumn leaves, and I forget which one my attention was on." He straightened up in his chair, and stared intently across the table at Daniel.

"You've come to us from a long distance, haven't you?" he asked.

Daniel shrugged, "Well, I don't really know. I just walked up the driveway from the brook." *What driveway?* He hadn't walked far, but he obviously wasn't in the log cabin. The priest must think him crazy.

"Oh, no," the monk said with a smile, "Not the driveway, not the, ah—what do you call them—the restaurant, either, was that it?"

"I'm sorry?" Daniel was more confused than ever, but the mention of restaurant had jogged something in his memory about a woman with strange eyes, and frying onions.

"Was it from the restaurant that you came?" The monk didn't wait for an answer. "No, of course not, you came from your home, from your—ah, your easy chair, yes? Right in your home, your, ah, dwelling, is that so?" He sat back, evidently satisfied that he had accomplished some feat of translation that he could be proud of.

"Yes, now that you mention it," Daniel began. Then he remembered the CD he was playing, and how the music seemed to morph into images, and then the images took over. And now he was experiencing everything entirely within the worlds of his imagination. *This is my imagination, isn't it?*

The monk was leaning across the table with a look of apprehension. "Now, don't worry about it," he began, tapping his finger on the wood. "Just forget I said that, for the moment. I'll tell you whatever you want to know." But the monk's apprehension seemed to grow, and he hastily added, "Wonderful things!"

Daniel wasn't paying attention. He was thinking about the CD, and wondering how it could have produced such a vivid series of hallucinations. He took his left hand in his right, and squeezed— it hurt, like a real hand. Then he tried to retrace his steps in his mind—the monk, the organ music, the table in the log cabin.

Where are my eyes? Daniel thought, in a sudden panic. *Where the hell are my eyes, my real eyes?* He jumped up and looked around the room while a wave of desperation and terror surged into his heart. *This is wrong! This is not real, and this body is not real! Where the hell is my real body?*

The monk was watching his frantic movements with sorrow and concern. He heard the monk say, "Oh dear. Please, don't be upset! You can open your eyes if you must. Don't be frightened, please, it would break my heart. I never meant to—"

Daniel did open his eyes, though it took some effort, and his living room popped into existence all around him, complete in every detail, right down to the headphones covering his ears, and the Brahms symphony he had just bought playing on the CD machine at his side. Still in a panic, he pulled off the phones and leapt from the chair, looking around desperately for—for what? His living room was *right;* it appeared just as it had a few minutes ago when he sat down to play the CD.

Everything was as it should be. Somewhere in the back of his mind, amid recent memories of seeing Jan and walking in the woods, the monk's voice was saying, "Next time just bring your mind. It will be easier."

Daniel hurried into the kitchen and poured himself a shot of scotch, downed it, and leaned back against the sink to collect his senses. His faculties seemed to be working properly, but he couldn't shake the memory of what had just happened. It was too real, too much like an actual experience, to dismiss it as a daydream.

Faint, tinny sounds of Brahms floated in from the headphones in the living room. The scotch burned in his throat and warmed his stomach, but there was still a faint, lingering smell of frying onions.

•

For several days, Daniel avoided the new CD, even the player and headphones and his recliner. He wasn't prepared for another leap into the unknown. He didn't speak of his dream to anyone, especially the appearance of the monk, because he wasn't even half convinced it was a dream.

Then, on another warm spring evening, he felt a subliminal urge for Brahms, and decided to try another listening session. He sat in the big easy chair and leaned it part-way back, donned the headphones, and turned on the player. The Brahms CD spun up, and familiar orchestral music began to flow.

What was it the priest had said? Something about "just bring your mind"? *What could that possibly mean?*

He settled back, relieved that an actual orchestra was performing Brahms this time—the Third Symphony, orderly and unambiguous. His muscles relaxed, and he sank gratefully into the cushions. When the horns began their stately theme, he reached down and lowered the recliner all the way back. With a bemused smile he thought, *I'd be happy to leave my body here for a while.*

Through the trees, the afternoon sunlight flickered and dazzled his vision until Daniel realized he was looking up at a forest canopy and the bright blue sky. He sensed that the Brahms was long gone, but somehow woodland sounds had filled in for the orchestra and he couldn't remember when the transition took place.

The forest was familiar, and he knew the cabin was up the hill, over the knoll, in its utilitarian clearing. He had forgotten about the dog, but it was still there when he approached the wooden porch; everything was as he remembered it. As before, the dog didn't look up when Daniel approached. But it wasn't until his first steps across the decking that he realized he wasn't making a sound.

Puzzled, he looked down at his feet. He wore the same shoes that were comfortably resting on the recliner's footstool a few minutes ago, but they were silent as he walked across the porch. Not muffled: silent.

He stopped and stamped one foot, and then wished he hadn't, since it would undoubtedly startle the sleeping dog. But his shoe made no sound and the dog continued to snooze, its legs still twitching in a dream of its own.

The forest sounds were complete; he could hear the wind overhead, and the rattle of a woodpecker echoed through the trees. But his footsteps were perfectly silent.

He reached out and knocked on the cabin door, this time not expecting anyone to respond. No-one did, but when his knuckles struck the hard paneling they made absolutely no sound. *What's going on?*

He pushed the door open and stepped inside the cabin. The door creaked softly, but his footsteps were inaudible against the floor boards. "Hello?" he called, and he heard his voice fill the large cabin space. A fire crackled inside the wood stove. And then he heard the faint hum, as on his last visit, and as before it was growing louder.

In a few moments the hum filled the cabin. Daniel took a few steps across the rag rug, and then realized the hum emanated from a flight of steps on the far side of the room, leading down into the basement.

This time he knew there was no point resisting the urge to explore. So he went over to the stairs, and peered down into the darkness. There was a light switch alongside the opening in the floor, and he flicked it on. The stairs were stout wooden planks, freshly cut and fitted together with evident craftsmanship, and after making a turn at the landing, they continued on down to the right. *Why not?*

The stairs led into a spacious room of poured concrete that supported the whole footprint of the cabin. A large door in the far end of the foundation stood open, and a warm glow spilled through the opening onto the cement floor. Daniel strode across the room, conscious that his footsteps were impossibly silent, and pulled the door wide open.

A tunnel stretched out before him, leading down into the earth, curving slightly to the right. It looked like a mine tunnel, supported with stout square timbers and cross-beams, with a rough dirt floor. It was lit by a long series of dim light bulbs wired with big loops of cable that stretched off into the distance.

Daniel tried to relate this to his previous visit, but he sensed there was something arbitrary about these places he was exploring. He remembered the monk's comment that Daniel had come a long distance, and then the monk had guessed about where Daniel had actually been en route. No doubt this was all happening in his imagination, but if so, why wouldn't the monk know where he had come from?

The tunnel before him was complete in every detail, totally convincing. He took a step onto the dirt floor of the tunnel. He could feel the dirt crunching under his shoes, but it made no sound. *Alright, not entirely convincing.*

Daniel continued walking along the passage, which ran on into the distance, angled slightly down and to the right. After some time, it seemed he must have gone full circle, and he wondered if the tunnel was a huge spiral curving down, deeper into the earth.

At last a corner came into view, and the tunnel opened up onto what looked like the side of a large rough wooden warehouse built into the earth. There was a long railing in front of the building, with a gate about fifteen feet wide. A huge door, large enough for heavy trucks or wagons, was set into the side of the building. In the massive wall to the right of the door, a smaller door, the size of a man, stood open, and Daniel stepped inside.

To his surprise, the interior of the warehouse was not a building at all, but a vaulted cavern whose stone ceiling arched overhead into the shadows, and a short distance away fast-moving water flowed past a broad dock with a number of stout mooring posts.

To the right of the dock a dozen round-bottom boats were stacked upside down, with wicker hulls that looked incongruously frail amid all the stone and heavy timber. Daniel walked over to inspect the boats, and saw that one of them was already in the water, bobbing gently against the dock.

This is obviously a mythic journey, Daniel thought, eyeing the dark waters and the primitive little boat. *But I suppose I'm not in any real danger, since I'm probably not really here.*

Still, it took some courage to climb into the coracle and feel its almost spherical hull slip and turn in the water. It seemed far too unsteady for practical use, but perhaps when laden with cargo it maintained a more seaworthy stance. Feeling an almost child-like thrill, Daniel untied the line from the post, and pushed the woven reed gunwale away from the dock.

The river current immediately caught the boat, and spun it slowly around, moving swiftly away from the dock and the cavern he had just left. Soon the river was speeding down its own tunnel, one of sheer wave-cut rock plunging ever deeper into the earth. What little light there had been was soon lost, and Daniel held to the sides of the coracle as it spun and rushed along in complete darkness. *This isn't very much fun right now,* he thought. But he slapped the tarred wicker hull with his hand, and when it made no sound, he was a little reassured that this adventure wasn't real.

The river seemed to be curving to the right, just as the tunnel had done, and it seemed even more likely that he was being swept around in a huge multi-layered spiral. This was soon confirmed when the boat burst out into a large round cavern dimly illuminated by a silver glow that came from the water itself.

The current here was moving rapidly clockwise, around the rocky walls and then—to Daniel's immediate horror—into a huge spinning whirlpool in the center of the cavern. His tiny boat was spiraling rapidly toward the center of the glowing maelstrom. There was no telling how far the water fell from there into the next section of the underground river.

As the boat raced around the whirlpool, the rotation became more and more dizzying. On one lap around the perimeter of the cave, Daniel noticed a rock outcropping that descended near the water, and at first he feared his boat would crash into it and be destroyed. But even as the speed of the whirling river increased, he saw that there were bits of rope hanging down into the water from the rock.

The boat was revolving so fast now that he could barely stand, and he would soon be overcome by vertigo. Blindly, he reached out as the boat spun past the rocky ledge, and he felt something slap against his hand. It had to be one of the ropes, so he reached out with both hands, and as the boat came around again, poised to plunge straight down the center of the maelstrom, he managed to grab hold.

The coracle fell away into ever tighter circles and for a minute Daniel bobbed and flailed in the roaring water, clinging to the rope with all his strength. Gradually, he managed to haul himself onto the outcropping, by clutching first one and then another of the ropes, and he finally made his way out of the river. As he did this, he saw the coracle twirl around a few more times, dizzyingly fast, and then it rolled onto its side, and dropped down the center of the whirlpool and disappeared.

Daniel lay gasping on the wet rock, staring at another tunnel that stretched away into the darkness. *Is there no end to this?* He rested for a few minutes and thought, *If this is entirely imaginary, why am I so exhausted?*

When he picked himself up, there was no other path available but this new tunnel, so he started walking. A short distance from the whirlpool cavern, total darkness enfolded him again and he had to feel his way, one hand tracing the rock wall, and his feet testing the floor before each step. He continued gingerly making his way through absolute blackness for a long time, measured only by the gradual fade of the river's thunderous plunge into unknown caverns below.

Later, for a time, the tunnel was almost silent: the river had faded to a faint echo in the distance behind him. Then his eyes detected a glow ahead, and the tunnel took another sharp turn to the right. He could see enough of the dirt floor now to walk at a normal pace without fear of tripping or falling into a hole, and soon the whole tunnel was aglow and Daniel knew the end was near.

Rounding another corner, the tunnel straightened out, and daylight blazed in from a large opening a hundred feet ahead. Daniel almost ran to the end and gazed, panting, at a steep mountainside overlooking a distant green valley. He felt a rush of elation. His spatial sense told him the tunnel couldn't possibly open onto the upper reaches of a mountain, but here he was, and the valley below was more than a little inviting.

It was reasonably easy to make his way down the steep hillside into the woods, and then into the compact rolling hills of the valley. A broad stream ran through the center of it, and he wondered if it was fed by the same underground river he had just left. Maybe this was where the great whirlpool emptied out. No, the topology was all wrong; they couldn't be interconnected.

At the edge of the first open field, Daniel found a broad avenue lined with tall, identical trees. He followed the avenue for a mile or more through the afternoon sun, until he came to a stone tower several stories tall. There was a small door at the base, in fact more of an access panel, about two feet square. When he released the catch and looked inside, he saw a cramped square room, like a walk-in closet in an antique house, with a small open window and a door on the adjacent wall.

He climbed through the hatch into the little wood-paneled room. Through the window, he could hear the distant sounds of city traffic: cars, horns, buses, air brakes, taxi and truck horns, the familiar din of a big city. *Am I back in the real world?*

He went to the window and looked out, but the scene far below (*Am I at the top of the tower now?*) looked like a 15th century village. *I must have been imagining things.* As if in response to his thought, the city sounds faded to chickens and the distant cry of fishmongers.

He turned, and the little room had become a large library lined with books, with a stone fireplace. The monk was sitting in an ornate wooden chair by the fire. "It's good to see you again," said the monk.

"Yes," said Daniel. "Something of a relief, actually."

"Well, you certainly took a dramatic route this time."

"It wasn't my idea."

"It wasn't?"

"I nearly drowned in that underground whirlpool."

"You did? Your clothes aren't wet."

Daniel looked down. His jeans and shirt were perfectly dry. His hair was dry. He frowned.

"When I said to leave your body, Daniel" the monk remarked, "I didn't mean you had to turn the journey into some kind of mythic quest."

Daniel shook his head, and sat down across from the other man. The monk laughed. "You seem to have brought most of your senses, too, which is also quite unnecessary."

"My senses?"

"You could have just come directly here," said the monk.

"How? This only happens when I play the CD. And I have no idea what's happening anyway."

"I know," said the monk. "I'm sorry you have become so confused. Let's try to sort things out, shall we?"

"Yes, that would be a relief," said Daniel. After a minute, he said, "How do you know my name? Are you just part of my imagination?"

The monk appeared shocked, even mildly offended. "Goodness no!" he said. "I'm definitely not in your imagination. What a concept."

"Well, then, what is all this?"

"This place?" said the monk.

"This whole experience," said Daniel. "What's going on? Why am I here? It's like a detailed hallucination."

"Well, yes," the monk replied. "I suppose it is."

Daniel waited for the monk to elaborate, but the man said nothing.

"Look," said Daniel. "You obviously know what this is all about, and I don't, so why don't you just explain it to me. OK?"

The monk looked up. "OK." He smiled. "Quaint expression, that one—oh kay. I gather it doesn't mean anything specific."

Daniel slapped the arm of his chair in frustration. "Could you please?"

"Alright," said the monk. "First of all, you apparently think I'm some kind of priest. But I'm not a priest, because I don't represent a religion anymore."

"Oh," said Daniel. "I'm sorry. You lost your religion?"

"Oh no, I didn't lose anything. It just became irrelevant."

"That sounds drastic. Your entire religion became irrelevant? How did that happen?"

"In your world," the monk said, "religion is something of a choice. In my world, it was mandatory. Everyone is either a monk, a priest, or a member of the laity. That is, everyone is part of the church."

Daniel nodded. "Just to clarify," he said, "what is your world? Is this the 15th century?"

"Oh no," said the monk. "It's not any particular time."

"But—" said Daniel.

"Or place," said the monk. "We're outside of time. I thought you already understood that. My mistake."

Daniel stared at him.

The monk continued. "In your world, a religion is a different kind of thing."

"How so?" What Daniel really wanted to know was what the monk meant by 'outside of time.'

"To your people, a religion is an institution, a hierarchy of wisdom and insight, an authority on the story of creation and man's role in it."

"OK, that sounds like a fair definition."

"Religions are open to all the people, and anyone can come and learn the ideas and practices, and join the faith."

"Pretty much," said Daniel. "Some religions are a bit more inclusive than others, but I'm with you so far." *Although I don't know why we're talking about this.*

The monk smiled and said, "But where do these religions come from?"

Daniel thought about it. "I suppose they always start with someone who's an emissary from God," he said.

"But what does that really mean?" said the monk.

"I don't know. I've never met a prophet or a saint. Or a savior. I'm not sure I'd even know if I did meet one."

"What do these luminaries all have in common?" asked the monk.

"Well, they all have different theories," said Daniel. "I guess the only thing they have in common is thinking they know the answers, even though they'd probably all disagree with each other."

"You really think they would all disagree?" said the monk.

"Wouldn't they?" Daniel spread his arms. "Where I come from, religions are always arguing with each other, sometimes to the point of starting wars. Or worse."

"Exactly," said the monk. "Religions are always arguing with one another. But we were talking about the luminaries, the founders."

"Well, I don't know. They're all dead, so they don't get to argue."

"The thing is," said the monk, "there's a big difference between the founder and the religion."

"There is?" said Daniel. "Like what?"

"The luminary who starts a religion has had an experience," said the monk. "He knows something. He's seen something. He's trying to help."

"And the religion?"

"The religion is an institution of ideas, a structured confabulation of dogma. When the luminary passes on, his followers have only his ideas, not his vision."

"So the religion has to interpret what the founder was saying?"

"Oh no, it's much worse than that," said the monk. "The religion isn't a person, it's an organization with members. An organization isn't anything like a person!"

"Alright," said Daniel. "You're saying the members of a religion are following a group instead of an individual."

"No, not that," said the monk, looking mildly frustrated. He scratched his tonsure and then said, "A real religion is founded on experience, the spiritual experience of someone who can see deeper into things. But this experience is his, and it's not part of the religion at all."

The monk paused. Daniel nodded, and then the monk continued. "The experience of the saint, luminary, savior, avatar—this is what other people see, or sense, or respond to. This is what they try to perpetuate. They create an institution, a religion, to preserve what they saw in the saint."

"Well," said Daniel, "what's wrong with that?"

"Nothing is wrong with it," said the monk, "But the thing they have created simply isn't the same thing the luminary was experiencing. Not in any way."

"OK," said Daniel. "So the religion is a set of ideas based on the experience of the founder?"

"Yes," said the monk. "But the experience itself is missing. The people go to the religion instead of to the experience. The saint expounded his actual, personal, spiritual experience, but the followers aren't having that experience—they're just talking about it."

The monk paused for a long time.

Daniel waited.

"It's two completely different things," said the monk.

"I guess it's inevitable," said Daniel.

"I'm afraid so. It's only on the basis of a really profound, revelatory experience that a true religion can be created, but the experience *of religion* isn't what creates a religion. Once the religion is created, its members must either have the founder's experience, or 'join the institution.' It's a tragic alternative."

"Is that why you lost your religion?" asked Daniel.

"As I said before," said the monk, "I didn't lose anything—I had the experience."

"The experience of creating a religion?" said Daniel.

"No, the experience which the saint had, the saint who created my religion."

"Wow," said Daniel. "How do you know it's the same experience?"

"It's obvious," said the monk. "But it takes a lifetime to explain that." He paused. "And the explanation is no better than a religion. It's just a description of ideas, concepts, distinctions, and it doesn't convey the experience. That's the whole point—it doesn't convey anything."

Daniel considered for a while. "So it must be very frustrating to be a saint," he said. "Never being able to share what you've experienced."

"It would be frustrating," said the monk, "if the experience weren't so divine. But the urge to share it, for many saints, is what leads to explaining it, and that leads to followers, and that leads to a set of tenets and beliefs. And it's those abstractions, concepts, that get institutionalized and become a religion. And by then, the saint is long gone."

"It sounds like religion itself is ultimately pointless, then," said Daniel.

"Oh my goodness no!" exclaimed the monk. "Not pointless at all. Most religions are full of wisdom and useful knowledge that can help the people avoid disaster and suffering. And a good religion can lead its people in the direction of that original experience. At least some of the people. If the dogma doesn't get too stultifying."

Daniel thought for a while. This was interesting, philosophically, but it didn't seem to have anything to do with his repeated journeys into other worlds. Including this particular world, with a monk at the end of a tunnel.

Daniel said, "Why are you're telling me all this?"

The monk smiled. "You asked me to explain why you're here, didn't you?"

"Yes," said Daniel. "But this doesn't address that question at all!"

"But it does," said the monk. "Telling you all this—that *is* why you're here."

"Really?" said Daniel. "But why the tunnels? Why the cabin in the forest? What were Jan and I doing in the city, last time? You're not giving me any real answers at all." He paused. "And why me? Why tell me?"

"Why not?" said the monk. "We are all in the same predicament, trying to build insight on a foundation of ignorance. That will never work. Knowledge comes from cognition inside and experience outside."

"But you didn't say why I have to go through all this fantasy business to get to talk to you."

"My heavens, you don't. You really don't."

"Then why does it keep happening?"

"It's not happening. Nothing ever happens outside your own thoughts."

"It's all a projection?"

"Absolutely. What else could it be?"

"Well, this weird world here may be a projection. That is, it must be just my imagination. But the real world isn't. It's—too real. In the real world, I do get wet, and when I stamp my foot it makes a sound, and when I do something, there are consequences."

"Oh, yes, there are always consequences," said the monk.

"Then it's not imaginary!"

"No, it's not *merely* imaginary. But it's still your creation."

"And the consequences of my actions?"

"All, all still your creation."

"Then how can I tell the difference between this fantasy journey into your world, and the real world I actually live in?"

"You can't. You can't tell the difference between the real world and a dream, either."

"Of course I can!"

"Not when you're dreaming."

Daniel put his head in his hands. "You're talking me in circles. I can't make sense out of this."

"You shouldn't expect to make sense out of it. You're using your brain when you should have left it behind."

Daniel groaned. "Then what do I do? You make it seem so important—so it should at least make sense, shouldn't it?"

"Not really. It's very complex, very rich, very much beyond anything brains can handle."

"So I'll never understand it? Doesn't anybody ever understand it?"

"You're confusing understanding and knowing."

"What's the difference?"

"You think that if you can't explain it, then you don't understand it. But that doesn't mean you can't know it."

Daniel fell silent. He was running out of words.

"Words don't help," said the monk. "Not after a certain point, anyway."

"Then what can I do?"

"You need them both. Understanding *and* knowing."

"But how do I get them?"

"You don't go somewhere and acquire them," said the monk with a chuckle. "You already have them."

"No I don't!" said Daniel.

"Sure you do. You know, in your heart, that you've been searching for something. And if you've been searching, then on some level you know what it is. Otherwise you wouldn't recognize it, and you wouldn't be able to search for it."

"I suppose so," said Daniel.

"And you have the experience," said the monk.

"Wow, that's not what I would say. I don't even know what this special experience is supposed to be!"

"It's not a special experience," said the monk. "It's just you, inside, seeing who you really are."

"Is that all? Inside I'm just me. I don't see how that could spark any great religions."

"Yes, they do become a distraction," said the monk.

"To say the least," said Daniel.

"Those two things—" the monk said, and paused.

"What I'm searching for?" said Daniel.

"Yes, and—" the monk paused again.

"Who I really am?" Daniel wasn't even sure what that meant.

"Exactly. Who you are inside," said the monk. "Those two things."

"What about them?"

"They're the same thing," said the monk. "This is gnosis."

Daniel tried to think this through, but so much philosophy had drained his mind and he didn't have any ideas left. His mind was a blank.

"I guess I don't get it," he said, but then he realized the monk was gone. The room had reverted to the closet-like chamber in the tower. He opened the door alongside the window, and stepped through into larger antique paneled room. But when he turned around after closing the door, he found himself in his own living room, standing by the armchair.

The CD player was still running. He wondered for a moment how a CD got into 15th century England, or wherever it was he'd just been. Clearly, it hadn't been England, and now outside the window, he could see his lawn and driveway; the door he just came through wasn't there.

He turned, and sat down in the chair, and put the headphones back on.

What I've been searching for, he thought. An image formed in his mind, and then immediately dissolved. It wasn't something one could imagine: only recognize. *And this is who I really am?* He looked inside again, at the silent fullness from which his thoughts arose, a place outside thinking, outside space and time, outside language and concepts; it was like nothing. *These are the same thing*, the monk had said. *This is gnosis.*

The last notes of the Brahms symphony faded, and the CD slowly spun to a stop.

Ω

14

Am Not / Am [performance 2]

Am Not

I am not God. I know, I know, certain prior materials may have created the impression, according to some scholars, that one voice in those papers was indeed God, and that the author, having written that voice, was therefore himself God. Of course, no-one believed that for a moment, so the inevitable conclusion (among scholars and critics alike) resolved to the inevitable: that the author was either deluded, or perpetrating an unspeakable hoax in asserting divinity devoid of any conceivable legitimacy. Unfortunately, it was politically expedient to uphold the original assertion for a time, even though such a position demanded celestial provenance, but it was thus affirmed *ad nauseam*. The critics of later years came to their senses, as everyone knows, and my position, stated above, at last rests unchallenged.

Lest readers be further provoked, this present material affords a completely different view of things from the aforementioned prior materials. It is at times something like a *dialog*, to be sure, but no represented voice thinks for a moment it is God. Neither of them (if there be only two) would dare to pursue such ridiculous fantasy. Let it be said now, to be perfectly clear: If, in the course of this erstwhile dialog, notions arise that some assertion is being made, tacitly, subliminally, by implication, or by some subtle logical maneuver, that any party to the dialog is anything other than a fabricated persona dwelling in the fingers of a fast typist, then an egregious error has been committed, for which all of us apologize in advance.

Thus the aforementioned dialog, which commences shortly, could never include the voice of God. It's too ludicrous to contemplate. Do not seek the sacred here; don't read between the lines, and don't interpret. Take these rants for what they are, simply, at first glance: just the blind deceiving the blind.

But this is enough preamble, nothing more than a prelude to prolapsed psyche. The sheer smallness of it all is overwhelming.

No, yes, I admit the *it all* is obviously not small in and of itself. It's the contrast. No end to the contrast. Everywhere I look there's something bigger and better and wider and taller and harder and thicker and richer and smarter and older and happier and healthier and—

Tautologies are all there is, all there can be. Eating my fake bacon and fried egg whites and drinking my Tang, looking over this whole situation from as far off as I can get, what's to see? Nothing but tautologies. Just as I said.

I'm looking at quantum fields, electromagnetic swirls and eddies that shimmer with existential pops and what do you know? Up shoots the stuff, the convincing stuff, a head full of this and that, billowing into every nook and cranny until the whole brainpan bulges with intolerable pressure, the scalp stretched tight and shiny, hairs standing straight up under the tension.

Have to keep going. Have to finish something before it's finished.

There's the cry of the ages, going raucously into the night, carping and bitching about every little detail. Who can blame us? We all do it. We all *will* do it, and nobody's the wiser for having done it. It just happens. The sickness sweeps up through the alimentary canal with gun and camera and bursts the explosive high-tension brain-pan and all the studied presentations disintegrate in confetti fluttering within a great blast of fetid air.

You protest. It can't be all that bad, can it? You insist there's more, there's an underlying explanation, there's a Good Story, there's an apologia from on high, woven with theological precision into an ethereal rationale for shattering every dream and ripping the flesh from the carcass while the beast inside roars and roars.

But you're right. Not bad, not bad at all. If you have to live in a swirling electromagnetic field of superpositioned wave-forms ten thousand thousand times bigger than the sun, all waving and constructively and destructively interfering in an n-dimensional symphony of unpronounceable rhythmic ditties that hide behind every little wrinkle of time, yes, if you have to live there, God bless you, then hey, it's not so bad. Could be a lot worse, couldn't it?

There's this: Surely such complaining, this constant complaining, comparing, weighing, judging, enumerating, all this badgering and conniving and endless fretting, every speech, every conference, each monologue and soliloquy, couldn't emerge from the mouth of God, could it?

I've proved my point.

Not that I ever doubted it; well, some time back I may have thought otherwise, but now, now that it's obvious and incontrovertible and unassailably obvious, now we can just say with utmost confidence that we're not God. *I'm* not God. Never was, never will be. What a stupid idea in the first place, right? What pompous nonsense. The sheer inexcusability of it proves it.

No god would be inexcusable, would he? How would that work? He has to be good, or at least a nice guy. He can't be the source of all misery and horror and emptiness because he's a creator, he makes the stuff, makes us, makes *me*. So it's someone else who rips it all apart and thwarts what God really wants. Has to be. Couldn't be any other way.

So, then, there's the devil. That's where he comes in. God is all the good stuff, and the devil is the crap. But of course God created it all, so he created the devil, and the devil is his only real main pain in the ass, and nobody can do anything about it, apparently even God, so this doesn't make any sense either.

Sorry, I'm doing my best. God creates some stupid negative force that blocks him at every turn, right? No way. I'm trying to remain somewhat lucid. And I'm trying not to speak for you, though perhaps I may have done, once or twice.

The thing is, it's so terribly unnecessary. That's the whole issue, ultimately, the unbelievably gross un-necessity of it. Of the devil, of the negative forces, of the balance of good and evil. The grossly unnecessary theory of social contracts with the divine, our unnecessary covenant with God, and the only real agreement is that we'll keep the sophistries going on and on and endlessly build sufficient blatherings to keep him from getting the blame.

So he *can* make everything and still not get the whole thing pinned on him, right? Just the good stuff. Fine. So, I'm OK with that. Have to be, don't I? No choice. I'm not complaining. I may have sounded like I was earlier, and maybe I was just a little, but really, I'm not.

Whoever suggested I was God in the first place? Not me. OK, it was me, I, who came up with that, but I heard it in various circles, you know, the critics, and before from certain not-to-be-named conclaves of like-minded folk who had built an enticing edifice of optimism and positive thinking, and then dumped it on me.

Well, not dumped—they fed it to me, wrapped in a tasty pastry shell with colored sprinkles and those crunchy tiny clear cubes of raw sugar. Man, it tasted good. I sucked on it for years, and admired the texture, and it always felt real good going down. But sooner or later, the food has to come out, doesn't it? Not a pretty picture, but part of the larger scheme of things, inevitable like every other little thing.

The scheme, of course, comes in other flavors, too, so it took me forever to realize that all the schemes are just schemes, stories, word-webs woven by our great spidery intellect, which apparently has nothing to do but wrap everyone up in big fur-balls of warm vermiform bullshit.

I apologize for the limits of my vocabulary. I wanted every phrase to ring with authority, to emerge from the chaos of my ramblings with a stunning aura of subtle credibility, so you'd know that even someone as mad and incompetent as I am, might have, like babes in toyland, accidentally uttered something magnificent. Or OK, not all that grand, but plausible, something with a shred of possibility that doesn't collapse at the first poke of a second thought, something a person could lean on for a little while and take a breath and pretend for one short evening that even though all the other schemes are hollow and cynical, here's at least one good poke at them all, a laudable jerk on the rug they all stand on, a sharp stick to jam into the chinks and at least worry a few particles of marble out onto the museum floor. The mausoleum floor, polished and cold, where all ideas ultimately crumble into dust.

But there you are, there I am, blowing the dust from my hands and watching my own meager spiderweb of sophistry just tangle itself up and come to naught. And the worst of it is that even this half-baked idea, that the schemes are all worthless, has to come across in one of the worst mixed metaphors I've heard in over an hour.

But then, or now, you were promised a dialog. Or threatened a dialog, or something akin to a dialog, perhaps a dialectic, or more than one voice, if not in conversation, or even at least a suggestion of the exchange of ideas.

In truth, however, the exact nature of this dialog will not be found in this section of the material. For this is part one of three, and the other two don't exist yet. They are, in fact, inconceivable to him who writes this first part. The other two transcend, as it were, the context of Part One, just as reality itself must transcend language, even though we know full well that language creates reality and reality would be a sorry mess without it.

So the putative dialog, if it is still worthy of the name, exists only in the counterpoint between the parts, or in a sense it exists in the temporal juxtaposition of the parts, since they must be experienced sequentially while only later, at the same time, or really subsequently, can they be considered all at once, in juxtaposition. And now I'll leave it there, to everyone's relief, since preambles can't be sustained forever.

And so for all, our thanks, with gratitude unbounded for bearing with us through this minor prefrontal trauma. The lobes will have at it, one step at a time, and once they subsume it all, *then* we can make some *real* progress and bring this weary exercise to an end. That's what progress is, after all, an end to things, to everything. Isn't it?

Am

Oh lordy, for heaven's sake, alright, Jesus, I give up. It's incontrovertible. There's no other possible conclusion. I was in error. Utter, devastatingly inexcusable error. I *am* God—I admit it, and I have made a terrible mistake.

God makes a mistake? We'll come to that. And how terrible must be the mistakes of a god, yes? But later. For now, know that the nature of the mistake is more calamitous than simply forgetting. My real mistake was in assuming this role of primate in the first place, and *then* not knowing; homo sapiens not-so-sapient.

How then, now, do I know? Well, therein lies a tale. We'll get to that all too soon enough, and I say that advisedly, since it's not something I'm proud of, or anything one would want to dwell on any time soon, once the whole truth of it is known.

The thing is, it's the only possible explanation for the notions that have been dogging me all this time, and it's the one denouement I would have most dreaded, had it not been by definition the antithesis of any possible scenario that I might have entertained. For someone so utterly bummed out by the stark knowledge, unbidden and unquestioned, that he is not God or anything vaguely celestial or even theological, for such a person to find himself forced to the conclusion that in fact the opposite is true, that he *is* ultimately the original of all that is, the wellspring of every impression that once seemed so obviously to come from an external dualism, that he is the fountainhead of every brush stroke of existence from planet-devouring solar eruptions to the dancing dust-motes in a sunbeam—this discovery, for such a person, such a soul, in fact, is a level of irony that transcends all reason, *and* the even greater irony that reason itself can be transcended by, of all things, irony.

The recursion alone is unbearable, as the crushed soul in question recognizes itself, in the final analysis, to be the uber-soul. The world-soul. The noumena. The godhead. The source. The eye of knowledge that peers in kaleidoscopic wonder through the spectrum of all beings.

But the worst is not this absurd overload of irony that annihilates reason, individuality, and hope. Yes, hope is obliterated in the absence of dialog, confirmation, counterpoint, of simple sharing, of pointing at something and just calling out, "Look at that!" No, the worst is that the first state could have existed at all. The abyss gapes when I try to fathom the previous supposed reality, that I am *not* God. Why? Because that previous mistaken notion was the result of *forgetting* that I am God. The implications are beyond horrendous.

I seem to have forgotten how it came about that I somehow concluded I am not God. Imagine, if you can, the scale of this misunderstanding: that I am God, in fact, but can no longer perceive it is true; nor conceive it. Imagine that I am the Creator, the origin of everything that exists or ever will exist, but my Self is barely human, at best human, consumed with fear and uncertainty, awash in endless trivialities that overwhelm all semblance of self-sufficiency or calm. Imagine being a king who has forgotten the location of his castle. Imagine a billionaire without a bank, Michaelangelo without a brush or chisel, Napoleon without even a slingshot. Imagine Christ with no disciples, no flock, no teachings, orphaned in Jerusalem.

And then imagine further that this forgetting, this getting lost in the atheism of pure reason, was entirely *my own doing.* And still I forgot.

I wonder if I did this to myself intentionally. Did I gaze at the universe one day, one eon, and think, "I must go into this. I'll enter into one sole tiny being, and see my creation through his eyes, and then I'll know what it's like."

Why would a God do such a thing? Isn't he already omniscient? Doesn't the answer to this question—a trivial one, mere voyeurism—already exist in his boundless cosmic mind? What could possibly be the point of condensing infinite knowledge into a bag of sticks and giblets that trembles at shadows? And then, pointlessly, wantonly, *forgetting?*

They say here, in this world of fearful manipulating bipedal omnivores, that God is a mystery, and the ways of God are unfathomable. This, then, must be the quintessential most terrible unknowable: why God inflicted the smallest unit of his Creation upon himself, and submerged in limitation.

There is a further conundrum, however, wrapped in a hairball, I'm ashamed to say (and I'll have to deal with a divine hairball and divine shame in another diatribe), and here it is:

Drowned in boundaries, though I now know I *am God,* I still do not know myself *as God.*

Big difference there, I can tell you. Because since you only exist in Me, and so do I, and there is nothing else, because I am the alpha and the omega, the beginning and the end, all things, the source of everything, the universe itself, yada yada, then—when I look out my eye-holes into the quantum soup—obviously I should see *myself,* right? Something more profound than selective seratonin reuptake inhibitor side-effect warnings and political sound-bites.

Forgetting you are God is in a different league from forgetting where you parked your car. But it's not *that* different, since both memory lapses are apparently really easy to achieve.

I woke up in this meat puppet, wandered around for decades, taking everything very seriously, and vigorously denied any connection to the sacred in any sense of the word. Then one day (is that not enough for you?) the inescapable conclusion rears its head and I'm off to the races, one thing leading to another, solipsism devoured by Gödel's incompleteness theorem with Heisenberg for dessert, and the reared head turns out to be mine, and there are no other heads, no matter how many colorful and devious personae I may have contrived in my capering disguise.

It's simple enough to come to the right conclusion, since there aren't any alternatives available anyway. Strip away the illusions and deceits and deceptions, shut off the busy blast of the senses, look down deep at the only thing that truly exists, and boom again, there you are, nothing left but God. No god but God because there isn't anything but God. God's the *stuff*, no more no less. Tag, I'm it.

Me

The issue these generations of imaginary beings have incessantly addressed is simple identity. There is no question that there may be a dialog, or a trialog or polylog; this is not in doubt. The question is, Who are the participants. Do we know them? Do we create them? Are they ourselves?

We sit inside our heads, angel on one shoulder and devil on the other, listening to their dialog, and we are the third party, the listener, wondering paradoxically which of them is the real me. But all along we know, in the adamantine center of cognition, it is neither.

How many of me are there?

On my left shoulder is the angel, the voice of God, the voice of Values, the voice of Better Judgment, the voice of Ought and Should, and this voice, we all know, we tell ourselves, is, must be, the voice of the Higher Self. It speaks only truth. It speaks only that which is preferred, better, prioritized.

And on the right shoulder, is the voice of Reality, the voice of Reason, the voice of stark Pragmatism, the voice of the world, the voice of the Devil, who says, *It's hopeless, don't bother, you know the voice on the left has no power, no influence. Nor do I, no-one has any influence. You go through this thing the way you go through it, and no-one has anything to say about it.*

And you, oh listener, sitting in your ivory tower, sitting on your golden throne inside that head between us, looking to the left, looking to the right, imagining the angels and devils on your shoulders carrying on dialogs—what an idiot you are. You have nothing to say, because you do not speak. You have nothing to understand, because you cannot act, and knowledge without experience is meaningless. And so the experience of action is denied you as you ride this silly chariot down the road toward nothing, from nothing, with nothing, achieving nothing.

The voice on the left says, *No, no, no, it's not so bleak. There is beauty along the way. Behold the field of daffodils, what could be more sublime? There are great people, great minds, great achievements, great poems, great paintings, great symphonies, great personal interactions, great conversations at a cocktail party that leave you thinking 'Yes, yes, there is more to it than this, there is something below the surface, something that matters, something I can't quite glimpse, which reaffirms and reminds me, whenever I encounter it, that there is more, that this is not just form, this is not just function, this is not raw action devoid of meaning.' The meaning comes from within,* says the angel, *the meaning is intrinsic, intrinsic to what is inside.*

Inside what? Inside me?

It is inside the head, in fact, sitting bodiless upon its throne inside the skull. It sits there, staring at a screen that fills with light from the lenses of the eyeballs, and sees the actions playing out. And it listens through the giant conchs, holes in the side that open out into the world.

Inside the conch on the left it hears the angel, and inside the conch on the right it hears the devil, and the two of them fixate in living stereo upon the song of the world, the song of dichotomy, of this and that, of is and not, the song of black and white, the song of day and the song of night. It is not right.

Where, in this perverted dialectic, is there anything remotely God-like? When I jumped from the celestial into the mundane, is this what I expected? Could I have wanted this? Could it have a purpose?

Not likely. Its only rationale must be the fulfillment of my cosmic curiosity to know—from both sides of the veil—every nuance of experience. I chose the scenic route, nothing more. And this, of all such paths through the myriad sensoria of living creatures, just happens to be a trap.

At least that's the only rationale this creature can conceive.

The trap's release, then, isn't inside—it lies *outside* the sensorium. The trap is not the question *Am I God,* nor the resulting dialectic *No / Yes,* nor the fog of reason that obscures the center itself and confirms the very dimensions of the field. No, the trap surrounds the mind but does not submit to language, conceptualization, or any kind of sensibility. This release can only be an escape from the mind itself, not to subdue it, or understand it, but to remove all attention from thought or mentation of any stripe. The mind is the trap.

What could exist outside of thought? In this beastly guise, there is nothing *but* thought. Thought from incessant stimulation of the senses, thought from the gurgling wet-ware which itself dwells outside direct perception, and thought from the never-ending dialogs of doubt, analysis, correlation, and confusion. No, a dialog is not what this is: it is the din from a restless crowd of incomplete personae, each desperate to confirm its own existence in a domain of partial, unverifiable identities.

And what remains? God or no god, there is nothing here but the faint glow inside the skull, emanating from this trivial pineal splidget that dangles at the center, awash in a galaxy of overlapping quanta, dwarfed among more galaxies like grains of sand, yet glowing with a faint joy so dim and inconclusive that if it were one erg more intense the heavens would explode in a new big bang within the last one. Nested bangs, recursive bangs, tsunamis that race across the tiny texture of Herschel's sandbox.

$$\Omega$$

15

Another Threnody of Hope

Desert Island

The tide was advancing and the waves, although only a few feet tall, now threatened Hal's beach towel. He lay face up in the shade of a large umbrella jammed into the sand, but the afternoon sun had moved the shadow almost completely off his body. The air was comfortably warm, but cooler now. As usual, the ocean sunset was going to be elemental—a huge yellow disc sliding behind a razor-blue edge.

Hal sat up abruptly, rubbing his eyes. "Where am I?"

Farther from the water, canvas deck chairs were arrayed in the sand. On the nearest one, Josef looked up from his book.

"Us?"

"Me," Hal said. "Where the hell is this?"

Josef went back to his book. "You mean us. It's New York. Manhattan."

Hal looked at the beach, which wrapped back around them on both sides. The island was very small.

"How could it be?" he said.

Josef snorted, still reading. "You would prefer Bali?"

"I just want to know where— Why do you always give me a hard time? What did I do to you?"

Josef put down his book, splayed open, and raised his glasses to squint at the other man. "You really want to know?"

Hal grimaced. "No." He glanced back at the setting sun. "Was I unconscious?"

"Well, passed out," Josef said. "Comatose. Oblivious, you might say. Unconscious, yes. Eyes closed. Breath deep, slow, and regular. No rapid eye movements. Complete loss of tonus."

"Always the sarcasm," said Hal.

"Oh, and you were out. Did I say dead to the world?"

"You have so little respect for people," said Hal.

Josef looked around elaborately. "What people?"

Hal lay back down. The shade had moved too far, so he covered his eyes with his arm. "In Kuala Lumpur I met the princess and dined with the emperor."

A perfectly formed curler broke lazily along the beach.

"I was a prized commodity," Hal continued. "Hors d'oeuvres were named after me."

"Yes, you talked a lot while you were delirious," said Josef.

"I've never been delirious! I'd know if I were delirious."

"Don't we all?"

Another wave rolled in, as perfect as the last. The sand fizzed quietly.

"In Rangoon," said Hal, "—or was it Tashkent?—I rode in the royal carriage, down the esplanade, and the crowd cheered me like a conquering hero."

Josef put his book down again and sat up. "Did you dream that?" He sounded genuinely interested.

"What a stupid question!"

"You have such a colorful background," said Josef. "I often wonder what color your foreground is."

"What's that supposed to mean?"

"Well, you're more than a little transparent at times."

"Transparent? Is that an insult? Are you mocking me?"

Josef smiled. "I may be seeing through you a little."

Hal snorted. "That's a laugh. You've never seen anything clearly."

[Josef to the reader: *Seeing is believing.*]

"And what's so especially clear to you?" Josef said aloud. "What do you know that everybody else has to guess about?"

Hal said nothing.

Josef went on: "What's your secret information we're all supposed to hold our breaths for? What's your Message, Hal?"

Hal remained silent, staring into his forearm. Sparkles played inside his eyelids.

"Well?" said Josef. "Come on, Hal, spit it out. We're all waiting. We're all ears. That is, he's all ears." He waited. "We're all agog." Hal didn't speak. "Eh? Well? Yes?"

Hal sat up and looked at the other man. "How can I ever explain it to you? I saw, I mean inside, in my—my mind's eye, a kind of, well, truth, that isn't the same as, isn't like what you usually mean by truth, I mean—it just is true, you know? That is, you just know it. It's like you don't have to think about it: you just know."

"You just know. In your mind's eye."

"Yes!" Hal said. "You can tell. You see yourself knowing it, and you can tell you're knowing something that's true, without thinking about it. You don't have to, you know, like analyze it, or, I mean, with rationales and proofs and, well, dialectics, postulates, corollaries. You know."

"So articulate! Why don't you just say you know something without thinking."

"Right!"

"How," said Josef, "can you know something without thinking?"

"I don't know."

They both were still while the sun moved half a diameter closer to the ocean.

"That's it?" said Josef.

"What's what?" said Hal.

"That's your big presentation?"

"Well, that's—it's what I experienced."

Josef opened his book and then closed it. "This is your vision of 'Life among the Humans'?"

"It's just what it is. It's not a vision."

"That's true enough. Not much evidence of insight."

"I told you," Hal said, "I don't have visions. I'm not like you, with your, your—your damned *perceptions*."

"Haven't any colorful ideas ever crossed your mind?"

Hal thought. "We drove across the desert—"

"Yes—"

"Ran out of gas—"

"Too bad."

"Had to sit in the car waiting for somebody to come along and bail us out. But nobody came."

After a long while Josef said, "How'd you get back?"

Hal jumped, as if someone had poked him in the ribs. "Oh, somebody came by eventually. But it was so hot. I mean, blazing sun, no clouds, no shade, much hotter than this, and that damn black car sitting in the middle of it."

"That's terrible."

Hal mopped his brow dramatically. "God, it was hot. We just sat there and sweltered. It was so hot, you couldn't move, you couldn't do anything but just breathe, and sit there."

"And sweat."

"No, not really. I mean it was hot so yes, you sweated, obviously, but it was so hot your sweat just disappeared, as fast as you could sweat it." Hal paused, remembering, and looked at his hands. "It was really hot, you know, not just like a hot day, not like when you think, 'This is too hot.' I couldn't believe it."

"That's horrible. Must have been really bad, out there. All day like that."

Hal wriggled into a cross-legged position on the beach towel. "Wasn't all day, but yeah, it was pretty bad. We just sat there and thought, 'When is somebody gonna come along,' you know? And bail us out? God."

"I know," Josef said. "That's terrible. It's too bad the car wasn't, um, white, or something, you know? Lighter, more reflective, so it wouldn't be so hot. Soaking up the sun."

"Yeah, I guess," said Hal. "But you know, it was so damn hot even if the car'd been white even, wouldn't have really made it any cooler. Nothing could have cooled it off out there. Could have had ten white cars, and it'd still been unbelievably hot."

"Yeah?" Josef frowned. "How'd having more cars would have made it cooler?"

"Whaddya mean?" said Hal.

"You said ten cars would have made it cooler."

"No, I didn't say that. I said ten cars wouldn't have been any cooler at all." Hal frowned, too. "It was hot, anyway."

"Ten cars wouldn't make any difference," said Josef. "It'd be just as hot. You must have meant ten times cooler or something."

"Don't tell me what I meant. I never said ten cars like that."

"Did too. You said, 'Ten white cars wouldn't have made it cool-er.'"

Hal shook his head. "Well, they wouldn't have."

"Right."

"And I didn't say it like that anyway."

Josef wagged his finger. "You said it. I heard you say it—ten white cars."

"Why are you harping on this? I know what I said." Hal put his head in his hands. "I'm not talking cars anymore."

"Don't deny it."

"I'm not denying anything. I know what I said."

"That's a small miracle."

"Lay off it, will you?"

Josef spread his arms wide and made a little bow. "Well, booga woola."

Hal gaped. "What?"

Josef smiled confidently and said, "Wogga mumbaloola. Stumpo lavaleema pooka."

"What the hell is that supposed to mean?"

"Mindaloobian porga furbish," Josef continued. "Squando." He paused again and then spoke in a conspiratorial tone, "Broggle?"

Hal grimaced. "Oh for Christ sake! Having one of your fits?"

"Havin' a fit," said Josef. "If the shoe fits."

"You're outrageous."

"Got you off it a little, though," said Josef.

"Why do you do that?"

"Why do I do anything? I do all kinds of things."

"Like babbling incoherently in front of people? In front of him?"

"Who? God?"

"Sure, right," said Hal. "Not God. Him. You know." He lowered his voice to a whisper. "*Reader.*"

"Oh. Sure, in front of all of us. But not like babbling. More like—well—like, gun to the head, muzzle in mouth, finger on trigger, trembling, perspiring, biting against the hard steel, fitting the sight into the groove in the upper palate, drooling a little down the barrel, trying to focus on the hammer so close, poised, chamber positioned, rim-fire brass casing round the slug, nestled at the breech, blunt tip soft and ready, black powder compressed in a little pellet of chaos, packed into the cartridge like peat in a tiny flower pot, the acrid taste of bluing on the tongue, of ancient powder burns, the salty sulfurous smell, the cold metal sweating in the reversed hand, the tiny give of the trigger against the thumb, the diamond texture on the handle, the cold stripe against the palm, between the wooden grips, the hard heavy weight awkwardly tiring, urging the final twitch of thumb, the tiny click as the ratchet releases, the inaudible sproing of the hammer-spring—"

Hal was on his feet. "Enough! My God, you go on so."

Josef stared at him. "And you just put a stop to it."

Neither man spoke.

"Ratiocinator," said Josef.

"What were *you* putting a stop to?" Hal said.

"Well, that's really just patronizing."

"No, really, I'm interested."

"Sure," said Josef.

"Please. Do continue."

"I haven't quite figured out the three of us, whether it's one schizophrenic guy or a bunch of actual people."

"But you actually did try to kill yourself?" said Hal.

"Well, yup."

"What did you do?"

"What did I do?"

"What did you do to kill yourself?" said Hal.

"You're asking me what did I do?"

"Yeah, obviously you did something—"

"Something."

"To kill yourself—"

"To kill myself."

"Right," said Hal. "What did you do?"

"I can't believe you're asking me that."

"I can't believe you're repeating everything I say."

Josef glared. "What the hell difference does it make what I did? What do you care what I did?"

"I'm not asking because I care. I'm asking because it may be helpful to talk about it."

Josef got up from the deck chair and put his hands on his hips. "Well, it won't be," he said.

"How can you be so sure?"

"For Christ sake, I did it, not you! I know what I did, and I find it upsetting, alright?" Josef turned away and stared at the horizon.

Hal took a step toward him. "It upsets you?"

"And I don't particularly feel like talking about it, OK?" He turned to face Hal. "I mean, if you don't mind too much," he added sarcastically.

"But it does upset you," said Hal.

"So what if it upsets me?"

"Don't you see that talking about it is part of getting better?"

"That's bullshit."

"It's catharsis."

"I'll get better? You're sure of that?"

"Well, you should."

Josef waved his hands in exasperation. "I honestly don't think you have the faintest idea what 'better' even is."

"But you'll know. I don't have to know. How should I know? Everybody knows." He paused, but Josef said nothing. "Better is happier, more successful."

Josef frowned. "If I get better, then I won't screw up, right?"

"Right."

"And if I don't screw up, I might try to kill myself and get it right, right? If I don't screw up again, right?"

Hal nodded.

"You want me dead?" said Josef. [To the reader: *That's a laugh.*]

"Of course not," said Hal.

"Of course not. You already said you don't care why I did it. And now you want to save my life?"

"It sounds to me like you're kind of turning things around here, don't you think?"

Josef waved his arms again. "Me turning things around? You're the one who likes to screw things up, not me. You keep up these questions so I can't get away from the things that upset me, and then when I get upset you tell me I'm not supposed to mind."

"Well, that's basically right, but—"

"Seems to me, getting upset and minding are the same damn thing. [Josef to the reader: *Rotationist.*]

Both men stared at each other while the waves rolled in, too small for surfing, but big enough to qualify as surf.

Hal spoke. "We've tried to get past this chapter before, haven't we?"

"This chapter?" Josef looked back at his book, lying in the sand by the deck chair.

"The point where you can't face these issues that bother you."

"Look, Hal, this isn't a novel, it's a desert island. [Josef to the reader: *It says so in the subtitle, right?*]

[Hal to the reader: *You stay out of this.*] "Changing the subject doesn't change anything—you know that."

"Hey, look. You know damn well that *how* I tried to kill myself—and that's saying I did actually try—happens to be a topic of discussion I don't particularly like to get into, OK? And it doesn't have a damn thing to do with whatever may have gotten me into that situation."

"What situation?"

"That I wanted to kill myself! The reason behind my actions, obviously."

"Well, that's what we're trying to get at, isn't it?"

"That's what you're trying to get at, I think, not me.

Hal's shoulders drooped. "Look, why do you bother going through all this if you're not going to cooperate? You know *I* can't do anything for *you*—*you* have to do it for *yourself*."

"I can't believe you just said that."

"Oh, Jesus. Never mind."

"OK."

They stood without moving, and then Hal repositioned his umbrella so the big towel was in shade again. Josef returned to his deck chair and picked up his book, but he didn't open it. The waves roared quietly, and the sand made soft frying sounds.

Hal spoke first. "You want to go on?"

Josef didn't look up. "That's a loaded question."

"Why?"

"You know why."

"You tell me," said Hal.

"I'll just go on," said Josef.

"Fine."

There was a long silence, and then Hal said, "Well?"

Josef looked at him. "You just gonna wait for me, right?"

"Unless you have a better idea. It's your nickel."

"Right," said Josef. "You wait. I'll go on. Sound familiar?"

"Sure, I guess so."

Josef waved his hands at the sky and rolled his eyes. He turned to face Hal. "You wouldn't recognize yourself if he came up and bit your face, would you?"

"Why do you say that?"

"I rest my case."

"We're letting it get fairly hostile today, aren't we?"

Josef frowned. "Yeah. Sure we are. Sorry. My fault. My apologies. My nickel. I bow to your superior sophistries."

"You were talking about why you killed yourself."

"I didn't kill myself. Only tried to. Allegedly tried to."

"But why? It's the why we want to get at, if you're up to it."

"My nickel, my suicide, my business."

"What?"

"My business. My nickel."

"I don't think I'm getting you."

"Right. You're not. Just my nickel."

"What are you trying to say?"

"What I'm trying to say, Hal, is this: I am trying to say that this whole game you are playing is a cesspool of self-indulgence—your self-indulgence—and you oughta be picking up on this yourself one of these days, without my help."

Hal tried to smile. "Don't you think suicide is self-indulgent?"

"Sure it is," said Josef. "But it's a solo performance. You have to drag other people into yours."

"No I don't."

"Do."

"So therapy feels like suicide then?"

"You want to talk about suicide. You want to talk about reasons for suicide—"

"Your reasons," said Hal.

"You want to turn everything into a product of something else."

"I what?"

Josef swung his legs over the side of the deck chair and pointed at Hal. "You ever see a brain? A real, live brain?"

"In medical school—"

"It was alive? In somebody's head?"

"It was in Dissection. A cadaver."

Josef spread his hands as if to say, So there you are. He stood and went round the deck chair and began speaking to it, as if perhaps to a cadaver lying there.

"Take a deep breath," Josef said to the corpse. "Close your eyes. Let your mind clear, thoughts fall away. Your pulse slows. The black behind your eyelids is sparkling, like it always does. Look past the sparkles, into the smoke. The heartbeat slows, oxygen consumption goes down, tiny synchronous pulsations wave from hemisphere to hemisphere, with occipital to frontal trends. Anaerobic metabolism diminishes, breath slows, breath volume drops, body temperature stabilizes, peripheral blood flow eases up."

Hal watched curiously.

Josef said to the corpse, "Something is forming past the smoke."

Hal waited.

Josef went on. "Digestion slows, cortical blood flow increases, blood pressure falls, hands spontaneously describe the appropriate mudras. You can see it now, with a wonderful clarity, the whole room, the furniture, the window, the clock, poised inside, through the eyelids, like seeing through walls. Are your eyes open? Did you remember this? The contact of pure knowledge directly with the naked mind without intervening mechanism of sense—cognition."

"Ignition?" said Hal.

Josef waved his hand over the cadaver. "We get these now and then," he said gently. "Even the room is a marvel this way. Such a marvel."

He stopped speaking and stared down at the empty deck chair. "And there are times when it isn't like that at all."

Hal waited, but Josef lay back down on the chair.

"I don't think I understand, but go on," said Hal.

"No, that's it. I've said it. You got what you want, but believe me, it doesn't make any difference."

"It's interesting, though," said Hal. "Seeing through your eyelids. You should continue. Tell me the relevance, is all."

"I can't. It's too late."

"Sure you can."

"Can't. It would spoil it."

"Oh, come on."

"No, Hal, I don't think so. It's so much bigger than you are. Than any of us. All of us."

"Oh, come on, come on," said Hal.

"It's a long story."

"Well?"

"I was in the courtyard, looking up at the house," said Josef. "It was my house."

"And?"

"I saw the men on the rooftop, capering about as if—drunk on some wild nepenthe."

"You were seriously polluted yourself, Josef," said Hal. "Not all that very long ago, if you recall," he added, in a broad aside.

"The walls became transparent. I saw through them, into the mist, like before, like—"

"Go on."

"I could see through the mist. Everyone was laughing. There

were people, and they were laughing and smiling, beckoning to me, and—and—"

"Go on."

"And—floating." Josef looked out at the ocean, and then put his head in his hands.

"That upsets you?" said Hal.

Josef looked up. "No, I—they were floating intentionally. And I—I could see how. Like three feet in the air. They were just there."

"Yes. Really?"

"Yes! Yes! Yes! What do you think, I'm making this up? Three feet in the air, dammit. And somehow I just knew."

"How they did it?"

"How who did what?"

"How they floated?"

Josef was suddenly very calm. "Yes, I knew how. And I could do it."

"And then you did it with them? All of you together?"

"Together?" Josef said. "No—they weren't real. But the knowledge was. I knew how, and I tried it, and—and—"

"Go on."

"It worked."

"It worked?" said Hal. "You floated?"

Josef nodded.

Hal stared. "You levitated?"

Josef nodded again. "Just that once."

Hal was on his feet. "Can you still do it?"

"I don't think so."

"Why not? Don't you remember?"

"Oh, I remember."

"But it doesn't work any more?"

"It works. But I can't do it."

"You can't, or won't?"

"I can't."

"Can't?"

"I can't make myself." Josef jammed his hands into his pockets, and then pulled them out again. He looked around for some place to put them, then gave up and let his arms hang at his sides.

"Why not?"

"I don't know. God!" Josef sat down on the deck chair. "We aren't in control, are we?"

"You'll forgive me," said Hal, "but this seems too convenient."

Josef glared at him. "Convenient?"

"That it worked then," said Hal, "but you can't demonstrate it now. How can you expect me to believe you?"

"I don't. But I did. And now I can't. Quite."

"But you seriously do think you floated?"

"Yes, I think I floated. I know I did."

"And you, ah, can't do it anymore."

Josef pouted. "I don't want to talk about it anymore."

"But you should!"

"It's too—It makes me feel like a rock, like a mound of dirt, like a goddamn anvil, a lumbering pachyderm for God's sake. A wall of mud, a pile of—"

"OK, OK. Take it easy. You can stop."

Josef settled down.

"Do you remember anything else?" said Hal.

"It came to me in the dream," said Josef. "You were on horseback, railing against an unseen foe. You danced about, too, but with your épée. Never did see what you were fighting."

"You couldn't see?"

"No, you couldn't."

"Why do you have dreams about me?"

"Are there other dreams?"

Hal mused. "A man is standing on one foot. A bright light is shining out of the doorway behind him. He falls to his knees. The light goes out."

"What's that supposed to mean?" said Josef.

"It not supposed to mean anything."

"Then why say it?"

"It just came to me."

"Where does that stuff come from?" said Josef.

"From inside. From the dark."

"From the light."

"What do you know about the light?"

"Sorry," said Josef, embarrassed again. "Nothing."

"People are drawn to you because you're smaller than I am," said Hal.

Josef emitted a short, explosive laugh. "People don't even know I exist!"

"Small people are cute, lovable," said Hal.

"I don't exist—never did exist—"

"Like dolls, like toys, pets, ashtrays," said Hal.

"You know what does?" said Josef.

"What does what?"

"What does exist?"

"What?"

Josef waved at the beach and ocean. "That stuff. Out there."

Hal pointed at the sand, the beach towel, his shoes. "This?"

Josef was gazing at the sky. "It's busy." He shook his head. "You know, frantically busy, roaring, screaming, growling, creeping."

"What, you mean nature?"

"Are B-52s nature?"

"In a way."

"You know they're up there, flying around, 708 of them, or something, right now, as we speak, while he just sits there reading."

"That's not very profound," said Hal.

"The bugs are out there, too," said Josef. "There are ninety-three million six-hundred thousand termites crawling around in every half acre, under the dirt, lifting tiny grains like boulders, moving and building channels through the dark moist ground. Through the peat."

"Disgusting, even," said Hal.

"The peat and the poop," said Josef. "The damn little hadrons and leptons, too."

Hal fidgeted and looked around randomly. "Abstruse," he said.

"Swirling vaguely at hyper-speed around probability wells," said Josef.

Hal suppressed a yawn. The sun was getting very low. "Is it soup yet?"

"Subatomic particles, wave-forms flashing blindly in and out of existence, fluctuations of the vacuum state of the quantum field. Busy, busy, busy."

"At this moment," Hal muttered to himself, "half the world is in darkness."

"Planets circling suns," said Josef. "Moons circling their planets, space junk from techno-states circling planets, bombers, balloons, blimps, blippos, baleen whales, blandishments, brazen buffoons."

Hal was counting on his fingers. "So about, say, one quarter of the people are adults in bed, and probably, say, at least ten percent are making it right now. Or even, conservatively, say, one percent."

"Blatant poltroons. Pewter spittoons."

Hal continued figuring. "The rest of us are sitting around while a hundred million people are humping and bumping simultaneously." He turned back to Josef. "I see what you mean. Busy, busy."

"I'm trying to express some insight concerning the nature of things, the incessant activity of the world," said Josef. "The oceans are evaporating, the air is condensing, the jet stream is bulging down over North America, and you turn it into something ridiculous."

"Sex is ridiculous? Now who's the humorless one?"

"A hundred million people? Bumping? Bumping? It casts the attention down, not out, or inside, or—or—up—"

Hal stiffened and a shadow swept across his face. "Up?"

Josef paused, embarrassed again, and looked down. "Well, in," he mumbled. "I mean out."

Hal was becoming angry. "Up? Up, you say?"

Josef's voice was almost inaudible over the soft surf. "I, well, you know."

But Hal was furious. "Up? Jesus Christ! You'll stop at nothing!"

"I'm sorry."

"God God God!" said Hal. "Just give me a goddamn break!" He glared at Josef and then said, ominously, "Watch yourself."

Josef's head was still down. "I apologize," he said.

Hal glared at him. "Remember our agreement."

"I will. I'm sorry."

"Hah!"

"I really am sorry." Josef's eyes were wet, and he blotted away a tear on his cheek. "Please excuse me."

Hal stamped his foot, but it made no sound. He looked down at the sand and stamped again, and shook his head. "Life is so damn difficult when things aren't going perfectly."

Josef looked down at his own feet and wiggled his toes. "One of us has to be a visionary," he whispered.

The sun had moved all the way to the ocean, just touching the edge of it like a balloon balanced on a knife-edge. A figure was coming toward them across the sand, a woman. She was carrying a tray with plates and little jars.

It was Betty. She walked up to the two men and grinned broadly at them, first one, and then the other. She held out the tray.

"Anyone want some hot buttered toast?" she said.

The Living Room

Hal sat on the rug; Josef stretched out in the easy chair, his feet up on a leather-covered footstool. Betty stood by the fireplace with a tray of toast and several little jam jars. The living room was cozy, but large enough for a small party. The fireplace was well-used, although there was no fire.

Hal looked at Josef excitedly, his eyes wide with surprise. "You what?" he said.

Josef shuffled his feet, feigning remorse. In a sullen little-boy voice he said, "I didn't do it, and I won't do it again."

Hal dropped his gaze and began examining the andirons in the fireplace.

Betty started forward between the two men, holding out her tray. "Anybody want some hot buttered toast?"

Josef looked hungrily at the toast, and savored its appealing aroma. "I'd love some."

Betty handed Josef a plate with slices on it. He accepted it gratefully, leaned back in the easy chair, and took a bite of toast. "Did we ask for this?" he said.

Betty shrugged and smiled. "I just thought you might be getting the urge for a snack."

"Well, that's very thoughtful of you," said Josef. He munched for a while and then added, "Thanks. It's very good."

Betty went over to Hal and held out the tray. "Hal?"

Hal continued studying the fireplace accessories.

"You want some?" Betty said.

Hal looked up, as if seeing her for the first time. "Eh? What?"

Josef looked over at them and started to say something, and then stopped.

Betty repeated her offer patiently. "Hal, would you like a piece of toast?"

Hal was staring at her. "Oh, yeah. Sure." He slowly took a slice of toast from her tray. It already had jam on it.

Still eating, Josef said, "Boy, a simple thing like toast really hits the spot when you haven't had anything for a while." He paused to swallow. "When you get caught up in things." He finished off one piece, and set the plate in his lap. One more slice of toast remained. "When things change," he added.

"Can we finish what we were doing?" Hal said.

"What was that?" said Josef.

"You were—"

"I was?" said Josef.

"No, I was—"

"You were?"

"We—I forget."

"So do I," said Josef, with finality.

Betty set her tray on the coffee table. "Well, I think I remember," she said brightly.

Hal groaned softly. "Please, Betty, we're having a conversation."

"It's OK, Betty," said Josef. "It wasn't anything."

Hal glared at him. "The hell it wasn't!" He paused. "What was it?"

"I think you were—" Betty began.

Hal cut her off. "Please! How can I remember if you keep interrupting?"

"Was I interrupting?"

"No, you weren't," said Josef.

"You keep out of this," Hal snapped.

"Out of what?"

"Out of this conversation I'm having with—" Hal groped mentally. "With—Beatrice."

Betty frowned and drooped her head.

Josef said, "Oh. I thought you and I were talking about something."

"We were," said Hal. "And I'm trying to remember what it was."

Betty said, "Well, I'm not going to stand here like a hitching post while you act like God almighty." She busied herself with the tray, fixing up some more slices with jam, spreading it neatly with a silver butter knife.

Hal looked back into the fireplace and sulked, still trying to remember something that must have been important.

Josef finished his third piece of toast, carefully set the plate on the end table, and slowly sat up straight. He looked around the room and sighed. Then he stood up and walked over to Hal and leaned against the mantelpiece.

"Hal," he said resolutely, "I think I'm going to go for it."

Hal looked away. "Leave me alone."

Josef watched Hal mope, now hunkered down on the thick throw rug. Then he said, "I've decided."

"Great," said Hal.

"I'm gonna go for it."

"Well, you can leave me out of it."

"No, Hal. I want to tell you why."

"I don't. Don't tell me anything."

"I'm going to float, Hal. I'm going to look through walls and see what's over there, on the other side."

Hal put his head in his hands. "Shut up! You promised!"

"Three feet up, Hal!" said Josef.

"You promised!" Hal cried.

"I'm breaking my promise," said Josef. "You deserve to know." He turned to Betty. "There's got to be more to this than just what Hal happens to know, doesn't there?"

She looked up from the coffee table. "Yes, I'm sure there is."

Josef turned back to Hal. "So just listen to me, will you?"

Hal jammed his fingers into his ears, shouted "No!" and began humming.

"You're acting like a jerk," said Josef.

"You calling me a jerk?" said Hal, his fingers still in his ears.

"Hal, I—"

Hal jumped to his feet and turned to glare at Josef, his face only a few inches away. Josef recoiled a little, but held his ground.

"I could tell you what you're trying to do," said Hal, "but I don't want to pull your flimsy little rug out from under you, understand? I could rip your pathetic ethereal world-view to shreds in a minute, but I don't, see, because I still have some hope you might get it together. So don't push it, Josef. Don't make me do something we'll both regret."

"I won't," said Josef.

"It's better that way," said Hal, quietly.

"That's your opinion, of course," said Josef.

"True."

"That's it, then, is it?"

"Yes," said Hal. "Someday we'll forget all of this."

"Yes."

"You'll thank me in the end."

"I'm sure," said Josef.

"Cela suffit."

"Indeed."

"It's all for the best," said Hal. He was getting into the rhythm of it.

"There's a little more toast and jam here," said Betty.

Josef made a stop gesture and said, "Not this time, but thank you."

Hal reached for a slice, and Betty held out the plate. "It's not hot anymore," she said.

Hal took a bite.

"I could go make some more," said Betty.

Hal grimaced. "No, no, not necessary." He glanced at Josef, but Josef was gone.

"What's to forget?" asked Hal, looking around. Betty recoiled a little and moved away from the coffee table.

"What's to remember?" Hal continued. He walked to the easy chair and bent to examine it more closely. "I remember history as a list of events, but they're all the same, like cuts of beef in a market. Why add things to the list? It's not my list anyway. I'm not shopping for myself."

Hal stopped and looked back at the fireplace. Betty stood to one side, watching him warily.

"What a stupid metaphor," said Hal. He looked all around the room again. "Josef?" He took a step toward Betty. "Josef?" he said again.

Betty said nothing, but began to examine everything in the room, pausing her gaze on each piece of furniture, one after the other.

"Where is he?" said Hal. "Is he gone?" He turned to Betty and demanded, "Where is Josef?"

Betty was startled and looked even more concerned. "I don't know," she said. "He's, um, left, I guess. I don't know."

"Left?" said Hal. "But where? I didn't see him go, did you?" Betty was mute. "Is he really gone? He's really gone? He really is gone."

"I think he is," Betty said, softly. Then she called out, timidly, "Josef? Are you there? Are you here?"

"I knew he'd slip away," said Hal. "Hah. He's really gone?"

Betty shrugged. "Gone. I don't see him anywhere. Do you see him?"

"Of course I don't see him! Why would I be looking for him if I could see him!" Hal cupped his hands and shouted, "Josef! Josef!"

Betty joined in. "Josef! Josef!"

They both waited in silence, hoping for the sound of Josef, perhaps.

"He must have gone," said Betty.

"He went."

"Gone where?" said Betty. "I can't imagine where he'd go. There's nowhere to go."

"Oh, he's alright," said Hal.

"You can't run away from it," said Betty. "There's nowhere to run."

"He's not run away," said Hal.

"Then where?"

"He's gone. He's killed himself. Damn! I was supposed to help him. I promised! Damn! What could I do?" Hal was close to tears, and his lip trembled. His eyes were becoming red.

Betty went to him and put her arm around his shoulders. They were shaking.

"We had a deal," said Hal.

"There, there," said Betty.

"He sneaked away, didn't he? He sneaked away and committed suicide, like before." Hal looked at Betty, and she saw the tears on his cheeks.

"Now, now," she said.

"The bastard."

"There, now."

"Why didn't he stay? Why did he have to do this now, when we were just coming to an understanding?"

"Come, come," said Betty.

"I can't bear it," said Hal. Betty stroked his head. "I didn't want it to end this way."

"Here, here," said Betty.

Hal pulled away and grabbed Betty's shoulders. "What are you saying?" he yelled.

"Now, now," said Betty, looking fearful.

"What in God's name are you saying?" Hal shouted.

Betty took a step backward, her face contorted.

Desert Island

The little surf was rolling slowly along the sand, and the blue sky was bright with mid-day sunlight. Two deck chairs were set up facing the ocean, and Hal was sitting on one of them. The other was tilted over, partially sunk into the sand.

In the distance, an old man with a cane slowly made his way along the water line. The rest of the beach was deserted.

Hal raised himself up and fiddled with the beach chair, pulling it into a more upright position. He had a yellow writing tablet in his lap.

"I didn't do anything," Hal said, to no one in particular. "I tried my best. It was inevitable."

He settled back into the chair, legs spread on either side of it. He glanced down and saw Josef's book lying in the sand between the deck chairs.

"His type always comes to a mysterious end." Hal watched the waves and the old man with the cane, slowly coming closer.

"I did enjoy his company, in a kind of a way, now and then. When he wasn't too difficult." He paused. "When it wasn't too difficult—" He paused again. "I did try, but I didn't do anything really wrong. It was wrong of him, though, to disappear like that."

The old man was closer now, and over the gently roaring surf Hal could just make out an unsteady voice calling, "Josef!"

"I dreamed I saw Josef—floating. Levitating, like a damn Arabian magician, only no carpet."

"Josef?" called the old man. "Are you out there?" His voice drifted on the surf like mist.

"He floated into my bedroom, can you believe it, and floated over the foot of my bed, and said— He said, 'I remembered how.'" I laughed at him.

"What's the point of levitating, really? I mean, what good is it? It doesn't make you a better person, does it? It just strains the damn imagination. It puts your back up against the wall and says, 'You think you know how it works? You think you know a single damn thing about anything at all? Then look at this! Take a good look at this, kiddo, because you don't know nuttin'!' And then they float up into the air like balloons, and you look up at 'em like a jerk, and they just float away, smiling and laughing—"

The old man could be heard more clearly, now. "Josef! I want to talk to you!"

Hal crossed and uncrossed his legs. "But he told me how he did it. In the dream, I mean. That is, he tried to tell me. He explained it, sort of, and I thought I could follow it. He saw through the veil." Hal laughed. "He met Sir Gawain! Goddamn looney! Jesus!"

The old man was waving his cane at the sea. "I want to tell you something!" he called. A trio of gulls flew past, low over the surf, just skimming the water.

"I can't quite get it right," said Hal. "I may have missed something. He explained it very patiently, but I got something crossed up, or left something out, or something. Something." He rubbed his hands on his pants for a minute. "I don't know. These things make me crazy. I just want to help people, you know? I can clarify things by asking the right question, help bring on a little catharsis—a little bullshit."

"Josef?" said the old man.

[Hal to the reader: *That's his father. Josef's. Thinks he saw him in the sky. God, this has gone too far.*] "Old man! Hey, old man!"

The old man turned, seeing Hal for the first time. "Whaddya want?"

"Nothing," said Hal. "Just thought you wanted to talk."

"I do want to talk," the old man said. "But not to you. I'm trying to find Josef."

"Who isn't?" said Hal. "What else is new?"

"What?" said the old man. "I can't hear you, boy."

"Never mind."

"What?"

"Never! Mind!"

The old man turned back to the sea.

Hal picked up his writing tablet and looked at the ruled yellow pages. "I wonder where Betty went."

He found his ballpoint in the sand by the deck chair, and started to write something. [Hal to the reader: *I was writing to pass the time, just a kind of informal dithyramb, wondering where it all leads. Then I thought, why not write to Josef, just to collect my thoughts. I thought, I could put my ideas down on paper, and give them a direction, a style, by making up a kind of imaginary letter to my old friend Josef.*]

Hal jumped up, angrily stamping away from the chair. "Damn!

He just kicks back and bumps himself off like a thief in the night—
and we all wait around for him, while he—his —father over there
calls his name over the surf all day long. The conceit! The arro-
gance!"

Hal stomped back to the deck chair, writing tablet in hand, and
sat back down. "One day, the same day." He scribbled as he spoke.

"Dear Josef, I hope this letter finds you—it seems strange, writing after—Let me start over.

"I envied the—your dreams, your vision. I know you could see
through your eyelids, that time, that it was real, part of my, my
perceptions, you might say—I think I said that—but it felt unfamiliar, and you went on with such, shall we say, not finesse certainly, with, Betty said, uh, 'finality.'

"Wait; I've mixed my prepositions here—" Hal erases and
crosses things out.

"But it's not the levitation," Hal said, turning over another yellow page. "God knows, certainly any trick of the light—any parlor
trick—you couldn't get this much interest worked up, you would
just go around it, not, uh, think, uh, try to ascertain permanent
affiliations, God knows, some kind of damn mystic visions, God
knows, wounds in the side, hanging, gazing down through sloe
eyes, gazing, grazing, the goats, the—oh. Goats.

"But I digress. Josef is gone. Have you seen Betty? I apologize.

"I'm writing to you, aren't I? It was never for me to talk to you,
face to face, with such an unfamiliar familiarity. They play with
words, too, those two, I mean you and—and—Betty.

"Wait, Josef—but I have seen things, Josef, I have traveled all
these years, well, some years, and then—One day, I remember,
there was light, gleaming over the grave as he said, gleaming, gazing, fields of waving fresh grass, sunlight, the sky, the twilight—I
think by now nearly everyone knows what twilights can do.

"Was it then, after you left, I remembered you? I never forgave
your damned questions, your preposterous posturings, yes, your
business, even your crepitations, like damn ticking viruses in my

blood, these temporal questions, these incessant insinuations of sequence historicity linearity diminuendo."

Hal stopped writing and looked up at the sky. He frowned, read some of his writing, and looked up again.

"I saw Betty in the moon, coming down over a cornfield, with you. You danced, sang, passed the hat. We all—cheered."

[Hal to the reader: *They bowed, we loved them, those light-hearted, intrepid performers, their giddy charm cheered us and warmed our hearts and gave a tiny direction to time. We all sang then, and raised our steins high, all in the high times; those were good times; remember the speeches? God, the speeches, swirling into the crevices of our brains, among the convolutions, the whorls, stirring the blood.*]

Hal continued reading as he wrote. "The blood. Yes, well, you could have made the first move, you know. I forgive you for that. I think I do. I do, yes, I do. 'Forgiveness is the treacle of the—Forgiveness giveth unto the masses the vision of—'

"Let me start over. Envy and avarice and acrimony are all beneath me. I graze I mean gaze down at them with disdain. Hal is above such base emotions. I am supposed to be the one who explains. I love my children."

[Hal to the reader: *Did the rest of this letter get through? Was there a breakdown among the letter carriers? The caryatids? The katydids? I look down, gaze down at them singing in the tall grasses, gazing down from my own lofty perch. I can afford to be magnanimous. We all have to carry our own victims.*]

Hal read aloud from his manuscript. "What do we do? We go on, right? We carry on, we flourish our tattered capes in the grey ocean wind. We leap about on the beaches like clowns drunk on the opium of history. We jump and fall, we hurl ourselves from high places, we crash headlong against the sea wall like the surf, we crush our own skulls between the boulders, under the weight of the buried and blackened synagogues and cathedrals, under the weight of earth, crushed underfoot by these spastic clowns, these screaming fools who light their way to dusky death.

"I digress." Hal laughed a little. "Let me start again. I apologize. I repel when I would cajole. I detest wheedling. I rise above these issues, these partisans, these caucuses. I must go, on."

Hal's voice had become a little shrill, with a touch of tremolo. "Where are you, Josef? Have you seen Gawain? I know you have. Have you seen Betty?"

Hal stopped reading and writing. He continued to look down at his yellow pad for a long time. Then he looked up at the sky and said, "Sand."

He sat in silence for a minute and then wrote, "Very truly yours, Hal."

He put the tablet back in the sand by the deck chair and folded his hands in his lap. The sound of the waves was endless and drifted into his ears and through his mind like waves of prairie grass or the rustling of crinoline. He looked back up at the sky, and it was still only early afternoon.

"I can't stop dreaming about you," he said.

•

The old man had shuffled closer, up to the beach towel that was almost completely buried. He dropped his cane and stood up straight and looked over at Hal sitting on the deck chair. Then he turned away and faced the ocean.

Hal didn't move. He seemed not to be breathing.

The old man took off his hat and dropped it in the sand. His long white hair drifted in the wind as he shrugged out of the big black overcoat. Then he reached up and pulled off his hair, a wig, and threw it down alongside the coat and hat. He reached into a pocket in his baggy jeans and withdrew a towel, and began to rub his face, removing layers of makeup and theatrical appliances.

When he turned and faced Hal, anyone could see it was Betty, no longer wearing her disguise. She took a few steps toward the deck chairs, stopped, and then turned back to the sea again. She felt the salt air on her skin, and was glad to be rid of the grease-paint.

[Betty to the reader: *It's a relief not to be anyone anymore. But you deserve some explanation.*]

Betty walked away from Hal and the chairs and the beach blanket. When they were just small in the distance, she said, "Don't laugh. This isn't funny." She was talking only to the reader now, without pretense of story or drama, or even context.

"Don't laugh. This is the way the world ends."

She waited while a flock of gulls swooped along the beach, crying raucously.

"Civilizations don't collapse," she continued. "They gracefully sag in a long, silent slide under the feet of their successors. You catch a glimpse of something, and you spend your whole life chasing it down. And sometimes it disappears—And sometimes it explodes in your face.

"And sometimes it just drags you slowly down, like Rome, like Minoa, like a Mycenaean artifact in the muds of Bodrum, until your heart breaks.

"But it can gleam in the dark distance, like a red glowing puff on a cigarette, like your mother's sister waiting to tell you something you never knew, about yourself, about your family, about how everyone always talked, discreetly, about your family, about your mother and you her child, and you never knew, and it couldn't have been your fault, and everyone else must have misunderstood.

"You know what I mean.

"Anyway, who cares?

"Kindness is the noblest of human virtues. All these comings and goings are nothing more than a distraction.

"Would anyone like some hot buttered toast?"

Betty stood patiently in the sand, waiting for the reader to reply.

Ω

16

Writing in Restaurants

Gustatory Sonatinas

1 A man walks into a restaurant and is seated at the last empty table. He begins his dinner and then puts it aside, half eaten, and starts writing in a notebook. Another man comes into the restaurant, but there are still no tables. The two men's eyes meet. A moment passes, and the second man leaves the restaurant. The first man continues writing, weaving the other man into his spaghetti.

•

2 Two women are drinking coffee in a cafe. One of them spills her coffee and seriously scalds herself. The other bursts into tears.

•

3 A woman and a small child sit down for lunch. The woman orders a chicken salad sandwich and the child orders a hamburger with fries and a soda. When the food arrives, the child doesn't like the hamburger because the bun has sesame seeds on it. The fries taste funny because of the off-brand ketchup, and the soda is Pepsi instead of Coke. The woman listens to the child's complaints for ten minutes and then whacks it on the side of the head, knocking it

to the floor. The child stops complaining and eats all its food. The woman glares at the other patrons.

•

4 A man is eating a ham sandwich at a lunch counter. The waitress asks him if he would like another cup of coffee. He tells her the coffee is undrinkable and shouldn't be served to alley cats. She asks him why anyone would serve coffee, even bad coffee, to animals. He glares at her and stuffs the rest of his sandwich into his mouth. She waits for him to reply, but he begins to choke on the food, and jumps up from his stool and staggers around, clutching at his throat. His face turns white, and his eyes roll back. Another patron in a booth rushes over and grabs the man around the waist and heaves violently, pressing his fist into the man's diaphragm. A great glob of half-chewed sandwich flies out of the man's mouth, and splatters across the lap of another patron, an elderly woman in a knit dress. She screams and leaps out of her chair, half falling, but another patron nearby catches her and guides her to the end of the counter, where she begins dabbing at the mess on her dress. The choking man spits out the rest of his sandwich and slaps some dollar bills on the counter and rushes from the diner. The waitress clears away his dishes and pours another patron some coffee.

•

5 Three teenagers are sitting in a booth with their schoolbooks. They talk loudly and coarsely, using all the dirty words they know of, as often as possible. The other patrons glance at them disapprovingly. The waitress takes their order, along with a dozen rude remarks, and returns to the kitchen. A man in a neighboring booth gives them dirty looks again and again. A woman with a small child hurries out of the restaurant. A man and a woman walk in, notice the loud teens, turn around, and leave. Three of the people dining at the counter grow annoyed and depart without dessert. The waitress brings their burgers and fries and soft drinks. They make fun of her uniform. She blushes and hurries

back behind the counter. A man comes into the diner with a large black bag slung over his shoulder. He sits at the counter and orders apple pie. While waiting, he notices the students and looks at them with disgust. They see his reaction and call out various childish insults peppered with the same old dirty words. The man gets up, opens his bag, and quickly stuffs all three teenagers into the bag and cinches it up. The bag bumps and jiggles violently for a minute or two, and then it stops moving. He shoves it under his stool and eats his apple pie.

•

6 Two small children walk into a corner restaurant. One of them stands on tip-toe at the counter and asks for two grilled cheese sandwiches. The counter man tells them to get lost. They explain that they are already lost, but the counter man gives them the bum's rush out onto the sidewalk. They run away. The counter man turns, but the restaurant isn't where he left it and he doesn't know where it is.

•

7 A limousine pulls up and an elegant couple enters the most expensive restaurant in town. The maître-d' seats them and the head-waiter brings their favorite drinks. Three sou-waiters hover discreetly in the shadows a few feet from the table. While serving the third course, a waiter trips, dumping a large dish of hot soup into the lady's lap. She jumps up and begins screaming rhythmically while the other four waiters run around the table screaming in unison with her. The maître-d' hurries over and begins beating time on the serving tray with a ladle. The waiter who spilled the soup climbs onto the table and kneels in the salad plates, moaning and beating his chest. The gentleman rises and pulls out a .38 caliber snub-nose revolver and shoots the kneeling waiter in the head. He falls over onto the place settings and the other waiters freeze. The gentleman and the lady sit back down while the room erupts in applause. The elegant couple and the waiters rise and bow to the

other patrons, and then return to their meal while the dead waiter is removed on a serving cart.

•

8 A tractor-trailer rig pulls into an all-night truck stop. The driver is huge and shabby. He sits at the counter and asks for three orders of hash browns. When he is finished, he orders three cheeseburgers with chili sauce. After the cheeseburgers, he devours three orders of apple pie à la mode, and then downs three chocolate milk shakes. The waitress brings a large mug of coffee and he drinks it all at once without cream or sugar. He lights a cigarette and the skinny man on the next stool leans over and points to the No Smoking sign. The truck driver immediately puts out the cigarette, pays his bill, and leaves.

•

9 Four little girls are sitting around a doll table set for tea. The first little girl puts her Barbie on a toy chair and pretends to feed it tea from a tiny cup. The second little girl has a larger doll in a fancy lace dress and she holds it over the table with a toy teapot, pretending to pour tea into the other tiny cups. The third little girl takes a lady Smurf doll and waves it up and down as if the doll table were a trampoline; she bounces it all around the table, knocking the table settings into disarray. The fourth little girl writes furiously in a tiny notebook.

•

10 A teenager and his girl friend get out of their car at a drive-in movie and walk up to the snack bar. The man behind the counter is very tall and has a hawk nose and pimples. He wears an orange bow tie and a dirty white apron. A big window behind the counter shows the movie playing outside. The teens order a large soda with two straws and a bag of popcorn. They take their food to a small wire-leg table and watch the movie through the big window.

As they sip soda through crossed straws, the planet Tirandia explodes in a shower of rocks and flame.

•

11 A middle-aged man walks up to a family restaurant on the edge of town. It is late at night and the restaurant is closed. The man takes a cardboard six-pack out of his rucksack and sets it on the ground. Each section of the six-pack contains a can of spray paint. For the next three hours the man paints an elaborate calligraphic mural on the restaurant wall.

Ω

17

Underground

You probably don't know who I am, or you'd already know whether or not to read my stuff. If I was famous, or did something bad, or good, or just something that caught a headline, then my life would mean something and people would want to know about me, where I came from, what I did, why I did it.

Well, maybe I am somebody, and maybe I did something, or didn't do something, or maybe I was there when something happened. You'll have to decide for yourself.

I got to New York at the end of the 1940's, when it was still cold in the summer and the whole city was dead frozen from October to March. Buildings were all heated with coal in those days, and at any moment you could hear the thunder of a full load clattering down a metal coal chute into a bin in the basement of some brownstone or apartment house, and there was a permanent tang of oily smoke in the air from the bituminous, the cheap coal in tenements and low rent buildings that couldn't or wouldn't pay for anthracite.

There was grit in the air, and when you walked on a hard floor like marble or linoleum, the grit crunched underfoot, and that was what you were breathing. Your nostrils got black from the soot and grime and that was how you could spot the street people—black nostrils and upper lips from living outside and never getting near a sink.

For the first few weeks, I hung out mostly in the subways, which were warmer than the street and protected from the wind. There were a lot of people living in the tunnels in those days, but you didn't see them much. I didn't get very deep into the underground. Maybe they're still there. A lot of New York has always been underground, probably even more now than back then. Anyway, it was getting on to the end of winter; it was still freezing every night, but spring wasn't far off. I didn't know anybody yet, or have money for a place to stay, but I was young so I made do riding the trains and dodging the transit cops.

Back in the '40's there was a transit cop on every third or fourth subway. They'd ride for a while and walk through all the cars, and then get off and catch the next train. At the end of the line they'd start back. One cop could run the length of Manhattan eight or ten times in a single shift. So if it was night-time and I wasn't looking for someplace to sleep, I'd track the first cop I found, riding the train after his. When I saw him on the next platform, I'd get off and take the next train. That way I never got rushed more than a couple times, and more important, I didn't get famous.

It didn't do well around the subways, getting famous. Cops see a million people a day, but once they take notice of someone, they get fixed on that face and they see it like there's a spotlight on it whenever the person turns up. Then you can't slip by, or fade into the crowd, or hurry on past with your head down. One glimpse and they'll roust you, no matter what you've been doing, or haven't been.

So I was tracking some transit cop, a few weeks after I got to New York, and he'd just changed trains, heading back uptown from the Bowery, and I was settling down on the platform to wait for the next train. It was a cold and windy night, with one of the first serious rainstorms of early spring, and I knew I wouldn't be seeing the light of day for a good long time, not until it stopped drizzling or warmed up a little.

Most stations have a couple of iron benches you can lie down on if there's nobody around, and so I stretched out on one of them to rest my legs. You get tired standing in the cars, swaying around all day long, and your legs go even before your feet. I was mindful not to fall asleep, though, or one too many trains could go by and leave me back in sync with my transit cop.

So I'm lying there with one eye open, so to speak, trying to think about why I came to New York in the first place, which was mainly to be a poet, or maybe a painter if I could get enough scratch for supplies, but a poet was more realistic, given the overhead, when the station got really quiet, and the hum of the city overhead evened out, and the scrape of distant subway trains on other lines was just audible away down either end of my particular tunnel, and my mind wandered a little too far inside, and the next thing I knew I was waking up to a sharp poke in the ribs.

Transit cops aren't real cops, at least that's what the real cops would tell you, maybe because they don't carry guns, or didn't back then in the 40's, but they did carry billy clubs and my personal transit cop was using his on me without much restraint.

He poked me again, hard, and I sat up, trying to fend him off.

"No sleeping in the stations," he growled. "Get yerself the hell out of here."

"Yes sir," I said, in my best subservient tone, keeping my head down to retain as much anonymity as possible.

"Don't make me take you in," he said.

"No sir," I said. "I'm going."

I got to my feet and started putting on my jacket, which I'd bunched up on the bench, under my head.

"I don't want to have to book you, kid. It's a fucking pain in the ass for both of us." He was still prodding me with his club, but less energetically now that I was cooperating.

"OK," I said, wincing and dancing away from his jabs. "I get it. I'm leaving."

"Well, get a move on," he said.

I started walking down the platform toward the turnstiles. He followed close behind, so close I could hear him breathing. I figured he'd be on my ass until I was upstairs on the street, but I still had some hope that he might lose interest and I could slip back under cover.

"Is it still sleeting outside?" I said.

"How should I know?" he replied. "I been down here all day."

"You didn't see anything up the stairs at Whitehall?" I asked. Some of the stations were small enough that there was a glimpse of sky if you were in the right car.

"Naah," he said. "It's too dark."

"Passengers coming in with umbrellas?" I said.

"Yeah, some of them. Not many this time of night, though." He was walking just a few steps behind me now, almost as if we were having a normal conversation.

As we reached the turnstiles, a loud clap of thunder echoed down the tiled stairway, and we both stopped. You could hear the sudden rush of rain up on the street and the echoes of thunder bouncing around the city.

I shivered and pulled my jacket collar up. It was a pretty decent leather jacket, with some quilted lining, but no damn good in the pouring rain.

"You got a place to go, kid?"

I hung my head and projected all the misery I could. "No sir. Just killing time until my uncle gets back from Long Island."

He looked up the stairs and back at me, sizing me up. I was still trying to be invisible; just a habit, hard to break even when it's a lost cause.

"OK, look," he said. "It's a mess up there. You can hang out for the next train, but you gotta sit up or walk around."

I nodded like I never thought about that before.

"No lying down," he said. "Not on the benches, and not on the platform."

I nodded again and mumbled appreciatively.

"My supervisor sees you, or anybody reports you lying around down here, I get burned. You get it?"

I shuffled my feet, wanting to grin and say thanks, but not daring to break character. "I got it," I said.

"OK then." He pointed at a bench back by the wall on the other side of the token booth. "Go sit over there and keep warm."

I looked at him, and he waved his billy club impatiently. "Get on over there."

I went to the bench, and he followed, doing that New York cop billy club thing with the leather strap, spinning the club around and catching it, like it was second nature.

After I sat down, he stood there for a minute, looking up and down the platform. It was late, and trains weren't running very often. We were both in for a long wait. I wondered what I was going to do once I got on the next train. He'd be expecting me to get off somewhere.

"Where you headed, anyway?" he asked, like he was reading my mind.

"Well, 86th Street, actually," I said. "But my uncle's not home yet, and I don't have a key, so I was just riding the IRT up and down to kill time."

It wasn't entirely untrue. I knew someone in a fifth-floor walk-up on 88th Street, and they were probably out of town, but I didn't know them well enough to crash their apartment at 2:00 AM anyway. So if I had to get off somewhere, that was as good as any other place. Besides, 86th Street had some dives and all-night bars where I might be able to sponge a little change and buy some coffee to stay awake till morning.

The cop scowled at me. "What's his address? Your uncle."

"268 East 88th Street," I said, proud to have something so factual and plausible to offer, and especially without having to think about it.

"That's what, between Lex and Third?" he asked, and I knew he was testing me. Fortunately, I knew damn well where George's place was because I'd been there a couple of times when I visited the city two years ago.

"No," I said, trying to keep the elation out of my voice. "It's between Second and Third. Just off Second, actually. Red brick building, corner restaurant called Sally's."

The cop relaxed, but he didn't say anything. He continued gazing up and down the platform, almost as if he was trying to look like a cop, but I knew he was just a transit cop, and if there was real trouble, there wasn't much he could do. I don't think he even had a radio. Even real cops didn't all have radios in those days.

After a few minutes, he sat down on the bench, at the opposite end. I was afraid to look over at him because I didn't know what he was going to do.

"Don't tell anyone I'm sitting down," he said.

I shook my head.

"I'm not supposed to sit down on the job," he added, and he sounded almost sullen.

Then I looked over at him, and he didn't seem much like a cop anymore. He was slumped, and his arms were just lying in his lap, the billy club dangling from the leather thong, and his feet were out straight, splayed apart.

"Long day," I said, cautiously.

"You have no idea," he said.

"Catch any criminals?" I asked.

He gave me a disapproving grunt, and I thought better than to get too familiar.

We sat in silence for a while, listening to the rain up above and the incessant sporadic squeal of subway trains braking in far-off stations, scraping around corners in other tunnels. I wasn't about to be the first one to speak.

"It's a hell of a job," he said.

"Yeah, I guess."

He was staring across the tracks at the empty downtown platform on the other side.

"Sometimes I can't believe I've spent another whole day underground, just riding up and down the island," he said.

"Been a cop for a long time?" I ventured.

"Ten years. You get promoted, little promotions, a tiny raise now and then, but the beat's the same. I'll never get out of here until I make sergeant, and there's sixty, seventy guys ahead of me."

"That's rotten," I said.

He sighed, and sat up straight for a while. After a few minutes, though, he slouched back down and stretched out his legs again, and let his head lie back against the tiled wall.

I wondered how long I could maintain my own sanity if I had to ride the subway up and down Manhattan, year after year. Not long. Maybe it was time to crash at George's for a few weeks, if he'd let me in, and get some actual writing done. Or at least find out what I could do for a little scratch.

The faint roar of the rain storm was still omnipresent in the station, but I could hear a train, far away down the track, shrieking to a stop at some platform downtown. It wouldn't be long before it got here, and my slow-motion dance with the transit cop would have to stop, at least for tonight.

The cop didn't seem to hear the train, and he was so motionless I wondered if now it was his turn to fall asleep. Should I wake him if he did? He probably wouldn't like that, but he could get in trouble if someone reported a sleeping cop sprawled on a bench next to some vagrant. I was mulling it over, imagining headlines in the *Daily News*, radio reports about city police mismanagement, trouble for Mayor O'Dwyer, who had just been elected, when I heard the uptown stopping again, this time just one station to the south, and I knew this was the next stop.

The cop heard it, too, and straightened up. He glanced at me with a blank expression, like I wasn't there, and I got a shiver and looked away. He stood up, and gave his billy club a few loop-de-loops, like he was practicing, and then he looked up and down the platform again with the air of an official observer.

I didn't say anything, but I sat up and shoved my hands into my pockets, ready to get on the train with him and get forced out on the street at 86th. You could feel the air in the tunnel moving now, pushed ahead by the advancing uptown local. There was a dim flash of light from the darkness to our left, and a faint roar was building.

The cop took a few steps forward and moved down the platform a ways, in front of the token booth and the turnstiles. The wind and the roar were growing, and the squeal and clatter of steel drowned out the rain. And then the train appeared and filled the tunnel with noise and light and motion, and the brakes came on with more grating of steel on steel, and the smell of oil and ozone. The train ground to a stop, exactly filling the station, from one end of the platform to the other, yellow light bulbs in each car, almost nobody on board.

I got up, and the cop turned and pointed his billy club at me. "You stay there," he shouted. "But get the hell onto the next train, or I'll be after you."

I stared at him. He looked fierce and almost military. "Yes sir!" I shouted back. He gestured at the bench with his club, and I backed up and sat down again.

I wondered if anyone was looking, if there was a supervisor evaluating his behavior, as he strode onto the train, checking up and down the car. He didn't have a gun, but he swung that billy club like a pro. The doors slid closed behind him and he didn't turn around as the train lurched into motion and roared on out of the station, up towards 86th Street. The lights on the train blinked out a couple times, and I could just see him marching through the empty cars into the night.

Ω

18

Deaths in the Family

First the One

The monster arrived at dawn.

Dawn was breaking like a yellow plastic cup thrown down by an angry child—a child whose dismay at the disruption of her expectations has not yet turned to fear. A child always expects another timeless sortie into play and wonder, but these are not on the monster's agenda.

The monster had been traveling for days or months, from a place, though distant, curiously coterminous with the immediate.

We need not know the monster; it is unmistakable when it reaches you.

•

Sally sat on the folding chair, knees tight-pressed, frills pulled out taut, curls stiffly posed with mommy's hair glue, patent leather shoes bright and black, with her lace gloves in her lap, fingers intertwined. She kept herself very straight, not touching the cold metal chair-back, and stared right at the coffin.

Sally had never seen a real coffin. On screens, maybe, but so fleetingly they never left a mark. Coffins got carried around a lot, and got driven in black station-wagons, or lowered into square holes in the lawn. She saw some pine boxes on the screen one time, tilted up against a cowboy building, with funny men sleeping in them, but those weren't coffins, and she didn't think of them right now. Coffins were such fancy boxes that she never even wondered if they had anything inside.

People liked to cry a lot around coffins, and most of them were doing that now. Crying was easy to do if you felt like it, but if you didn't, you never even thought of it. Having so many people doing it all at once was very unusual, and Sally kept herself especially straight, just in case. Every so often one of them would come and bend over and stare right into her face and then suddenly start crying. Usually old women. The first time, Sally got really startled, but there were a lot more all morning. One time a woman burst out crying so hard that it was like when milk goes up your nose, and Sally had to wipe her face with the lace hankie that matched her gloves. Mommy might not like using the hankie because Lace is for Looks, but the lady's nose drips were right on Sally's cheek. And she knew it was gross to let it dry.

•

Late in the morning, long after the monster arrived, someone announced the Viewing.

Sally's legs were sore and twitchy from sitting on metal for two hours, and her back ached. She was also hungry and fabulously bored. Daddy wasn't here, but he wasn't much fun anymore and either growled or turned away. All her aunts and uncles were here, even the ones who never came for holidays, and some other people Sally never saw before.

The monster headed straight for Sally, timing its arrival for the exact moment when she was about ready to climb down off her chair and curl up on the floor. Daddy let her do that in the living room, but this was somebody else's room so she knew better. The grown ups would all make a fuss instead of letting her disappear into the fur.

•

Today, this morning, she would be toasted just right, parboiled to perfection, ready for the monster's bite.

It only takes one bite.

•

The announcing man wasn't one of Sally's uncles. She had never seen him before, and his voice was very low like rocks in a bucket. He went up to the coffin and rang a tiny tinkling bell and suddenly all the crying and whispering stopped and Sally sat up straighter than ever.

He said something about starting the Viewing, and mentioned mommy's name once or twice, her first name, which only daddy used and some other grownups who came to visit. Everybody else called her Mrs Devon. Sally called her Mommy, unless she felt really bad and just called her You, but she never used her actual name. There was something very not mommy about having a regular name and Sally didn't like hearing the man say it.

After he talked for a while in his low stony voice, he lifted the edge of the coffin lid and raised it up. Half the lid opened, and Sally could see pink satiny quilting inside. The coffin was dark shiny wood like a piano, but inside it was bright and soft. Sally wondered what the bottom part was like, and why they would make a box that was like a bed inside, so she made herself as tall as possible, but all she could see was the underside of the lid.

•

The monster stood behind Sally and slowly arched itself up and over her, still invisible like everything behind you. Its head went upside down, pointing right at her like all the women who cried, but its jaws were open wide enough to consume her all at once, including the folding chair.

•

Some man went over by the open coffin and put a little wooden stair on the floor. Each step was covered in dark leather.

Aunt Norma came up and bent over the opening in the coffin for a minute and then stood up and started crying. She looked right at Sally, and cried even harder. Uncle Don put his arm around her and led her away. He glanced into the coffin very quickly as he left.

Sally wondered why everyone was sad, and she wondered if the coffin made them feel bad. It was just a box, but maybe it was magic. Maybe looking inside was like medicine and made you lose all your sadness at once. Sally couldn't decide how much sadness she had, because usually it comes from something that happens and you just feel it inside.

Aunt Dillie came over and took Sally's hand and Sally was very glad to stand up. She knew everyone was looking at her like they always did when she got dressed up, so she stood very still and tried to look serious.

Aunt Dillie led her to the wooden steps and Sally realized she could climb up and look into the coffin. That would be interesting, so she climbed the steps one at a time, holding Aunt Dillie's hand.

•

The monster was wrapped all around Sally like a big snake and its huge mouth opened in a wonderful monster smile. Yes, monsters can smile, sometimes quite nicely.

•

Sally put her hands on the side of the open coffin. Even standing on the top step, she still had to go up on tiptoe to see into the box.

Mommy was inside.

Something like mommy. Mommy like wax. Not mommy. Wrong, wrong not-mommy.

•

The monster closed its jaws around Sally's little body and engulfed her in its hot inescapable mouth. It was dry and dark inside the monster's mouth, with teeth all around her, and lots of wiggling tongues that bumped against her all over. Sally screamed, but nothing came out. She twisted around and hit against the monster's teeth and tried to fend off the twisting tongues. The monster tasted all the colors of her little life and swallowed her whole.

•

Aunt Dillie wrapped her arms around Sally and lifted her up so she could see better. Sally was so light and pliable. She didn't understand, but later in life she would want to know that she said good-bye to her mother.

Sally stayed limp in her aunt's arms. Uncle Pete came over and gently took her and she hung over his shoulder like a doll in her lace dress and shiny black shoes. Her arms went around his neck and she clasped her hands in the pretty lace gloves.

Uncle Pete carried her out of the chapel and put her in the car seat and drove her home. Aunt Norma and Uncle Don were already there, and they took her upstairs and put her to bed even though it wasn't even lunch time.

Sally stared at the ceiling, but she saw only the monster's stomach, red and dry, with nothing in it but her.

The grownups smiled sadly at Sally's upturned face and tiptoed from the room.

Then the Other

Ward 4C, end of hall, Room 28: Harold Grosvener. Inside: Marjorie his wife, son Kendrick, daughter Beverley, and a few friends from the Legion Hall who just dropped in to say hi.

Also: rack of colorful flat-screens with requisite sine waves and other graphs of Harold's primary bodily functions, get-well cards propped open on credenza next to fat-straw beverage container, and day-before-yesterday flowers.

Marjorie was staring at the far wall, lovely pale green with desaturated orange stripe across middle, interrupted by huge doorway with heavy windowed panel that swings both ways. Her thoughts had gone random a few days ago, and she spent most of her time staring, while her personality whiplashed among several dozen intolerable scenarios. All the scenarios radiated from a single point, Harold's imminent death.

Kendrick and Beverley were arguing, fulfilling the promise of siblings just entering their third decade of life, while the Legion Hall crowd tossed awkward anecdotes back and forth like a medicine ball.

A sudden hush fell over the room as Nurse Polticci entered, bearing a tray with half a dozen syringes. The Legion Hall men watched uncomfortably while she emptied the syringes, one after another, into the tap on Harold's I.V. line. As the third one mixed into his drip, the display on one of the monitors sped up, numbers increased or went down, and certain indicators started flashing. The family members looked at each other in horror. When the fourth syringe's contents joined the flow, the colored numbers and graphs settled back down, and Harold's family did the same. The Legion Hall men remained paralyzed with empathy.

"What are they doing?" whispered Kendrick to his mother, but she just turned and stared at him, imagining his face aging and turning black before her eyes.

"They all just die on you," she said.

"What?" Kendrick took her arm. "Don't say that, Mom."

"It's no use," she said, pulling away. "You're dying, too, my sweet beloved darling. Everyone is. Oh lord." She put her head down and stifled a sob while more tears seeped from her eyelids into the caked makeup on her cheeks. Her mascara was waterproof and did not run.

Beverley watched helplessly, unable to think of a single consoling remark, admiring her brother's ability to mumble something appropriate even when nothing useful could possibly be said. Her chair was too far away to take her mother's arm, so she took her own arm and pressed it to her chest.

The nurse finished injecting things into the tubing that kept Harold in his present state, whatever that might be, and marched from the room with a curt nod at the men. They turned as one, watching her leave, and then looked at each other. A silent consensus formed among them, and they turned abruptly toward Mrs. Grosvener, tipped their heads respectfully, and then hurried out of the ICU into the general population.

"It was nice of them to come," said Kendrick. His mother swallowed. "Yes, I guess it was," said Beverley.

A few hours later, Dr. Bower came in. The family perked up, watching him check Harold's chart. A wave of unfounded optimism swept through each of them, and was immediately dashed by the resigned look on Dr. Bower's face.

"He seems to be resting comfortably," he said in his unusually deep doctor voice. The family nodded and waited for his next pronouncement.

"I don't think he has long to wait," Dr. Bower said. "Harold's slipping away naturally now." He paused, observing the family's dazed stare. "Probably just a few more hours," he said. The family lowered their eyes. "If that." They sighed audibly, in unison.

Dr. Bower strode to the data panels and checked the knobs and selector switches unnecessarily, tracing his finger along one or two of the glowing graphs as if to absorb just a little more information. It wasn't good to appear perfunctory.

Then he turned and gave the family a taut smile, and rose up on his toes a little. "I must be going," he said softly. "But I'll be back."

Marjorie looked at her children, her face slack and without hope.

"At least he said Dad's resting comfortably," said Kendrick, and Beverley nodded.

•

Harold stood on the cliff. The sun was painfully bright as he looked out across the Grand Canyon at the north rim, 1000 feet higher than he was, and imagined the whole area rising up over the aeons while down below the Colorado river cut deeper and deeper through the strata. Now the river looked like a piece of blue yarn dropped into the chasm thousands of feet below.

And then he screamed. He screamed for Marjorie and he screamed for Kendall and Beverley. He screamed the names of his friends, his distant relatives, his acquaintances, and all the people he knew and remembered. None of them was with him in this stylized geological surprise.

And then, helplessly, he screamed for the tens of millions who had died while he lived, from old age, from disasters and car crashes, from diseases, from hatred and war and senseless violence, and from accidents, from the buffoonery of fate, the pointless buffoonery of natural laws entangling the limbs of innocents.

He screamed again the name of his wife, who would not die for decades hence, but whose light had already faded in the dark hallways of his imagination. She might have never existed, or the children. He could no longer know. Knowing itself was fading, fading like the lights in the corridors, fading like the sunset, bleeding its color into the blue-black night.

•

The thermocouple in Harold's oxygen cannula warmed past the trigger point, and a beeper went off at the nurse's station down the hall. In Room 28, two yellow numbers on one of the ICU panels turned red and began blinking.

The family members gripped the bed frame, watching the enigmatic data readouts anxiously. A nurse hurried into the room and began checking the tubing that ran into and out of Harold's body.

Harold's chest rose and fell very slowly, and only just a little. The rest of him did not move. Marjorie reached for his hand, but the nurse was in the way.

Another nurse came in, and a few minutes later Dr. Bower returned, looking professional and engaged. The medical people moved around the bed, doing little things that the family didn't understand, speaking occasionally to each other in soft encoded phrases. The family looked at each other and then looked back at Harold.

Around 4:00 PM, some more beepers started up, and other colored lines and numbers began blinking and changing color, and the nurses moved around faster, checking everything. Dr. Bower didn't come back, though, and the family thought maybe this was just a phase. But it wasn't.

•

Harold's soul slipped out into the room through his nostrils, with his last dying breath. It circled the room a few times, looking down (in a manner of speaking) or just looking, at the room and the people clustered around the bed.

The soul then spread itself out, conforming somewhat to the shape and size of the ceiling, and it seemed to peer at the whole room at once, with a meta-geometric view, seeing from all the angles from all possible positions on the ceiling at the same time.

Then with a diaphanous shudder it expanded farther and gained depth, thickness if you will, and rose up higher, enveloping Room 28, in fact gradually engulfing the hospital wing, inside and out, and surrounding it for 50-100 feet in all directions, even into the ground, through the basement, permeating the storage rooms, permeating the HVAC plant and the pathology labs and the morgue, down into the soil, around the perimeter drains and the building tile which surrounded the foundation of the hospital, down below the tips of the taproots of the trees on the front lawn.

Harold's soul expanded upward, too, far above the nearby manicured treetops of the hospital grounds. Birds flew through Harold's soul as it expanded, and high-drifting tufts of dandelion fuzz floated within it, as it moved into a roughly spherical form, and then held for a while, looking again at the lifeless body on the bed surrounded by people.

It looked at the room, the ICU ward, the wing, the basement, and the tree roots and trunks and the leaves blowing in the upper reaches of their branches. It looked at the birds and dandelion fluff flying through itself. It looked at all these things from all points and all perspectives within the sphere it encompassed, and then with another kind of shudder it contracted a little, to a sphere perhaps no more than 30 feet in diameter, barely enclosing Room 28, barely descending past the far corners of the ICU. Perhaps for one last look.

Then in a matter of seconds it expanded rapidly and steadily, encompassing more and more of the buildings and the city and the region until its size was irrelevant, its size was beyond size and it had no more corporeal analogies to represent itself. And still it grew.

Beyond the solar system, it paused again as it looked down into the planets, into the heart of the sun, and savored the fusion fire fueling the great orb. In like manner it savored the delicate motion of the moons swinging about the planets they served, and it saw the motions of the planets circling the sun on a timescale that was no longer biological.

Then after basking in this vision it spread much farther out and within a short time subsumed the Milky Way galaxy and all its billions of suns and planets. Not long thereafter, on a scale of less and less relevance to any frame of reference, it encompassed the galactic region, the inter-galactic fabric, and finally the entire family of galaxies, stretched over 15 billion light-years of growth and evolution.

Harold's soul looked down now on *Hiranyagarbha*, an almost egg-shaped notion of a creation whose reality is only dimly hinted at by words, now beyond the conceptual, now beyond the now, and Harold's soul was at last emptied of tension, devoid of compression, of definition, of all boundaries, of duality itself, at long last relaxed and free.

Ω

19

No Brainer

Harlan MacDavies Sandovar was the first person, and may well prove to be the last, to be subjected to the now controversial Brattleboro protocol, in which such drastic procedures were conducted upon the physiology of the human brain as to raise ethical concerns in every sector of the scientific community, and indeed well beyond the borders of science into the nation as a whole and humanity at large.

In the era of the Brattleboro experiments, medical science had progressed in many areas, but a clear functional geography of the brain remained elusive. Indirect means had been employed for decades, notably functional MRI and related scanning technologies, but these methods disallowed normal activity and interactions. Lying motionless inside a giant donut-shaped electromagnet permitted only the most perfunctory psychological testing, which left a considerable gap between the science of fine brain anatomy and the subjective reality generated by that organ.

Alternative approaches were often put forward by various physiologically oriented neuropsychologists, who conjectured that by disconnecting certain sections of the brain, using some hypothetical procedure, a research subject could be studied in his natural habitat, as it were, performing a variety of human behaviors and submitting to an array of standard psychological tests. Presumably, it would soon become obvious exactly which mental functions are performed by which sections of the brain.

Somewhat comparable research had been done, on a rather crude basis, through hemispherectomies, callosotomies (the slicing of the corpus callosum), and other remedial surgeries performed in the removal of tumors and repair of damaged areas of the brain from stroke and disease. In such cases, however, a prolonged conscious interaction with the subject before and after these various functions and faculties were impaired was completely impossible. Tumor removal or callosotomy are a one-way street. Furthermore, the "before" state of such a brain was pathological and therefore wholly inadequate for comparison with the subsequent post-op state.

In the long run, a method for the temporary and systematic deactivation of sections of the brain had never been found, and was widely considered something of a pipe dream. The determined neuropsychologists of the Brattleboro Institute, however, eventually hit upon a technique which could do just that—switch off functional sections of the brain without harming the patient, and then switch them back on again.

After their prompt and well-deserved Nobel, doctors Bruce Jacoby and Hiram L. Myer set up the laboratory in Southern Vermont and prepared their landmark study of Harlan Mac-Davies Sandovar—the Brattleboro Project. The foundational technology invented by the two doctors was a new form of stereotactic bio-magnetic-encapsulation, which is now popularly known, to the annoyance of neuropsychologists everywhere, as "shrink-wrapping."

By means of this encapsulation process, a temporary magnetic boundary could be set up enclosing specific regions of the brain. Because of its inherently electromagnetic mode of functioning, the brain's own role-specific boundaries, based on the topology of long-term neural pathways, tended to "snap into alignment" with the enclosing field. This resulted in tremendous accuracy in mapping, by encapsulation, the various operational sections of the brain. Moreover, once magnetically encapsulated in this way, the enclosed brain region could be deactivated, rendered fully inoperative, by simply reversing the polarity of the field. The encapsulation field was itself bi-stable, which meant that although a very powerful electromagnet was still required to set up the initial encapsulation, it could be maintained in its present polarity by means of a very small circumcranial coil that would fit inside a baseball cap.

Using this technique, sections of Mr. Sandovar's brain could, in theory, be turned on or off like a desk-lamp while he was fully conscious and interacting with the experimental team. But the ultimate breakthrough, hitherto completely unexpected, as so many leaps of fundamental science tend to be, only emerged after several weeks of preliminary experimentation had taken place.

It happened that during one of Sandovar's preliminary sessions with the MRI machine, modified of course to generate the required bio-magnetic-encapsulation field, a team of R&D technicians had been working on a second MRI machine in the next room. Unaware that a live subject was undergoing the encapsulation protocol, they happened to switch on their partially-assembled MRI for a few seconds. As luck would have it, the second MRI was facing in the opposite direction, and a reversed magnetic field briefly pulsed through the field being tested on Sandovar. The result was a kind of magnetic bubble inside the primary target in Sandovar's brain, a stable field-within-a-field, if you will. Once the researchers realized what had happened, they were able to design a new dual-magnet MRI device that could generate a primary outer encapsulation with a second region of encapsulation inside. This inner field served as a kind of "exclusion" area, a portion of the brain that was left "on" while the surrounding volume was switched "off."

It would be difficult to overstate the profundity of this refinement of the technology, which gave rise to our contemporary

Compound stereotactic Bio-Magnetic-Encapsulation field generator, or CBME. With a compound field, researchers could not only turn on and off specific parts of the brain, but they could also leave on targeted regions while turning off everything else. Suddenly, the dream of generations of neuropsychologists was realized.

In effect, a researcher could use his CBME to outline any section of the brain on a 3D rendering and then (figuratively) seal it with Saran wrap to isolate exactly that section. He could then toggle this section—or the rest of the brain—on and off, so the selected portion was either deactivated, or was the only part of the brain which remained activated. With a research tool of this novelty and precision, innumerable profound and unprecedented discoveries could be made.

Over the course of the Brattleboro Project, the first phase was the simplest, in which various numbers and combinations of segments of the brain were disconnected, leading up to the ultimate tests during which, in effect, virtually the entire CNS would be operating on the limbic system alone.

The first phase of the final experiment involved dividing each hemisphere into a dozen or so primary regions, treating the corpus callosum as a distinct body straddling the center line, and then switching these sections off one at a time in precise sequence until the entire brain was shut down. During later trials, researchers would note the patient's response to various questionnaires and conversations, involving both conceptual and perceptual experience, and an assessment would be made of the overall functionality of his conscious mind. At some point, it was expected, linguistic skills would be lost. Indeed, consciousness itself might be lost, but it was not clear when, and for what reasons, these things would take place. Indeed, this question was the main focus of the experiment.

•

Harlan Sandovar lay on a gurney, loosely strapped down so he could be wheeled into the CBME. Nurse Kettle had inserted his I.V. and attached EEG and ECG patches, and now a large bundle of colored wires ran from the gurney to a life signs monitor on a wheeled stand. She stood to one side, watching the flashing numbers and bar-graphs that showed Harlan's current physiological status.

The two principle investigators, Dr. Jacoby and Dr. Meyer, stood by the master control panel, a large desk covered with knobs and sliders, under an array of color display panels. The largest panel displayed a detailed diagram of Harlan's brain, brightly lit and pulsing with fine dotted lines which indicated the encapsulation regions that had been mapped so far.

"Well, Mr. Sandovar," said Dr. Jacoby, "we're ready to begin. Are you?"

"You bet," said Harlan. He was a jovial man, and seemed to enjoy the attention, and perhaps even the strange experiences brought about by turning pieces of his brain on and off. Nurse Kettle looked at him with a maternal smile.

"Then let's get you into position," Jacoby said. He and Meyer wheeled the gurney under the massive inverted U of the CBME. They latched the gurney in place, and then stretched elastic straps around Harlan's head and shoulders. Once the encapsulation was complete, of course, in subsequent sessions he could be removed from the CBME and sit normally in a chair, wearing the field-control baseball cap, while they interviewed him and administered various psychological tests.

"Are you comfortable?" asked Dr. Meyer.

"I feel ready for the luge," said Sandovar. "Where's the ice?"

"We're very grateful for your participation, Mr. Sandovar," said Dr. Jacoby. "We'll get you out to the Olympics as soon as possible."

Everyone laughed politely, but stereotactic compound bio-magnetic encapsulation was a new discipline, with potentially serious consequences, and they were all well aware they were entering uncharted waters.

"Hey," said Harlan.

"What?" said Jacoby.

"I trust you guys," said Harlan. "Let's learn something new."

•

A few minutes later, Harlan Sandovar's brain was shutting down, one precise region at a time. Meyer confirmed each disconnect on the big brain map, while Jacoby watched their experimental subject, maintaining a light conversation with him as the subject's internal machinery gradually turned off.

When his left hemisphere went dark, Harlan began to hum a little tune, and he joked with Dr. Jacoby about his evident lack of musical prowess. Later, without prefrontal lobes, he began to tell surprisingly off-color and inappropriate jokes; Nurse Kettle blushed and turned away.

As the researchers switched off more and more of his brain, Harlan Sandovar remained perfectly conscious, but his dialog with Dr. Jacoby became increasingly peculiar (yet interesting). Toward the end, normal verbal communication became impossible, and they switched over to an interpreter mechanism that converted faint neuroelectrical impulses for processing by a speech synthesizer, thereby enabling whatever verbal impulses there might be to emerge in a raw, uninflected voice. This speech interface was based on a complex decoding system that Sandovar had spent several weeks learning, explicitly so that he might be able to communicate with the researchers when there was virtually no conscious connection to his musculoskeletal physiology.

After a while, the entire brain display was dark, except for a thin stripe of light across the narrow gap separating the two hemispheres. The view from below showed this to be a broad band interconnecting the two halves of the brain. No person had ever survived for long with such an extreme reduction in brain anatomy. Without all these higher centers of the CNS, only a dysfunctional vegetative state was possible.

There was a soft thump from the speaker. "What is that?" said the transcollator vocal system, in a metallic monotone.

The doctors looked at each other in surprise. This was more than anyone had expected.

"Harlan?" said Dr. Jacoby.

"That," said the machine connected to Harlan's corpus callosum.

"I'm sorry," said Jacoby. "I'm not sure what you mean. What is that?"

"I'm that," said Harlan, through the transcollator.

"With whom am I speaking?" said Dr. Jacoby.

"Har-lan," said the transcollator.

"Are you aware of what is happening right now?"

The transcollator was silent for a moment and then said, "Lab. Brain. Off."

"Excellent," said Dr. Jacoby. "Is it possible for you to tell us what part of your CNS is now operating?"

"Yes," said the transcollator.

"What portion of brain anatomy is that?"

"Corpus," said the machine, and after a pause, "Callosum."

Jacoby stared at Sandovar, seemingly unconscious on the gurney, and then at his partner. Meyer was shaking his head in amazement.

"Is this really possible?" said Meyer. "We're talking to just the corpus callosum?"

Jacoby pointed at the big brain map panel. "That's the only part still lit up," he said. "We've deactivated everything else." He shook his head. "The real question, though, is how the hell can the corpus callosum be talking to us? How can it possibly have enough resources to manage language, even with the transcollator?"

"Beats the hell out of me," said Meyer.

"Are. We. Done?" said the transcollator.

The scientists both jumped. Mr. Sandovar should be a vegetable now, having effectively been subjected to a double hemispherectomy. All the vital sections of his brain were shut off: both hemispheres, his frontal lobes, parietal lobes, cerebellum, and even the upper portions of brainstem, right down to the medulla.

Jacoby frowned. "Well, no, Mr. Sandovar, not quite, if it's all the same to you. We'd like to find out a little more about what conscious faculties are still operational."

"Rather. Not," said the transcollator.

Meyer and Jacoby looked at each other. "How so?" said Meyer.

"Difficult," said Sandovar's corpus callosum.

"Are you in pain?" asked Jacoby.

"Not. Pain. Strain."

"I see," said Jacoby. "Then are you asking us to turn everything back on?"

"On. Yes." After a second, the transcollator said, "Or. Off."

Jacoby was writing furiously in his notebook, while Meyer fingered the control panel, reluctant to stop so soon after this astonishing session had begun.

The transcollator said, "Chaos."

"What's that?" The doctors exchanged concerned glances.

Harlan didn't speak; the audio system remained almost silent, but for a faint hiss. But the hiss was growing louder, like the noise between FM stations.

"Are you still there?" said Meyer, his finger poised over the switch that would end the experiment.

"Given. Existence." Harlan said. The hiss grew louder.

"Are you asking us to stop the protocol?" said Meyer. Jacoby was still writing.

The hiss grew louder still. Then Harlan's words emerged again, fainter than before. "Of. Personal."

"What's that?" said Meyer. "Are you still with us?"

"God," said the machine, and the hiss continued to increase. Faint words and phrases seemed to whisper within the noise, but nothing more that either scientist could recognize.

"Harlan?" said Meyer. "Are you OK? What's happening?"

The hiss from the transcollator was quite loud now, but the voice buried within was so faint they didn't dare turn down the volume.

"Harlan!" said Meyer, again reaching for the termination switch.

Far off in the hiss, Harlan said, "Outside. Time."

"What's that" said Meyer.

Jacoby said, "Something about time?"

The hiss had become too loud to tolerate, and Harlan's words were almost totally inaudible, so Jacoby turned down the audio system until the hiss could barely be heard. He switched on the print interpreter, and a small white rectangle blinked in the center of the language display panel.

"I hope it can pick out what he's saying," Jacoby said.

Meyer shook his head. "We should turn him back on."

"Just a few more seconds. He seems incoherent now, but if he's got anything left to communicate, it could be worth months of further research. We may not be able to put him through this again."

Nurse Kettle pointed at the monitor with Harlan's vital signs. They were not good. Harlan was fading fast. "He's not going to maintain his autonomics," she said.

The print panel suddenly lit up with letters, random syllables.

"A few seconds more," said Jacoby. Meyer frowned and Nurse Kettle shook her head.

Then, amid the nonsense, a bit of syntax appeared. "MAN WASTES PINES."

"What does that mean?" said Jacoby.

"I have no idea," said Meyer. "We should turn him on now."

"Wait, there's something more," said Jacoby.

Two more words blinked across the display. "WASTES PINES."

The life monitor started beeping and whistling, and Nurse Kettle grabbed Jacoby's arm. "We're losing him," she cried.

"OK," said Jacoby. "Turn it all back on."

Meyer hit the switch, and a complex series of readouts appeared on the main control display. One by one, Harlan's brain functions were reactivating, and corresponding lights appeared across the brain-map panel.

The life system alarms continued, and Nurse Kettle fretted with Harlan's I.V. and checked the electrodes glued all over his head and torso. "He's not responding," she said.

Jacoby scanned the displays, watching Harlan's CNS coming back to life, piece by piece. The real Harlan lay motionless on the gurney, like a man in a coma, which, in effect, he was.

Then another big section of the left hemisphere lit up, followed by various nodes in the left parietal region. The life monitor stopped beeping. Nurse Kettle sighed loudly. Harlan's chest began to rise and fall more vigorously. Both scientists took a deep breath.

"I think he's back," said Jacoby. Meyer nodded.

"I thought we were going to lose him," said Nurse Kettle.

"What was that last bit he was saying?" said Meyer.

"Something about god, or trees, or something. Just verbal noise."

"He got pretty incoherent," said Meyer.

"What did we expect?" said Jacoby. "He was operating on nothing but the corpus callosum. It's incredible there was any linguistic function there at all. I still can't believe it."

"He didn't sound much like Harlan," said Meyer.

"No, but that's not surprising. The corpus callosum just wasn't nearly enough brain resource for his psyche to work with."

"Still," said Meyer, "we turned off everything else, and his persona remained, in between the hemispheres." The scientists looked at each other for a long moment.

"Maybe that's where he lives," said Jacoby.

"In the corpus callosum?"

"Right. Maybe we were really talking to his essential self," Jacoby said. "The I inside. I wish he could have stuck around longer in that state."

"It's too hard on the subject," said Meyer. "We can't do this to people, even volunteers. We have no idea what the long-term effects might be. And if his left hemisphere hadn't come back on line when it did, he probably would have died."

Jacoby nodded grimly.

"It was a close call," said Nurse Kettle, looking down at Harlan's body, entangled in tubing but now resting in deep sleep. "He was lucky."

•

Over the next few weeks, Harlan Sandovar was found to be in perfectly good health: mental, physical, and emotional. The temporary loss of 99% of his brain function had done no harm, and he was enthusiastic about continuing the research.

The final and most paradigm-changing experiment of the Brattleboro Project took place 22 days after Harlan's first interaction as nothing but an activated corpus callosum. The end state of the protocol this time around was the complete deactivation of Harlan's brain, including his corpus callosum.

Harlan Sandovar was brought into the CBME laboratory feeling quite chipper, and he appeared to be delighted to participate in another session of brain deactivation.

Once Nurse Kettle had adjusted all the monitoring electrodes, Dr. Meyer latched the gurney in position under the CBME coil, and Harlan said, "Have at it, boys."

One by one, the doctors switched off every major portion of Harlan's brain. Then they deactivated the minor regions, and finally nothing but the corpus callosum remained lit on the brain-map.

"Ready?" said Dr. Jacoby.

The transcollator was already routed through the audio system, and the same hiss was rising in intensity. Harlan's mechanized voice said, "Set. Go."

Jacoby nodded to Meyer, who pressed another button on the

control panel. The bright stripe on the brain-map dimmed and extinguished. Nothing but the dotted lines delineating Harlan's brain regions remained illuminated.

The transcollator said something like, "Nothing," and then the hiss faded slowly away and the audio became silent. Harlan's brain was entirely off.

The linguistics panel showed an occasional random consonant where text might appear.

The three researchers then conducted a complete battery of tests to confirm that Harlan Sandovar was indeed in full vegetative coma.

Meyer was about to suggest that it was time to start switching things back on, when the linguistics panel lit up and a large burst of random letters appeared.

The audio system was utterly silent, and then Harlan's voice came through the speakers in high fidelity.

"Hey guys!" he said.

All three researchers jumped and spun around, looking to see who spoke.

"I see you," said Harlan.

"You what?" said Jacoby, stunned.

"Peek-a-boo," Harlan said. His body lay motionless on the gurney, eyes closed, barely breathing. Nurse Kettle was frowning while she fiddled with Harlan's adhesive electrode patches.

"Where are you?" said Meyer.

"Right here, you silly," said the transcollator. The voice from the speaker was extraordinarily clear and realistic.

"But your eyes are closed," said Meyer.

"Not all of them," said Harlan.

Ever the scientist, Meyer held out his hand in the traditional V for Victory sign. "How many fingers am I holding up?" he said.

"Two," said the transcollator.

Meyer started to change his finger positions, but Harlan's voice said, "Three, one, all five," as fast as Meyer could move his hand.

Jacoby stared at his associate in shock. "But there's no CNS at all!" he said.

Meyer shook his head. "How is this possible?"

The transcollator said, "Anything is possible."

"But where are you?" Meyer asked again.

"Where aren't I?" said Harlan.

"Are you inside this laboratory?" said Meyer.

"You bet," said Harlan. "Outside, too." The voice sounded almost giddy, bubbling with more than the usual dose of Sandovar's characteristic humor.

"Are you OK?" asked Nurse Kettle. "How do you feel?" The scientists scowled at her intrusion into the protocol, but didn't interfere.

"Feel?" said the transcollator. "Bliss."

"Bliss?" said Meyer. "What's bliss?"

"You're such a kidder," Harlan's voice said.

Jacoby looked up from his notebook. "Last time, in the corpus callosum, you said something about god. We didn't catch your meaning."

"Oh yes," said the transcollator. "I remember that."

Meyer was trying to silently mouth the word "memory?" to Jacoby, but the other scientist ignored him. Meyer mimed slapping his own forehead and walked around in a circle, shaking his head.

"What were you trying to say about god?" Jacoby said.

The transcollator was silent, and the researchers noted the total absence of hiss from the audio system. Then it said, "I was unhappy."

"Why unhappy?" said Jacoby.

"My corpus callosum is a pretty crappy substitute for a whole brain," Harlan said. "It was a big strain to hang onto it. Kinda threw me into a funk about the human condition."

"Really?" said Jacoby. "And you feel better now, with no CNS at all?"

"Gosh yes," said the transcollator. "What a relief!"

"To not be trapped inside the corpus callosum?"

"To not be trapped at all."

"By the equipment?"

"No, by physiology. The whole thing is a trap. It's just a really, really big one." The audio was silent for a moment. "Until you start shutting it off, of course. Then it's like a prison, and then a cell, and then a cage that's shrinking around you."

"That sounds horrible," said Meyer, coming back to the gurney. "I'm sorry we put you through that. You should have mentioned it afterward."

"I didn't remember much," said Harlan.

"So what would you say about god now?" asked Meyer.

"Ha!" said the machinery. "That's a good one."

"What do you mean?" said Meyer.

"What would I say about god! What the hell can anyone say about god?"

"Do you think there is one?" said Meyer.

"Sure!" said the transcollator.

"What makes you think so?" Meyer asked.

"It's me," said the transcollator.

"What is?"

"God."

The scientists exchanged glances. Jacoby said, "You think you're God?" He rolled his eyes at Meyer.

"Think I am?" said the machine. "No need to think. And by the way, I saw you rolling your eyes."

Jacoby looked around the room. "How is that possible?" he said.

"Like I said," said the transcollator, "Anything is possible."

"Fine," said Jacoby. "Philosophically. We need to know—physically—how you can see us. I wasn't even looking toward you just now."

"It's not philosophy," said Harlan. "Not to me."

"But you have to admit, Harlan, what you're saying sounds

pretty unusual. Are you sure you're OK? You've never even talked about god or philosophy with us before."

"I'm quite OK," said Harlan. "And I'm not Harlan anymore. Just a pinprick of me is Harlan."

"But how did you see me just then?" said Jacoby.

"I'm everywhere," said the transcollator.

Jacoby started to speak, but the transcollator interrupted. "By the way, another little pinprick is you," it said. "And Meyer. And Miss Kettle."

The three looked at each other.

"You don't believe me, do you?" said the transcollator.

"Well, frankly, Harlan, it's pretty hard to swallow, in spite of your inexplicable ability to see us. And we're not getting any closer to understanding how you can function at all with your entire brain turned off."

"How's this?" said the transcollator.

The brain-map display suddenly lit up, showing all sectors fully activated. Jacoby and Meyer jumped back, staring in amazement. Nurse Kettle studied Harlan's life signs, but they all still showed deep coma.

Then the brain-map display went black; the entire diagram disappeared. Jacoby reached for a reset button on the console, but before he could press it, there was a flicker on the right edge of the display. The Energizer Bunny appeared, banging its tin drum and turning its head from side to side. The bunny rolled across the screen and disappeared off the left edge.

"Believe me now?" said Harlan from the audio system.

"My god!" said Jacoby.

"It's just a cartoon," said the machine. "No need to get religious about it." The transcollator laughed.

"How did you do that?" said Meyer.

"Never mind how," said Harlan. "Watch this."

All the displays suddenly went black, but none of the alarms went off. The scientists stared in awe as a single image formed, spread across all the panels. It was a galaxy, bright and colorful, its spiral arms slowly rotating.

"What the—" said Meyer.

"Oh, and this is even better," said the transcollator.

The entire room went dark, all the displays and the ceiling lights, even the red button on the telephone. Then the galaxy reappeared, encompassing them. The room had no walls, and everything in it had disappeared but Harlan Sandovar's body floating where the gurney had been, and the three researchers, standing in empty space. The galaxy spun slowly all around them.

"Holy shit!" cried Jacoby. Meyer was reaching out like a blind man for something to grab onto. Nurse Kettle had gone rigid with fear.

"Sorry," said Harlan, and the room suddenly blinked back, with all the lights and displays working normally. "Didn't mean to scare you."

"You scared the shit out of me," said Jacoby. "Shit!"

"What the hell?" said Meyer.

"Oh god," said Nurse Kettle, clinging to the rail on Harlan's gurney.

"That was nothing, really," said Harlan.

"No!" shouted Jacoby, waving his arms.

"Don't worry," said the transcollator. "I'm not going to do it again."

"Thank god," said Jacoby. "Please don't."

"I think I should go back now," said the transcollator.

"Back?" said Meyer.

"Back into my body," said Harlan's voice. "It's been fun, but this isn't my time."

Jacoby looked at the loudspeaker. "You want us to turn everything back on again?" he said.

"Yup. Sure do," said the transcollator. "Not dying to wedge myself back inside, but it's the right thing to do. Maybe later."

Meyer had his finger on the switch. "You ready?" he said.

"Yowza. Go for it," said the transcollator.

Meyer pressed the button, and the inactive regions began to light up again on the brain-map, starting with the corpus callosum and working outward into the larger processes. The life monitor perked up and showed Harlan was returning to normal sleep state. A few seconds after the brain-map was fully lit, Harlan opened his eyes and looked around.

Meyer unlatched the gurney from the CBME while Nurse Kettle unplugged the EEG and ECG cables. A few minutes later, Sandovar was sitting in a chair, wearing a bathrobe, smiling and looking unusually refreshed.

All three researchers clustered around Harlan's chair, examining his demeanor. "Are you sure you're OK?" said Jacoby.

Harlan nodded and continued grinning. "It was good?" he said.

•

The Brattleboro Project was shut down the following week, voluntarily, by the principal investigators. The CBME machinery was repurposed for therapeutic and diagnostic applications, and Drs Jacoby and Meyer returned to private practice. Nurse Kettle took a position in an assisted living center. The final report by the Brattleboro Project's principal investigators made only passing mention of Harlan Sandovar's extraordinary performance, and the conclusion of the paper stated what is now known as the Jacoby and Meyer Conjecture—that in fact the corpus callosum might be the ultimate seat of consciousness. The paper concluded with the even simpler assertion that "... nevertheless, once everything is shut down, nothing remains. A coma is simply a coma."

Ω

20

The Beginning

It all started, as it always does, with the mind-body transfer. This is not science fiction, although it might be more satisfying if it were. The mind-body transference I'm referring to really happened—not in a mad scientist's lab, but it could have been a mad creator's lab. Alright, no shit, it was my mother's womb. That's what I've been told, as have we all, and by sheer testimony it's hard not to accept it, however impossible and bizarre the process might seem. The trick is not to think about it in too much detail.

This particular fetus had been growing in there, following its natural course of mitosis, steadfastly recapitulating phylogeny, and somewhere around the three-month mark, this particular mind (mine) got transplanted into the fetus's non-functional recently-embryonic central nervous system. That's about all anyone is sure of. Since then, things have gotten increasingly incomprehensible.

Naturally you may inquire as to why I would say transplanted—metempsychosis, transmigration, reincarnation?

Here's why. Before I began inhabiting the fetus, with its woefully inadequate physiology, floating helplessly in its little sack of bodily fluids, I was definitely not Genghis Khan or Paul Revere—and yet I can say that I definitely was. That is, I existed, although I wasn't inhabiting anything. Inhabiting anyone, I should say. Unfortunately, I cannot elaborate on what I was doing, as there doesn't seem to be any doing in that prior state, but it definitely didn't involve inhabiting. I'll have to say that I just was, and leave it at that.

But this isn't really where my story should be going. I wanted to start at the beginning, because that's where one might expect to find some answers to the forthcoming questions, which I'll get to soon enough. But as you can see, starting at the *absolute* beginning has its own pitfalls, and we're already failing to answer even the simplest of questions, and there's no point going any further in this direction.

Later on, you'll probably be thinking I should have spent more time on this, because there simply must have been some clues that an astute reader could pick up on. Because then you could contact me, through my publisher or whatever social medium is ubiquitous in your day and age, and try to shed light on at least one or two of the conundra which have made such a muddle out of what could have been a perfectly normal, even productive, life. And I would be so grateful to escape the traps of my imagination, and you would feel so good, being able to help.

At this stage, after so many years, I'm quite convinced that there can be no help, but I shan't blame you for feeling compassionate. For now, please just trust me—don't waste your time second-guessing what's going on here. I'd love to think it is just a story, a contrivance for nothing but simple entertainment, but it is, after all, my life, and I'll stake my reputation on the conclusions I've reached. Conclusions I've been forced to. If you can even call them conclusions.

Continuation

For several more months I languished in the vat, cooking up a full-fledged human body with a lot of help from my mother. Again, this is just what I was told, but I'm not arguing with it, although from what I understand the vat was more of a bladder. Eventually, my body was extruded into the world, smacked on the back, and I began to spread out into the newly-minted brain of this burbling little proto-person.

Things went fine for many years after that. The people in my little world were successful in convincing me that I was a person. It (the person) was named Allen, and it lived in a body that was also named Allen. The distinction between Allen the person and Allen the body was moot—by now they might as well have been one and the same. But my intuition, and later on innumerable layers of experience, told me unequivocally that there were two of us. At least.

Still later, well into my second or third decade, it became apparent that the body had a mind of its own, and that raised new and unwelcome questions. For one thing, if the body had a mind of its own, whose mind did the person have? Were there two minds? Or was the body's mind actually another kind of person? It was very confusing, like everything else during those decades, so I concentrated ferociously and tried to make sense out of everything.

Unfortunately, it wasn't very long before I realized that the mind, too, had a mind of its own—several, in fact. But we'll have to get to that later on in the story.

In sum, having a mind of its own isn't any better than not having a mind at all, but that, too, took a while to recognize. You can thank me now, dear reader, for telegraphing all these profound messages early on in the process.

Aside

We should ban the first person singular from our vocabulary. I, me, mine—they imply there's only one of me. What nonsense.

Prelude to a Slight Digression

Here I must digress slightly. There was an interesting side-effect of concentrating ferociously, or of trying to make sense out of absolutely everything, and it revealed something that might be important.

For most of my school years, people told me I was one of the smart ones. I knew that was a big misunderstanding, but who was I, a shy kid, to argue with adults trying to praise me? They thought I was smart because of my language skills, but language skills have nothing to do with being smart. Expressing smart, maybe, but not being smart.

Although I correctly assumed that these flattering adults meant I was more intelligent than some average kid, I knew quite clearly from innumerable social failures and breaches of protocol that obviously most people were a lot smarter than me. The only difference was that I could explain myself. This, it turns out, goes a long way to make up for not being brave or strong or an especially adept center-forward on the soccer team.

Years of schooling conditioned me to stay smart, or risk actually being the nothing I assumed I actually was inside.

Now don't get me wrong—I wasn't a sad, existential kid. I had a great childhood, and my parents did everything they could to encourage my smartness, and they succeeded in building a pretty solid foundation of self-esteem. But self-esteem is a judgment call, an intellectual evaluation of one's self, and has little to do with one's experience of life. It doesn't mean you're not also scared most of the time. But you draw on this deeply implanted judgment and do your best to explain yourself, and after a while people just assume that your tone of voice represents a solid rock of courage and certainty that can't be easily shaken.

Somewhere in the beginning of my second or third decade, I noticed that I could think about myself with the same analytical tools I had been taught to use on frogs or the Louisiana Purchase. This meant that my penchant for understanding everything now had to include understanding myself, and a great paradox-ridden feedback loop got started. This self-energizing recursive compulsion is still running full tilt, and I've had lots of fun and frustration over the years trying, without success, to extinguish it.

The Digression

Which brings me to the digression itself. Concentrating ferociously to make sense out of everything is a dangerous and pointless practice. I speak from experience, not to discourage anyone from being cerebral if they like that sort of thing, but to warn anyone who does like swimming in the convolutions, and keeping the taxonomy sorted, that too much of a good thing can make you barf. Of course, too much of this particular good thing is likely to make your friends and associates barf long before you even notice yourself preparing to hurl.

It turns out that the brain, which is more or less responsible for the physical side of mental activity, is a lot like a muscle. It consumes plenty of oxygen when it's working hard, and it kind of scrunches in on itself when you really force it. And if you strain it enough, it gets cramps.

Not many people recognize a brain cramp when they get one, and for good reason. A brain cramp feels like something unknown and invisible is about to devour you, and your blood chemistry suddenly floods every neuron with the brain's version of lactic acid, cramp-juice. Subjectively, this is experienced as sheer, pure, elemental terror. Not fear, which is anticipation of something dangerous that might have an effect on you, but terror, which is more like the certain knowledge that you will almost immediately be totally obliterated, and the resulting oblivion will be absolutely unacceptable. And final. Terror doesn't make you nervous like fear does. Terror consumes your awareness and feels a lot like standing on the most crumbly edge of the tallest cliff in a hurricane with nothing to hold on to.

All this terror was of course totally debilitating, and I fought against it without success. When it struck, within seconds I was hanging on by my proverbial fingernails, the fingernails of my persona, I suppose, or those of my ego, and it took a huge amount of effort to keep the persona or the ego or my whole damn body from being most utterly obliterated. The best possible outcome was being reduced to a squirming idiot gabbling incoherently on the floor of a padded cell. The effort to resist this, in turn, caused more brain cramps, which brought on more terror.

But hidden in this wretched cycle of terror and resistance was something unexpected. Remember that terror is anticipation of oblivion, dread of the imminent loss of everything. So consider for a moment, just what is this "everything"?

In a weirdly retrograde way, terror provided my first glimpse of everything, of the totality. It was my first opportunity to connect an experience of any kind to the categorical word "everything." It didn't give me an experience of everything, but it did afford a colorful sense of the opposite—oblivion. Oblivion is what you get when you remove everything. So, perversely, my dark night of the soul was also my first glimpse in the direction of nirvana.

Another more mundane effect of the terror was to provide a memorable disincentive to ferocious concentration on understanding everything, on integrating every single experience into a massive intellectual overview. I didn't perceive this connection for a while, but once I learned to stop, it was obvious.

Post-Digression Continuation

After living with terror, born simply of trying too hard, and then learning to stop, I also realized that most of the people I knew had been telling me to lighten up for years. It was one of those realizations that suddenly makes sense out of a lot of confusing history, and also makes you want to crawl into a hole. You want to tell everyone about your new discovery, but you don't want them to find out it took so many decades to catch on to the obvious.

Now back to the main story, which I may as well admit is not going to continue the way it began, as a long chronology. It's a story, but it's not a history, and if I were to continue to chronicle all the formative moments of my life, we would both soon run screaming from the room.

Note from Author to Writer

The dweller wishes to expound briefly upon the ironies and joys and angst of the attractions, so many of them, so powerful, so hard-wired, so inexorable, so seemingly fulfilling, so impossible to fulfill. But worse, each attraction, in its pursuit, renders its attainment less satisfying, and reinforces the impossibility of the utter ownership and union that the desire spawns in the heart.

Why is the other, the object, the unattained, so perfect? It is because of the way the senses are skewed, to find a perfect emulation of a pre-recorded internal model, not because of any particular perfection that might be present in the object and presumably missing in its alternatives.

Why is food, why air, so compelling and irresistible? It is because it is against the most basic chemical laws of the body to avoid it, to be anything other than obsessed by it, not because there is anything fundamentally appealing about seared muscle fragments or dead plants. Where is meaning in all this? There is none.

Possible Postscript

I think I should have waited a bit longer. Writing this now, at this stage, has to be merely, I don't know, premature. The only proper way to address all this is to write it after I'm dead. Otherwise there is no way to properly sum it all up. To sum it up, you see, that's what I need to do here—find the common thread, discern the real pattern of my deception, my self-deception, not that it didn't fool everyone else as well. Then, moving that aside, there's nothing left but the real self. But how can I know the full measure of my delusion while it's still going on? Can't. Have to put this off a little longer, just until death is at the door, coming inside, approaching my chair, gently but irresistibly pushing the notebooks and yellow pads and tablets and smartphones and laptop computers off the table onto the floor, wiping away stacks of paper and file cards and post-it notes, reaching slowly for my hand—

Scenario 921,864 of 13,977,251

As I drove down my street, I decided to park at the curb in front of the house so I could wash the car later on. I pulled into the driveway, hitting the garage-door opener button as I turned the wheel, mildly proud of this minor multi-tasking maneuver. The garage door had almost closed behind me when I noticed that I had not parked at the curb.

I walked into the kitchen, thinking, "I'm definitely not going to have any ice-cream tonight; putting on too much weight." As I opened the freezer side of the refrigerator, the thought came, "I'm not going to do this. I really shouldn't do this." Minutes later I walked into the living room with the whole container of vanilla. "I'll just have a few spoonfuls," I said to myself.

While surfing the cable channels, I thought, "I should call Linda. We haven't spoken since her operation. I hope she's doing alright." There wasn't much on tonight, so I kept switching around. "I really should call her, but I'm not sure if I will. It's always a bit awkward." A huge black fishing boat was plowing through high seas in a gale, with crew members staggering around on deck trying to launch crab pots without being swept overboard. "I'll call her after this show," I thought. When the crab men were done, I returned to flipping channels.

Much later, I noticed it was after midnight. I'd eaten all the ice-cream and hadn't called Linda. I also hadn't washed the car, but it was obviously much too late for that. "I really should get to bed before 2:00 tonight," I thought. There wasn't anything interesting on the TV anymore, but I started one more scan through the channels, just in case. Around 3:15 I woke up in my chair and went to bed.

It takes only a moment's reflection to see that every day is the same, no matter what I decide. Whoever is running things isn't me. Deciding makes no difference at all. Whatever I think about doing, somebody has other plans.

What is most frightening is that the plan is apparently to perform exactly the same pointless, deadening actions, and never to do anything else. The tedium is overwhelming, although only in the region of my brain that is aware of the repetition. Somehow the rest of the system is perfectly content to eat and vegetate itself into spherical oblivion. Perhaps this is abetted by some deep but misguided faith that oblivion is different from death. Oblivion is a recurring theme.

For most of the day, now, I study every conscious moment, watching to catch the intervention of some doer, some inner entity who is the real author of an action.

I sit at the kitchen table, sipping a cup of hot coffee. Looking at my right hand, which holds the cup, I think, "Pick up the cup." The cup lifts.

"There," I think. "I had the thought to do something, and then the hand did it." Simple, like everybody already knows.

Then I try thinking "Pick up the cup," but without actually doing anything. My fingers still hold the handle, and I still know the difference between picking and not picking, but I don't pick it up.

So there it is: I have authored an action and an inaction. And yet, when I examine the details, when I take a close look at the difference between raising the cup and just imagining that I will raise it, I see nothing. There is no difference. The one in charge is the one who tells the mind to think about raising and then tells the body not to. The distinction is so fine, so thin, so tenuous, so inscrutable, that it might as well not exist.

Transcript from Radio Received Last Thursday

I don't know if you can hear this, but we're transmitting on our last battery. We have no more power for our transmitter or for any of our equipment. The entire station has been buried in what we fear may be four or five hundred feet of snow and ice. Only a small portion of the station is still intact, and our collective body heat is all that keeps us from freezing. The face of the glacier began crumbling two days ago and we started collecting our supplies to attempt an escape before large portions of ice fell near the camp. Unfortunately we didn't have enough time, and we believe the section called Maria's Node is the one that broke off yesterday and collapsed alongside the camp, with a great deal of additional snow and ice. Judging from the signals we were able to receive before the generators quit, we feel there are now probably several hundred feet of glacial rubble above us. Please give our families our best and if it's possible to send a rescue party, that would be great. Of course we realize the chances of that are not very good. And even if you sent a rescue party it would take a very long time to dig down to us. And we have no spare oxygen in this part of the camp. So, from all of us here at the research station, it's been great, and have a nice day. Signing off: Team Six.

$$\Omega$$

21

Glass Onion

It was late afternoon. I had fallen, and I couldn't get up. "Help!" I had cried, followed by the usual description of my plight, but no help was near, and I had no panic button. There was no scheduled visit from Meals on Wheels, so I knew I would likely remain fallen for a long time—or at least until I could get up.

•

There was a silent summer night on Indian Island in central Maine where the lake was so motionless you could see the stars reflected as in a softly undulating mirror. The moon had risen a few diameters above the mainland, silhouetting the trees against the silvery darkness. At the far end of the lake, a loon warbled hysterically for a moment, and its cousin, nearby, dove under water with a soft ploosh. In a few minutes, it would silently return to the surface hundreds of feet away.

At the near end of the lake, little more than a mile North of the island, the shadow of Mt. Phillip clove into a deep V cut almost to the horizon. In the center of that gap in the blackness of the mountain was a comet, motionless, posed for privileged viewing. In a tiny distant swoop, the curved fading tail simulated actual motion, but the comet hung in the sky like a photograph, as still and silent as the lake.

Great Pond lies close to the northern extremes of the continental US, and enjoys more frequent displays of aurora Borealis than most of us get to see. Blue and green curtains hang and sway from high above Mt. Phillip, and on a calm night they reflect in the lake in a vast silent animated Rorschach symmetry.

One night, some weeks after the comet, there were no northern lights, but the sky offered a strange performance I had never seen before. High above, toward the East, rusty bursts of cloud appeared, like faint silent explosions very far off in the sky. Each one looked like a cartoon bomb blast, a ball of cloud with short red rays shooting out, and each burst bloomed and faded for several seconds while others waxed and waned all around nearby. This went on for an hour while I considered a dozen explanations and then gave up to the inexplicable.

•

Great Pond bubbled and swirled against the old wood hull of the *Vircona* as I lay back against a pile of anchor rope. I could see the bright blue sky through the tiny hatch in the Vircona's bulkhead. There was just room enough under her deck for a six-year-old to curl up among an antique kapok life preserver, an iron mushroom anchor, coils of rope, and an empty gas can. Everything smelled of gas and oil, and the in-line six rattled and roared amidships, driving the thrumming hull through clear water.

Later, I sat on the bed in Dad's cabin, looking due North out the cabin door. The August stillness had darkened and a summer rain approached from the North-West. The lake was calm again and I could see the line of the rain advancing across the still water. As it approached the island, the hiss of uncountable droplets arose, sweeping softly closer and louder until it filled the world. For a moment the drops fell on the nearby blueberry bushes, slapping their wiry leaves with a new spatter of sound, and then the whole cabin submerged in a din of rain on the roof and walls and the world dimmed for a minute. Then the tiny storm moved on down the lake, its thrum and hiss disappearing into the distance, and in the ensuing silence I heard individual drips from the cabin's eaves, and then another loon, so far away I almost couldn't hear him, and yet the echo lasted for hours.

I can hear it now, although I can't get up.

•

My friend George was coming over to play—well, not play, exactly, because we're too old for that now—but I was looking forward to it because he's kind of mischievous, and when we get together we usually cook up something interesting, like the time when we were five or six years old and we stomped all my older brother's lead soldiers into a jumble of flat painted metal that looked like old dead leaves on the floor. I was so young I didn't get in serious trouble for it, but in a grand irony of adult reasoning it was my brother who got scolded, because he had left his fragile toys out and should have known better with a pair of sixers prowling around.

Anyway, George was coming over any minute now and I figured we'd have a drink, maybe go out and see a movie, maybe hit a bar on the way home and see if we could pick up some girls. Sometime around 5:30 PM the doorbell rang and I opened it. There was an old man standing there, quite old in fact: 75, 80, or more.

"Can I help you?" I said.

"It's me," he said.

"I'm sorry. I don't think I recognize you," I said. "Do I know you from somewhere?"

"It's me," he said again. "George. You told me to come over."

I was flabbergasted. "But you're—"

He looked at me with a funny expression. "I'm what? What's wrong with you? You really don't recognize me?"

I squinted and looked at him again, really close. I guess I could see some George in his face. Maybe a little of George's mischief in the corner of his eyes. "How can you be George?" I asked.

"What are you talking about?" he said. "You called me a couple hours ago and said come on over. So here I am. What's the problem?"

I looked at this little old man standing in my doorway and I didn't like the way it made me feel. Why was he so old? I blurted it out. "Why are you so old?—You look 80!"

He gave me another funny look. "Well, I am," he said. "I'm 82."

My jaw dropped. I stared at him.

After a while, he said, "Hey. What's wrong with you? You're 82 yourself. We're the same age, remember? What the hell's wrong with you?"

I stared harder. It was true, we were the same age. But he looked 82 and I was only, what, 19? 25? I couldn't quite remember, but it wasn't 82. That would have been impossible. I would never be 82.

•

I must have dozed off.

I think I might have been seven years old. I'd been sent up to bed a little early because we had company and grownups with guests don't want kids around.

I was trying to fall asleep, but I could hear the jumbled sounds of conversation and tableware from the dining room. They always sat around for a long time after the meal to have a few drinks and talk.

I thought I heard my mother's voice. She wasn't speaking loudly — no, she was shouting, screaming, in fact. I sat up and strained to hear, but all I could make out was one phrase, "Well, I don't!"

There was a crash, a splintering sound like something smashed and broken. I tried to imagine what was going on, but it was impossible. My mother and father never screamed or yelled. Nobody ever smashed anything.

Everything had gone quiet. I lay in bed, absolutely motionless, listening to the tiniest sounds in the house. I could just make out some people speaking very softly.

The screen door slammed, and someone began walking along the gravel driveway under my window, very briskly up the hill.

I heard another set of footsteps, hurrying. They were heavier and it was probably Dad, going after Mom.

Something terrible must have happened; something really terrible that could make her scream. And somebody smashed something.

Did one of the guests throw a platter and scare her? Did she smash something because she was so angry? What could possibly make her that angry? She could get mad at me, for things kids do, and she could snap at my brother or sister for things older kids do, but she never yelled.

She certainly never screamed. And nobody, nobody, ever, ever smashed anything.

Hushed voices floated up from below, into my window, my father's voice. He was saying something, his voice urgent but very quiet. We had no nearby neighbors; dad probably knew I was listening. The two sets of footsteps continued up the curving driveway, to the top of the hill, and out of earshot into the woods.

I continued lying there in absolute silence, listening for the tiniest sound. There were no more clues from downstairs. The guests must all be whispering, or they might have gone away. No, they came in cars, so they couldn't have left without a sound, without driving under my window.

I lay very still, listening and listening, my eyes scrunched shut. Were Mom and Dad OK? Was something happening I should know about? Was something terrible going on?

I listened and listened, but after a while I heard only crickets and katydids in the soft summer darkness. The windows were open: the wind moved softly through the trees on the upper lawn, but there were no footsteps. Mom and Dad were gone into the night, away into the woods, urgently whispering.

Mom had seemed to be walking as fast as she could, almost running, and Dad had been hurrying along to catch up, mur-

muring something, maybe something about what had happened, whatever had made her scream. I didn't know what was going on. I didn't know what to make of it. My mom lost control of herself, and now they were both gone.

•

Several years later in winter, my parents and I were back at our house on Storm King Mountain, as always, up through the snow for the Christmas holiday. The house was still chilly, closed and shuttered since our last weekend visit, and the radiators hadn't been hot long enough to catch up. The lights were on in the kitchen and I don't think any of us had even gone upstairs yet.

I was just standing there, leaning against the hot radiator while the snow fell all around outside and the evening light faded away. My mother and father were in the living room. Dad had built a fire in the big stone fireplace and I could hear it crackling.

And slowly an unfamiliar realization crept over me that this— what I was experiencing right now—was definitive happiness. Even at ten years old I knew there was something special about what I was feeling: everything was right. My parents were content in the living room. We had made the slippery trek up the Palisades Parkway from New York, and we were now safely ensconced in the big shingled house surrounded by trees and white blanketed lawns, probably to be snowed in for at least a day or two. We had plenty of food, and the furnace worked and the house was warming, and mother and dad were at home.

The thought came to me, *I have to tell someone about this.* So I picked up my glass of ginger ale and put in a couple of ice cubes, and walked into the living room feeling, perhaps for the first time in my life, like a complete person. I had something to say.

Dad had just finished putting another log on the fire, and Mom was sitting in her chair, just resting and gazing into the fireplace. A few soft incandescent table lamps were on, and the ceiling was lined with paneled rafters with deep shadows between them. A huge concrete mantelpiece was set into the stones of the fireplace and a dark smoke stain reached up from the arched opening, across the chimney, all the way to the ceiling.

A painting of a sailing ship hung over the fireplace. We had found it in the log cabin nestled in the woods a few hundred yards from the house. It was a very old log cabin, with horse-hair chinking between the logs. The painting of the sailing ship had real starched cloth sails that bulged out from the canvas, and very fine threads had been strung from the tops of the masts like real rigging. A tuft of cotton had been artfully glued at the bow of the ship to simulate the spume and spray. It was a three-masted schooner and my dad always viewed it with fondness, remembering his teen years in the merchant marine in the early 1920s.

I sat down on the couch and sipped my ginger ale and I could tell that my parents were also aware that all three of us were in a strikingly idyllic scene at that moment. Christmas wasn't far off and there was a special charm in the air, and this big old house with the crackling wood fire was almost too perfect.

I spoke up after a while; I had to say something about how this seemingly ordinary experience felt. "I just wanted to tell you guys," I said, and then I paused. Dad looked up questioningly, perhaps anticipating a comment about something interesting I'd read, because we tended to talk a lot about stuff we had learned. He was a surgeon, but he still acquired new knowledge every year, every week, pretty much every time we talked. Right now my mom was probably glad nobody was arguing about anything. For her, when there weren't any intense discussions going on, we could all just savor the moment. "What is it, dear?" she said.

"Well, I don't know. This is going to sound kind of funny but I really wasn't sure what I wanted to say. It just felt so good, so right, that I had to say something."

"What did you feel, dear?" my mom said.

I was a little embarrassed. "It's just so good right now," I said. "I'm really, really happy."

My parents glanced at each other and smiled. They looked back at me. "Well, that's great," said my dad, with a big grin on his face. "There's nothing like sitting in front of the fire on a cold winter's eve."

"Yeah, I guess that's it," I said. "But, well, part of it is that I'm just really glad to be here with you guys. It just feels really good to be at home."

My parents looked at each other again, a bit longer this time, and I know now, thinking back, that their hearts were swelling. This was an unspeakably perfect moment for all three of us.

A couple days later we were still snowed in and I spent the afternoon at a neighbor's house. By the time I started to walk home, it was night. It was just a short trek past an old tennis court and then through the woods to the top of the hill overlooking our house. A fat moon had risen, and I was admiring its clear cold light on the snow.

It was the kind of snow that crunches and squeaks; it came just over the tops of my boots and every step sounded like styrofoam. The leafless trees wove intricate silhouettes against the sky and the whole forest seemed to glow with its own luminescence. The air was clear and crisp, and bright stars speckled the sky around the moon, which shone like a floodlight on the snow-covered hillside.

Looking down at the house, I could see that Dad had finished putting up the Christmas tree in the bay window, so it seemed to be half inside and half outside. The glare from the living room spilled out from all the windows and cast glowing trapezoids of warm interior light onto the snow. I could see faint splashes of color from the Christmas lights on the lawn outside the living room, and the crystals on the hillside sparkled with moonlight and reflected ornaments.

Snow covered the roof and all the shrubbery around the house and barn, and there were no tracks of vehicles on the driveway, no footprints in the snow anywhere, except just ahead, where widely separated perforations betrayed a deer that had recently passed by.

The house and the whole world were all aglow, and the season was in the air, and this was another perfect moment.

Many decades have passed since that evening walk through the snowy woods, and I've remembered those two moments again and again. I didn't know at the time how important they would become. I recognized their perfection, but I had little sense of how rare they were. Now, each time I think of either scene, I think of both. I remember being young, living in a world where perfection was possible, where someone could be truly at home and the outside was safely outside. Nature could be cold or hostile, but only beyond the glass, and all it took was a pane or two and a crackling fire to achieve perfect refuge from the cold. And all it took was two adults, a mom and a dad sitting in their favorite chairs in the living room while the firelight flickered and glowed across their faces, and a Christmas tree casting dashes of color onto the snow in another white, dark, wonderland of perfection outside.

Each time I remember this, it adds another layer to a stack of a thousand recollections. Each layer holds the same pair of scenes, and each scene is perfect and simpler than the last, so that now there are really only two tiny bright diamonds of recollection left to see. These scenes now live outside of time, and each one represents that feeling of safety and satisfaction and perfection and happiness, joy even, that sustained me during those two moments, a few days apart, one winter when I was ten.

These thoughts now are only moments. The thought itself lasts only a millisecond, and then the next thought comes and it, too, has barely any duration. Each one is like a momentary button-press flashing a brief brilliant light of unforgettable warmth and happiness that cannot exist in reality and, amplified by half a century of layered recollections, never existed, even then, when I was ten.

A memory is nothing more than a name, a label on what was once an experience that consumed time and space. The memory is just the sudden flush of recognition of the momentary feeling that once arose during some long past and even unknown original experience, and has no dimension or duration.

•

My childhood friend and I sat in the dark, on folding chairs of aluminum tubes with nylon webbing, chairs with a unique metallic creak I could recognize a mile away. Summer was peaking, and the hot sun had gone for the day, and there was nothing planned for this evening, so we just sat by the pool at the edge of the woods and listened to the rustles in the underbrush and watched the stars reflected in the water. The late-night katydids and peepers were in full song, and if you said nothing you could be overwhelmed.

We watched the sky, waiting for shooting stars, and told each other sparse adolescent affirmations of our emerging self-awareness. We were patient and calm, because infinite life and infinite summer lay before us—and because it was night. But in our hearts we were waiting for a beautiful girl to silently take our hands and lead us to the promised land. We sat by the pool, and listened to the world, and spoke occasionally, affirming our continued existence in the boundless night.

•

No one had come to my aid, as I expected no one would, but the afternoon had turned itself into evening while I lay helpless on the floor. By then I had noticed a little relief in my lumbar region, and I managed to turn over. For a few minutes then, I had continued to lie without moving, worried that I still lacked the strength to get up, but then I did raise myself into a crawling position with no more than a minor twinge or two, and a few minutes later, with the help of a nearby chair, I was back on my feet.

Ω

Afterword

A few notes on the stories may be of interest. In particular, there is the matter of truth and fantasy, which interleave wantonly in some stories. In that context, I should point out that although real people are named, they are fictionalized simulacra rather than the actual people, and the apparently historical sequence of things is almost always distorted and bent to the will of the story. Even blatantly autobiographical elements (such as in the story "Glass Onion") are not to be trusted. There are also a few allusions that may be too obscure to decipher; some of those will be clarified below.

•

"16 Degrees of Correlation" turned out to be one of the most interesting writing experiments I have undertaken, not so much in the story itself, but in what inspired the story and what came to light upon writing it. The initial idea came while watching a documentary on the Discovery channel, in which the narrator tied together a series of scientific and technological breakthroughs as if some science writer had planned out the whole thing in advance. The documentary provided an entertaining view of the history of science, and illustrated how things come about, one discovery feeding the next. But real life isn't as neat and tidy as that documentary implied. I wondered what was making the whole chronicle seem so convincing, and I realized that it had a lot to do with the tone of the piece. The writing and the narrator had created a sense of absolute authority and plausibility, and it worked so well that most viewers would be unlikely to experience even a shred of doubt.

Intrigued by this technique, I decided to write a short fake narration, in which nothing tied together at all, but which used tone and style to make everything seem perfectly logical. Upon closer inspection, the reader would see that all the connections were in fact illegitimate, and that nothing actually held together at all. Then we would all, the reader and I, have a good laugh.

As it turned out, it was surprisingly difficult to write something that makes no sense. Each fictitious event would tie itself onto the previous event, and onto the next, in spite of my concerted effort to make the chronology leap inexcusably from one scene to the next. Try as I might, unjustifiable breaks in the sequence would fill themselves in against my will. It took several rewrites to remove the reasonable connections and make sure everything was as illogical as I intended.

The next surprise was that whenever I spoke to a reader, or read the story to an audience, everyone just bought it. The tone was sufficiently "official" to render the nonsensical series of events so plausible that the joke was a complete failure. At some readings, I explained what I was doing in advance, and still, at the end many would remark, "Wow, what an amazing set of coincidences. Did you make any of that up?"

This short piece, like a voice-over for a documentary, was sparse and skeletal in style, but some interesting characters had emerged, so I decided to flesh it out and turn it into a readable story. In the process, again against my will, certain non-sequiturs melded themselves together into an actual sequence of events that could make sense. The leaps of randomness became just colorful wrinkles in an otherwise still unintentionally plausible story. So I gave up, and allowed "16 Degrees" to assume the guise of a rational history, part fiction and part reality, although in the end, as the conclusion suggests, it still doesn't entirely make sense. Perhaps it illustrates that the journey can be more relevant than the destination.

•

"The Knock" deals with a real sleep disorder, exactly as described in the story. Now and then I've experienced this strangely mischievous mental behavior, and when I discovered it is officially called Exploding Head Syndrome in the psychological literature it was too good to be true. When a writer researches a seemingly trivial mental quirk and discovers a name as good as that, it's like manna from heaven, and a bizarre little story was unavoidable.

•

"The Journalist" explores one of the recurring unfocused themes of this collection: identity. There is significant skepticism as to the reality of Multiple Personality Disorder, so much so that the syndrome has been renamed "Dissociative Identity Disorder" to deprecate the notion of multiple actual personalities. I find this ironic, since we all manifest multiple personalities throughout our lives. Perhaps these personas vary only in certain details or modes of behavior, but they are nonetheless real enough to leave us all wondering who is driving the car, at least some of the time.

I thought it would be interesting to explore this idea in a different way—instead of different personalities inhabiting the same mental environment, how about multiple *instances* of the *same* personality? To avoid a ten-page realistic setup that might justify Dr. Borman's condition, it seemed more fun to let it be a spontaneous affliction. Having the personality alternations speed up also highlighted the inadequacy of our definitions of personality, but it was interesting to consider how even identical personalities would eventually diverge from the inevitable differences of daily experience. Finally, making the whole thing contagious was just a bit of perversity I couldn't resist.

•

"Interview with the Zombie" just begged to be written. We're inundated with vampire and zombie fiction these days, but there's barely any depth of character in the literary treatment of zombies. This seemed unfair, and I endeavored to correct things. Turns out there's really no depth to begin with, which (along with the fact that zombies can't speak) made for a *very* short story.

•

"Our Lady of the Ellington" Though of little import, the large man's room number, 1509, is the year Henry VIII assumed the throne for a 38-year run. His first queen was Catherine of Aragon; our lady's name, at least one of them, is Cathy. His last queen was Catherine Parr, another Cathy. Why do writers do this with impossibly obscure details in their stories? I wish I knew; perhaps it just adds a subliminal hint of depth.

•

"The Meaning of Life" is a kind of morality tale. The salient observation seems to be that although there are hundreds of ways to get past our own limitations, none of them seems to work very well. Worse yet, even the easily attainable glimpse of nirvana afforded by drugs is intrinsically so fragile that a few moments of trivial, clumsy social interaction can completely destroy it. The quest, therefore, turns to some form of altered consciousness that is not only more centered, or cosmic, or capable, but is, above all, sustainable.

•

"The Mirror" is a horror melodrama, plain and simple, with room for a sequel, or a whole series. It just seemed to be time for a dip into the classic genre of wet and weird voodoo badness. It was terrific fun to write, with complete disregard for any deep theme or literary merit. I hope on some dark night at least one reader gets a good shiver from it.

•

"Hoobner on the Post" is entirely true, drawn from the life of a real dog, but all the names have been changed in the hope of averting violent reprisals.

•

"Barnaby Goes Home" shows that you can go back, although the quest is long and the goal may not be what you thought it would be, and yet it still may be just fine. I still love central Vermont, and I fully expect to go back myself, one of these days.

•

"Signs" arose from a combination of two lingering impressions. First, when I worked at McGraw-Hill decades ago, there was a street person who often sat on the curb and drummed on an inverted plastic bucket. He ignored the throngs of pedestrians and the jammed traffic in front of him, and just played on, accompanying his inner experience, whatever that was. He was also incredibly dirty, and his skin was blackened with city grime. The other impression was of a suggestibility demonstration, in which a group of people were allowed to see certain intentionally placed visual and written cues, and were then given a creative task that was substantially influenced by the planted cues. I wondered what might happen if fate (or a higher power, suggested by the man on the 50th floor, who does nothing) combined the drumming man (without his drum) with random verbal suggestions from the environment. The result was most unfortunate, but perhaps to some degree we are all influenced in this way.

•

"Little Torments" is torn ruthlessly from the personal experiences of myself, or someone not that different from myself, while enrolled in an "ivy-league" preparatory school in the 1960s. Since writing it, I have found it necessary to ensure the readership that Holden Caulfield could not have been further from my mind. In fact, I never connected to *Catcher in the Rye*, perhaps because I had lived in that milieu and had never met anyone who would have tolerated Holden's bland, pointlessly disaffected narcissism for a minute. At Starkfield, he would have been considered something of a jerk. Perhaps there are people like that, but they aren't at all representative of the rebellious youth of *my* youth.

•

"Rocky Mtn High" does not refer to a drug-induced high. It might have done, and the reader is free to presume that it does, but in fact it doesn't. It's altitude. This piece was written as a performance, to be read or recited aloud to a live audience. I believe it still works in book form, but for best results I encourage the reader to find a safe place and read it out loud with gusto.

•

"The CD" explores both the unreality of the world and the unreality of religion as a gateway to the sacred. Daniel's internal odyssey meanders through familiar scenes and romantic impossibilities, en route to a theological discussion that apparently needs to take place far removed from the quotidian world. The circuitousness of Daniel's path to the monk is itself dismissed by the monk, because in theory we *could* just address these concepts directly. But we never do. Any discussion of the distinction between true religious experience and "religion" *per se* is likely to go nowhere. But it seems important to point out that a religion doesn't provide the direct experience of God or spirituality on its own: only the person can have this experience, inside, and it can't be handed to you any more than it can be rammed down your throat.

•

"Am Not / Am" is the second performance piece, and should also ideally be delivered out loud—as loud as possible. More adventures grappling with cosmological theology. The conclusion contains an allusion from astronomy that I couldn't resist injecting into a literary context: "Herschel's sandbox."

Herschel refers to a deep-space infrared observatory operated about a million miles from Earth, at the second Lagrangian, by the European Space Administration and NASA from 2009 until 2013 (named after Sir William Herschel and his sister Caroline, who discovered Uranus in 1781, along with the infra-red spectrum itself). Although its official mission ended in mid-2013, in January of 2014 the Herschel discovered water vapor surrounding 1 Ceres, a dwarf planet (and largest body) in the asteroid belt between Mars and Jupiter. A probe is en route for a rendezvous with 1 Ceres in 2015.

Sandbox is what Herschel's camera sees in a particularly "empty" extra-galactic view of deep space (the Lockman Hole). The image is packed solid with a granular texture, which is actually

tens of thousands of galaxies twelve billion light-years away (a light-year is about six trillion miles), packed together like grains of sand. With luck, one such image can still be found at *oshi.esa.int/image. html?id=36.*

•

"Another Threnody of Hope" could have been a play. Perhaps it's better as a story. If so, it's a story with little respect for the Fourth Wall, and little need for plot. Two characters search for unattainable abstractions, and perhaps for each other, but the harsh reality seems to be that we're all out here on our own, and there isn't much of real consequence beyond Betty's unceasing and simple kindness.

For those familiar with Beckett, I freely admit to several oblique references to *Godot* (going on, and such). Going on, of course, is something of a last resort, and perhaps that's the same resort in which we find Hal, Josef, and Betty. The story's title comes from a beautifully eloquent blurb on an early Grove Press edition of *Waiting for Godot,* taken from the *London Times*:

"...one of the most noble and moving plays of our generation, a threnody of hope deceived and deferred but never extinguished; a play suffused with tenderness for the whole human perplexity; with phrases that come like a sharp stab of beauty and pain."

Unfortunately, even with the stupendous resources of Google, Wikipedia, and the web in general, I have been unable to locate the original article or the author of the quote, but I do keep looking.

•

"Writing in Restaurants" was inspired, or perhaps triggered, by the existence of a book of the same name by my old classmate David Mamet. I should perhaps emphasize that it wasn't triggered by the *content* of David's essays, but by the title of his book. For some reason, when I first saw it on the shelves, I thought, "What a great title. I should have written one of those." Some years later, here they are: eleven little stories so short they're barely even discernible. The first one, as it turns out, is the only one *about* writing in restaurants, but the last one, should the reader not have noticed, is actually about writing *on* restaurants.

•

"Underground" returns to the New York subway system, which we briefly visited during the vivid death-dream of our lady of the Ellington. I have spent many hours in the subway, and even in the Third Avenue Elevated (the "El"), a subway that's twenty feet above ground and should have been called a superway, or hyperway if you prefer Greek. One night I rode the subway out to Far Rockaway, where I discovered the only way out was through a turnstile that required another token. I didn't have another token, so the experience was not soon forgotten. In the present story, we find that even exhausted, unappreciated transit cops have a streak of human kindness, which gleams all the brighter in that cold, damp, impersonal subterranean world.

•

"Deaths in the Family" has been a bit rough on some readers, and for that I apologize. We all deal with death sooner or later, but here we see how it can silently demolish the world of a child, while it can also release the soul to its true nature as unbounded pure consciousness. In the latter case, I couldn't resist playing with the Vedic notion of *hiranyagarbha*, from ancient India. The universe is said to resemble a vast cosmic egg, as seen from "outside," by the Creator, who is at once the source of hiranyagarbha, its substance, and its dissolution. So death ain't all bad, but it can help to have some living under your belt. Then again, we all know Sally will outgrow the loss of her mother, and soon she'll be just fine.

•

"No Brainer" is one of those stories that sneaks up on a writer in the middle of something else. I was playing with the "encyclopedia article" style, that impersonal, authoritative tone of voice that makes everything so definitely true. It's the voice of Someone Who Knows, and brooks no disagreement. To my surprise, I discovered this wonderful piece of machinery that lets researchers turn portions of the brain on and off. What a great toy! Like "exploding head syndrome," it was impossible not to find out what would happen when the brain is entirely turned off, but the "dweller in the body" is still there, unfettered by physiology. A significant number of readers ask if the science and technology parts are based on reality, but as of 2014 they are definitely not. And again, it's no accident that the transcollator, during the corpus callosum episode, emits the central syntax of Lucky's speech in *Godot*.

•

"The Beginning" celebrates (or flaunts) the conundrum of personal identity. It seems to hinge on doing things: thinking, acting, putting one foot in front of the other. But when you look deep into the phenomenology, even *doing* isn't knowable. Authorship of action is entirely invisible, if you get up too close. What else is there? We don't really know, at least not through thinking and remembering and analyzing, who the hell we are, or even *what* we are, and eventually, if we try too hard to figure it all out, we end up buried in an avalanche.

•

"Glass Onion" takes a somewhat opposite view of what we are: we are memories, we are the conviction that we remember who we are. The story appears to be told by someone quite elderly, almost helpless, it would seem. Memories at an advanced age take on increased color and depth and saturation, until they become more vivid and meaningful than reality ever was. And thus, as beautiful as those memories can be, ultimately they can be seen to be little more than points of light on a field of silence.

Also by Allen Cobb

Cave Paintings: Collected Poems
ISBN-13: 978-0-9792104-5-7

This collection reveals the wide variety of styles and idioms of the inner world—the cave of the human interior. These poems emerge from spaces seen by the poet through many eyes and many epochs, laced with humor, understanding, and surprise.

The Rules: for playing the game of life
ISBN-13: 978-0-9792104-2-6

That "voice in your head" has something new to tell you. A novel, a parable, a glimpse into one man's internal dialog, revealing unexpected rules from an unverified source. His life is punctuated by tantalizingly cosmic insights—from God, from an alter ego, or possibly just a big misunderstanding. "The Rules" takes the reader far from homilies and aphorisms into a surprising existential form of spiritual clarity, where expectations are up-ended, and theology is boiled down to its essentials. Notions of 'how it works' become intimate and personal, brought down to earth but at the same time revealed in a quiet grandeur that transcends conventional thinking. "The Rules" is a light-hearted journey into a new vision of the sacred permeating the mundane, offering inspiration without sentimentality, realism without emptiness.

www.ingramcontent.com/pod-product-compliance
Lightning Source LLC
Chambersburg PA
CBHW032239010726
47494CB00002B/548